Praise for To Kill a King

"Hawkin seamlessly weaves prehistoric Irish history (300 BCE) and Celtic mythology in this compelling Historical Fantasy. With fluid prose, well-developed characters, jealousies and romance, the reader will be caught up in the magic." —GAIL M. MURRAY, *Ottawa Review of Books*

"This novel has the sweeping emotions and meticulous but seamlessly integrated socio-cultural backstory of a historical romance, the sharp edges of a psychological thriller, and the exhilaration of an epic adventure." —JUNIPER ASHE GREER

"A vivid time travel thriller with romance and gorgeous descriptions of ancient Ireland." —SIONNACH WINTERGREEN, *Love Songs for Lost Worlds Series*

"A wonderful blend of fantasy, horror, sci-fi, and mystery, author W.L. Hawkin does a marvelous job of crafting a narrative that speaks to the reader and eloquently paces the story." —ANTHONY AVINA, *Readers Entertainment Magazine*

Novels by W. L. Hawkin

The Hollystone Mysteries

To Charm a Killer
To Sleep with Stones
To Render a Raven
To Kill a King
To Dance with Destiny

Lure River Romances

Lure: Jesse & Hawk

To Kill a King

A Hollystone Mystery: Book 4

W. L. Hawkin

BLUE HAVEN PRESS

To Kill a King

Hollystone Mysteries (Book 4)

Copyright © 2020 W. L. Hawkin

Tattoo Edition, 2020

Issued in print and electronic format

ISBN 978-0-9950184-9-5 (paperback)

ISBN 978-1-7772621-0-5 (kindle)

ISBN 978-1-7772621-1-2 (epub)

All rights reserved. No part of this book may be used or reproduced in any manner whatsoever without written permission, except in the case of brief quotations embodied in critical articles or reviews. This is a work of fiction. Resemblances to persons living or dead are unintended and purely co-incidental.

Published by Blue Haven Press

http://bluehavenpress.com

Edited by Eileen Cook & Wendy Hawkin

Author Photo by Debbi Elliott

Original Art & Cover Design by Yassi Art & Design

Dedicated to my Muses all—
Without you there would be no stories.

---

is ó mhnáibh do gabar rath nó amhrath
It is women who fortune or misfortune give.
— Irish proverb,
(The Colloquy of the Ancients)

Glossary & Pronunciation Guide

We don't know what dialect the Iron Age people of Ireland spoke. In some cases, I've used spellings from the myths and, in others, modern Irish.

Adamair: **A**-*da-mer*. King of Tuath Croghan

Bean Rua: *Bawn* **Roo**-*ah*. Red-haired Woman. The song Conall composes for Sorcha

Bres: *bress*. means competitor. Bres was an unpopular Fomorian king who became king of the Tuatha de Danann and treated them poorly.

Capall: ***caw***-*pull*. Conall's spirited white stallion

Cernunnos: *ker*-**new**-*nos*. The ancient Celtic fertility god

Conall Ceol: **Conall Coo**-*el*. Conall means strong wolf. Ceol means music.

Criofan: **Cry**-*o-van*. The oldest druid at Tuath Croghan

derbfine. ***der***-*vi-nah*. The kin group composed of the male descendants of a common great-grandfather, they possessed important legal powers relating to its members' affairs, the control of kin-land, and the election of the head of kin.

Emain Macha: **Ow**-*an* **Ma***ca*. One of the great royal sites and a prehistoric ritual complex west of Armagh in Northern Ireland. It's now called Navan Center. Loughnashade (Lake of the Treasures) is nearby. There are several mythological stories concerning Macha, the goddess for whom it is named.

Ériú: *Err-oo*. The ancient way to say Ireland

Fearghas: **feer**-*goss*. Fear means man in Irish and ghas, force, vigor, strength. Our Ox is a man of strength and force, but also intelligence.

geis: *gesh*. A complex concept related to the casting of certain prohibitions or taboos. A man who violated his geis often met with a tragic end in the myths.

giolla rua: *gillaroo*. Red Fella. A type of brown trout that inhabit freshwater lakes in Ireland.

Gundestrup Cauldron: a silver cauldron with gold gilding dug from a peat bog near Gundestrop, Denmark in 1891. It is believed to have been an offering to the gods during the Early Iron Age (150-1BCE.) Cernunnos, the Celtic Fertility God is embossed in the silver holding a torc and a horned serpent. The vessel is thought to have been created in Thracia and likely traveled north with the spoils of war. It's currently housed in the National Museum of Denmark.

Loughnashade Trumpa: **lock**-*na-shed*. Lake of the Treasures. Four huge sheet-bronze trumpets were uncovered in 1978 beside the lake. The surviving trumpa is on display at the National Museum of Ireland in Dublin. It's embossed with a lotus flower motif that originated in Egypt. It arrived in Ireland in the early Iron Age. Simon O'Dwyer has a replica that you can experience online. The trumpa was played in ceremony or to lead armies into battle.

maoled: *moiled*. A native cattle breed, the name derived from the Gaelic *maol* or dome that stood atop its head.

Máire: **My**-ra. A young Irish girl who captures Dylan's heart

Púca: **Pooka**. Ruari's big black horse. The púca is a shapeshifting Irish faerie that can take several forms including that of a big black horse.

ruaim: **roo**-*im*. A powder of crushed berries that could be used to highlight lips or cheeks. Ancient Celtic makeup

Ruairí Mac Nia: Rory son of Nia

Ruairí Coś Fuil: *Rory Cus Foo-ill*. Blood Foot

sidhe: *shee*. An Irish term that refers to the earthen mounds which are thought to be home to the faeries or old gods (Tuatha de Danann) who disappeared underground. Today it often refers to the faeries themselves.

Tarbfeis: *tar-uh-vesh*. The ritual choosing of the king. A white bull is killed. One druid eats his fill then sleeps while four druids chant a spell of truth over him. The druid dreams and then awakens knowing the identity of the new king.

Tuatha de Danann: *too-ah day danon*. Tribe of the Goddess Danu. Mythologically, they inhabited Ireland prior to the Milesians (the current Irish). Danu's children, who were a race of gods, had supernatural powers and were skilled in magic. In legends, they were a faerie people who interacted with humans.

Weary-hearted

Autumn Equinox

Estrada rose through the gray veils between night and morning with images of Michael flooding his mind and firing his body. Dozing on his side, he basked in the heat until desire overcame him and he flung back an arm to draw his lover in. The hair on his arms quivered with the cool rush of morning air and then his hand hit a dent in the sheet where Michael should have been.

Shocked fully conscious by the reality of the moment, he rolled into the empty space, sniffed, and rubbed his eyes. Tears came unexpectedly and at the strangest times. A whiff of espresso could trigger an aching throat. The scent of a cigarette on the wind or the click of a Zippo could send silent tears streaming down his cheeks. He still carried Michael's silver monogrammed lighter in the pocket of his leather jacket.

Jesus. How long has it been? Long minutes marked off days. Days stretched into weeks. *August ninth*. That was the night Michael sacrificed himself to save Estrada's soul.

Bloody hell, Michael! Why did you do that?

They'd cremated him three days later, in secret.

Images flashed through Estrada's mind. That bloody vampire drilling its beak into Michael's brain. The knowing look on Nigel's face when he saw his grandson's body limp in Estrada's arms. The billiard table in Nigel's den, where they'd laid Michael out—his pale perfect face, all shadows and harsh angles, a black scarf tied around his forehead to hide his shattered skull.

Six weeks had passed and Michael wasn't coming back.

Estrada flexed his bicep and stared at his latest tattoo. *Corvus Corax.* The raven's back broke into a flurry of feathers and deranged birds to remind him how he'd split the terror asunder with the force of his right arm. He could still feel the damp steel, the hot blood, the hollow pit of his pulsing gut as he struck. The raven held a bloody rose in its beak, so he'd never forget how close he'd come to losing his baby girl. How he'd lost his best friend and lover.

Ah, fuck it! Enough wallowing.

Rising naked from the bed, he wandered into the kitchen and took a long drink from the tap. His mouth tasted like a tar pit. Grabbing an apple from the bowl on the counter, he bit into it. He remembered smoking a joint last night—it was the only road to sleep now—but there were three fat roaches on a saucer in the sink. He shrugged. What difference did it make how much pot he smoked? What difference did anything make?

His cell phone was still in the inside pocket of his leather jacket. He retrieved it and turned it on—5:52 a.m. He'd missed a call from his friend, Dylan, back home in Vancouver. There was a message. Probably Dylan wishing him a happy Mabon. The coven would've gathered for ritual magic last night at Buntzen Lake, while he'd done nothing to celebrate Autumn Equinox but drink and smoke too much after his Saturday night show at the winery. *Damn.* This was the first sabbat in seven years he hadn't been with his Wiccan friends to celebrate the change of season.

A year ago, all he wanted was to be High Priest of Hollystone Coven and now he couldn't even handle hearing Dylan's message. He'd cut himself off from them all. They who knew the truth. The vampire had wanted *him* and had kidnapped his baby girl and killed innocent people in his obsession to claim him. But he hadn't because of Michael.

Estrada's throat tightened and he exhaled through pursed lips. He needed to perform a ritual. There was still time. A man who believed in the power of the gods, he couldn't let this sabbat pass unmarked. If he went out into the hills now, he might, at least, cast a sunrise circle, call in the dawn and invoke the gods and goddesses. Ask for forgiveness. For peace. Because, like Yeats, these days Estrada found peace came dropping too fucking slow.

He took another drink and splashed cold water on his face, then padded out the door naked. The guest flat was simply furnished in expensive California *boho*; perhaps to offset the fact that it was built over a barn. He paused to take a deep breath and stretch at the top of the stairs. No one had started work in the winery and night still clung to the vines.

This wasn't exactly Los Angeles, but it *was* southern California and a place to retreat with his memories of Michael. Southeast of the sprawling city, the Abracadabra Winery was carved into the hills. A billionaire named Lucas Fairchild had built an exotic nightclub here to showcase his magically themed wines. Michael's grandfather had talked Fairchild into hiring Estrada to perform his magic act. "You need a real magician to promote your brand," he'd said, and Fairchild had agreed. Nigel knew Estrada couldn't perform at Pegasus. Not now. Perhaps never again. Since Nigel was a man Estrada respected, he took the gig and drove his Harley south. That was three weeks ago.

Padding barefoot through the grassy paths of the vineyard between masses of plump grapes provoked a strange melancholy. The sun crested the hills in a golden arc, illuminating the long, staked rows as rigid and precise as Fairchild. But the dewy green leaves spun a magic all their own. It was a hot, sultry morning. No breeze, and the grape vines were festooned with tiny spider webs.

"It's beautiful here, amigo. You should be here. I miss your poetry and our talks and, well, I miss *you*. All of you."

Some men enjoyed time alone. Estrada wasn't one of them. This was his prison sentence. Self-imposed solitary confinement. If he chose to analyze it, he supposed he was suffering from what they called "survivor guilt." If he hadn't left Michael alone so much ... If he'd known that Michael loved him ... If the vampire had taken *him* instead ...

Spying a black fleck in the sky, Estrada's heart flashed back to Don Diego and his nest of bloodsucking vampires—men who could transform into birds. But this was no pterosaur like Diego. No raven like his minions. Only a vulture, long-tailed and long-winged with splayed-feather ends like fingers. Then there were more. He counted six. Wheeling in low circles at the crest of a far hill. They'd sniffed out carrion.

Slick with the surge of adrenalin, Estrada loped toward them. He was in no mood for a body but someone might be hurt. Here, on the outskirts of Los Angeles, anything was possible.

It was a deer. An immense black-tailed deer with a full wrack of antlers. Twelve prongs. It sprawled on the ground, tethered to the earth, its hind leg caught in a snare of bloody rawhide. There was no obvious movement but perhaps it was still alive.

Estrada waved his arms and jeered at the dark brown vultures who postured like a gang of anxious thieves, their naked blood-red heads and pale beaks uttering silent threats. "Leave him, you fuckers! God damn you."

When they backed off, flapping and fretting, he knelt in the wet grass to examine the rawhide. It was embedded so deeply in the animal's flesh, he couldn't pry it loose with his fingers. He'd need a knife.

Who would set a snare in the paths of a winery? Fairchild's entitled son, Guy, and his boys? Perhaps deer came down from the foothills and browsed among the grape vines. Guy craved his father's favor and killing a marauding stag could win him points.

Moving to the animal's head, Estrada felt for a heartbeat and found it. Faint and weak, but still pulsing. He exhaled loudly. The ground around the deer was gouged by cloven hooves. It must have fought for days until exhaustion and dehydration finally took it down. *Fuck.* Grinding his teeth, he punched a fist into the earth. *When I find out who did this, I'll kill him.*

The stag's tongue was caught between its teeth, a small pink crescent. Estrada took a deep breath to calm himself, then laid his palm along the dark dry muzzle. When the eyes flicked open, he flinched. They were coppery, kohl-edged eyes. *Cernunnos eyes.*

Touching the bony-tipped antlers, Estrada remembered the Celtic god he'd conjured twice before—first in Scotland and again on Hardwicke Island. The god who'd come to help. The god who loved him. A voice, like wild honey echoed through his mind. *Know that I am with you, shaman.*

"*Are* you with me, Cernunnos? Because I could use a hand right now." Standing, Estrada surveyed the area. The base of the hills hid a dark shadow, the remnants of a pond. Perhaps the run-off from Fairchild's irrigation system? If he could get the buck down to the water and revive it, there was a chance.

"Don't die. I'll get a knife and free you." No creature should suffer and die like this. Bound and alone. Staring into those deep brown eyes, Estrada's throat tightened. He couldn't swallow. Had to conjure saliva to push past the lump. And when he did, the tears surprised him again.

Jesus Christ. Stop fucking crying, man. Go get your knife and do something useful.

His bare feet cut prints in the grass as he sprinted back through the vines. Though an athlete, the sudden exertion left him winded. By the time he hit the steps, he was panting and pissed. At whoever set that inhumane trap. At himself. At the world.

His boots stood at the top of the stairs. He touched the leather side-sheath that housed the knife he'd just bought at a hunting store in Oregon. *Empty.*

A chill swept through his body. Estrada wasn't a careless man, especially with weapons. But last night he'd kicked his boots off at the door and left them. Too drunk to care. Too cocky to think anyone would come here. Unless. *Did someone pinch it at the bar? No, I'd have felt a hand in my boot, no matter how drunk I was. Wouldn't I?* His knife was gone and the deer was still out there. A deer with the eyes and horns of Cernunnos. A deer he could save.

Grabbing a butcher knife from the counter, he turned and padded back down the wooden steps and through the trellised hills.

Halting twenty paces from the buck, he blinked hard. Blood now pooled where the buck's antlered head had been. *Decapitated? How could that happen in the time it took to run to the flat and back? How long was I gone? Twenty, thirty minutes? Are the bastards still here, hiding in the bushes?* He glanced around in all directions but didn't see anything unusual. No flash of color against green. No dark shadows. Squeezing his eyes shut, he tried to sense something.

Fuck me! Raising his arm above his head, he bent back his forearm and sent his frustration flying through the air like a spell. The blade twirled once and stuck in the ground quivering.

Then, another thought. *Maybe I'm dreaming. Slipped inside some kind of vision. Maybe none of this is real.*

He approached the carcass gingerly and knelt on the grass. When he touched the wound through the warm hide, his stomach clenched. The blood was cooling. Thickening. He stared at the sticky red fluid on his hands, brought it to his lips and tasted it. Salt and copper. *Real. If this is a vision, it's the most authentic fucking vision I've ever had.*

Slipping to his hip, he sat down beside the body. Blood drizzled from a stab wound in the heart. That was odd. The buck was nearing death when he left. Why bother to stab it in the heart? He could understand a trophy kill—a twelve-prong rack was a prize—but this stabbing was senseless and unnecessary. Overkill.

Placing his palms over the wound, he closed his eyes and conjured a pink cloud. He could, at least, send it on its way with reverence and respect. When the energy began to swirl, he stayed with it until an image appeared in his mind's eye. It was a memory really. The horned god, all sexy and sheikh, swaggering around the fire on Hardwicke Island just as he'd done that night. Those tense muscles. Those purple lips. That kiss. And again, those words. *Know that I am with you, shaman.*

Leaning back, Estrada held the image in his mind. Was this some elaborate message from Cernunnos? What could it mean? The horned god loved drama, but why this complex violence? Touching his hand to his own heart, Estrada heard three more words. Loud and distinct. Spoken in the god's honeyed voice.

"She needs you."

She? Opening his eyes, Estrada stared down at the deer's carcass. *Who? Who needs me? My daughter? Her mother?*

He retrieved the butcher knife and sprinted toward the house. He should never have come out here without his phone. Or his jeans. After what they'd just experienced on the coast, he should have known better. But surely his daughter, Lucy, couldn't be in peril again?

He'd have to call Sensara, though he didn't like the idea. He'd left things in a bad way and they hadn't talked in weeks. They'd exchanged a few terse texts, but that was all. They both needed a break after the events on the coast and his rushed and desperate marriage proposal. He wasn't surprised she'd said no. Just embarrassed.

Sensara was a wise woman and knew him better than most people. Knew he was grasping and grieving. Knew marriage would never work. Then he'd run to California and just three days ago, her ring had arrived wrapped in tissue in a small white envelope. The note said, "I hope you find peace in your freedom." How did a man respond to that with anything but tequila?

But Lucy. Lucy might need me.

The rumble of an engine disrupted his thoughts as he neared the barn. Then there was nothing but the song of morning birds. When he turned the corner, he spotted a red ATV parked at the foot of the stairs beside his Harley. The door was wide open.

Guy Fairchild. What the fuck is he doing coming into my flat uninvited at seven a.m.?

Estrada walked in naked and angry and brazen as hell.

Guy Fairchild was slumped in a corner of the pale gray chaise looking like he hadn't gone to bed yet. Though his lids were heavy, his pupils loomed the size of garbage can lids. Estrada's jeans were still draped over the back of the couch where he'd left them the night before and Guy's hand was on them. The fingers of his other hand moved erratically, as if he were playing a guitar solo—something he did when he was high. The kid wasn't half-bad and kept a Fender Stratocaster at the bar for opportune moments.

Guy's gaze ran blatantly down Estrada's naked body. Then he rolled his eyes and tossed over the jeans.

Estrada batted them to the ground. He didn't take anything from the younger Fairchild. Not orders. Not suggestions. "What do you want Guy? Come to beg for a date, again?"

The golden boy had propositioned Estrada twice when they were alone, and twice he'd been rebuffed. Nicely. He *was* the boss's son. The rest of the time, Guy made homophobic jokes with his boys—something that infuriated Estrada.

At Pegasus, there'd been lots of *guys* around. Men who, like Fairchild, wanted their first time to be with someone experienced and in Michael's case, legendary. Estrada didn't mind propositions. What he minded was the guile and arrogance and homophobic bullshit. Men died over such talk. Only a year ago, a man he cared about—

"Like I'd ever beg." Guy flicked his head to get the blond fringe out of his eyes. "I came to deliver a message."

"So, do it."

"Someone was looking for you last night."

"And?"

"He seemed upset."

Estrada glanced around suspiciously. He'd spent a few years living in Eastside L.A. when he was a kid and had no friends here.

"Relax, man. He called the bar and I didn't give him your cell number. I wouldn't do that."

No. You'd rather use it as an excuse to come here and harass me. Estrada set the butcher knife down on the counter but left it close enough to snatch. "You couldn't leave a message at the bar?"

Guy sniffed and rubbed his nose. He looked like he was itching for another line. Lowering his chin, he flashed those clear blue eyes. "He said it was urgent."

"Urgent. So?"

When Guy pouted, Estrada felt a sliver of rage ripple through his fingers. He wanted to slap those downturned lips. Instead, he picked up his jeans, climbed into them, and zipped up slowly. "What is it you want, Fairchild?"

Guy shrugged his left shoulder and glanced down at Estrada's crotch.

"Fuck, man. I'm no whore, and I'm not going to break you in. There are plenty of guys on the street that'll sort you out."

"You can't stay alone forever," Guy mumbled.

"What'd you say?" Estrada lurched forward but Guy opened his fist to reveal a buck knife—the buck knife that should have been in *his* boot. Guy popped it open.

Growling, Estrada picked up the butcher knife. "You think I won't stab you because of your daddy? You've seen me throw a knife.

You really want to play *that* game?" He was an expert marksman and had taken to piercing a bull's eye of grapes in his new winery routine.

Fairchild smirked. "You underestimate me."

"How did you get my knife?" If someone with Guy Fairchild's skills had managed to swipe his knife right out of his boot, it was time to up his game. Or stop drinking.

"Like I said, you underestimate me."

Estrada shook his head. "You're a sneaky little thief and I was pissed."

The two men locked eyes and then Guy's cheek twitched in resignation.

He tossed Estrada's knife and it clanged against the coffee table. "Dylan McBride is trying to reach you." He sniffed and waited for Estrada's reaction.

"Are you fucking kidding?" Estrada picked up his cell phone. There were now two more missed calls from Dylan and a text. **Call me NOW. Urgent.**

"Get out Guy."

"You sure you don't want—"

The action was faster than Fairchild could perceive. With one hand Estrada grasped the knife and with the other, he yanked the surfer boy up by his button-down shirt.

Guy gasped when the blade grazed his Adam's apple.

"I *want* you to leave. What? You think all guys who have sex with other guys just do it because they can? That's a stereotype, man."

"I just—"

"Look. This"—he pointed between himself and Guy—"is never going to happen."

Guy's eyes flashed something akin to unrighteous indignation and then he saw Estrada's fist and lurched backward. But not fast enough. A dozen weeks of grief and guilt hammered through Estrada's soul into that fist and right through Fairchild's jaw.

Guy hit the barn door with a thwack that rattled the cutlery.

"You know anything about that fucking deer?"

Guy spit blood. "What fucking deer?"

You Cannot Change History

When Estrada returned Dylan's call the phone rang and rang. *Fuck! No voicemail.* Dylan was a great friend but he lived in another century. Why leave a text like that and then not answer your phone?

Estrada tapped his thumbs against the glass. **Call me.**

His knuckles throbbed from Guy's jawbone and his hands were still stained with the buck's blood. He left thumbprints on the screen. After turning up the ringer, he took it into the bathroom with him and sat it on the counter. He wasn't surprised by the surly face in the mirror. He hadn't shaved since Michael died. Or slept much. His eyes were shadowed, his dark hair unruly. He wasn't thinking straight and knew it.

But the cold water numbed his sore knuckles. He washed off the blood, then splashed water on his face. When he ran a damp hand through his hair, he got a whiff of his armpits. Grimacing, he glanced at the shower. No, there wasn't time. *She,* whoever she was, needed him.

Surely, if Lucy were in danger, Sensara would find a way to contact him. They were witches, and Sensara was a professional psychic. And he'd *know* if something was wrong—except he hadn't known the last time.

Just make the call, asshole. Sensara has every right to be mad. After saying all you wanted to do was be a family, you left them again.

"You're always leaving me," Michael had said, and it was true. Estrada was always leaving someone. He picked up his phone and cleaned the blood off with a towel. He started to punch in Sensara's number, then saw Dylan's messages and decided to listen to them first. If something was wrong back home, Dylan would tell him straight. After everything they'd been through, there was no lying, or hiding, or softening the truth.

"Hey, Estrada! Happy Mabon. Everyone here is fine. We met last night. Sensara and Lucy send their love. But, uh, we need to talk. Call me when you get this."

Okay. Good. Letting loose a deep sigh, Estrada walked back into the kitchen. Both mother and daughter were fine. The other women in Hollystone Coven were fine. As he set down his phone, he noticed his hands were trembling. *Coffee.* He needed coffee.

But who the hell was *she*? And why a slaughtered deer with the eyes of Cernunnos?

Dylan knew. That's why he'd been calling. Estrada skipped anxiously to the last voice message.

"Just leaving Vancouver. Air Canada Flight 232. Arriving LAX 9:30 a.m. I'll call when we land."

Ah. No wonder Dylan's not answering his phone. He's in the air. Well, that's good. If he's coming here, there's no danger there.

Estrada checked directions on his phone. It would take him two-and-a-half hours to reach Los Angeles airport, riding northwest on Highways 15 and 91. It was now 7:45. Rush hour. Dylan would need to clear Customs. He might just make it.

He replied to Dylan's last text. **On my way. Wait outside arrivals.**

There was a faint knock on the door and Guy's face pressed up against the screen.

"What do you want now?" Estrada had calmed down slightly, now that he knew Lucy and Sensara were safe.

Guy huffed. "The ATV won't start."

Estrada bustled around the flat, collecting his things—wallet, leather jacket, sunglasses. He sniffed his pits again. "Call your boys, or the fucking auto club, or your father."

"You have blood on your ..." Guy gestured to Estrada's chest with his chin.

Glancing down, Estrada saw the remains of a bloody handprint. His bare feet, too, were spattered in blood. *Shit.* He hadn't looked down. He really did need a shower. "Sorry, man. No time. I can't help you."

He sauntered over and started to close the door in Guy's face, then noticed the kid's red, swelling jaw and glanced at his own bruised knuckles. He cleared his throat. "Ice will help that." He really *was* sorry about that punch. Guy was an arrogant son-of-a-bitch, but he didn't deserve that. Estrada closed the door and turned away.

Ten minutes later, he thumped down the stairs, damp but no longer bloody, and dressed all in black—T-shirt, jeans, leather jacket. He found Guy sitting on a log beside his bike looking like a kicked puppy.

"Get on. I'll take you to the bar." After pulling down his visor, he geared up his Harley.

Guy's hands gripped his waist and Estrada felt the sharp edge of his chin resting against his shoulder. *Fuck. Michael always did that.* Guy reminded him way too much of Michael, with his blond hair and sunken cheeks. His love affair with cocaine. Was that why he reacted so harshly?

But they were different men. Michael didn't have a tan and surfer tats, and he wasn't a hustler. Whatever shit he did, he did honestly, while Guy lurked beneath the surface like a shark. He'd probably tinkered with the ATV just so he could get a ride on Estrada's Harley. It was the first thing he'd wanted when they met just weeks ago. If he wasn't the boss's son, and if the boss didn't pay so well …

Estrada hated this place and the gimmicky performances Lucas Fairchild insisted he do. He wasn't pulling rabbits from a hat but it was close enough. He was a whore. A god-damned magic whore. A god-damned depressed magic whore. Making reams of cash and sending it home to Sensara. Guilt money for her and Lucy.

He squeezed the throttle. The bike pitched and spit out a dirt storm. Caught the curve at a bad angle. Guy squealed, and Estrada almost lost it. As he took control again, a sign for Abracadabra appeared at the top of the hill.

Lucas Fairchild had more money than taste. His architects had designed a launchpad for his winery that was part factory, part marketplace, part exclusive club, and all swagger. Abracadabra was built in the shape of an upside-down magician's top hat. The gleaming vats of production were housed on the first floor and open to the public by guided tour only. Guests could peek inside via large windows set into the exterior walls. The second floor was the glitzy showroom where wines were displayed, tasted, and purchased from sexy salespeople dressed in black evening attire. The floor above housed the theatrical restaurant with stage and bar. Everything was decorated in black, white, and shades of gray, including the employees, except for gold and silver accessories. The restaurant ceiling opened up to allow for the ambiance of sun and stars while accommodating the weather. Still above that, resting on the brim of the magician's hat, was a circular balcony garden with outdoor patio and a spectacular view of the winery. Twin elevators and staircases allowed customers to traverse both sides of the building. They called it "The Hat."

Upscale country club wasn't Estrada's style, and he missed the dark sexy throb of Pegasus where he'd been performing his edgy gothic magic act for the past several years. Maybe one day he could go back and try again when Michael's shadow had lifted.

He stopped at the service entrance, and Guy slid off. His yellow Porsche convertible was parked in the back lot with a surfboard sticking out the back.

"I hope things are cool with your friend," Guy said.

Estrada didn't raise his visor, just took off and left the surfer boy coughing in a cloud of dust. Weaving in and out of rush hour traffic, he kept thinking about that buck. Had some hunter killed it and Cernunnos merely taken advantage of the situation or had he staged the whole thing? Like Fairchild, ostentatious was the horned god's style. But why decapitation? And why stab it in the heart? That wasn't normal. Not that anything about this was normal.

Dylan was standing on the sidewalk holding a backpack when he pulled up and turned off the bike. Estrada swung his leg over, pulled off his helmet, and ran his fingers through his damp hair. He hadn't seen Dylan since their ordeal on the yacht. Now the feelings all came rushing back. The fear. The terror. The overwhelming sadness.

He threw an arm around Dylan's shoulder and the two men embraced and thumped backs. Within it, Estrada felt their bond—a bond forged from fighting monsters—and he bit his lip to hold back the tears. *Damn. Not now. I can't fall apart now.* He cleared his throat. "Sorry I'm late. I came as fast as I could."

"Aye. It's brilliant, man. I thought I might be catching the Greyhound to Temecula."

"Jesus. Don't *ever* do that." Shaking his head, Estrada pulled his light helmet from his saddlebag and handed it to Dylan. He'd taken to wearing fuller face protection lately—was sick of eating bugs in the hills, and the black visor created a barrier between him and the rest of the world.

Estrada chewed his bottom lip. "Listen, man. I didn't get through all your messages. It's been a really fucked up morning. But there are no coincidences so you must know who's in trouble. Who the fuck is *she*?"

Dylan cocked his head. "She? Oh, aye. Sorcha."

"Sorcha?" That was the last name Estrada expected. He hadn't heard anything about Sorcha since they'd been on Hardwicke Island several weeks ago. He'd conjured Cernunnos to help him find his daughter and the horned god had casually mentioned that *she* hadn't returned. He didn't say from where. At the time, Estrada had been alarmed by that statement but then life had taken over. "Right. Cernunnos took her somewhere at Beltane."

"Aye, and that was five months ago." Dylan flushed, simmering beneath his cool exterior. "But I *saw* her during our ritual the night before last. I was thinking of the stones and …" He paused, perhaps remembering his time with Sorcha at Kilmartin Glen. He swallowed and then spit out the news he'd been holding—his reason for hopping a red eye to L.A. "She was bound with branches. Someone's got her, man. She's scared and you know Sorcha doesn't get scared. We have to find her."

Estrada pulled on his helmet. "Let's go."

All the way back to the winery, Estrada was haunted by that deer—a deer with the eyes of Cernunnos. *She needs you. Sorcha.* It was all connected and the only way to find *her* was through *him*. They'd need to conjure the horned god again.

Estrada made coffee as soon as they arrived back at the flat. He handed Dylan a cup and chugged his black. "I saw something myself this morning."

Dylan put down his cup. "Something to do with Sorcha?"

"No doubt." Estrada was collecting his ritual tools.

As they walked out into the hills to where he'd left the buck's body, he told Dylan what had happened. This time there were no vultures and when they hit the top of the rise, the ground was pristine. No carcass remained. Not even a drop of blood.

"Well, he got your attention," Dylan said. "Do you think Cernunnos sent me the vision of Sorcha too?"

"Probably. You and Sorcha are connected. He knew he'd get a reaction." After he was released from prison, Dylan had spent the rest of the summer as Sorcha's lover. They were both archaeologists and she had a camp at Kilmartin Glen in Scotland. Dylan was in love with her. But Sorcha? Sorcha just loved life—which is how she ended up spending three days cavorting with the horned god at Beltane. "You know Cernunnos can never just ask for what he wants. He has to make a production of it."

They stopped at the base of the hill beside the pond and Estrada looked around. "Cernunnos likes fire. That night we conjured him on Hardwicke Island, he jumped right out of the ritual fire." It was hot and dry and static. The trees and shrubs were suffering in the drought. He kicked at the dry branches scattered on the ground.

"Aye, I remember. He uses it like some kind of portal."

Dylan busied himself by digging a small hole beside the pond and banking it with dirt to keep the fire contained, while Estrada gathered dry branches and kindling. The last thing they needed was to start the vineyard on fire. Finally, he knelt and lit it with a flick of Michael's lighter.

Estrada walked clockwise with a long crystal wand and cast a circle of containment, while Dylan knelt beside the fire with four vials and sprinkled handfuls of dried herbs on the flames. The smoke of sage and cedar, lavender, and dragon's blood, whirled through the air with his words. It was a spell Sensara had taught him years ago.

"I conjure this circle as sacred space
I conjure containment within this place
Thrice do I conjure the Sacred Divine
Powerful goodness and mystery mine
From the east to the west,
From the south to the north,
I cast this circle and call magic forth."

With the circle cast, Estrada knelt across the fire from Dylan and called in the elements of the four directions. As he did, he put a handful of salt in the North along with the skull of a rabbit he'd found on one of his walks. He placed the feather of a hawk in the East to give them safe flight and strong vision and honored the fire element in the South with a chunk of volcanic stone he'd picked up in New Mexico. Then he dipped an oyster shell into the pond and placed it in the West.

Reaching across the small bonfire, he grasped Dylan's hands and they began to chant. "We invoke Cernunnos. Ancient Horned God, join us in this sacred circle." Estrada closed his eyes and felt the energy zapping through him as they chanted. Louder. Faster. Stronger. "We invoke Cernunnos. Ancient Horned God, join us in this sacred circle." His body was riveting when—

"Shaman." The sound, like the roar of a hurricane, ripped through him, and he opened his eyes to see the horned god rising like a plume from the fire. Releasing their hands, the two witches skittered backwards. Cernunnos leapt from the flames in a flourish of sparks and pranced about on cloven hooves.

Estrada shook his head. Nothing the horned god did could surprise him now. It was evident how the story of a hellish Satan had evolved. In his full manifestation, he was tall, stretching over twelve feet. But as he drew closer to Estrada, he shrunk to half his size, so they were standing eye to eye and heart to heart.

"This is the third time you've invoked me, shaman."

Estrada thought of the deer and those eyes. "You invoked yourself, and perhaps us."

"Aye, that sounds about right."

When the god heard Dylan's voice, he swung around and grinned.

Dylan's face was flushed and there was anger in his voice he didn't bother to mask. "What have you done with Sorcha. Where is she?"

"*Sow-r-ka.*" Shaking his head, Cernunnos made a *tsking* sound with his tongue. "I gave her a gift. The chance to meet the tortured king."

"What tortured king?" Now Dylan's voice shook. His ears streaked red, and Estrada wondered how long he'd been suppressing this rage. Estrada didn't want to upset Cernunnos; at least, until he knew who and what they were dealing with.

"The king whose body was unearthed from a bog. The king she's longed to know. The king—"

"The bog body," Estrada said, with sudden understanding. "She told me about him. He was ritually killed and his body parts thrown into a pond below a hill."

Dylan raised his hands. "*Which* bog body? They've found several in Europe."

"One she saw at a museum in Dublin when she was a kid. He was wearing some kind of armband with metal decorations. When she touched it, she saw a vision of his face. That's why she became an archaeologist." They both knew Sorcha had a gift for psychometry.

"When did she tell you that?" Now Dylan was indignant.

"One night when we were telling stories. That's all. *Just* telling stories." Dylan had accused Estrada of sleeping with Sorcha when he was in prison. The bond Estrada had formed with the fiery archaeologist during the time he was incarcerated was obviously still a sore spot.

Cernunnos cleared his throat and they both stared at him. He rolled his eyes as if their trivial human emotions were beneath him. Then he stamped one cloven hoof and sighed. "Sorcha is in Ériú."

"Err-oo?" Estrada cocked his head. "What's Err-oo?" He was imagining other planets, galaxies, dimensions.

"It's the old Irish Gaelic way of saying Ireland." Dylan stood with his hands planted firmly on his hips.

"Oh. Well, that's not *so* bad. Sorcha's *from* Ireland, isn't she?" Estrada remembered stories of Irish whiskey, peat, and faeries.

"Aye, but not *Iron Age* Ireland. If she's gone to meet the owner of a bog body, he'd have died some two thousand years ago."

"What? You took her back through time?" Estrada was both amazed and amused by this possibility.

"She pleased me." The horned god shrugged.

Estrada nodded once. "Right. Three days and nights at Beltane. I remember."

"Christ! Why the hell would you do that?" Dylan kicked at the fire with the toe of his sneaker; perhaps embarrassed that the woman he loved had willingly spent a long weekend with the horned god. "Sorcha's brilliant, but time-travel? Couldn't you have just bought her flowers?"

Estrada considered. "I can see why Cernunnos might be so appreciative of Sorcha's enthusiasm, he might want to give her a unique gift."

Dylan fumed. "But why would you leave her in Iron Age Ireland with a bunch of Celtic warriors? Do you know what that culture was like?"

Cernunnos scowled and rolled his eyes. Of course he knew. Those warriors worshipped him. "I told her the rules."

"Rules?" This, from both Estrada and Dylan.

"I warned her she must not change history. And I gave her three days with the man. That was only fair as she had given *me* three days. But she defied me and refused to leave, so—"

"So, you left her there." Dylan's voice shook. "Why didn't you just make her come back?"

"I cannot interfere with the destiny of humans."

"Oh, fuck off!"

Estrada sent Dylan a cautionary stare. It wasn't a good idea to rile Cernunnos. They needed him. But the god only smirked. He was enjoying this. Estrada was still trying to make sense of Sorcha's predicament. "So, she's been in Iron Age Ireland all this time and—"

"Time is nothing."

"To *you*, maybe." This from Dylan. "Do you know Sorcha at all? Leaving that woman alone with Iron Age druids will do more than change history. She can create a dust storm from a pinch of sand."

"Bring her back. Bring her back now." Estrada was tired of the god's drama.

Cernunnos shook his head. "As I said, I cannot interfere in the affairs of men."

Dylan raised his fists and Estrada thought he might punch Cernunnos—not that it would do him much good. "Ach, come on. That's a load of crap. You interfered when you took her to Ireland!"

Estrada jumped between them and grasped the horned god's bare shoulder. "Listen. If you can't bring Sorcha back here, take us there."

Cernunnos dropped his lower lip in consideration. Is this what he'd wanted all along? A rescue party to clean up his mess?

"Listen. Whatever you want I'll give you but take us there now." Estrada remembered a bewitching kiss on Hardwicke Island and something the horned god had said about destiny.

Cernunnos smiled. "An interesting proposition, shaman. One I accept. But know that the same rules apply to you and your *friend*." He glanced over Estrada's shoulder to where Dylan seethed behind him.

"Go on."

"You cannot change history. The king is destined to die, and die he must."

Sorcha would be upset but they could manage her. "What else?"

"Do not develop bonds with anyone. That is what happened to Sorcha."

"Bonds? Christ!" Five months in Iron Age Ireland with a Celtic king destined to be ritually murdered. No wonder Sorcha was in trouble. It was a miracle she was still alive.

"How do we get back home?" A practical question from Dylan—one Estrada hadn't thought to ask.

"Circle back to the place where you begin and call my name three times."

Should we click our heels together too? Does he think he's the fucking Wizard of Oz? "And ...?" Estrada asked. There *must* be something else. There was *always* something else when it came to the horned god and his riddles.

"I cannot come with you or intervene while you are there." He touched Estrada's arm. "So, do not die. For then you will have changed history."

"What happens if we change history?" Estrada couldn't imagine Sorcha living in a place for five months and not doing something to change history.

Cernunnos interlaced his fingers. "Births and deaths are intimately connected. Change one thing and everything changes like the ripple of a spell. Bonds are forged. Bonds break." He pulled his fingers apart. "And that is not allowed."

"Not allowed by who?" Dylan asked.

"Don't worry about it, man. If we're dead, it won't fucking matter that we broke the rules."

The Cattle Raid at Croghan

The Previous Beltane

When the shiver struck Sorcha's belly, she opened her eyes. Something was off. It seemed she'd awoken inside a Van Gogh painting. Spiraling masses of stars studded an indigo sky. Dawn was breaking, creating a liminal golden glimmer on the horizon. Leaves fluttered, caught by the night breeze, and the sweet scent of apple blossoms perfumed the air. Also, the scent of fresh cow manure.

With a gasp she sat up, wrinkled her nose, and glanced around to see just how close they were to the patty. Then a branch snapped in the undergrowth and the curious face of a cow appeared.

Its nose and ears were as red as her own ginger hair; its white face flecked and freckled. An Irish Moiled cow. She'd seen them once at the agricultural show in Galway. A native breed, the name derived from the Gaelic *maol* or dome that stood atop its head. The beast flicked an ear and Sorcha giggled. If she were ever to be reincarnated as a cow, surely this would be the creature.

She turned to Cernunnos who slept beside her. "What've you done, man?"

Her whisper stirred the horned god, who sat up, gathered his long black hair in his fist and let it fall over his right shoulder. In his human form, the god resembled Estrada, the man from Canada she fancied but had never had, and she suspected this was no accident.

Cernunnos ran his fingers across her cheek and over her lips, then turned her face to his. His black eyes flashed deviously. "I'm not a man. I'm a god, and I've given you a gift."

"A gift?" She caught his hair in her hands and began spinning it into a fishtail. Her mind was spinning much the same. The horned god had come to her camp at Kilmartin Glen in Scotland on the eve of Beltane and offered to take her anywhere in the world, to any culture or time she desired. But an Irish moiled cow? Had they just blown across the sea? In all her years in Ireland she'd never seen it look this verdant, this fecund, this pristine.

Turning his face to hers, she stared into his eyes. "Tell me what you've done."

"You're home, *Sow-r-ka*." He said her name the ancient way, drawing out the vowels and trilling the *r* with a breathy flick of his tongue.

"Home?" The red-haired archaeologist had traveled the planet uncovering and analyzing ancient civilizations, but no place felt like home except ... "So, it's Ireland, is it?"

"Ériú," he said, pronouncing each syllable.

"Err-oo," she echoed, and suddenly realized that, although she'd grown up speaking Irish at her school in Galway, they were speaking a dialect she'd never heard before.

A corner of the god's lip turned up in a grin as he watched her face. "You wanted to meet your ancestors."

"Aye?"

"And see the tortured king you envisioned as a lass."

"The tortured king?" She'd studied cultures throughout time in Ireland, but could it be *him*? Old Croghan Man? The king who was ritually killed atop Croghan Hill? Whose body was mutilated and sunk in the bog over two thousand years ago?

The god's face twisted thoughtfully. "But a glamor is needed. We must appear in the fashion of the day."

"A glamor?"

Suddenly, a cow crashed through the bushes, its hooves coming within inches of Sorcha's face. She jumped up and out of its path, but it was followed by another near miss. She'd never seen cows move so fast.

Veering right, she raced into the trees and dashed behind a tall ash. Moiled cattle were everywhere. Careening through the grass, into the trees, and on over the rise of the far hill. Red and white blurs against the emerald green of the land and the gold-streaked morning sky.

Then near-naked riders appeared among them, waving their arms and whooping astride stout horses, their hair flying free or sticking straight up from their scalps in terrifying spikes.

"Cernunnos!" *Where the hell is he? He didn't leave me here in the middle of a feckin cattle stampede?*

She decided to go back to the place she'd last seen him and finding an opening, made a mad dash through the trees and into the glade. That's when she saw them—two horsemen bearing down on a huge white bull. The top of its skull was crowned in an enormous white *maol*. Red nose pointed down; it was barreling straight at her.

A voice in her head screamed *run!* but her feet were stuck to the earth. Then an arm wrapped around her belly and she was hoisted and flung onto the front of a horse veering sideways at a gallop. Her face hit the animal's sweaty hide and bounced and all she could smell was horse. The rider's knees pressed against her ribcage and hips as he steered the animal out of the path of the charging bull.

When the horseman stopped at last in a thick grove of trees, he shoved her down to the earth. As her feet touched the ground, Sorcha fell backward and smacked her tailbone. "Feckin hell!"

"*You* shouldn't be here." His amber eyes flickered as he huffed like an angry bear. "Why are you here?"

Embarrassed, she stood up, rubbing her sore back. Then, hands on her hips, she glared back at the horseman. "That's none of your business!"

He nudged his horse with his heels so it pranced about nervously, sides heaving, its jet black hair curly with sweat, and she had to get out of its way. But her retort had unnerved the man and she smirked. Perhaps a woman had never addressed him in such a tone.

"What're you called? What's your clan?" he asked, voice raised but composure back intact. This was a man who led. A man who asked questions and got answers.

"My name is *Sow-r-ka*," she said, pronouncing it as Cernunnos had, in the old Gaelic way. "And I ..." Stopping, she backed up a step and blinked.

She knew his face. Had seen it before in the National Museum in Dublin. In a vision. When she'd touched the copper mounts on the twisted leather armlet he wore above his elbow. The armlet he wore *now*. She'd seen it countless times in the museum where it still encircled his arm, though his torso was as flattened as a leather jacket. That armlet signified his nobility and had survived over two thousand years in a peat bog.

To see the tortured king you envisioned as a lass, Cernunnos had said. And here he was.

Sorcha's gaze dropped to his hands—the enormous hands of a man, six-and-a-half feet tall. Hands that had been photographed and published in endless articles.

Old Croghan Man.

His torso had been pulled from the bog in 2003 when she was fourteen years old. Standing before her was the reason she'd become an archaeologist. A rush riveted through her body and she wavered, unable to breathe.

He was staring at her, waiting for her to finish her sentence, and she couldn't. The sun had risen behind him and backlit this vision who seemed too beautiful to be real. But was. She could smell his body, had felt his hands as he swept her off her feet, had heard him speak in the old Gaelic tongue.

He was clean-shaven, nose long and straight, cheekbones high and shadowed. His glittering amber eyes swept up at the corners, both amused and annoyed. The sides of his head were shaved close around his ears, but his copper hair was gelled up in eight-inch spikes that made him appear over seven feet tall. Mud and sweat were smeared across his chest. He was a huge man, broad, muscular, and naked save for a leather loincloth.

Sorcha released her breath and swallowed. When at last she found her voice, she asked timidly, "What's your name?" It was a question that had haunted her for fifteen years.

"Ruairí Mac Nia."

Rory, she repeated, trilling the consonants in her mind. *Rory, son of Nia.*

Sliding down from his horse, Ruairí approached her and feeling suddenly threatened, Sorcha backed up.

"You're safe with me." His eyes swept over her body and she followed his gaze. Seeing her watching him, his face flushed and he turned away. "Fine. If you'd rather stand with your cloak in cow shit."

Sorcha glanced down then and took in the glamor Cernunnos had created. He obviously meant for her to be regarded as a woman of rank. This was a stratified society and the Brehon Laws were clear about who could wear what. Only kings and nobles were allowed to wear multiple colors, purples and blues, and slaves wore only brown.

Her long, woven sapphire cloak was fringed in gold and fastened by a circular gold brooch at the breast. The bottom dragged in the grasses and, aye, dangled in cow shit. Fortunately, the patty was not as fresh as the first one she'd seen. Beneath the cloak she wore a long, narrow saffron jacket as bright as the sun. Underneath, a soft white linen frock fit tightly around her breasts and was drawn in at her waist by a woven leather belt and purse. Soft leather sandals covered her feet. She couldn't wait to see how they'd been constructed.

Her hand strayed to touch the gold brooch and she choked back a gasp. It was La Tène, a culture that had crossed the sea from the mainland with the Celts. Images of gold hordes and wood-framed skin boats flashed through her mind. Decorated in the triple spiral, it was more beautiful than anything they had in the museum.

Nervously, Sorcha touched her hair, then realized it was drawn up and plaited elaborately, and held in place with pins. Thin gold bangles jangled at her wrists and sent small sparks up her arms.

She was nobility, as was he. Ruairí Mac Nia would not harm her. But someone intended to harm him. That was a fact. She'd seen the evidence.

"I'll come," she said. As she walked toward him, he leaned down and made a stirrup with his entwined fingers. She placed her foot in his hands and he lifted her gently onto the bare back of the black horse. He needed no help to mount but rather raised his leg and leapt up behind her in one fluid motion.

She felt his broad chest against her back and his arms encircling her as they rode through a forest more enchanting than any she'd ever seen before. It was primordial. Virgin. Even the air seemed drunk with untainted oxygen. She felt drunk herself. Intoxicated by the moment.

"Why are you out here alone?"

The question startled her. "I-I came here with my brother-in-law. I'd never traveled this way before, so he brought me along. When the cattle stampeded, we got separated."

"Brother-in-law?"

Did they not have such terms? She'd have to watch what she said. Just because she spoke their tongue didn't mean she understood their ways.

"Cern is ..." She paused, wondering what to say. There was a good chance Cernunnos would appear at some point. She was surprised he hadn't yet. He wouldn't bring her to a place two thousand years in the past and leave her there. This adventure with the tortured king, as he called him, was obviously part of the gift. Sorcha sighed. "My older brother married Cern's sister so ... It's complicated."

He laughed. "When is family ever *not* complicated?"

The sound of his laughter sent a shiver up her spine and put a smile on her lips. Ruairí Mac Nia was a man—no different than any man she'd ever met despite his appearance.

As they left the shelter of the forest the land opened up and far in the distance, she spied an Iron Age hill-fort atop Croghan Hill. The hilltop where he would be inaugurated as the Sun King and then ritually murdered, severed, and sunk in a bog.

Sorcha squeezed her fists in the horse's black hair. She'd seen the scars on the bog man's leathered chest, the slit nipples, and the stab wound to his heart. She couldn't let that happen. *Feck history!* At the very least, she must find a way to warn him of his fate. If he knew what was coming, he could change destiny himself.

A Horse With No Name

The cattle had settled now. After being corralled into various farms and pastures around the surrounding hillside, they were cropping the rich green grass. Sorcha bounced along on the back of Ruairí's black horse, feeling oddly secure in the arms of this stranger who seemed more like an old friend. And why wouldn't he? She'd dreamed of him over the years, read articles about him and his pagan culture, and gone to the museum to see his torso several times since that summer it had been unearthed in the bog.

When the horse stumbled, she tensed and clutched its mane tighter with both fists. It was dirty and sweaty and stunk. The horse was one creature she'd never loved, unlike many girls she knew growing up. She'd excavated intact equine skeletons, seen paintings on ceramics and cave walls, even bet on them at the Galway Races. But she'd never learned to ride. Give her a motorcycle, a camel, even an elephant, but not a horse. Her butt was sore already from bumping along with no cushioning between her arse and the animal's bony back. How these horsemen were able to ride bareback for hours was a mystery.

She felt Ruairí's inner thighs tighten as he squeezed his legs around the horse's belly. The animal picked up its pace and she started to slide right. His bicep bulged as he pushed her back. With a shiver, she suddenly realized that if she injured herself here, she couldn't just dash off to the emergency room. They had healers but people died young from illness and injury. She was an old woman here—twenty-nine—and that was close to the average life expectancy of a woman in this culture. It was a hard life, fraught with danger. She didn't know the exact year, but Old Croghan Man was thought to have lived and died roughly between 300-200BCE.

Sorcha had no idea what had become of Cernunnos. But, for the moment, she didn't care. Her dalliance with the horned god was a pleasant obligation incurred last summer when Estrada, the High Priest of a Wicca coven in Canada, had invoked him to ask for help and protection. Their friend, Dylan McBride, had been arrested for murder in Scotland and Estrada vowed to free him. Since it was her fault Dylan had been imprisoned in the first place, she felt it was her duty to oblige Cernunnos and, well, he *was* a god—a god who could satiate all her desires, both physically and emotionally. Hadn't he brought her here to meet the man of her dreams?

She stared down at the large smooth hands that held the leather-plaited reins. Every article she'd read about Old Croghan Man ran a photograph of these hands. *Clearly the ritually killed man dug from the bog had been nobility. His nails were manicured and his hands showed no sign of manual labor.*

In a stratified Druidic society such as this, the king held the highest position of authority. Surrounded by his druid advisors—judges, teachers, healers, prophets, musicians and storytellers—the king was venerated and called the shots. Below this noble class on the social ladder were chieftains and warriors. Then tradesmen, including the indispensable blacksmith, who forged the weapons of their warring culture. Lastly, came the craftspeople, farmers, and brewers who kept them fed, clothed, and pissed. As they rode, she saw their round wattle and daub houses scattered across the countryside, raucous with children and animals. Finally, there were slaves. The king and his retinue need never lift a finger.

And yet, here was Ruairí Mac Nia on his way home from a cattle raid—those manicured fingernails stained black with dirt and horse sweat. Perhaps the scholars got it wrong. What else did they get wrong? Her academic curiosity eclipsed her terror and filled her with a kind of wonder.

The smoke of mid-day cooking fires drifted skyward from farms dotting the fields. Ahead, Sorcha spied two horsemen driving the white bull toward the fort. One rode on either side. They'd looped ropes around its neck and were prodding its flanks with sticks. Not far beyond that, two stout horses drew a wagon up the rutted road. They were surrounded by somber horsemen and it felt like their own black horse followed at the rear of a grave procession.

As they cleared the dense forest, the ring-fort appeared. Sorcha had been to Croghan Hill, hopped the fence from the Community Center and climbed the 768 feet to its summit. Once a volcano, some 300 million years ago, it rose from the Bog of Allen in County Offaly and was nothing in her time but a cattle pasture surrounded by peat bogs, with a small village at its base. Groves of trees sprung up around the hilltop and their appearance gave it the look of a park. Archaeologists had found the remains of an Iron Age ring-fort but she never imagined it would look like this. She'd walked the hill in all directions that day, to see with her own eyes, the view Old Croghan Man would adore at his inauguration and abhor at the time of his murder.

It seemed absurd to call him Old Croghan Man now. For one thing, he wasn't old. He was younger than her, perhaps in his early twenties. But, more importantly, he'd transformed from a mummified artifact consisting of flattened torso, arms, and hands, into a flesh and blood man with a name. Ruairí Mac Nia. She'd longed to know his name for fifteen years and, now that she did, kept repeating it in her mind. *Rory*. The *r*'s rolled off her tongue and made her smile.

She glanced at the dark pools at the base of the hill as they passed. Over time, these pools would layer with decaying vegetation and sphagnum moss to form raised peat bogs. A man digging a tunnel had unearthed his torso here in 2003. His remains had been preserved by the oxygen-free, acidic peat bog. She wondered what other offerings had yet to be uncovered—a gold torque, a vat of butter, or perhaps the other pieces of his mutilated body.

As they climbed, Ruairí urged the horse on with his bare heels and it cantered slowly up the switchback. The angle of the incline pushed her back against him and she smiled when she felt him stiffen. Ruairí Mac Nia was a flesh and blood man as real as any she'd ever met. In a way, she'd loved him since she first touched the brass and copper mounts on his armband in the Dublin museum and an image of his face appeared in her mind.

Estrada was the only person she'd ever told about that incident. He said she had a gift for psychometry, which meant she could read the energy of a metallic substance when she touched it. Since then, she'd used that gift many times in the field. Wrapping her hand around the gold bracelets on her arm she experienced a sudden surge of color and sound—cloaks and swords, horns and pipes. Letting go, she leaned her head back against Ruairí's chest. She'd rather be at *this* party.

They crossed the lower ditch and then the upper embankment, and soon approached the circular timber structure that protected the people inside from other warring tribes. Some one hundred and fifty kingdoms existed in Iron Age Ireland gathered around particular clans like this; their boundaries defined by the landscape and marked by posts and standing stones.

As the wagon and its horsemen approached the gates, people fell to their knees. Some began to wail. Sorcha assumed they'd be elated at what, she assumed, was a successful cattle raid on a neighboring tribe. But they weren't. Women and children ran hysterically from the hill-fort. When she glanced around, she noticed that a stream of people were following them up the hill from the valley.

"What's wrong?" she asked, loud enough for Ruairí to hear above the wailing, but he merely shook his head and urged the horse on.

A woman in a purple cloak stumbled from the hill-fort and headed straight for the wagon. Ruairí tensed and pulled the black horse up short. When the driver stopped, the woman climbed into the back. They were close enough now for Sorcha to see that inside the wagon lay a man with dark hair, beard, and mustache. A piece of pale linen covered his body, but his face was exposed. His eyes were shut, his skin white.

Two horsemen rode at breakneck speed across the hill and up the rutted road, dust flying in their wake. When the first threw down his reins and leapt from his horse, a shiver ran up Sorcha's arms. Sharp and angular, his head was shaved, his eyes as focused as a hawk's. A double-forked beard grew from his pointed chin.

Climbing into the wagon beside the woman, he threw a consoling arm around her and she disappeared from view.

The other was a giant, well-fleshed and ruddy-skinned. Picking up the reins of the horse, he drove the wagon forward.

"Ana." The word escaped Ruairí's lips as a kind of sigh.

Ana. So that was her name. What was between her and Ruairí and the dead man in the wagon?

All eyes were on what Sorcha now realized *was* a grave procession. A man had died. A man of rank. Inside the fort, all stood with eyes downcast.

"Who was he?"

Ruairí looked at her strangely as if she should already know the answer. "Adamair," he said, at last. "Though I do not like to speak his name and risk calling him back." Turning slightly, he raised an eyebrow. "You don't know our king?"

"My brother-in-law mentioned him once," she lied. "I'm sorry." She *was* sorry, not only that a king had died, but because that left a job vacancy that Ruairí might fill—a job that would lead him a step closer to his own death. "What happened to him?"

Ignoring her question, Ruairí slipped off the black horse. She wouldn't have minded his sudden exit if he hadn't left her sitting astride the creature who, sensing his rider gone, pawed the ground and trotted toward a wooden water trough. Grasping the braided leather reins, she pulled back to no avail. Once at the trough, the horse dipped his long neck and began to slurp. Unbalanced and top-heavy, Sorcha slid forward headfirst into the water.

"Jesus, Mary, and Joseph!" She was half-in, head submerged, arse dangling over the side, when a pair of strong hands grasped her by the hips and hauled her out. She ran her hands over her wet face and tried to smooth back her hair. Then, she unclipped the Celtic brooch at her shoulder and removed the sopping blue cloak.

"Sorry, my lady." A handsome man with long chestnut hair stood awkwardly in front of her. "Ruairí is my best mate, but he doesn't always think before he acts." He took the reins of the wayward horse and tied it to a fence. "You're not a horsewoman, I take it." He couldn't hide his smile.

"No, I never learned." *A Celtic woman who couldn't ride a horse? That was a mistake.* "Thank you for coming to my rescue." She looked around for Ruairí and found him comforting the king's widow.

"We best find you some dry clothes. I'm sorry, I don't know your name. I'm Conall Ceol."

Pronounced *cool*, she knew it as the Irish word for music. *Conall Ceol.* "I'm Sorcha, and I'm fine. The sun's shining. I'll be dry in no time."

Conall's smile grew wider when his gaze strayed to her white linen shift which was now wet, transparent, and glued to her breasts. Her large rosy nipples protruded like the paps of Anu.

Throwing the cloak back over her shoulders, she gathered it in her hands and tried to cover herself. *So much for stealthy entrances.*

"You're not from around here." It was a statement, not a question. "Who's your clan?"

"O'Hallorhan." The name had no sooner left her lips when she wondered if it was even in use. Who knew for certain how and when surnames evolved? Worse still, what if it was and there were other O'Hallorhans in this fort? Others who might know she wasn't local or who might ask more pointed questions like who's your father? A question her mother had never actually answered.

When telling lies, it's better to stray no further from the truth than is absolutely necessary. That's something her mother always said and she was skilled in the art of deceit.

Sorcha had been born in Galway and grown up on the west coast of Ireland so that much *was* true. Galway was a far ride from here and with a hundred and fifty kingdoms across the island, the chances of someone appearing from there must be slim.

"O'Hallorhan from Inishmore." She'd gone to the Aran Islands many times as a child and thought it must be remote enough that they'd never have heard of it.

"Inishmore?"

Sorcha startled at the sound of Ruairí's voice and turned to face him, her cheeks flushing with the warm rush of blood.

"Where's that?"

Damn. He was suspicious. "It's a small island off the west coast," she said confidently. "In Connacht."

"Connachta?" He cocked his head skeptically.

"What happened to the king?" Sorcha asked, anxious to shift the focus from herself. She'd need time to concoct a believable story to explain her sudden appearance with no belongings and a brother-in-law who seemed to have vanished. The dead king had been removed from public view and the desolate crowds were drifting. A time of mourning would no doubt ensue, but she sensed a lightening around the fort as people returned to their business.

Conall pulled a face, while Ruairí simply shook his head, and she guessed she'd made some cultural faux pas in mentioning the dead man again. *Mistake number two?*

Her blunder was diverted by two young girls who rode up together astride a painted horse. "Ruairí! Father says you must come to the council right now!"

For the first time since she'd met him, Ruairí's mood lightened and she saw a flash of strong pale teeth. "These two warriors are my sisters, Donella and Winnie." The younger and fairer of the two had given the command. "Winnie is bossy for a girl of ten years. You would do well to stay away from her and believe nothing she says."

Sorcha smiled. Ruairí had sisters—sisters whom he loved. Of course he did. No doubt he had brothers and all manner of relations. "And what of Donella?" The older girl was dark-haired and elfin, as shy as her younger sister was bold. She looked perhaps fourteen or fifteen years old.

"Why are you dripping wet?" Winnie asked impertinently.

"Hush, sister."

The child rolled her eyes.

"Donella will look after you; at least, until Aengus arrives. She'll soon be wed and forget about us." The girl flushed and glanced away. Sorcha couldn't see her face and wondered if Donella had been bartered for a price or chosen for love. She'd always believed that Celtic women were strong and independent, yet marriage was a business and the sisters of a man who would be king could command a fair bride price.

"Ruairí! You *must* come. *Now.*" If she'd been standing, Winnie would have stamped her foot. Instead she merely scrunched up her face and glared. "And Conall too. Father says—"

"I'll come, Winnie."

Was the girl impatient or fearful? She had her older brother's features, even his coppery hair.

"Donella, will you take Sorcha to our hearth? See that she gets dry clothing, food, and a place to sleep? She's visiting from an island in the west." He said it warily and with a sarcastic edge. "It's a very long way away and she's misplaced her traveling companion."

"Yes, I hope he wasn't injured during the cattle stampede." She feigned a look of concern.

"Oh! The Western Sea! I'm going to ride there when I'm older. Come with *me*, Sorcha. You can sleep beside *me* tonight." This from Winnie.

"Sorcha will sleep where she chooses. We'll meet again soon, Sorcha O'Hallorhan," Ruairí said, his gaze softening to meet hers.

"Aye." Why did he make her heart beat faster and her skin sweat? Was it just because she knew his fate?

He turned and walked away with Conall, leaving her standing beside the painted horse that carried his two sisters.

"Are you hungry?" Donella asked.

"Of course she's hungry. She's traveled all the way from the Western Sea!" Winnie's hazel eyes were wide. "We were just going for a picnic in the woods. We have bread and cheese. You must come with us."

"Ruairí said I was to take Sorcha to our hearth." Donella's face reddened. Her sister was obviously an ongoing source of irritation.

"Ruairí will be gone for hours. He must comfort *Ana*." She said the queen's name in a sing-songy way that intimated they were in some kind of relationship. Miss Winnie was a tease.

"Don't talk like that." Donella glanced around furtively as if they could be caught for uttering something untoward.

"I think my frock will dry in the sunshine if you could just find me another cloak?" Sorcha said to distract poor Donella and ease her fears. She glanced around the fort hoping for one more glimpse of Ruairí, but it seemed Winnie was right. He'd vanished inside the large circular structure that must house the nobility. Loitering near the gates of the fort; however, was a man who resembled the horned god. Though his back was to her, Sorcha had little doubt it was Cernunnos.

"I have something I must do and then I'd love to see your home."

"Just wait. I'll bring you one of my cloaks," Donella said, and leaping off the horse, she sprinted toward the structure. Annoyed by the change in plans, Winnie huffed and cantered off on the painted horse. Sorcha had barely time to breathe when Donella appeared again, out of breath and carrying an emerald green cloak.

"How gorgeous," Sorcha said, taking it from her hands and swinging the woolen fabric over her shoulders.

"It's my best one," the girl whispered. "I wove it myself."

"I'll be extra careful. No horses. No water troughs. And no more shenanigans. I promise."

"You're safe here. Just stay close." Donella smiled and Sorcha breathed a sigh of relief. She'd found, at least, one friend.

Outside the main gate, she spied Cernunnos in a grove of trees. He was lounging on the grass with his back to an old, twisted thorn tree. The sickly-sweet scent of hawthorn filled the air. But what caught her attention were the bits of spun wool and linen threads tied around its branches.

"I saw a tree like this on the Hill of Tara," she said. "Funny, I didn't notice it when we rode by." Around it were others, a tall ash and a magnificent oak.

"Faerie tree," Cernunnos said. "Comes and goes like the *sidhe*."

"Aye, sure it does."

"Or perhaps you were temporarily blinded by seeing your man in the flesh." He stretched his neck from side to side and the cracking of his bones made her shiver. "You must come back with me now, Sorcha. You've seen your king."

"No, I can't. I need more time." Just the thought of leaving made her pulse race.

"You're in danger here. You know nothing of their ways and I cannot interfere in the affairs of men."

"From what I've heard, you've done nothing *but* interfere in the affairs of men." Cernunnos had gloated while telling her how he'd aided Estrada's lover when he was lost at sea. How later, he'd saved Estrada's daughter from a vampire. How the shaman loved him. Seeing the look of longing on his face, she'd thought perhaps it was the other way around. It was the same look the god had given her that night near the Ballymeanoch Stones. He certainly desired the handsome magician.

Cernunnos clicked his tongue as if reading her thoughts and reaching out, ran his thumb along her jaw. "Nevertheless, you will come."

She clenched it in response. "I will not. I cannot leave Ruairí here to suffer such a brutal death." To read of ritual murder or study the remains in a laboratory was one thing, but to meet the man who would experience such a horrendous execution? That was entirely different. Though separated by cultures and millenniums she'd always felt close to the bog man. And now that she'd met him, she knew their fates were intertwined.

"Sorcha, you must."

She snorted. "You're a god. Don't tell me you're jealous of a mortal who's destined to be murdered and thrown in a bog." She gestured with her chin to the black water pooling at the base of the hill.

"You cannot save him, Sorcha. There are rules." The horned god was arrogant and proud and didn't like his dictums questioned.

"Rules? What rules?"

"I cannot change history. Nor can you. What befalls Ruairí Mac Nia is his destiny."

"Destinies change. Why did I come here if not to save him?"

"Sorcha, he's just a man."

"No, he's not. He's ..." How could she explain the rush of feeling she felt for Ruairí? Was it infatuation? Love? Fate?

Cernunnos grasped both her hands in his and they locked eyes. "I could take you back right now—"

"No," she cried, wrenching her hands free and leaping back. "Please, Cernunnos. I must, at least, warn him."

Cernunnos scowled. "You gave me three days of pleasure. I give those days back to you."

"You do?"

"But do not test me." He walked toward the hawthorn tree, then glanced back over his shoulder. "I will come for you in three days and if you're not here, I will leave without you. I will not return."

Sorcha's eyes widened. Did he dare do such a thing? How would she ever get back to her own time? To visit druidic Ireland was one thing, but to live here? She was old. She wouldn't last. "Cernunnos! Wait." She dashed behind the tree, but the horned god had vanished.

Three days then. She had three days to gain Ruairí's favor and save him from his fate. And if she got delayed, she would die here.

From Kiss to Kiss

Ruairí rode beside Ana in her chariot, tall and solemn, their arms touching, as regal as any pair could be. They were both dressed in their finery. She was wrapped in an indigo robe that shone as brightly as her raven hair, and he, in a cloak that riffled like the waves of the Eastern Sea.

The craftswoman who'd made it for him was an artist from a land southeast of Gaul. Dark-skinned and foreign, she'd arrived aboard a trade ship as a girl, brought along her own woad seeds and planted them near her hut. When she married a leather-crafter from their tuath, she taught others her art and the two created incredible garments together. For Ruairí's cloak, she'd extracted the blue woad from her young plants and mixed it with the yellow flowers that grew in the pasture to produce this intense shade of blue. She called it *turquoise*. It was, she said, the color of the sea she'd left behind.

The cloak streamed out behind Ruairí as he drove Ana's chariot and set him apart from the others as in the red of the setting sun it drew out the golden streaks in his spiky copper hair.

He knew that Ana could have chosen any of the druids to drive her today. But she chose *him*. That alone, made him puff out his chest like a bull as he drove the chariot. Bres clung to Ana like a second skin. Fearghas was her protector. Ailill, her gossip. Ruairí hadn't been close to her the last four years—not since she'd chosen to become second wife to the new king when she was just seventeen. She was a woman who craved power and he wondered what he suddenly had to offer. He wasn't naive enough to think she was interested in anything else.

In the chariot that preceded them, King Adamair's body, now stiff and glittering in gold, stood tall between Bres and Fearghas, who clutched his arms and propped him upright. He'd been dressed in his full regalia. A thick gold torque gleamed around his neck. His dagger hung from a leather scabbard draped across his right shoulder. But his sword was held aloft in a stiff, cold hand held tightly by Bres.

Many of the old kings and queens of story were buried standing upright, ready for battle, their eyes seeking the sun. A king was the manifestation of the sun, for without it the people could not exist. This tuath now cremated their kings, allowing their spirits to surge to the Underworld in a blaze of glory. For fire too was an element of the sun. Only after his purification would the king's remains be collected and entombed in the cave beneath the hill with those of the ancestors.

As they approached the small rise where the people gathered around the funeral pyre, Ana touched Ruairí's hand, signaling him to halt the horses. Her five crows circled around their heads cawing and flashing sharp quick shadows on the ground. Ruairí hated them. He'd seen what they'd done to men who defied the queen. Fearghas wore their scars on his face.

Ana's hand remained on his as she turned to face him. "How did Adamair die?" she asked, and her dark eyes blazed.

Ruairí knew he couldn't lie and heaved a sigh. This was not the time for such talk. Eyes were on them, people waiting. But that was Ana. Queen of Arrogance. One of the crows flew behind his head, so closely its wingtip razed the flesh of his neck. "The-the white bull," he stammered. "Adamair saw it alone in an enclosure and wanted it."

"Go on."

"Ana, the people are waiting." She knew of Adamair's lust for power. Why must he explain now? Their red bull was potent and strong, but the king would add to his wealth and legend with the theft of the white bull. He should have known better. They'd all grown up with the story of Queen Maeve of Connachta, whose desire for the brown bull of Ulster had resulted in tragedy.

"I'm waiting for your answer, Ruairí."

He sighed, caught between Ana and propriety. "I don't know what happened. I found him in the bull pen. He'd been gored but also struck by iron as you saw. We couldn't stop the rush of blood. We fought the men who guarded the white bull and Bres took one man's head."

Ana would have seen it. Bres had tied it to the mane of his horse and ridden home with the man's blood drizzling down its shoulder. One man's head for a king. It was not enough. In the next raid, they would take more.

Ana's lips narrowed. "The gods give us fitting ends. Adamair was a bad king and a worse husband."

Not knowing what to say, Ruairí stared at the beautiful queen and waited, his heart pounding. Ana had been his first lover and taught him many secrets only women knew. He knew every inch of her body and wanted her. When he was a boy, he'd hoped they'd wed. Once, long after they'd begun meeting in the woods, her belly had swollen, but no child came. He asked her what had happened but she wouldn't speak of it and, after that, she didn't call on him again.

Then Adamair had come from the north with his wife and child, bringing much wealth—a herd of cattle and a horde of new treasure they'd never seen fashioned before. Riches from the Continent. He was a hero, who'd fought in the wars at Emain Macha. And when the old king died in battle, Criofan dreamed of Adamair at Tarbfeis and chose him as the new king. To show his allegiance, he'd married Ana and made her Goddess of Sovereignty.

But Adamair was an ambitious, reckless adventurer, who spent months away from the tuath. Ana had not conceived by him or any of the other men she bedded in his absence—men who, like Ruairí, feared her as much as they desired her.

When Adamair's wife and child died agonizing deaths within days of their arrival, the people feared her more. It was said to be some form of plague they'd brought with them but the sickness didn't spread among the others and there were whispers. Ana had been seen meeting a woman in the forest. If it were true and could be proven, Ana would be banished. Women and children were priceless and their lives could not be bartered in cows.

Ruairí didn't want to believe that Ana could do such a heartless thing to gain power. But the part of him that feared her knew it was possible and that made her all the more tantalizing. He hated himself for wanting her so much but how did a man turn off a desire that burned so deep? Ana was the woman he dreamed of most in the dark. His heart ached but more than that, he missed the sex. Ana was wild and he'd found no one to match her. Leaning forward, he breathed in the perfume of her skin, then caught himself and fell back. "We must go. They wait for us."

Raising a finger, she touched his cheek. "*You* could have stolen the white bull and lived, Ruairí Mac Nia. *You* are a hero—a hero and a prophet."

Ruairí's skin tingled and words caught in his throat. It was true he was a dreamer. The night before the cattle raid, he'd seen Adamair lying dead in a pool of blood and warned him not to go—not on the raid or after the white bull. But Adamair refused to listen. *"I've crossed the great sea through storms and killed countless men in battle. A cattle raid is nothing to me. I am the Sun King,"* he'd said, dismissively. Adamair's arrogance had cost him his life.

"Come to me tonight," Ana said, drawing Ruairí back. "I will wash this bad king from my bed with your sweat."

Ruairí's eyes widened as a stream of lust surged up his inner thighs. She scraped the back of her fingernails boldly across the ridge in his cloak and he spurred on the horses. As the chariot lurched forward, she was forced to grasp the front railing and cast him a menacing look. But he knew that dash of danger would only fire her blood all the more. Ana wanted him and, after many long years of wanting her, he could hardly wait to have her.

As King Adamair's funeral pyre raged against the darkling sky, Ruairí stood with the other druids in a ring of nine around the fire. He stole a glance at Ana, who looked on solemnly from her chariot. She didn't love her husband. Not when she married him and certainly not now. But did she love anyone? Was she even capable of love? Ruairí glanced around the circle of druids who stood with arms raised as Adamair's spirit flew in smoke and ashes to join his ancestors in the Underworld.

Bres watched Ana and Fearghas watched Bres.

I, too, must watch Bres, Ruairí thought. They all knew Ana slept with Bres when Adamair traveled. So why had she not chosen him today? Bres was obviously insulted and jealous and that made him more dangerous.

Ruairí shrugged. Bres need not worry. This thing with Ana wouldn't last. When the druids met for Tarbfeis, Criofan would eat of the white bull. It had already been slain and was roasting in the pit. After Criofan had eaten his fill, he would sleep and dream of the new king. Criofan was uncle to Bres and would, no doubt, dream of the sister's son he fostered. Then Bres would marry Ana and produce an heir. That was the way of it.

Ruairí would make the most of tonight and then court Sorcha. She was even more beautiful than Ana and he thought she must be fey. A woman who'd arrived alone from the ethers with nothing but the clothes on her back in the midst of a cattle raid? A woman who knew no one in the tuath? Who couldn't ride a horse?

She even wore the mark of the sidhe on the back of her neck—a dazzling fey butterfly that exuded freedom and power. He'd seen it beneath her fiery red hair; its wing tips hiding beneath her gown and teasing him. He wanted to see more. He wanted to touch it.

Sorcha was haughty and powerful and a seductress. If she'd traveled from the western isles, it was by magic. Sorcha O'Hallorhan was sidhe. Of the Tuatha de Danann. Of that he had no doubt. And that made her all the more alluring.

Hours later, Ruairí ran his fingers through Ana's long dark hair, pulled the scented tresses to his nose and breathed in her perfume. She hung over him, skin moist and slick above the flare of one honeyed candle. She was still panting—had ridden him like a racehorse and mounted him still.

Leaning forward she breathed in his ear, tickling him with her tongue. When he snorted, she slapped his cheek. "Shush, they will hear."

He hoped they'd heard. Especially Bres and the de Danann woman. Their breathing, sharp cries, and the swish of skin on skin showed his skill as a lover.

Straightening up on her knees, Ana pulled free of him and Ruairí gasped. Had she done with him so soon? Reaching out, he touched the pink tip of her breast and grinned. The first time he'd touched it, he'd ejaculated before his parts were even free. Ana had laughed and taught him how to last and last and last.

Curling up behind him on the soft sheepskin, she bit the back of his neck and shoulders, and then the soft muscle between his shoulder blades. All the while, her fingers massaged his buttocks, exploring the hidden places, tickling and stroking and reaching through, re-awakening his lust.

Then, pushing him down on his back, she ran her tongue over each of his nipples. "You see, my lord, I submit," she whispered.

To kiss a king's nipples showed submission to his rule. At the new king's inauguration, each of his nobles would come forward to do this very thing. Ruairí couldn't imagine either Bres or Fearghas ever kissing *his* nipples. They'd bullied him since boyhood and would never submit. As he would never submit to either of them. He'd rather fight to the death than allow either of them to ever have power over him again.

"I'm not your king. Nor will I be. Criofan will dream of his nephew, Bres. He is closer to him than to his own son, Ailill."

Ana's teeth clamped down, warning him not to defy her, and then released. Smiling up at him, she touched his lips with one pale finger. "Does it matter? He would be king in name only and I will always submit to you, Ruairí." He opened his mouth in surprise as she rose above him. Moaning, she flung back her hair and set his hands upon her breasts. "You must trust me," she breathed.

He closed his eyes and thought: *but how can I? I know you are as fickle as the wind.*

"I want a child, Ruairí. You gave me one once before. Give me one tonight. Give me the son that no one else can." It was a demand and his first instinct was to fight her. But the idea was irresistible. *This is why she chose me. Not because she thought I might become king, but to father her child.* Leaning forward, she kissed him with such passion, he growled.

As long as Ana lived, she would remain the Goddess of Sovereignty, wed each new king in succession, and augment her power. Adamair had given her this position when he agreed to marry her, which was why his first wife had to die. As the Goddess, Ana had more sway than anyone in the tuath, including the king. Even the druid council listened when she spoke. The Goddess of Sovereignty was directly connected to the Earth who fed, clothed, and sustained them. To father her child would only increase his power and prestige among the druids.

Yes, Ana. I will give you a child. A son. I will give you a son.

Flipping Ana onto her back, Ruairí took her again loudly, thinking only of this prince he was creating. "Here is your son, Ana," he whispered in the last second. Everyone in the hall would know whose child this prince would be. Ruairí's bloodline would be ensured and no matter what happened at Tarbfeis, his son would live on as a prince. He could almost hear Bres whimpering in the hall.

A Fatal Image Grows

Several families ate and slept in the same hall heated by the same hearth, so the whole house could hear Ruairí and Ana making love. *Hah! Making love!* That was a euphemism. What Sorcha heard through the crepe partition was a desperate widow celebrating her freedom with a young virile stud—one that Sorcha had been hoping to ride herself. *Damn him.* She'd waited for him to come to her, to make some excuse to get her away from the others. *"Sorcha can sleep wherever she chooses."* Why say that and then choose Ana?

And bloody Cernunnos had given her only three days. *How can I get close enough to him in three days to warn him of his peril?* It wasn't the kind of thing you could just blurt out. *"Oh, by the way, I'm an archaeologist from the future and I know these people are going to ritually murder you and throw your body in a bog. I don't know exactly when or why, but it's going to be brutal."* She'd spent half the night cursing him and the other half wondering how to save him from his fate—a fate she was warned specifically not to change. And now he was feckin the bloody queen!

Did he love Ana? She was beautiful and powerful, that much was true, and she was the highest-ranking woman in the tuath. Donella had told Sorcha at supper that Ana would wed whoever the old druid chose to be their new king and she must produce an heir. Apparently, she had yet to do that. Ana was the embodiment of their Earth Goddess and the king was like a god—their Sun King. Donella didn't say what would happen to Ana if she failed to produce an heir but there were plenty of dead queens in history who could illustrate the hazards of that position.

Apparently, Adamair was a distant relation to this clan and the druids had wanted to re-introduce his bloodline to keep their people strong. Sorcha assumed that by breeding cattle, they'd become aware of genetics. But it hadn't happened. Ana hadn't conceived and the tribe believed that was why the goddess had taken his life. At least, the failure had been attributed to Adamair rather than Ana. That was progressive. The king took lengthy excursions and was well-connected in both Gaul (modern-day France) and Britain. Donella said, Adamair had many women on his travels and in the tuath, though she hadn't mentioned children.

It seemed the king was a playboy except where it involved the queen. With walls this thin, their lack of sexual activity was public knowledge. Donella thought that Ana had been neglected, even spurned, and her plight evoked a great deal of sympathy among the nobles. Sorcha thought that, although he'd brought wealth and prestige and they'd fussed over his death, Adamair was not loved.

Ruairí *was* loved. It was evident in their smiles and respectful nods. He would be a good king. A loved king. If he lived. She had only *three days* to warn him of his impending murder. Sleeping with him seemed the quickest way and would prove no hardship. But now that he was with Ana. *Feck!*

Sorcha thought again of the horned god's warning. "*You cannot change history*." How would history change if Ruairí Mac Nia remained alive? Would he sire sons who would alter the course of events in Ireland? Surely, he was only a minor king and his actions would have no lasting impact on the world? And then a wild thought: what if she did manage to save his life and he lived to the ripe old age of thirty-three or was killed six months from now in a cattle raid? If she'd never seen his torso in the Dublin museum, never touched those copper mounts, never envisioned his face and fallen for him, would she still be an archaeologist? Of course, if Cernunnos left her stranded here in the past, he'd have changed history, wouldn't he? Him and his rules! Time-travel was mind boggling.

Jesus, Mary, and Joseph! They were at it again. Sorcha could hear the thrust of his hips, feel the vibration of his very bones through the quaking earth. Did no one care that the queen's husband had died only that morning?

"The king is dead. Long live the king." Is that how this phrase evolved? A tribe was vulnerable without their king. Perhaps, the official mourning period was brief and ended at Adamair's cremation. They would choose a new king soon. It might be Ruairí but then again, it might not. According to Donella, it could be any one of the nine druid nobles who surrounded the king, or even a man from another tuath if he was *derbfine*. True kin.

It could be months or even years before Ruairí became king, but Sorcha knew he would eventually. The death he'd suffered was that of a deposed king. A king's rule could be short, subject to politics, religion, and greed. Many kings were killed using their own sword by their successor. Still, Ruairí needed to know his eventual fate. "Forewarned is forearmed." Wasn't that the old saying?

Sorcha snorted and opened her eyes in the smoky room. She was perseverating—her mind racing in circles. She needed to walk. The sheepskins on which she lay gave off a musky odor. Their bed was raised off the earth floor by a wooden palette and Winnie and Donella were curled up beside her. It was warm and comfortable, but between the rutting next door, the midnight symphony of snores and farts, and the bad air—smoke, ale, and undigested meat—she'd had enough.

After extracting herself gently from the heap, she clutched the green cloak around her shoulders. The unbleached linen frock Cernunnos provided had dried with sun and fire. It fell just below her knees and provided enough cover for a brisk walk on a May night. She'd be safe enough. The dead king's subjects had toasted him well into morning and many had simply fallen where they sat. No one else would be about. After threading her way through the bodies, she pushed open the wooden door and stepped outside.

It was dark and cold. Too cold for an Irish May; more like March in her time. A waxing moon and canopy of starlight peeked from behind a low ceiling of shifting cumulous clouds and provided just enough light to distinguish shapes. She wished she'd thought to grab her shoes. Too late now. Shivering, she pulled the green cloak tighter and crossed her arms over her chest.

The chill reminded her of a fact from a textbook that seemed strangely pertinent. Though she had no idea what year this actually was, Old Croghan Man's torso had been radiocarbon dated to sometime between 300-200BCE. Some archaeologists believed he'd been sacrificed to the Goddess of the Land because of bad weather and ruined crops due to climate change. A cold epoch on a grand scale. The king had displeased her in some way and she'd retaliated by destroying their food. *Is that what's happening here? Climate change? Could that be key to changing Ruairí's fate?*

But how did you convince a culture to change their beliefs? Especially when you'd been warned not to interfere? And you only had three days? Well, she'd just have to cross that bridge when she came to it. *If* she came to it.

The fort was deserted as she expected and Sorcha wandered among the circular houses with their thatched roofs. The king and his closest nobles lived in the largest of three. There were other buildings. A grainery. A shed where meat hung beset by flies. A storage shack for ale. If ever they were besieged, they could survive for weeks, perhaps longer. A beast slowly roasted in a massive fire pit and the aroma of barbecue made her stomach growl. The white bull's hide was spread on a curing rack. From what she'd seen at dinner, meals consisted of grains, meat, wild honey, butter, and cheese. Oh, and ale. Plenty of ale. There was nothing here she hadn't read in every scholarly paper ever written about prehistoric Ireland.

In a back corner, she opened a wooden gate and entered into a lush garden built with labyrinthine pathways. An oval man-made pool stood at its center. This was something she'd never seen mentioned in her Irish research and it caught her attention. They had no running water on the hilltop and she wondered how they kept it full in dry times. Slave labor, perhaps. Tonight, it was near overflowing from the rain. A humungous flat stone altar stood at the far end, strewn with branches—hazel, rowan, and yew. Brass cauldrons burning rendered animal fat illuminated chiseled markings in the stone and around the sides, pine pitch torches cast a romantic glow. Above the altar, a thatched overhang had been built to protect it from the elements. It was extraordinarily peaceful and beautiful. *Druid magic.*

Her half-fey druid friend, Magus Dubh, would appreciate and understand these druids. As would Estrada, with his Wiccan beliefs and mystical abilities. Sorcha had watched with awe last year when he'd conjured the old Celtic gods and his woman, Primrose, had appeared as a faerie. If they were only here now. She accepted that Cernunnos had somehow spun her through time but she had no inkling as to *how* these miracles occurred. She was a scientist who relied on evidence and facts, and realized she was out of her depth when it came to understanding druid culture.

The waxing moon cast a silver haze around the heavy cumulus clouds. It would rain again soon. Perhaps even snow. Timber gates had been dragged across the main road leading into the fort to ward off intruders, but she spied another smaller gate just large enough for a horseman to enter. It was guarded by a lump of a man who'd also succumbed at the dead king's wake.

Sorcha whispered through the passage without disturbing him and padded down the path toward the stand of trees where she'd found Cernunnos earlier. Accustomed to white noise, her ears rang with the silence. The odd bleat of a sheep, the croaking of frogs in the black pools below, and the cries of crickets in the pastures, all seemed oddly comforting. She glanced around as she dashed along the path, clutching the cloak tightly to her breasts, her bare feet tingling on the cold earth.

As she entered the forested glade, she grew more confident. "Cernunnos," she whispered. Nothing. Perhaps, she should try something more formal. The ancient Celtic fertility god was just arrogant enough to demand an appeal to his power and position. "Hail, Horned God. We need to talk." When he'd first abandoned her during the cattle stampede she'd been angry, but then she reckoned he was giving her time alone with Ruairí and she'd forgiven him. Perhaps, he'd even orchestrated their meeting. She had no idea what a god like Cernunnos was capable of, or what his agenda might be. But she still had two more days. Where was he?

Following the sickly-sweet scent of the blossoms, she found the hawthorn tree where she'd discovered him earlier. Examining the edge of Donella's cloak, she looked for a thread that she might tie around a tree branch and make an appeal. She'd done this very thing at the Hill of Tara two years ago, and the gods had answered with a vision of an Egyptian princess in Scotland that had made her career. But there were no loose threads and she dare not damage the cloak Donella had worked so hard to perfect. In the old days, Sorcha imagined women used ribbons from their hair. Though Cernunnos had created an elaborate plaited updo for her hair, she could feel no ribbons, only pins.

But why not a hair? It contained her essence, her DNA. Surely that would impress the gods. She pulled one long red hair free and yanked it out, then spun it between her fingers and bound it around a hawthorn twig. Then she prayed. She'd never been a Christian, but she'd always known there were spirits and now she knew there were gods. Someone would hear.

"Benevolent spirits"—it was best to distinguish between good and evil in a place like this—"help me find a way to warn Ruairí of what will befall him. Convince Cernunnos to let me stay beyond three days. Help me save—"

"Summoning your spirits?" The deep raspy voice shivered up her arms. Sorcha could smell the brew from his breath. Hear its effects in the man's slurred speech.

Turning, she took a quick inhale and stepped back against the hawthorn tree. *Bres.* He'd shaded his steel gray eyes in charcoal so appeared to wear a mask. His cheekbones crested dark hollows and his long sharp nose pointed down. Even his ears, so visible on each side of his slick bald head, were pointed. It was difficult to see his mouth, which was hidden beneath a dark mustache and beard that fell in coarse tangles nearly to his waist and covered most of his naked hairy chest. He'd split the beard below his chin in a double-fork and tied each tail with a leather thong. His tight-fitting breeches were held by a leather belt which housed a sheathed knife.

Sorcha swallowed to compose herself. He'd surprised her, but not unnerved her—even knowing he was armed. He was just another drunk and she could best him if necessary. Having spent years living on university campuses and at archaeological field sites around the world, Sorcha was no stranger to drunken men who felt it their prerogative to harass and assault a woman caught alone. So far, none had prevailed. A course in women's self-defense had seen to that.

She dug her bare feet into the earth, softened her knees, and tested her balance. "I don't believe we've met."

"I know who you are, or rather, who you *say* you are, Sorcha O'Hallorhan from Connachta."

She thrust out her chin. "What do you mean? Who I *say* I am? Why would I claim to be someone I'm not?"

When Bres lurched forward, she stepped back and to the right, which sent him bouncing off the hawthorn tree. Then he turned, his furious face weakening her knees. She took another quick breath to regain her strength.

"You are de Danann. I will have you and your power."

De Danann? He thinks I'm a faerie. The stories said the Celts intermarried with mortals to produce strong and powerful children. Is that what he wants? Feck!

The hand that grabbed her linen shift was quick. She'd underestimated his drunkenness. Pulling her in, he shoved her hard against the tree, grabbing her breasts roughly and scratching her neck with his stinking beard.

She lifted her heel high and brought it crashing down on his bare foot. He yelped, drew back, and raised a fist.

Then. A glint of metal. He'd drawn the knife.

She struck quick with the side of her hand and knocked it free. Surprise showed in his cocking head. *Had he never seen a woman use a hand strike to defend herself? Well, then.* Sorcha brought up her knee.

He jumped clear and chuckled. "You're a wild cat, you are."

"If you touch me, I'll curse you." Surely, he knew the fey could be just as evil as they were good. Malevolence was their middle name.

"But you won't. Because if you do, I will take Ruairí's youngest sister and work the bossiness right out of her."

Winnie? Surely Ruairí would kill him if he ever—

"And I won't wait until she comes of age. Her mouth needs a stopper. When I'm done with her, she'll never utter another word."

Leering, Bres yanked down his breeches to expose his erection.

She'd seen enough of them not to flinch and this was no impressionable cock. She rolled her eyes.

Sensing a moment of consternation, Bres leapt, spun her, and shoved her face into the tree. Sorcha's forehead cracked against the bark and she winced and wobbled but didn't go down. Pinned by his biceps, she screamed and struggled as he fought to penetrate beneath her gown. Her clothing proved solid enough a barrier but infuriated him.

Bending down, he grasped the bottom of her linen shift with both hands and ripped. Spiking on adrenalin, her terror turned to rage. Dropping her weight and leaning forward, she lowered her head. As he rose, she threw back, smashing the bony back of her skull against his mouth and lips. It hurt like hell and her eyelids riffled, but Bres yelled and clutched his bloody face, and that spurred her on. Turning, she grasped his bearded tails and yanked him forward, then hammered her knee into his crotch.

A flash of fire by the tall oak tree and they both turned. *Cernunnos.* The horned god appeared as Sorcha had seen him that first night at Ballymeanoch, standing tall on cloven hooves, his rack of antlers stretching up. His eyes were lined in kohl. His lips a deep dark purple. He was beautiful and terrifying and—

"Really feckin late." She heard water trickling and glanced down to find Bres pissing himself. He seemed dumbstruck—mouth open, eyes wide, body still bent forward to clutch his aching balls. "Jesus Christ!" she said, shoving Bres away.

"F-f-fey," he stuttered.

"F-f-feck," she replied mockingly. "Didn't you just accuse me of that? Wasn't it the *fey* you were all about seeing? Maybe you want to take *his* power you misogynist son-of-a-bitch!"

Bres was more shocked than injured having come face-to-face with the stuff of story. In the firelight, she caught the glitter of his knife on the ground. Grasping it, she squatted and held it beneath his balls. "Can you hear me, Bres?"

He nodded, blood running from his broken nose.

"You'll not touch Winnie, and you'll tell no one what happened here tonight. If you do, I'll curse you and castrate you, so you'll *take* no one ever again. Do you know what I'm sayin'?" She stared into his irate eyes. "Aye, sure you do, cowboy."

Turning to Cernunnos, who still stood bathed in fire like a rock star awaiting his Grammy, she sniffed. "Show's over, mate. You may as well go back where you came from. I won't be leaving Ruairí. Not now. Not two days from now. Not with these bastards."

Tarbfeis

Bres's nose was swollen and bloody, flattened and slightly twisted. He was subdued and surly, like he'd lost a fight he expected to win. Ruairí glanced at Fearghas, Bres's stepbrother and usual opponent. The big man was contently slurping porridge at a keen rate from his burled bowl. His knuckles weren't swollen or bruised and he appeared to have no injuries. That was odd. Perhaps, he'd cracked Bres with a chunk of wood. Once he'd broken Bres's nose by shoving him into a wall. Ruairí found that amusing. There'd been many times when he'd wanted to shove Bres into a wall himself. Together, Bres and Fearghas made one formidable bully but separately it was any man for himself. The scowl on Bres's fat lip was one of humiliation. Perhaps it was a woman.

Ruairí stuffed a piece of lamb in a flatbread along with a hunk of cheese and opened the door. It was still raining. A cold, hard rain mixed with chunks of ice. When Ana had sent him from her bed before dawn, he'd stumbled outside to piss and felt its fury. Perhaps the weather would improve with Adamair gone and the promise of an heir. Surely the Goddess of the Land would be pleased that he'd given Ana a son.

Stuffing the food in his pocket for later, he pulled the hood of his dark gray cloak over his head and stepped out. He was anxious for the ritual to begin. Until their new king was chosen and inaugurated, chaos would rule. The people were restless, gambling on who Criofan would choose. The white bull had not bellowed when Fearghas slit its throat yesterday, just stood calmly waiting for the knife. That was a bad omen. And now this driving rain.

Carpenters had built a wooden shelter over the massive fire pit to keep it dry, but the dampness had slowed the roasting and the ritual had been delayed.

The woman he'd rescued from the stampede sat on a log underneath an overhang out of the rain. *Sorcha O'Hallorhan from Connachta.* Distracted by Ana, he'd neglected her. She'd pulled her legs and feet up beneath her cloak to cover herself completely and was watching as the roasted beast was hoisted from the stones in the fire pit. Perhaps, she was hungry. Had his sisters not tended her?

He walked over, ducked in out of the rain, and shook back his hood. At six-and-a-half feet, Ruairí was the tallest man in the tuath and never quite fit under anything.

When she raised her head, her own hood slipped back and he startled to see her face so clearly. He knew it, had dreamed it. But not like this. Her cheeks were red, and her forehead swollen and purple.

"What happened?" he asked, but Bres came to mind.

Sorcha pulled the hood forward to cover the bruise and shook her head once. "Nothing. I slipped and hit a tree when I went out this morning in the dark."

A tree named Bres. Pulling the food from his pocket, Ruairí offered it to her. She shook her head. "Take it. We won't feast on this beast until after Tarbfeis."

"*Tar-uh-vesh.*" She spoke the word as if she'd never heard it before. Then she rolled the meat and cheese firmly inside the bread and took a bite. She nodded. "Thank you."

Sorcha made him uneasy. His body ached for her but his mind was plagued with questions. Surely, she dwelt among the *sidhe* and was of the Tuatha de Danann. But why had she come now? A woman whose face he'd once seen in a dream? Was it because it was close to Beltane when the veils collapsed between the worlds? Was destiny at hand or did she play a game for her own benefit?

Ruairí had heard stories of sidhe women who seduced and married mortals. They had much power but were wild and dangerous. They'd all heard the tale of The Morrigan, a shapeshifter who incited wars. She'd slept with The Dagda in the Second Battle of Mag Tuired to ensure victory for the de Danann. Perhaps Bres thought Sorcha had similar potential and had tried to tame her.

"You don't know of Tarbfeis?" His tone was accusatory though he tried to mellow it.

"Of course I know." She sounded peeved by his testing of her knowledge. "After eating the meat of the white bull, one of the druids will sleep. Four of you will witness. Whoever he dreams about will be chosen as the next king."

Ruairí nodded. King Adamair had died stealing the bull and now the bull was dead and the circle nearly complete. Through its flesh, the spirit of the divine white bull would provide Criofan with the insight to choose the next king. Ruairí glanced at the cooks who'd turned the roasted beast and were carving the flesh into fat strips. It was nearly time.

"Do you love Ana?"

The question surprised Ruairí and he felt his cheeks flush. "What do you know of Ana?"

"Nothing more than the whole house knows." Sorcha stood and tossed her head like a wild horse, then leaned toward him. "I thought ..."

Though her eyes were as green as the grass in the cattle pasture, they flashed fire. She'd heard his moans and was jealous. One side of his lip twitched in a lopsided grin. And when her lips puckered, his mouth moved toward hers. "You thought ...?"

"Jesus, feck!"

Ruairí cocked his head. Some of her expressions he'd never heard uttered, even by a foreigner. She was reckless and bold and titillating.

When she reached up to touch his cheek above the beard, he bent forward with a rush of lust. She stared into his eyes. "Are you with Ana or are you a free man?"

Of course he was a free man, as were his fathers before him. And Ana? Ana was Ana—as impossible to understand as Sorcha seemed to be. He shrugged, not knowing how to answer.

"I thought you wanted *me*," she whispered.

"I *do* want you." His cheek fell forward into the warmth of her palm and he leaned in, drawn to her as if by invisible cords. Her lips were full and pink and open and his but inches away. She raised her other hand and held his jaw with both palms, pulling him down, down, down ... and then he panicked.

She is De Danann. A seductress. A faerie. Reality intervened and he jumped back, raising his hands to break the spell.

"What's wrong?" she asked, her hands still raised and reaching.

"We have offered hospitality to a stranger, as is fitting, but now you must go." He said the words without emotion, knowing he didn't want to say them, didn't want her to go, but that he must. The de Danann were dangerous and must be treated carefully. If he gave in to Sorcha, he could lose himself in her charms. He'd already dreamed of her and that alone unnerved him. Destiny was at play but before anything could happen between them he must find a way to keep his power. He dreaded to think he'd already succumbed to her charms, but that was how he felt when he was near her. And he couldn't be thinking about Sorcha with Tarbfeis about to begin.

"Go? Where the feck am I supposed to go?"

One of the carvers called out to him and Ruairí turned. "Is it time?"

They stood, their sharp knives stained with the blood of the bull, its flesh and joints laid out on a giant wooden trencher carved from a cedar tree. "Yes. We've prepared Criofan's platter." After setting it on a flat stone beside the pool, they all disappeared.

Sorcha was still standing there staring at Ruairí with her big green eyes when the gate opened. "You must leave now," Ruairí said. "No one is allowed to witness Tarbfeis but us."

"Ah, well, aren't *you* special. Don't worry. I won't spoil your ritual." Turning, she stomped off, passing the other four druids as they entered the garden.

Criofan appeared first in a pale linen shift that fell to his bare feet, his long gray beard and thinning hair meeting at his elbows. He walked through the sleet somber-faced and entered the pool at the far end where flat rocks had been placed as steps. The water bubbled and misted around him as he waded to the altar and settled among the branches.

Bres picked up the feasting platter and followed, gave Criofan the bull's flesh, and came to sit at the edge of the pool beside his stepbrother. Ruairí and Conall took their places along the other side as rain hit the thatched roof and fell in sheets at their backs.

Ruairí shivered in anticipation. His world could change today. If Criofan dreamed of him, he'd take his place as king and stand proudly beside Ana. He'd love her and honor her and be a good father to his son. He'd look after his people and do whatever was necessary for the good of the tuath. But if Criofan dreamed of Bres or Fearghas, Ruairí knew he must leave his family, his friends, and his home here at Croghan Hill. He would not submit to either of them. Ever. The only way his life would remain the same was if Criofan dreamed of his own son, Ailill, or one of the other druids.

Conall held his wooden pipes to his lips and breathed an intricate melody as Criofan picked up the first chunk of flesh and began to chew. Conall had been born with bardic gifts that surpassed them all. His mother said he'd picked up a flat stone by the lake when he was still unable to walk. It had three tiny holes mysteriously carved right through it—a gift from the goddess. First, he stuck his fingers through the holes and then he put the stone to his mouth and breathed a note. He laughed and blew through each of the holes. Different sounds came from each. They rose and fell and quivered and Conall laughed more. Then he composed his first tune.

A traveling bard from the eastern mountains had given him the pipes he played now. Six narrow tubes of differing lengths, they were made of hollowed-out yew wood and bound together. Conall's lips flew over the holes caressing the instrument with his breath. His music could make a man laugh or weep.

Ruairí had no such gift but was not jealous of his best friend. Criofan said every druid had a unique gift that was of benefit to the tribe. Ruairí was a dreamer like Criofan. One night, he'd dreamed of the low land surrounding Croghan Hill covered in water so high their fort was nothing but a small circular island in an immense silty lake. The water licked the timbers at its gates and the people shivered and wailed inside. He'd awoken gasping for breath, wet and trembling and terrified. A few nights later, he'd dreamed of the hill as a barren green pasture cropped low by strange black and white spotted cattle, the land below nothing but flat black ridges that had been hacked into strips by a giant blade. Both dreams frightened him and he kept them to himself. How could either dream be of benefit to the tribe?

When he looked across the pool, the sheets of water flowing off the thatches reminded him of his dream. What if the rain didn't end and summer didn't come? Was the Goddess of the Land still so angry at Adamair? Whoever Criofan dreamed as the next king must appease her, and Ana, who embodied her as their queen. If not, they would starve.

Ruairí glanced across at Bres, his face cut and bruised and mean, and didn't want him to be Ana's husband. Women whispered of his cruelty. Adamair was cruel to Ana but in a different way. Ignorance and neglect were his weapons. Ruairí could see Bres's thoughts spinning as he squatted near the trees in the copse, watching with disinterest as Criofan ripped the meat with his soft old teeth and chewed and chewed and chewed.

Bres was an arbitrator, his judgments cold and based only on the facts of the case. At times, that was needed and he'd helped the tuath in many ways. They were rich in cattle due to his raiding strategies. His arguments and debates were skillful and his mind never stopped. Right now, Ruairí knew Bres was fixated on the fey woman; his thoughts as sharp as the iron blade that hacked the black ridges of their land into strips. Sorcha had humiliated or offended him in some way and he'd have his revenge. Ruairí blinked twice. De Danann or not, he couldn't allow her to become Bres's prey. He must protect her. The only way she'd be safe was if she left their territory. As much as he wanted her, he hoped he'd convinced her to go.

Criofan patted his belly and licked his fingertips, then pushed the platter aside and stretched out on his back on the stone slab. Some people thought Fearghas was Bres's inferior but Ruairí thought the big ox's gift came second only to Conall's. Fearghas had envisioned and engineered this place with its sacred pool, then built it with his own hands. There would be no stone on which Criofan could dream, no trees, no pathways, no pool—nothing would be here but the beaten earth on the curve of the hilltop without Fearghas's vision. The ox understood how nature could be shaped and bent to create beauty and purpose. He could envision it and then build it, and that was truly a gift.

Rain continued to pour off the sheltering rooftop Fearghas had constructed to protect the garden, and collect in the pool. It was close to overflowing but Ruairí knew there was no danger of a flood because Fearghas had constructed the pond with a corbeled base much like the roof in the tomb near Tara, only upside-down. At the very bottom of the pond, he'd left one stone that could be removed so the water could drain down into the earth. The big man dove down regularly with an iron shaft and pried up the stone to let the water drain.

As Conall's tune deepened into the lower reaches, Ruairí closed his eyes and his mind sunk below the surface of the pond. Slipping along the edges of the stones like a rivulet, he followed the water past the drain stone and down into the crater below. At first, there was nothing but darkness, a black hole sunk deep into the center of the hill. Then he imagined fire and torches appeared stuck into fissures in the sides of the rock. The stone itself was mottled and streaked, deep browns and blacks, white and gold, with splashes of red, the shade of their cattle, where the sacred flesh of the goddess had been bruised and her blood pooled. The crater loomed bottomless as he slipped down its fissured sides with the dripping water. He could see small cracks in the edges where the black water from the base of their hill poured into the crater and he knew he was entering a place he'd never been before. A sacred place below the skin of the earth.

An image of Bres arose in his mind then, an image he'd dreamed three times before. Dressed in a purple cloak, he stood with arms upraised, an iron sword in each of his fists. Blood streamed from the blades and heaped around him were the butchered carcasses of cattle. The stink of blood and carnage tainted the very air. And beyond the cattle was a brash whiteness. Looking closer, Ruairí could see that bone littered the earth, bone so dense the earth could not be seen. One skull, and then another, a leg bone, a ribcage, a foot. These were the skeletons of people. *His* people.

Ruairí startled then and the vision collapsed inwards. The music stopped abruptly, a signal from Conall that Criofan had awakened.

Opening his eyes, Ruairí saw Bres, across the pool, his neck turned, his black eyes staring at something in the trees beyond. Ruairí followed his gaze and gasped.

Sorcha O'Hallorhan stood there watching them.

Cruel Claw and Hungry Throat

Sorcha had spent her life brushing bones and shards from the earth, testing, analyzing, radio-carbon dating, recreating, theorizing and re-theorizing what prehistoric life might have been like. The druids left no written records and everything known about them was tainted with Roman bias or constructed from mythic tales visioned and revisioned by Christian scribes.

Nothing in this sanctuary would survive to find its way to a laboratory. The only things that remained from this time and place were Ruairí's headless torso and the remnants of a hillfort. A fort in which she now stood with Celtic druids. Of course, they called themselves neither Celtic nor druids; nevertheless, *real* Celtic druids were conducting a ritual Sorcha had only ever read about in journal articles.

Tarbfeis or *Tar-uh-vesh*, as Ruairí pronounced it, was so sacred no one but these druids had ever witnessed it.

How could she *not* watch?

She tucked away as best she could in the leafy bushes and stared through the pouring rain. If they caught her, she would plead ignorance and hope that Ruairí would support her. The look in his eyes told her he would. Even if he didn't, the actual experience was worth the risk.

What's the worst that could happen? They might berate her, but surely, they wouldn't beat or kill a woman of noble birth just for spying on them?

Here were five druids meditating on the destiny of their tribe. After eating a plateful of meat, Criofan had stretched out in the corpse position among the green branches and promptly fallen asleep. Warriors must be trained to sleep whenever and wherever they can. Sorcha could see his chest rising and falling, his mouth open in a soft O, his eyelids riffling in dream.

From where she stood, Sorcha could see only the backs of Bres and Fearghas and was glad of it. Bres obviously meant *ugly* in their language. What else could it mean? And the white bull would have made a far more pleasant companion than Fearghas, Bres's giant sidekick.

Conall and Ruairí faced her. Both had shut their eyes. Conall's melody seemed to emerge from some faerie world—the muse of music. His lips and breath brushed the keys like it was a woman. A fortunate woman. Conall was handsome and gentle, talented and charming—the prettiest of them all, truth be told. She wondered if *he* had a woman. She hadn't seen him with anyone. In fact, none of these men appeared to be married. She didn't understand their domestic rules and yearned to know more.

Adamair had taken Ana as his second wife while he was still married to his first, so they obviously allowed for multiple partners; at least, among the nobility. She wondered if the same held true for women. Could a woman have more than one husband or lover? Ana certainly had wasted no time bedding Ruairí after her husband's funeral. Even Winnie, at the age of ten, knew there was something brewing between Ana and Ruairí.

Perhaps, the druids were polyamorous. The word triggered thoughts of Estrada, who loved both Michael Stryker and his fey lover, Primrose, then fell for that Glasgow cop. The only reason he'd rejected Sorcha's advances was a promise made to his friend, Dylan. Loyalty was another quality that drew her to him. Aye, Estrada would appreciate these druids. He'd fit right into this culture.

She wondered if each of these men hoped to be chosen as the next king. Though she feared for his life, Sorcha knew Ruairí would make the best king. He exuded honor and courage, patience and wisdom. Now he appeared to be in a deep sleep though he sat rigid, his legs crossed, hands flat on his thighs. For a tall man, Ruairí's hip and knee joints were flexible. Perhaps he'd been trained to sit this way since childhood. Her mind drifted to the image of Cernunnos on the Gundestrup Cauldron. He also sat in this yogic posture. Ruairí wore a gold torc similar to the one the horned god held up in his right hand. Perhaps it was this connection to the ancient horned god that provoked her passion and drew her to him.

Suddenly, Conall stopped playing the pipes. Bres and Fearghas turned their heads. Ruairí's eyes opened and they all looked straight at her.

Feck! Ducking down, Sorcha tried to slip out of the bushes and into the fort. She'd managed to stand, turn, and take one step when Bres caught her. Crushing her shoulders in his bony fists, he yanked her backwards against his chest. As she struggled, he repositioned, looping one arm around her neck and the other around her belly. "You are caught, faerie, and your threats hold no sway with me." She thought he was going to snap her neck.

"Let her go, Bres." Ruairí spoke with authority. "I brought the woman here and I will guard her until she can appear before the council."

"You are too soft. Fearghas and I will—"

"Ruairí is right." Criofan's low husky voice reverberated through the trees and Sorcha released the breath she held.

"I've never seen such a beautiful place," she said, feigning innocence. "I'm sorry. I stumbled in here. I didn't know I was intruding."

Ruairí stared into her eyes as he pulled her free of Bres and she hated herself for lying. She'd broken his trust.

"Surely *this* can wait," Conall said, his brown eyes as gentle as his song. "The woman broke a rule but the people await Criofan's proclamation. If Ruairí guards her, what harm can she possibly do?"

"None," Sorcha said quickly. "I meant no harm and I promise to break no more rules." She'd been stupid and taken too big a risk. She wouldn't do that again.

Criofan had not yet risen from the stone but Sorcha heard his voice as clear and loud as if he stood beside her. "Call the people for the feast. Ruairí will bring the woman and we will decide what must be done."

Sorcha didn't like the sound of that and opened her mouth to object, but Ruairí squeezed her arm and she shut it. He hauled her roughly through the garden and out into the hall. They were both soaked from the downpour which showed no sign of stopping.

When he presented her to Donella, who was engaged in a pleasant conversation with her fiancé, the girl seemed unimpressed at the interruption. "Find Sorcha something dry to wear. She is not to leave."

"I won't leave, and I'm sorry to cause such trouble. I meant nothing by it."

"I told you." His eyes blazed.

"I know you did, but ..." Sorcha shrugged. Couldn't he understand her curiosity, her wonder, at being able to experience something like Tarbfeis? "What will happen? Not torture or death?" Somewhere she'd read that the druids had no death penalty, but then there were all those stories of sacrifice.

Ruairí shook his head and took a deep breath. "The council will convene after the feast and make a decision. Bres will argue for your banishment."

"Banishment?" Should she just tell him where she'd come from and why? On her own, away from the fort, she could be captured by another tribe, or die. How would she survive alone?

"And I will agree with him." Ruairí turned his back on her and walked away.

"No! Please Ruairí ..." Sitting down hard on the floor, she dropped her head in her hands, bit her lip, and squeezed her eyelids tightly together to stop the tears. She was to be driven off and there'd be no way to change anything. At least Cernunnos would be happy—him and his "you can't change history" rule. But what of *her* history if she died alone here? Wouldn't that change something?

"Don't despair." Donella was suddenly beside her patting her shoulder. "My brother is pig-headed but he's kind. He won't let Bres hurt you *again*." She glanced at the bruise on Sorcha's forehead sympathetically. "I've brought you dry clothes. After you change you can sit with us." She pointed to her man. "This is Aengus." Her face beamed. "He is my One Love."

One Love? How beautiful. Sorcha had never thought there could be just one love for anyone, but looking at Donella and Aengus, she thought it just might be possible. And how she ached for it—for Ruairí. The thought surprised her and she felt a pain in her chest.

Then, Conall walked by carrying an immense bronze horn shaped in an S-curve and nodded his head. Sorcha's eyes widened. She'd seen the famous Loughnashade Trumpa at the National Museum in Ireland and this could be its twin.

Donella smiled at her unexpected delight. "Conall's going to call the people to the feast."

"Where? Can we watch?"

"If we're not too close and cover our ears. King Adamair brought the horn from the north as a gift to our tuath."

"Conall can play anything," Winnie said, proudly. She'd appeared suddenly beside them and was looking longingly at the bard as he crossed by the hearth.

"Winnie loves Conall," Donella teased in her sing-songy way.

They were no different than any girls Sorcha had ever met. "Come on," she said, grasping Winnie's hand. "Let's go watch Sir Conall play the horn." She needed this moment of normalcy. Of hope. Truth be told, she felt closer to this family of strangers than to any she'd ever had in her world. No siblings and a single scholarly mother who traveled. A lifetime of boarding schools, academia, and shifting allegiances. Had she fecked it all up just to witness a ceremony?

Conall stood under the thatch and held the bronze horn to his lips. It rose six feet above his head in a lazy S-shape. The bell, which pointed out toward the gate, was decorated in embossed swirls. They all covered their ears as Conall blew a low tone that could be heard for miles and miles. Sorcha held her breath as he blew and just as she was about to gasp for another breath, the pitch rose an octave. The girls all cheered and laughed and Sorcha thought *I want to stay here with these people. Please do not let Bres banish me.*

With the entire tribe packed inside the hall, there was little room to move. Sorcha knew they followed a strict caste system and wondered how often they gathered together like this. Tradesmen and craftspeople, farmers and brewers, were all pouring into the hall with warriors and druid nobles. Whatever Criofan had to say, he wanted everyone to hear at the same time. There was something about the old druid that Sorcha admired and she was curious to hear his proclamation, even if the name that left his lips was Ruairí Mac Nia.

Sitting cross-legged on the skin and rush-strewn floor, she ate and watched. Immense trenchers had been laid out all around the hearth. Donella and Aengus had gone before her, piled their flatbread with meat and then maneuvered through the crowd back to their cozy corner. The rain had lessened but the stench of damp skins, smoke, and roast beef permeated the room.

When Sorcha discovered they were passing around several bronze cauldrons full of ale, she put out her hands and grasped one as it went by. It was yeasty and grainy, dark and delicious. *The original Guinness.* She gulped and gulped. If she was to be banished, she'd do so drunk. She finished the cauldron and passed it back, hoping it would be magically refilled and appear again before her.

When Bres stood and raised a hand, she felt an icy rush ripple through her core. People stopped talking, even chewing and drinking as all sat anxious to hear Criofan's decree. "We eat the flesh of the white bull here tonight, as Criofan did this afternoon. We are grateful to the Goddess of the Land." He nodded to Ana who sat in the center of the raised platform with the other druids around her, Criofan at her right and Bres at her left. "She nourishes the earth so our tuath continues to grow strong. She makes our cows fat *and* our women!" He puffed out his cheeks and mimicked pregnancy and the crowd cheered.

Sorcha saw Ana's eye twitch in irritation at Bres's ironic comment. She was the physical embodiment of the Goddess of the Land but had failed to conceive. And, for a moment, she felt a rush of sympathy for the dark queen.

Criofan stood and wiped his mouth with his hands. The people hushed and waited as the old man took a breath and collected his thoughts. "I had a dream." There was a loud dramatic pause. "I had a dream of Bres."

Bres stood and raised both fists and there were raucous cheers all around. Sorcha released a breath, she didn't know she was holding, and glanced at Ruairí's face. He was neither smiling, nor frowning. She couldn't read him. What was he thinking?

Criofan settled them with a downward movement of his hand. "In my dream, Bres stood holding two raised swords in the midst of a herd of slain and bloody cattle. Beyond them, the land was littered with bleached bones. The bones of our people." Whispers flew from mouth to mouth, brows furled, and then it grew silent as they awaited the old man's interpretation. "This is a bad omen. Although I dreamed of Bres, I do not choose him as our king."

Bres stood amazed, and then, when he found his voice, screamed over the crowd. "It may be that Criofan dreamed this dream, but it did not come from the gods. It is the work of the fey! This woman," he said, pointing directly at Sorcha. "This woman is *de Danann*. I've seen her call her spirits. *She* has poisoned Criofan's dream!"

"No, I-I-" Sorcha stammered. What could she say? What would they do? She wanted to stand up and run but her legs felt disconnected from her body. She couldn't move.

"This *faerie,* who claims to be Sorcha O'Hallorhan from Connachta, lies. She appeared among us the day our king died. One could argue, *she* is responsible for King Adamair's death."

There were gasps among the crowd and people all around Sorcha pulled away. She sat alone and vulnerable. "I didn't kill—"

"I caught her in the glade last night summoning her spirits and when I accused her of this, she used supernatural strength to beat me." He pointed to his bruised face.

Ah feck. The ale churned in Sorcha's guts and she hunched over, hand to mouth, in case it came back up.

"Then this afternoon at Tarbfeis, as Criofan slept, she stood in the bushes and poisoned his mind. This fey creature is the cause of all our suffering. *She* will bring ruin raining down upon us."

At this, two warriors grasped Sorcha's arms and hauled her up in front of Criofan.

"Is this true?" Criofan asked. "Were you in the garden watching while I slept?"

You know it is, she thought. *You saw Bres catch me. God damn courtroom drama for the spectators.* Still, she couldn't speak. The muscles in her jaw were so tense she couldn't form words. She had no breath. This was more than minor rule-breaking. Bres was accusing her of killing a king and poisoning the mind of the chief druid. Surely, those charges could only end in death.

"It's true," Fearghas said, backing up Bres. "We all saw her."

Criofan looked at Ruairí and Conall.

"I saw her there when I awoke," Ruairí admitted, and Conall nodded reluctantly. "But she appeared to be just watching, not casting spells over Criofan as he slept. I do not think she is malicious. Nor do I think she had anything to do with King Adamair's unfortunate death."

Sorcha released a breath. *Please, Ruairí, if you care anything for me, save me. Save me from this lying pontificator who spins a web of lies and dares to call it truth.*

Bres thrust back his bony shoulders and raised his hands above his head. "She summoned the Horned God. I saw him with my own eyes. He wore a full rack of antlers and naked and cloven-hoofed, he stood in a blaze of fire."

There were gasps and whispers among the crowd.

Cernunnos, if you want to put on a show, now's the time.

"*Can* you summon the gods?" Criofan asked, his old eyes flashing with wonder.

What's the correct answer to that question? Sorcha's mind raced. *Was it better to be fey or not fey?* She glanced at Ruairí, hoping he would somehow come to her rescue, but his poker-face was back. She heard her mother's voice echoing in her head. *Tell the truth or as close to the truth as you can get without drowning yourself.*

Taking a big breath, she thrust out her chest and exhaled. "I am Sorcha O'Hallorhan from Connachta. I was born on an island off the West Coast and traveled here with my brother-in-law. But we were separated during the cattle raid and now I fear he must be dead. I almost died in the cattle raid myself."

"That's true." Ruairí finally spoke. "If Sorcha is de Danann surely she would not have stood in the path of a raging cow." Everyone chuckled at that and the mood shifted slightly. "Perhaps, she's just an ignorant woman from Connachta who doesn't know our ways." Again, a chorus of laughter rippled through the room.

"If Sorcha O'Hallorhan is de Danann, as Bres claims, she must not be harmed," Criofan said. "If she is not, as Ruairí suggests, then she is just an ignorant woman who has broken our laws. Either way, it's best for us all if she leaves our tuath."

Bres was indignant. "She poisoned your sleep."

"There is no evidence of that," Criofan said. "But I will think on this, and the council will meet and talk more of both this woman and my dream."

Bres grew suddenly quiet and then his voice trembled with emotion as he spoke. "According to the rules of Tarbfeis, whatever man you dream about will become the next king. There is no clause for interpretation in the rules. I am that man and I claim that right!"

"No," Criofan said, shaking his head. "I do not sanction it, and I state that publicly while all are here to witness."

Bres picked up a cauldron full of ale and hurled it at Criofan, who shifted so quickly to the side, Sorcha couldn't believe her eyes. She'd thought, as Bres did, he was just an old man.

"I see that I've made the right decision," Criofan said, smoothing down the sleeves of his linen sheath. "As for you—" He stared at Sorcha. "You are banished from Tuath Croghan."

"No. Please, I promise—"

"Ruairí Mac Nia, since you brought this woman here, she is your responsibility. I trust you will see her safely from our land."

"I will." Ruairí left his place with the druids and took Sorcha from the warriors who held her.

She struggled to break free from his grip, mostly because she refused to be man-handled by anyone.

Ruairí growled. "Do not fight me, *faerie*. You will not win."

Not a Crumb of Comfort

Sorcha was back bouncing on the knobby spine of a horse. This time, it was not Ruairí's black horse—he rode that monster himself. Hers was a short, brown, furry horse with a fat belly. It was a pony really. He'd lashed a sheep's hide over the creature's back but it made little difference to her comfort.

She wore a dark green skirt and a new linen sheath—parting gifts from Donella—along with her saffron jacket and royal blue cloak. She'd pulled the skirt up between her legs to provide some cushioning and protection from the sweaty beast. The women didn't wear undergarments—no pantaloons and corsets, thank God—but rather, dressed for comfort and freedom. Ruairí had tied packs behind her and she wedged herself against them for lower back support. She was especially grateful that Donella had given her a pair of soft knee-high boots that had stretched to cover her ample calves.

Ruairí hadn't spoken since they left the ring-fort, but she could feel his angst. Perhaps, it was humiliation. Who knew with him? If she asked, she would most certainly just get *the look*. So she bounced along quietly gritting her teeth and wondering what "banishment" really meant. Would he escort her to the edge of their territory, turn his horse and gallop away? Or could there be some softening of this edict? Some distant friend in another village that might take her in.

They'd left shortly after sunrise and she'd been following the sun's slow movement as it rose through the mist over what she assumed were the Wicklow Mountains. For once it wasn't raining, though it was still overcast, bone damp, and threatening. At times, it was like walking through a ground level cloud. She pulled the hood of her cloak tighter around her head. It must be mid-afternoon by now. They'd been riding at a slow pace for hours. She was hungry and thirsty, her arse aching, and her bladder full. And now that she'd escaped the threat of Bres, her moxie had returned.

"How long before we get to wherever the hell we're going?" When he ignored her question, she wanted to smack him. "Ruairí, can we stop? I have to pee." They'd passed a farmhouse surrounded by moiled cattle and dark plowed fields a few miles back. Now, they were entering a mixed wood. The pony continued to plod along as Sorcha fumed beneath her cloak, and then, exasperated, she yanked back on the reins.

To her amazement, the wee brown pony stopped and stood still flicking its tail. She flipped her leg over its neck in a flourish of color, jumped down and scrambled into the copse. She could see Ruairí through the branches as she squatted, a grin spread across his face. *So, I'm a joke to him, am I?* Reaching out, she grasped a velvety mullein leaf to dry things off, then straightened her clothes and walked boldly from the woods.

As she passed, Ruairí offered her a bull's horn stoppered with a leather plug and bound with a braided cord. She opened it and sniffed. *Ale. Aye, why not?* This silent treatment was driving her mad. She took several gulps, tied the cord, and handed it back. "Don't piss off the faeries," she said, narrowing her eyes. "That's what my gran always said." It was a vague threat she couldn't back up, but it made her feel better.

"There's shelter on the other side of these woods."

"Oh, he speaks!" she said sarcastically, and stared at the woodland that seemed to go on forever. She glanced at the brown pony and then up at Ruairí. Sitting astride his horse, with his mohawk glued straight up, he seemed fifteen feet high.

Imagine that figure bearing down on you in battle, naked and brandishing an iron sword. And then a random thought. *How many men had he killed?* Goosebumps rushed up her arms.

Ruairí gave his horse a kick and it started forward. "Hey, wait. Aren't you going to help me up?" His horse kept walking. "Oh, for feck's sakes." Grabbing the pony's reins, she walked along beside it as they entered the woods. Ruairí's horse walked slowly, picking its way carefully through the fallen branches. But there was no way Sorcha could keep pace.

Finally, she pulled the pony over close to one of the downed logs and used it as a step-up to get back on. As soon as it felt her weight, the little thing began to trot, anxious to catch up with the black horse. Bouncing along, holding the reins and mane in her hands, she squeezed her legs around its fat belly and tried to keep her balance. All at once, she seemed to find a rhythm and sunk into it. When they came abreast of him, she looked over. "It's not so hard."

This time his smile was wide and genuine. "Not bad for an ignorant woman from Connachta." He gave his horse a hard kick and it took off at a gallop.

"Jesus. Feck!" As her pony raced to keep up, she crashed down hard with every surge and felt her bones might break.

When at last they stopped, he was laughing, his amber eyes twinkling. "This is the edge of our territory." As they left the woods, they passed into a grassy narrows that edged a lake. The horses smelled the water and pawed at the ground. Sorcha was so thirsty she could smell the water herself. Ruairí pointed to a series of wooden posts driven into the earth as far as she could see. From one hung the skull of a man.

"Who left that there?"

He shrugged. "It's always been there."

Boundaries. They were crossing the line to her place of banishment. A chill ran up her arms. What if the neighboring tribe, on whose land she'd been banished, patrolled this place? She'd rather be on Ruairí's side of the line, even if it meant living in the woods like a hermit. She glanced back over her shoulder. *Could I find my way back to that farm? Surely, they would take in a lost woman.* Any hope she had of Cernunnos coming to her aid was gone and telling Ruairí the truth now would only complicate things. How could she confess to traveling from the future with the horned god? It would only affirm Bres's accusations. All she could do was make the best of a hopeless situation and hope that Ruairí still cared something for her. Her feelings for him had intensified with his gallantry and good will. She knew unequivocally, that, without him, Bres would have hung her out to dry.

Beyond the trees, a lake appeared, offering space where there was none, and they followed its edge along a trail thick with brambles. She recognized the small green leaves of bilberry and farther back, soft stands of birch, willow, and rowan. The black water rippled with the slight breeze and only when she saw it stippled did she realize the sky was spitting drops of rain again. *Water worship*, she remembered.

The Celts named their rivers after gods and goddesses—the Boyne for Boann, the Danube for Danu—and they left votive offerings like vats of butter and gold hoards. Coming out of the dense woods to this dark tranquil space with its unknown depths, Sorcha suddenly understood why. *What lies beneath? What creatures hide in its shadows?* Her thoughts drifted to the dragons of myth—the Loch Ness monster and Finn MacCool's salmon of wisdom, and sacrificed humans weighed down in the bog, like himself.

She watched him sway on his horse as if he'd been born to ride and wondered if, given time, she might one day ride like him. *Ah, but who am I kidding. I'm banished. He's about to dump me off and ride away into the sunset, to his death.*

When the trail veered slightly left and opened onto higher ground, she was glad to be out of the shrubbery and bugs and her own dark thoughts. A small circular wattle and daub structure perched by the edge of the lake. Around it, the ground was sandy, as was the small beach before it. Large flat rocks were strewn along its edges. It was a dreary place but might provide some shelter and protection from the clouds of midges who'd trailed them from the bush. She had itchy bites on her neck and hands that she was trying not to scratch.

Ruairí slipped off his horse and draped the reins over a post that had been hammered into the sandy ground. Relieved to be taking a break at last, she swung her right leg over the horse's neck.

Catching her knees in her skirt, she tumbled down. He laughed and shook his head.

"Ha ha. Ignorant woman falls off horse. Again." She wiped herself off and straightened her clothes, then draped her reins over the same post. Sorcha thought she was doing amazingly well for a woman who'd never ridden a horse in her life.

As Ruairí pushed open the wooden door, he disturbed a family of swallows who were nesting in the thatch. "Bring the packs." He didn't say *woman*, but Sorcha heard it. Scholars said, women had power in this society but she'd yet to see it. Even Ana seemed subject to Criofan.

"Is this it? Is this where we're staying?"

"This is where *you're* staying."

A pain struck her heart and for a moment she couldn't breathe. *This* was banishment? Was he expecting her to live here all alone in this derelict cow shed? When he stooped and took a step inside she hesitated, then stuck her head in the door. It was small, dank, and dirty. There were no windows and the only light came from the smoke hole above the central hearth, which also let in rain and birds and flies and God knows what else. And there was no furniture, just a dirt floor big enough for two people to lie flat, a couple of slanted stumps, and a pile of dry wood and twigs.

She shuddered thinking of the creatures that must live in the wood pile and in the thatch—wasps and mice and spiders and— "I can't stay here," she said, backing out. "I'd rather live in the woods." As if on cue, the rain poured down buckets. "Oh, for Christ's sake, Ruairí!" She stamped her foot and shook her fist and promptly collapsed outside under the thatch overhang in a fit of tears. It was just low blood sugar and a sore arse and this infuriating man.

The longer she stayed, the more she regretted her decision to stay. *I should have just left with Cernunnos.* But then she'd see an image of Ruairí's curled mummified fist and know she couldn't leave this beautiful bastard to a fate like that.

He poked his head out the open doorway. "Come in, Sorcha O'Hallorhan. I believe you."

"What?" She wiped her face and blew her nose on her linen shirtsleeve, and when he offered his hand, she took it. His eyes were huge, amber flecked with gold, and spoke reams. "What do you believe?"

"I believe you intend no harm and that is enough for now."

"Oh. Good." Standing just inside the doorway, Sorcha watched him. When he squatted and built a small fire, the heat and light and sputtering orange and blue flames answered all her questions about prehistoric man. She knelt before it, as if it were a god. This answer to darkness. To fear. To despair. The rain slapped the thatch, streamed down the open doorway, and pounded the sand. But as the fire grew, the hut emanated an aura of comfort.

When Ruairí stood, the tips of his mohawk brushed the thatch roof. "When Conall and I built this hut, I was much shorter." He unplugged the bull horn and took a drink, then leaned over and passed her the ale. Settling down on the dirt floor in front of the fire, he pulled his cloak around him.

"The two of you built this. How old were you?"

"Six or seven. We came here often to escape Fearghas and Bres."

"Feckin bullies." She took another swallow of ale and passed it back, then settled down across from him and watched his face through the smoke. "Who else knows about it?"

"No one. You're safe here."

"But it's not *your* territory. What about the lads from the other tuath?"

Ruairí shook his head. "The lakeland is watched over by the goddess and is no one's territory."

No Man's Land. A liminal border between territories, like twilight.

"But do they come here to fish or ...?"

"They're a day's fast ride north and have no reason to come. There are plenty of lakes and plenty of fish."

To the east were the mountains and the Celtic Sea. Sorcha knew that much. She reckoned they'd covered twenty or thirty miles today. The lake was at the base of a hill, not far south of where Dublin would one day be built. She tried to remember if there were any lakes in the area. Of course, the landscape would've changed over two millennia. Lakes dried up, filled with sphagnum moss and became raised bogs. Like the ponds around Croghan Hill where they'd sink Ruairí's body.

"What about Bres?" she said, and goosebumps rose on her wrists. "Will *he* come here? Will he send Fearghas?" The big ginger-haired goon was intimidating, but she'd met men like him before and survived. Bres, though, he was different. He was the stuff of nightmares—a strategist, interrogator, psychopath.

Ruairí shook his head. "They don't know about it."

She felt the muscles in her face tighten and glanced away. Bres had it in for her and he wouldn't stop.

"No one knows about this place. You must trust me."

Something small and black scurried along the floor and she screamed, jumped up, and brushed her arms with her hands. "Jesus, Ruairí, I can't stay here. This place is crawlin'."

"They're just curious."

"Curious what I'd taste like."

"Is that so bad?" He raised his eyebrows.

Ah, jeez. In the midst of all this squalor is he flirting? Ruairí was a hard man to read, but there'd been that moment in the garden when he'd almost kissed her.

He opened one of the packs and took out a roll of bread and meat. "Eat. You'll feel better."

"Why are you always trying to feed me?"

"You heard Bres."

"Ah, yes. We like our women fat like our cows." That summed up Bres's misogynist attitude quite nicely. Women, to him, were useful only as vessels and a means to power. "Bres means you harm." She blurted it out suddenly and then she couldn't stop. If Bres took out Ruairí, God knows what would happen to her. "If Criofan chooses you to be king, don't accept. Bres will—"

"If it's offered, I *must* accept. I have no choice."

"Damn you." She raised her hands in a pleading gesture. "There's always a choice."

He cocked his head. "How do you know what Bres will do? Are you a seer?"

A seer? Aye. Why not? Better a seer than a witch or a malevolent faerie. Criofan was a seer and they respected him. "Aye. Sometimes I dream, like Criofan. That's why I came here."

"You came all the way from Connachta because of a dream?" His eyebrows furled.

"A dream about you." She felt her heartbeat quicken. Here was a man she'd imagined for fifteen years. It was almost like she knew him.

He took off his cloak and spread it on the ground. "Sit here, Sorcha, and tell me about your dream. I'll guard you from the spiders."

Stepping around the fire, she settled down on his cloak and pulled her own tightly around her shoulders. "It's more like a prophesy."

"Go on. What did you see?"

She took a deep breath. This was it. What she'd come here to do. Warn him. Save his life. "I saw your face and I-I knew things."

"Things?"

"Aye. In the future, you'll become king, and then later—I don't know how much later—you'll be deposed. They'll kill you. Sacrifice you to the Goddess of the Land."

"Sacrifice?" His amber eyes flashed.

"Aye, so you see, you must *not* become king. If you do, they'll bind you and stab you in the heart and cut off your head."

A sense of relief flowed through her limbs and then, leaning back, he smiled. "But *that* is a great honor."

"To be decapitated, cut into pieces, and sunk in the bog?"

"To be sacrificed and reborn with the Goddess is the greatest honor." He seemed to stretch even larger and she felt his happiness at hearing this dreadful prophesy.

"I don't think it happens like-like *that*," she stammered. "There's torture and pain and ..." She glanced at the leather-braided armband he wore and remembered the hazel branches strung through his upper arms to bind him. Had he been alive in that moment?

"There's always pain. That's a warrior's life. But to be the Sun King and then given to the Goddess. *That* is truly a gift." Reaching across the smoke, he laid one of his large hands on her shoulder and squeezed gently. "You risked your life to come here and tell me this?"

Reaching up, she placed her hand across his. "After I saw your face, I couldn't forget you. I had to warn you."

"You're a good woman, Sorcha O'Hallorhan, and that you are de Danann intrigues me. I confess, at first I feared you, but now I know you are a blessing. That's why I brought you here to my secret place."

"But I ..." She started to say that she was not de Danann, that she was from the future, and then she thought how ridiculous that conversation could become and she let it go. He believed her and that was all that mattered for the moment. "I'm afraid—"

"You're safe here. There's nothing to fear." He squeezed her shoulder again, then let go and prodded the fire with a stick. "I'll bring you food and no one will harm you. Once Criofan has chosen a king, I'll ask him to lift the banishment so you can return to us. Do you understand?"

A ripple of excitement raced through her limbs. She could return to them. She could stay.

"But, what if Bres is king?"

"Criofan will not allow Bres to become king." He said it with such confidence, her body softened.

"Aye, all right. But tell me. You saw me at Tarbfeis. How did you know I didn't poison Criofan's mind with that dream about Bres?"

"Because I had the same dream as Criofan at Tarbfeis and Beltane and Midwinter and Samhain. Always the same. Bres standing among slain cattle and the bones of our people. Three times *before* you appeared."

"Oh." She lost her words when he caught her chin in his fingers and brushed her bottom lip with his thumb.

"I, too, am a seer, Sorcha O'Hallorhan and, once, I dreamed of you."

Giolla Rua

Leaning forward, Sorcha felt the fire's heat bathe her face. How could they be so entwined that Ruairí Mac Nia, an Iron Age druid, could dream of *her* two thousand years before she'd even been born? She stared across the flames at his granite face, jagged with edges and shadows and resolve. "You dreamed of *me?*"

A corner of his lip curled up slowly as he narrowed his eyes to replay his vision. "You are standing in a field of yellow flowers. It's Midsummer. Your hair is long and wild, blowing back in the wind. You're dressed like a farmer in long breeches and dull shades the color of sand. You see something in the grass, reach over and pick it up, then smile and tuck it away. Do you remember a moment like this?"

"No, I don't think so." Was it a moment she'd forgotten, an image from the future, or simply a metaphor? "What could it mean?" she asked, knowing one thing—he'd seen her in her own time, in the clothes of her profession. She often wore khakis. They were comfortable on digs and easy to pack and she was always stuffing something in the pockets. But why that particular dream?

He touched his heart and his eyes glittered as he stared into hers. "Whatever you lose will not be lost forever."

"I feel better already," she said, wondering what she might possibly lose in this place besides her life, and *him*. She'd always romanticized the past, but the truth was, she was cold and wet, dirty, hungry, and afraid. And she didn't want to think about losing him. "Did Donella send any other clothes for me?" she asked, reaching back to claim the reality of the moment.

"My sister is a good woman. I'm sure she thought to pack everything you might need."

"I *need* a bath," Sorcha said, looking out the open doorway toward the lake. The rain still poured down, but a quick dip and some fresh dry clothes were what she craved most. Having spent much of her life living in tents, she was used to dirt and dust, but whenever the luxury of a lake appeared, she was first in and last out. She dove and swam like a dolphin and could float for hours if the sun was shining and the water warm.

"A bath?"

"Aye, and you're welcome to join me." Not that she minded the raw scent of him. The combination of leather and horse and manly sweat was strangely erotic.

Ruairí crossed his arms over his chest, then uncrossed them and ran a hand through his long, straight hair. The resin had been washed away by the rain and it fell over his right cheek like a silken curtain. "But the lake is—"

"I know. Freezing, but the fire's warm," she said, tugging off the leather boots. Then standing on his cloak in her bare feet, she turned. Skirt, jacket, and linen shift all fell away easily beneath the cloak. She could sense the chill of the cold lake water already.

"Sorcha …" Reaching over, he clutched her ankle.

"What? Is there a monster?" she teased, pulling free of his grip and dashing out the door with her cloak billowing out behind her.

Of course, there *could* be a monster. Some scientists were still trying to prove that Nessie was a long-necked plesiosaur who'd somehow escaped extinction and been trapped in Loch Ness. But the water called her so strongly she couldn't refuse it.

At the edge, she hesitated for just a moment, turning back to see Ruairí's anxious face in the doorway, and then she stepped off the rock into the sandy shallows. "Jesus, Mary, and Joseph! It's feckin freezing!" Her feet tingled, and she knew if she didn't go now—

Flinging the cloak onto the rocks, she ran babbling, knees high, into the frigid water. "Holy feck! Holy feck!" When she was up to her waist, she took a breath and dove, screaming inside her head. Then, she swam out into the lake. Oxygen flooded her bloodstream and numbed her soul. She took a big breath of sweet, unsullied air, as turning to face the hut, she treaded water.

Ruairí was standing on the rocks by the shore some thirty yards distant, waving his arms, and shouting.

"Come in," she yelled. "It's brilliant!"

And then something long, chill, and slick slid past her leg. She blinked, then held her breath and dove. Better to know than imagine a scene from *Jaws*.

Opening her eyes, Sorcha searched the hazy world below. It wasn't deep. Maybe fifteen feet. She could see weeds swirling on the rocky bottom and above them, shapes. Hundreds of shifting shapes, slipping through the water, dipping and rising all around her, kicking up sediment. *Trout!* They were feeding, nabbing fly larvae from the weed bed.

Breaking the surface, she gulped air and dove down again for a closer look. They were tawny and gold, their sides dotted in a dark red, that she knew would shimmer crimson in sunlight. Her uncle lived in Donegal and every second summer her mother had sent her fly fishing with him in Lough Derg. *Uncle Emmett, if you could see this*! He'd surely have a heart attack to see the sheer numbers of trout feeding on sedge fly larvae in the bottom of this lake. She rocketed up for another breath, then dove back down again, swam into their midst, and ran her hands along their flanks. *If I only had a net, I could scoop one up for supper.* She didn't really even need a net; a yard of linen would do—just something coarse to hold the slippery bugger.

She swam to the surface, swept her hair back from her face and looked toward the hut. Ruairí was no longer waving from the rocks. *Feck! If he's gone off and left me, I'll kill him.* She dove back in and swam hard and fast toward the shore, watching the bottom rise as she pumped her arms and legs. It was only a few feet deep and yet the trout were still all around her, dipping and nipping, feasting on the larvae. Stopping, she found her footing on a rocky shelf and squatted beneath the water. And then, she saw him.

Head and torso visible just above the water line, Ruairí was walking toward her.

She stood up, catching the shock her naked body produced on his too-often sober face. "Ruairí!"

"I thought you were—" His hands were balled up fists. The skin around his eyes veiled in sweat.

"Drowning or being devoured by brown trout?" She tried to make light of it. Judging by the grimace on his face, she'd scared the poor man half to death.

"The Giolla Rua," he said.

"Aye, the Gillaroo." *The Red Fella*. "I used to fish them with my uncle back home. I'm fine. You needn't worry. Have you got anything to fish with?" She thought for a moment, then noticed he'd stripped down to his linen loincloth. "Never mind. That'll do."

"What?"

"That." She pointed. "That loincloth. Don't worry. I won't hold it against you. I know the water's cold."

"What're you going to do?" he asked, untying the cloth and turning slightly away from her to shield his shrunken bits. *Oh Lord, is he shy? He didn't sound shy last night with Ana.*

"Just go in and stoke up the fire. I'll bring you a surprise."

His eyebrows drew together in one intense copper line.

Sorcha shook her head. "Ah, don't worry about me. I'm fey, remember? We've an affinity for the water and air and all such things." Without waiting for his response, she turned and slipped into the lake.

It was easy enough to grab a trout that had never been grabbed by a woman with a loin cloth on a rainy day in May. By the numbers of them, she reckoned there were no predators here. A secret lake that no one fished. She couldn't imagine a spot like this existing anywhere on the planet.

Back in the hut, she found Ruairí, tucked back into his leather breeches and linen shirt. She proudly presented the fish to him, still wrapped in the loin cloth, its mouth opening and closing as it struggled to survive. "Gotta knife?" she asked, eyebrows raised. She was totally pleased with herself.

"I cannot touch it. The Giolla Rua are forbidden. Bres's grandfather put a *geis* on the men of our tuath years ago."

A gesh? "On all of you?" That seemed odd. As far as she could remember, a geis was an *individual* taboo or prohibition doled out to keep a warrior in line and it didn't usually pass through generations. Warriors lived by an honor code and in the old tales, a man who broke a *geis* met with tragedy. But stories in books and stories from real people were two different things and Ruairí certainly didn't need any more misfortune coming his way. "That's a shame. I fished it from the lake just for you." She bit her lip. "Well, there's no geis on me and I'm sick of jerky. Can you stoke up the fire while I gut it?"

Ruairí's gaze had fallen to her breasts. She hadn't had time to pick up her cloak and glanced down at her pink naked skin, all ravaged by goosebumps. "Aye, it's cold when you get out." Once she'd spit out the words, her teeth chattered. "Lend me your knife?"

He followed her outside and stared like he'd never seen a naked woman gut a gillaroo.

"This fella must go ten pounds." She pulled out the organs but decided to leave the head on. "So, was Bres's grandfather anything like him?"

Ruairí shrugged. "He was king for many years as were several of his sons including Bres's father."

"I see. What happened to the old man?"

"He drowned during the spring floods long before I was born."

"Drowned?" Likely drunk and en route to one of his conquests.

Ruairí scraped his fingers through his beard. "Aye, but not before he sired thirty-nine sons."

"Thirty-nine sons! Christ! The fort must be teeming with Bres's kin."

"The fort and half the country. He traveled and fought."

"How many wives?"

He raised his hands as if to say, *who knows? Who cares?*

Perhaps wives were inconsequential unless you were married to the Goddess of Sovereignty, which he undoubtably was. Like Adamair, he likely slept with whoever he pleased. But why slap a taboo against eating trout on all the men of Croghan? It made no sense unless somehow it benefited him personally. She'd heard that Vitamin B increased sperm motility and trout were a good source. Had Bres's grandfather figured that out or perhaps been told by a seer? Skew the gene pool and rule the tuath?

"The old man probably forbid you all from eating the gillaroo so he could steal their power for himself. I'm sure these red fellas would give a man keen strength and endurance. Eat more fish. Make more babies." She winked and caught a flash of interest in his eyes.

She sat the trout on a flat rock and brushed the hair from her eyes with the back of her hand. "Can you rig up something to hold this red fella out of the fire as he cooks?"

Ruairí looked around and settled on some green branches. Taking back his knife, he wiped it clean in the sand and began to whittle. She glanced at his hands—the famous hands of the deposed king who'd never done any manual labor.

She followed him into the hut carrying the gutted trout on a slab of wood. He'd whittled two Y-shaped prongs from branches and stuck them in the ground on either side of the fire—cooking tools that would decompose organically and never make it to the archaeological record. She placed the gillaroo in carefully, making sure it was secure, then went back outside to wash in the cold lake.

By the time Sorcha returned she was thoroughly frozen. After rummaging around in the pack, she pulled out the emerald cloak. "Ah, Donella. Give a banished woman your best hand-made wrap." With it was a clean linen shift, which she slipped over her head and left hanging open and loose.

Ruairí had gone outside again to do God knows what. He didn't talk much. She wondered if he was anxious around her or if this was just Ruairí.

Cuddling up by the fire, she assessed her hair. Her up-do was down and hanging by one gold pin. *I've lost the other three in the lake*, she thought. *Two thousand years from now, some archaeologist will dig them up and say, "Look a votive offering."* She pulled out the single gold pin and did the best she could to comb out the tangles with her fingernails. At least, it was cleaner than it was before. She left her hair hanging down, long and free, to dry by the heat of the fire.

The fish was starting to flake and Ruairí hadn't come back into the hut, so she peered out the door. The rain had lessened to an acceptable drizzle. Ruairí was rubbing down his black horse with what was left of the loin cloth. Her wee brown pony was sheltering under a rowan tree and she decided, right then and there, to name her Rowan. Ruairí her friend, and Rowan her pony. If she had no one else in this place, she had them.

She watched the muscles in his back and arms stretch and contract as he worked. When he considered the black horse to be sufficiently groomed, he suddenly lifted a leg and leapt onto its back.

"Where are you going?" she asked, sprinting across the glade.

Ruairí looked down while his horse pawed the ground anxiously. "Home."

"Ah, not now." When she touched his calf, her fingers crept around in a light hold. She didn't want him to go. Couldn't bear to be left alone in this place.

"They'll be looking for me."

Who? Ana? Criofan? Bres? "If you go back now, Bres will know how long you've been gone and he can tell how far you traveled. If it's not far, he might send riders. He hates me, Ruairí. If he comes when you're not here …" It was a flimsy argument, since it took far longer for them to get here than it would for him to gallop home, but her show of emotion trumped her logic.

Ruairí slid down from the horse. "If I stay any longer it will be too dark to ride home tonight." He stood staring at her, biting lightly at his lower lip, his eyes a maze of questions.

"Good." She turned and walked into the hut without looking back, knowing he would follow.

As she slipped the trout from the prongs and onto a wooden slab, Ruairí watched intently. Had he been a dog, he'd have been drooling. She flecked off a piece of sizzling white flesh and popped it in her mouth. "Mmmmm, *so* good. I've never eaten anything so fresh. I feel bad eating it in front of you but damn, you can't break a geis."

He sniffed and cleared his throat, then broke off a piece of trout and popped it in his mouth.

"What are you doing?"

Ruairí's eyes stretched wide with pleasure.

"Good? Yeah?"

He nodded. "Better than tough dried bull."

"But the geis."

"You fished for me. You cooked for me. How can I turn down your food?"

Ah, feck! I caught him between two social taboos—the geis and the need to be gracious and accept hospitality. He can't turn down a meal made for him. "But the geis? Will it hurt you?"

"I'm a warrior. *Everything* hurts me." He laughed cavalierly. "Don't worry so much, Sorcha. Eat."

They ate the trout off the wooden slab with knives and fingers, flecking off pieces of tasty white flesh and washing it down with ale. Ruairí seemed to have an unlimited supply of bull horns.

When they were both full, Sorcha covered what was left with cedar branches—she was sure bugs didn't like cedar though she wasn't so sure about mice—and placed it in a corner of the hut away from the wood pile. Then she took the bones down to the lake shore. After washing her hands and face, she cleaned her teeth as best she could using a twig.

When she returned, Ruairí had spread his cloak on the floor and was leaning back against a split stump. He gestured to the space between his knees with a tilt of his head.

"Looks cozy," she said, catching his meaning. She settled in easily between his legs and eased back against his chest. She'd left the door open to the night and while it grew dusky outside, inside the firelight drew shapes against the walls.

With his right hand, Ruairí pulled a pine branch from the fire, held it up and watched it burn slowly like a torch. With his left, he stroked the curve of her hip. She sunk into the sensations his touch created in her body.

She could also feel the braided armband he wore on his left arm just above the elbow and wondered what would happen if she touched the copper mount again, as she had in the museum. *No, not now.* She wanted no tragic scenes to interrupt this peaceful moment. She watched the torchlight and dancing shapes a while, hypnotized by their shifting shadows and the feel of his heart beating against her neck. Then her eyes closed and the beating of his heart lulled her to sleep.

When she awoke it was pitch black outside. Their fire still burned on a bed of orange embers, but a slight breeze caught the smoke and sent it shimmering out through the hole in the roof. She'd slid down and Ruairí's chin was now wedged in the dip above her collar bone. His beard tickled her cheek. She could feel the soft sough of his breath. His right arm was sprawled across her breasts. Tilting slightly, she stared at his chiseled face, then leaning in, she kissed him lightly on the lips. He didn't wake up, but his mouth moved with hers and his breath quickened as he began to stir.

When she took her mouth from his, he growled. "Don't move."

Her muscles tensed. *Are we in danger? Is someone here?*

She fell forward with his weight as he moved behind her. Then his fingers began a slow dance across her breasts—one hand creeping beneath the linen shift, while the other swept the hair from her shoulders. His lips brushed the fey butterfly tattooed on the back of her neck sending a rush of promise down her spine. With his tongue he traced the leafy veins on its wings. Then, with those long fingers, he reached down her left side, pulled up her skirt, and gently teased.

God, she wanted to move, to flip over, rip off his clothes, and take him.

"I mean it," he said, hearing her thoughts. "If you move one muscle, I'll call all the spiders in this hut and they'll crawl all over you. I know a magic word. It's me or them."

"Spider whisperer." The hand that stroked her breast crawled upwards like a hungry spider and touched her lips, ending her thought and sending another. She opened her mouth slightly and he touched the edge of her lips and tongue, then trailed his fingers back to her breasts. With his other hand, he reached behind and tarried between her thighs, traveling slowly in her deep warmth.

"Jesus, man." Impulses raced through her body and sprang from her open palms. She was right there, hovering on the edge, body purring, when he dropped his hand to shove down his leather breeches.

"Oh, hell. The cold water didn't do you any harm." Lifting and tilting her hips with both hands, he found his way. "Jesus, man ..." she cried, and then his fingertips began their magical dance again so he seemed everywhere at once.

His lips explored the back of her neck, her shoulders, her ear, and then she heard his voice, low and rough, like the growl of a fox. "*Now* you can move."

The Fox & The Ox

Ruairí stared at the flaming twig he held in his hand and knew he'd been beguiled. Mesmerized. Like a moth who, ignoring the danger, still flies into the fire. Sorcha O'Hallorhan, the woman who fit so perfectly against his body, was undoubtably de Danann. Why else had he dreamed of her? She even wore the mark of the fey on the back of her neck: a faerie woman with butterfly wings imbued with magical symbols. He'd watched her dive beneath the lake and return to the place of her people—the old gods who'd been driven underground. And when she surfaced, bathed in a circle of light, he'd felt her power. She emerged with the ability to tame the *giolla rua* and everyone knew the red fish had deep magic.

Once, when he and Conall were boys, they'd built a coracle of bent wood and skins and paddled out into the lake. The red fish had rushed to the surface and swarmed their boat. The motion caused such waves, the coracle tipped and they fell into the fish-infested lake. Ruairí breathed in a mouthful of water, his nose burned, and he panicked. Even then, he was tall and thin and gangly with a body that didn't take to swimming. He beat his arms, madly splashing, then sunk beneath the surface.

Conall dove down and hauled him up, hooked his elbow under his chin, and carried him along until they reached the shallows. Ruairí couldn't look Conall in the eye for days after that, such was his shame, and they didn't speak of it ever again. He could still remember the stiff nibbling mouths of the *giolla rua* against his skin, and the stiffer leather strap his uncle beat him with when they returned to the fort. Though they hadn't told him, he knew. Ruairí had never gone into the lake again until today, and it was concern for *her* that had sent him.

Even a glance at the red fish made his skin crawl and when he'd stood in the lake they'd nibbled his legs and thighs just as they had that day long ago, filling him with terror he could not reveal. But she'd not only swum among them, she'd picked one up with her bare hands.

That's why he'd made up the story of the geis. Better for Sorcha to think he feared the geis than falling in a lake of red fish. But she knew things about the *giolla rua* and he couldn't resist a taste anymore than he could resist tasting her. And if she was right, if it made a man more potent ...

Tossing the pine torch into the fire, he continued to stroke the curve of her hip. As her muscles relaxed, she sank back against him. Her skin smelled of wildflowers and honey. No human woman smelled like this, and he'd smelled many. Sorcha was a fey goddess who could bring him good fortune or ill. She must be handled carefully. He knew what she wanted. Sensed it the moment she took human form in the glade. Like all fey women, she'd come to seduce a mortal man. The longer he made her wait, the stronger her need became. He'd made Ana moan to titillate Sorcha and show his skill as a lover. Breathing in her scent now, he could barely hold back.

When she emerged from the lake, her power had washed over him and his strength tripled. As did his desire. In truth, she frightened him. But it was a thrilling fear like the moment before he climbed on the back of a wild mare—a mare that could become the horse of his dreams, or his death. He'd never met anyone with such power. She'd seen his future, stood up to Bres, and walked beneath the waves.

If he could master Sorcha, he could rule Tuath Croghan as a druid-king. Stop this cold rain. Build an unconquerable army. Steal more cattle than any kingdom on the island. Reap a more bountiful harvest. And make his people fat and rich and happy.

The *child* of such a woman could perform miracles or wreak havoc. Bring blessing or misfortune to the tuath. To couple her power with his own would create a child destined to be High

King—unstoppable, invincible, celebrated—a king who could rule the entire island.

He heard the change in Sorcha's breathing as she awoke. Felt her nipple stiffen beneath his hand. Felt her face turn. Felt her lips against his own. Opening his mouth, he returned her kiss.

"Don't move," he whispered. Her heartbeat quickened as he played her body, teasing all the sweet fleshy spots Ana had taught him to touch. Arousing her, but keeping her on the edge, his body in full control of hers. "If you move one muscle, I'll call all the spiders in this hut and they'll crawl all over you." His fingers crawled over her body and when he sensed she was fully ready, he pushed inside. It was her time to conceive. He could sense it and feel it in the softening and opening of her ripe body.

In his mind, a vision appeared of the child he would give her tonight—a slick red-haired babe with green eyes and fighting fists and a cry like a fox kit. His name was Rónán. It echoed in his mind as he made love to Sorcha far into the night, filling her time and again.

In the dusky light of predawn, he extracted himself from her grip and crawled out the open door, glancing back only once. In the firelight, Sorcha's beauty made him stagger. He wanted her power, yes. He needed it to lead his people. But something had changed. His heart ached at the sight of her as if he'd been pierced by a sword. He'd had many women but the only one who'd ever made his knees tremble was Ana, and that was many years ago when they were just kids. Now his whole body throbbed and burned.

Sorcha had pierced his heart and now carried his child. He knew it in his core. This woman he'd dreamed was his destiny. He must protect her and to do that he needed Criofan's blessing. She would be safe for a few days in the hut and the time alone would deepen her need for him. And so, he left.

Criofan had still not made a decision on the kingship. The council convened each day and talked and talked and talked. Twenty-seven men had joined together, ignoring social taboos to discuss this business—the nine druids of the inner circle who advised the king, plus warriors, blacksmiths, craftsmen, and farmers. Each man had something to say. There were no interruptions. No judgments. No talking out of turn. The circle went round and round. The arguments were crafted and civil and Bres always spoke last. No one dared argue against him, so he always won. He'd even won Ana.

It was known that she'd been bedding Bres since before her husband died and was now with him often. Though he didn't understand it, that was Ana's choice, as it was the choice of every woman.

The third day was Criofan's birthday. He'd passed thirty-nine winters and was the eldest among them. Their families came to join the celebration. Criofan's son and daughter sat on either side of the old man, and they toasted him well into the night after the council adjourned and only the members of the inner circle were left. Between them, the party had drunk several casks of Gaulish wine along with the usual vats of ale, and the energy bubbled like a slow kettle. Another log or two on the fire and it would begin to sizzle and burn.

Fretting over Sorcha, Ruairí had drunk more than he intended. Then Ana slunk in, looking stunning in a silk dress that glowed like a purple sunset, crow feathers in her upswept hair. She cast him a cold glance and his skin prickled. He'd told no one that he'd spent the night with Sorcha, yet he was sure Ana knew. Her glare unnerved him and he went to sit by Conall, who'd picked up his lyre and was tuning each of the six silver strings.

"Play a drowsy tune," Ruairí said. Conall's music could make them laugh or cry or sleep. Ruairí loved to fight, as did the other warriors, but not with Ana. And not when there were pregnant women and children in the room. He'd rather they all fell asleep.

Bres was particularly anxious and engaged in an animated discussion with Ailill, as Conall slipped his left hand through the leather strap behind the strings and plucked a few notes. As the tones resonated, people stopped talking to listen. Conall's fingers danced on the back of the strings to change the tones as he picked a sultry tune with his long sharp fingernails—dips and jumps and slips, punctuated by sorrowful chords.

Closing his eyes, Ruairí envisioned a man riding home, battle-weary, blood-smeared, and bruised, but belly trembling to see the smoke of his home fire once more. When the melody shifted, he opened his eyes.

Conall was entranced, traveling in the heartrending realm of his muse. Sometimes, other musicians joined him, playing skin drums or rattling crotals or blowing wooden flutes, but tonight he played and sang alone, his breathy voice modulating in perfect attunement with the moment. Eyelids, already heavy with Gaulish wine, fluttered as people drifted. Mothers put their babes to sleep and fell in beside them. Still Conall played, his deep, rasping voice resonating harmoniously with the metallic twang of the silver strings.

Bres was speaking in low tones with Ana. The man never stopped talking. Ruairí watched her shake her head and touch Bres's bruised nose. She was teasing, the corner of her mouth pulled up in a smirk. Bres jerked back angrily and began to rave about Sorcha, how she'd attacked him and used the force of the gods to pummel him.

And Ruairí was too drunk for diplomacy. "Beaten by an ignorant woman from Connachta!" he shouted.

Bres shook his fist and the next thing Ruairí knew, Fearghas cracked the right side of his jaw and he went flying sideways over several bodies.

One punch was never enough for that great ox. So before he could get in a second, Ruairí shook it off and bounced back up. He came at Fearghas with his head down, bulling him in the gut and sending the big man sprawling.

Then Bres had a knife to Ruairí's throat. "The Goddess thirsts for fey blood but yours will do."

"She'll have to make do with bastard blood," Ruairí said and turning, he brought his knuckles up into Bres's bruised nose. Bones cracked. Blood spurted. The look of shock in Bres's eyes was worth the slit jaw when the knife slipped. Ruairí wrenched the weapon from Bres's hand and wrestled him to the ground, fingers squeezing the weasel's skinny throat. Grasping each of his beard tails, he pulled Bres's face up to his naked chest. "Kiss my nipples, Bres. I'll never kiss yours."

When Ruairí shoved Bres's bloody face against his skin, he struggled and spit and then broke free. Lurching away, Bres wiped his bloody nose and sneered. "You'll pay for this." He stalked over the bodies and filled several goblets of wine, then set them down on the board in front of Criofan. The old man was reminding his children of some man he'd gutted at a party when he was just a lad.

Conall came and tied a piece of linen around Ruairí's bleeding neck and he fell on his ass. "So much for drowsy," he said.

Ruairí was awakened by a scream. Following it, he stumbled over bodies until he found Criofan's daughter kneeling over her father's corpse. "He's gone. He's gone."

Indeed, the old druid's face was frozen in a terrified grimace, as if he'd seen the end of the world. Ruairí leaned over and touched his forehead. Cold. A faint fungal odor permeated the air.

"I fear the excitement last night strained his heart," she said.

Murder, Ruairí thought, but knew better than to shout it to the house. Instead, he pulled Conall aside, the one man he trusted. "I fear Ana has done this for Bres." He hated to think it. He still loved her but knew it was possible. "Mushrooms." She might not have put the poison in the old man's hand but she knew how and where to obtain it. Perhaps Bres had coerced or threatened her. He was capable of anything.

Conall's eyes flashed wide in disbelief, silently asking, *"Are you sure?"*

Ruairí nodded once and searched the room. Ana and Bres were nowhere to be seen.

But within the hour, Bres reconvened the council, though his eyes and nose were black and swollen. Ruairí sat beside Conall, watching and listening, as the murderer spun his magic cord around the minds of all the men.

"We are a people who follow the traditions of our ancestors. My father and uncles led this council for many years and my grandfather before him, so I know better than anyone how things should be done. We followed the rules. Along with Ruairí and Conall, Fearghas and I witnessed Tarbfeis. Criofan ate the meat of the white bull and, observed by all four of us, he dreamed.

"He dreamed of *me*. Slaying cattle for my dying people. He dreamed of *me*. Feeding them as any good king would do. He dreamed of *me*. But—" Bres paused dramatically—"Criofan's mind was *poisoned* by the de Danann woman. A woman Ruairí Mac Nia brought to our fort. So, the old man did not interpret the dream correctly."

There were gasps around the circle and Ruairí squeezed his fists into tight balls.

"Last night, I met with Criofan after his party," Bres continued. "Ana was there too, who you all know is the embodiment of the Goddess of the Land and beyond reproach?"

Heads nodded, and the edge of Ana's lip quivered so subtly only Ruairí could detect it.

"Criofan told us then of his error. He said that today he would announce *my* rule. 'Bres,' he said, 'like your father and uncles and grandfather, you will be king.'"

Ana sat expressionless, glittering in her silver-trimmed cloak and bejeweled hair.

"The fey woman must have been there lurking in her invisible form and heard his proclamation. When the magic she used to poison Criofan's mind failed, she poisoned his body with curses. Murdered him! Murdered our most honored druid *as he slept*. What warrior's death is that?"

There were more gasps around the room but still no one spoke.

Ruairí's muscles clenched as he fought to keep his seat. Blood pounded in his ears and filled his vision. Bres's blood. He would have the bastard's head for this outrage against Sorcha. Shut his lying mouth forever. But he must choose his time. The council teemed with his kin. And if something happened to him, what would happen to her?

"Though banished, Sorcha O'Hallorhan sought revenge by taking the wisest man among us, our beloved Criofan. This de Danann seductress must be found and brought before the council to pay the price for her crimes. How can Criofan rest in the Otherworld with his *murderer roaming free?*" He banged his fist against his palm to punctuate the last three words.

How indeed, when his murderer sits in this room? Turning to Conall, Ruairí whispered, "Leave now, and go to our secret place. Warn Sorcha. Tell her to stay hidden there until I return." As Conall stood, he grasped his arm. "She carries my child. I have seen it."

Conall nodded, and Ruairí glanced around the room. No one had noticed. They were all entranced by Bres's diatribe.

"We all know the Tuatha de Danann are gods who make themselves visible to mortals at their whim." He threw up his hands. "They slew the Fomorians, and then our ancestors triumphed and forced them underground. This woman came to Ruairí Mac Nia to seduce him and find her way back into our midst. She tried to seduce me too, but I fought her off and have the bruises to prove it." He pointed with both hands to his blackened face—a face that had been broken by Ruairí. "Criofan banished her because he knew that living among us, she would only cause dissension and the people of a tuath must not fight amongst themselves. We are strong only when united."

Interlacing his fingers, he held his fists to his heart as if in prayer.

"The Goddess of the Land weeps and our fields drown in her sorrow. A Sun King must be crowned or we are doomed."

When he paused everyone exhaled.

"I am that king. Messengers have been dispatched. When twelve dawns pass, we will celebrate my inauguration. Until then, know I am your king and I will deal with Criofan's murderer. Whoever finds Sorcha O'Hallorhan, bring her to me. You will be rewarded."

Fists pounded wooden benches and booted feet stamped the floor as the audience expressed their glee. Most of the nobility shared a common great-grandfather, but Bres's kin unbalanced the fort. With a shared goal and charismatic leader they would unite and no one who dared push against this tyrant would be safe.

Ruairí stalked out of the hall, pulled his hood up over his head, and walked into the rain. From the gate, he could see Conall on his white mare flying down the road, his loose hair streaming out behind him. No one else knew where he'd hidden Sorcha. She'd be safe with Conall for the moment. Glancing back into the hall, he saw Bres, drinking and posturing, with his small army surrounding him. *How can I stop him? There must be a way.*

After crossing the fort, Ruairí entered the garden through the back door. This was where he went when he needed to pray. He could feel the gods in this sanctuary in the water, and the trees, and in the pine torches that burned and shivered in the cool breeze. He took his usual seat on the far side of the pool and closed his eyes. It seemed hopeless. The only way to successfully depose Bres would be to reveal his lies. Honor and ethics were esteemed in the order. But he'd need proof to do that or someone to back his accusations.

What about Ana? Did she still float on the surface like a leaf caught in the ripples of Bres's diabolical plan? Or had she sunk below the waves and sworn him allegiance? Ruairí couldn't imagine Ana giving her power to anyone willingly. Perhaps he could win her trust and discover the truth. Their dalliance told him she still cared for him and with Ana to help him he might have a chance of castrating the tyrant. Unless she wanted the bastard intact.

When she called his name, Ruairí shivered and opened his eyes. "Ana. I was just thinking of you."

She stood across the pond, a black cloak covering her raven hair. When he blinked, he could still see the maiden who'd taught him about love beneath the oak trees in the glade. He stood and walked around the pond to stand beside her.

"What were you thinking? Of our night together or something more malicious?"

"Truth, Ana. I was thinking of the truth." He looked into her dark eyes. "Did you poison Criofan for Bres?"

Her eyes widened as her jaw dropped. "That's what you think? Criofan was like an uncle to me."

"That's why it sickens me. I've killed men in war, but to poison an old man in his sleep and on his birthday!"

Shaking her head, she touched his arm. "There are things you do not know, Ruairí."

"Then, tell me Ana. Tell me the truth. I will protect you."

"Ruairí, I can't. But please believe me. I did not murder Criofan."

"You were seen in the forest with a healer right before Adamair's wife and child got sick."

"Go inside, Ana. You're not on trial here and Ruairí has no right to interrogate you." Bres, who'd suddenly appeared behind her, took her arm and turned her sharply. Ana took one look at his somber face and walked away.

"This is a place of sanctuary, Bres. You know that." Bres was one of the most devout druids Ruairí had ever met. He prayed here alone every day at noon and observed all the rules of rituals. Ruairí hoped to appeal to the heart of him.

"As do you, and yet you stand in this sanctuary accusing our Goddess of Sovereignty of murdering three people." Bres stood with his arms crossed over his chest. "What say you to that?"

"I say, that if Ana didn't poison Criofan, you did."

"Prove it. You cannot." Bres rubbed his hand against his arm and glanced at the water. "Your fey woman has caused this unending rain and cold. If you want to help your people, tell me where you hid her. You've been with her. I can see it. I can smell it."

"You're just jealous that Sorcha gave me what you could not take."

Bres's eyes shifted to the left as a great hulking shadow appeared. The flat back of Fearghas's sword caught Ruairí just behind the knees. When his legs buckled, he lost his balance and fell forward. Then Fearghas hoisted his foot and kicked him hard in the ribs just as Bres's fist came up and caught him in the temple. The force of the dual blows sent Ruairí reeling backward into the pool. He hit hard and sank half-conscious, water flooding his nose, burning and filling his lungs.

Panic seized him, as it had that day in the lake. And then he popped up like a giant cork. Choking and gasping, he gained his footing and backed up against the edge of the pool. Through a gray haze, he could see Bres standing at the opposite edge stroking a bloody bronze spear butt. Ruairí tasted the blood that streamed into his mouth and spit.

Then, Fearghas was on him, the crook of his fat arm squeezing his neck, choking him, and yanking him up and back. Ruairí's jaw felt like it would rip from his neck. He felt himself slipping into darkness as the ox squeezed and dragged him from the pool. The last words he heard were those of Bres.

"Take him to the bull pen and lock him in. He'll tell us where he's hidden Sorcha O'Hallorhan or he'll die there."

The Road to Croghan Hill

Estrada glanced around, bewildered. One moment he'd been staring into the solemn eyes of Cernunnos, and the next, he was surrounded by the most verdant forest he'd ever seen—an intensely green maze that seemed to stretch for miles in all directions. He'd expected some painful transformation on a molecular level—the shifting of atoms and tearing asunder of his mind and body—but the time shift was more like awakening in a strange bed, jet-lagged after several days of travel and wondering for that split second where the hell you were.

Dylan stood beside him. The top half of his hair was slicked back and bundled up behind his head and a coppery beard hung down below his Adam's apple. Dylan's hair, which Estrada had never seen before, since he always kept it military-short, was a thick and wavy auburn streaked with gold.

"A half-up man bun?" Estrada chuckled. "You're wearing a half-up man bun?"

Dylan felt the back of his head, the bun and wild waves that hung below, and made a strange noise something between clearing his throat and a grunt, which Estrada took to be disapproval.

"You actually look pretty sexy for a nerd. Sorcha will probably jump you. I might even jump you."

Dylan's non-reckoning of Estrada's bisexual nature was something of a plaything for the magician who loved to tease his straight friend. It's not that Dylan was homophobic; he just didn't appreciate the pleasures a man's body could provide. Happily *hetero*, Dylan had been newly initiated in the craft of love by the very woman they were seeking.

"At least I don't look like Katniss Everdeen with a beard." Dylan pointed to the long black braid that hung down Estrada's right shoulder.

"Who?"

Dylan rolled his eyes. "Cernunnos is something of a sadist, isn't he?"

Estrada laughed. The horned god had obviously chosen a glamor based on what he thought would suit them and really, he hadn't done a bad job. Estrada had worn long braids for years before his coercive head shave and had no problem being compared to someone he assumed was a girl. "You actually look good, man. I think you owe him one." He winked and was not surprised by a firm punch in the shoulder.

Dylan's pale linen shirt fell over brown leather breeches and boots. A bright copper jacket hugged his chest, and around his shoulders was draped a moss green cloak clasped with a bronze brooch. He looked like a flinty wood elf.

"Seriously man, this ranger look suits you. Especially the beard and man bun. It's hard to resist."

"Shut your gob and stay focused. We don't want to stay here any longer than we have to."

"Right." Estrada took a deep breath. "So, this is Iron Age Ireland?"

"Aye, judging by that patch of shamrocks you're standing in."

Estrada stared at the thick mass of greenery at his feet. "I thought Ireland was beautiful when I visited two years ago but this is spectacular." Picking up a shamrock, he ran it under his nose. An intense scent, akin to freshly mowed grass, oozed endorphins through his brain. "Fuck, man. I feel like I'm on E. Does everything look and smell better to you?"

Dylan sucked in a deep belly breath and glanced around. "Aye," he said, exhaling. "It's pristine. Pre-Christian. Pre-Industrial Revolution. There's no pollution and the ozone layer is still intact."

"No wonder she didn't want to leave." Estrada remembered the night Sorcha told him her secret about the bog man, how the experience had changed her life, how seeing his face made her want to know her ancestors. And this was their world.

When Estrada had wandered through Taynish Nature Reserve on the western edge of Scotland, he'd experienced something like this. It was magical too, but it didn't explode his senses; at least, not until he discovered his fey lover hiding in the bushes. He didn't want to leave that day either.

But something was off. Though they'd left California at the end of September, here birds were singing, leaves unfurling, and bees buzzing inside newly opened blossoms. This world was just bursting into ... "Spring," he said aloud.

Dylan nodded. "Aye. Early spring. Cernunnos must have sent us back to a specific moment."

"How does he do it?" A part of Estrada was curious but the blissed-out part was being rhetorical.

"Through a wormhole," Dylan said.

Estrada wandered around sniffing his shamrock and reaching out to feel the energy of different trees and plants as Dylan talked. He always knew plants were sentient beings but this bonding was mind-blowing. He could see their auras connecting and pulsing in flamboyant color as one massive entity. "*Fuck.* I'm just amazed."

"Aye. If you travel at an accelerated speed, you can start in one place and time and land in another. Einstein figured it out in 1935. It may seem physically impossible, but that's physics."

"Is there anything you don't know?" It was another rhetorical question. As Estrada spun the shamrock between his fingers, he observed the shifting patterns of energy around it. Shamrocks were good luck charms. He went to tuck it in his pocket, then realized he didn't have one. His black leather breeches were soft and smooth and his long white linen shirt, plain and open at the neck. The edges of a scarlet jacket peeked from behind his black woolen cloak. Comfortable and rather dashing—the whole ensemble would work well in his magic show—but there were no pockets. There was, however, a leather belt and from it dangled a draw-string bag with a few pieces of silver and a knife-sheath. He stuck the shamrock in the bag and drew the knife.

It was a strong, sharp, ten-inch iron blade capable of slitting a man's throat. He felt the heft of it and was just about to try a toss into a humungous oak tree when Dylan shouted, "Look out!" and shoved him so hard he spun several feet. Concentrating on not being skewered by the iron blade, his toe caught a vine and he flipped over onto his shoulder, rolled, and landed in a thorn bush. "Fuck me!" His words disappeared in the thunder of pounding hooves as a dozen horsemen galloped by. Coughing in the dust, Estrada stared after them.

"Warriors!" Dylan had landed on the far side of what appeared to be the rutted tracks of a trail. The last two riders veered off and circled back.

Jumping up, Estrada fingered his iron blade. The horsemen were all wearing scabbards slung over their shoulders from which iron sword handles projected. He felt entirely underdressed. Had Cernunnos forgotten to give him a sword or was he expecting him to pull one from a stone?

The horses skidded to a halt, nostrils flaring. "Have you seen anyone on the road today?" Up close, the speaker surprised him. He was small and fair and looked no more than thirteen. A glint of snot showed above his bare upper lip and he wiped it with his sleeve. He was just a kid. Too young to be riding with an armed posse. Estrada shoved the knife back in his sheath and shook his head. He was not prepared to kill a boy. He'd ridden with his own posse at that age and lived to regret it. This boy might not be so lucky.

"No one," Dylan said. "Who are you looking for?"

"A red-haired woman. She may be with a man."

How many red-haired female outlaws could there be? Had Sorcha somehow escaped her bonds?

"What's she done?" Dylan asked.

"The king wants her. You must ask *him*!" The boy laughed as if the king wanted her for something obscene, and the two riders turned their mounts and rode off after the others.

"It's gotta be Sorcha. Do you think this king that's searching for her is the bog man?" Estrada stared after the warriors.

Dylan shrugged. He was walking in circles around the area where they'd first appeared.

"What are you doing?" Estrada asked, following behind.

"Cernunnos said, we have to come to this same spot or we don't get home. It all looks the same. How are we ever going to find it again?"

Estrada glanced around, then closed his eyes and let his inner senses expand. Sometimes, he could see heat images and if he could see heat, he could also see light. He turned in slow circles waiting for signs in the blue-veiled darkness. And then. "The oak tree, there," he said, pointing. "There's a gold blaze on its trunk. Antlers."

"Antlers?"

"Yeah. It's two feet square, just below the first set of branches."

"Aye?"

Estrada turned a half-circle and pointed again. "There's another one on this oak across the way." He opened his eyes and stared at the magnificent trees, then went over and ran his palm along the blaze. It felt as warm as the slow-burning embers of a fire. The other tree was directly across from it and the rutted road ran down the center. "Between these two oaks is some kind of gateway. Those warriors ran right through it."

"It's a wormhole. A door through time. Cernunnos must have to open it." Dylan scratched his beard. "It's oddly logical. They used to build doors from oak because of its strength. Harder to bash through with an axe, I suppose. The word door comes from the Gaelic, *duir*."

By nightfall, Estrada would know everything there was to know about Iron Age Ireland. He was glad Dylan was a nerd but time was ticking. They had to find Sorcha before that posse did. "Which way?" he asked.

Dylan surveyed the landscape. "The sun is setting in the west, which is the direction that search party rode. They were likely heading back home for the night." He shook his head. "I don't remember where Croghan is exactly, but two of the Irish bog bodies were found quite close to each other, both in the Midlands. I don't think there's much east of here but mountains and sea."

"Let's follow the posse then. If they do happen to find Sorcha, we might be able to intervene before they get her back to this king."

Dylan's flushed face blanched.

After fighting vampires how bad could an Iron Age king really be? Then Estrada remembered the final scene in *Braveheart* and touched his belly.

They walked for a good two hours without seeing anyone. The forest opened up onto grass-covered hills where white and red cows grazed. As they passed, the cows raised their massive heads and stared, chewing rhythmically beneath reddish noses, their tails twitching.

"Will you look at that? The original Irish moiled cow. Breeders have always claimed they were the first breed on the island and here they are."

"Do you think there's a bull?" Estrada had heard stories of frisky bulls defending their territories.

"Most likely. That's how they make baby cows."

As if they'd heard, three of the younger cows began walking toward them. Their eyes were big and brown and curious, their flicking ears as brash as their noses. All were patched ocher like islands on an Arctic map.

"Why are there no fences?" Estrada asked, nervously. A half dozen more had joined in and the cattle were closing the gap.

"It's open pastureland. The cattle free range. The nobles own them and farm them out around the tuath."

Dylan had taken to pursing his lips and pulling at the coppery hairs of his new beard whenever he was about to deliver an Irish fact. It was a trait Estrada had seen Dylan's grandfather do when he stayed with him in Scotland. He was well into pursing and pulling, and Estrada knew something important was coming.

"They use cattle as currency. If you kill a man, depending on his status, you have to pay up in cows. A judge might be worth say fifty cows."

"Really? So, if you had a large herd you could neutralize your enemies as long as you paid up?" The cows had clustered about ten paces in front of him and were slowly chewing. Estrada lunged forward and shouted, and the beasts panicked and ran, kicking up their heels.

Dylan took a few steps and looked back over his shoulder. "You'd decrease your herd right quick if you used that strategy. Everyone is related here. With one murder you'd increase your enemies exponentially."

Familial allegiances. He'd have to watch out for that. Estrada could see a few people in drab brown clothes working around the farm. "Do you think they might feed us?" He hadn't eaten since yesterday and his belly was rumbling.

"After you scared their cows? Not bloody likely." Dylan glanced at the farmers. "Besides, they don't look like they have much to spare. If I remember correctly, the king and nobles control everything. The farmers pay food-rent and are given a few cattle and horses to use on their allotments."

They continued along the rutted track several miles and were just cresting a hill when a lone horseman pounded seemingly out of the sky in a whirl of pink and gray.

Dylan leapt clear but Estrada was one second too slow. As he turned to avoid the collision, the rider's knee caught the edge of his shoulder. He heard a pop.

Then, through sudden searing pain, he felt himself flying. There was nothing he could do to stop the inevitable crash. As he landed on his hip, he rolled inward, grasping his elbow and pulling it tightly across his chest. *"Fuck!"* The pain surged down his arm and up into his head.

Dylan was suddenly there, leaning over, eyes bulging, mouth open. And then he felt the thunder of hooves and glanced up to see the rider vault from his horse.

"I'm so sorry. I didn't expect anyone to be on the road. Are you all right?"

"Do I look all right?" Estrada growled. His voice sounded shaken and weak and incensed him still more. Clearing his throat, he clutched his arm tighter. Trust this maniac rider to hit his bad shoulder, the one that had been dislocated several times before.

"What can we do?" Dylan stood beside the horseman with his arms crossed over his chest.

The rider pulled a vessel from his satchel that appeared to be made from a bull's horn and unwound the leather stopper. "Here, this will help with the pain." Kneeling, he held it to Estrada's lips as he guzzled the bitter, grainy fluid. He'd hoped for whisky but it was closer to ale. "Now, let me help you. I can see where the joint has slipped from the socket."

"You know how to fix a dislocated shoulder?" Estrada was skeptical. But then again, this was a warrior society. No doubt, injuries like this were common.

The man nodded. "I've fixed my own from time to time but it's easier with help."

Estrada laid back in the grass and clutched his arm to his chest. He focused on the man's face. Watched him gather his long brown hair in one hand and jam it into the back of his collar to keep it out of his eyes.

"Let me help you," he said, as Estrada pressed the arm against his chest, refusing to give it over to this stranger. "I can't make it any worse."

That was inaccurate. The man could easily tear muscles and tendons, or damage the nerves and blood vessels. Last summer, Estrada had dislocated this same shoulder in Scotland and fixed it himself. But he'd been dosed with faerie blood then.

"Trust me. The pain will lessen."

Trust you? Estrada took a deep resigned breath and let go of his elbow. The man slipped his hand beneath it. Then, grasping Estrada's wrist with his other hand, he held out the injured arm at a ninety-degree angle.

"I'm going to pull now."

"Slow and steady. Don't jerk it or I'll kill you."

"Don't mind him," Dylan said, embarrassed.

The man lifted a corner of his lip, then planted his booted feet firmly against Estrada's hips and slowly began to pull. Estrada held his breath, grimacing with the pain, and then, all at once, he felt the humerus slide under the bone of his shoulder blade and back into place. The pain lessened immediately and he exhaled. Sitting up woozily, he rubbed his shoulder.

"I really am sorry," the man said.

"It's not your fault. It's happened before."

"Where are your horses?" the horseman said, glancing around.

"Stolen in the night," Dylan said.

Estrada raised his eyebrows. He wasn't used to hearing lies from his moral friend. And delivered so quickly.

"We must find the culprits. Horse theft isn't tolerated." He pulled his chestnut hair free of his cloak and ran his fingers through it. "Are you on your way to Croghan?"

"Aye." Dylan held out his hand but the man just looked at it. "My name's Dylan McBride and this is—"

"Estrada."

"Iberian?" The man cocked his head curiously.

Is he puzzled by my name or my dark skin? Estrada thought. *Or is it something else?*

The man, despite his dark brown hair and beard, had pale skin. His nose was long and wolfish, his eyes slightly slanted at the edges. He was beautiful and more a man's man than a woman's, if Estrada was reading him right. The Greeks were known for their homosexual liaisons—especially older men and younger boys—but he didn't know about the Celts. Dylan hadn't got that far in his Celtic trivia.

"Aye, we met in Britain," Dylan said, "and since we were both coming this way, we decided to travel together."

"You'll never make it to Croghan by nightfall on foot, especially with a shoulder like that." He glanced at Estrada and then over to the farm. "Wait here."

They watched him mount his white horse, with the ease of one who's ridden his entire life, and gallop down the hill through the spotted cattle toward the farm.

"Iberian? What's Iberian?" Estrada asked.

"The Indigenous People of southern and eastern Spain. There are Celts in the north of the Iberian Peninsula, so he'd know of them. It's a good fit for you with your ancestry."

Estrada sniffed. His mother was Mayan. His father Mexican. He supposed it did make a sensible cover.

They watched the man speak with the farmer and canter back up the hill leading a stout black draft horse. Slipping off his mount, he smiled. "This is Ebony. She's strong enough to carry you both."

He approached Estrada with a long strip of unbleached linen. After folding it into a triangle, he tied Estrada's arm in a sling.

"Here, take the reins and I'll give you a leg up," he said to Dylan. Estrada had talked with his friend on several occasions about his early life. There'd been stories of boats and the sea and stones and bagpipes, but the subject of horses had never come up. Now, seeing the discombobulation on Dylan's face, he assumed his friend had never ridden a horse. That made two of them. But it couldn't be much different than a Harley. The man was standing with his fingers interlaced by the belly of the black mare, waiting.

"Here, I'll go." Estrada shoved his booted foot into the man's hand and sprung onto the back of the beast. His shoulder ached, but the pain had lessened some and the sling took most of the pressure off his muscles. He caught the reins in his good hand. "Come on Dylan, or we'll never make it to the fort by dark."

"Aye, sure," Dylan said, and accepting the leg-up, he landed awkwardly on the back of the horse.

"I must warn you," the man said. "The chief druid at Croghan died this morning and things are rather chaotic." He leapt back on his white horse, shouting as he turned. "When you reach the fort, ask for Ruairí Mac Nia. Tell him I ran into you on the road and he's to take care of you."

"What's your name?" Dylan asked.

"Oh, it's Conall." The man nodded. "Conall Ceol."

Bean Rua

Sorcha lay on a flat granite slab by the lake with her cloak spread beneath her. She'd taken off all her clothes, rinsed them in the clear water, and hung them on tree branches. After days of continuous rain and enforced shelter in the dark dank hut, the sun was so hot and bright as to be blinding. A decent breeze was not only drying her clothes but keeping the midges at bay. She'd had a good swim and a stretch and felt like a newly emerged butterfly broken free from its angsty cocoon.

The moment would've been grand had Ruairí been there beside her. She missed him. The smell and taste of him. His stature and style. And more than that, his gentle intensity. He was a man who commanded quietly using few words. *Don't move*. Those two words were like a shot of adrenaline and, uncharacteristically, she found herself obeying. He kept her hovering on the edge of ecstasy and then, with four small words, released her invisible bonds and sent her reeling. *You can move now*. And move she did.

It may have been just a one-night stand brought on by proximity and the sight of her naked body rising from the lake. He was, after all, a young warrior laced with testosterone and a good deal of ale. But she thought not. Beyond the physical chemistry was an emotional magnet based on their shared ability as what he termed, *seers*. He'd dreamed of her and she'd envisioned him, and that foreshadowed something beyond sex.

Then she awoke and he was gone and she was banished. Condemned and commanded to remain here in this no man's land to await his return. She wanted to pummel him for abandoning her and considered mounting the poor pony, who would undoubtably race back to the fort. But to what end? Criofan would only send her packing again or Bres would do something worse. And it wasn't *so* bad here at this lakeside as a temporary solution. She had to believe Ruairí could convince Criofan to reverse his edict. He must. She was stuck here now. Trapped in a time not her own.

The horned god had abandoned her, likely amused by the drama he'd spawned. Of course, she should have known better than to trust a trickster god. Mythology was rife with gods who toyed with humans for their own pleasure. And that's just what she'd been. A sex toy. She thought of Zeus and his affairs with humans.

If you're watching and can hear my thoughts, know this Cernunnos. Ruairí Mac Nia's a better lover than you'll ever be! I don't care if you're immortal, you narcissistic bastard!

There. That felt better. She'd had the last word at least and made her own choice to stay in this world and save Ruairí from himself. She stretched again, then interlaced her fingers and settled her head in the pillow of her palms.

When a shadow fell upon her, she thought it was only a passing cloud, until she heard a quick intake of breath. Rolling off the rock, she sprang up ready to defend herself.

"Conall!"

"I'm sorry if I startled you. I was just appreciating your *beauty*. It's rare to see a woman lying naked in the sun. I mean both to see a naked woman *and* to see the sun." He was nervous. Babbling.

"Where's Ruairí?" she asked, straightening up.

"He couldn't come and sent me." He pointed to the leather satchel that sat on the ground beside him. "Donella sent gifts—clean clothes and some jewelry."

"Are you sure you're alone? You weren't followed?" she asked, glancing around. She was in no mood for Bres and his goons. A white horse ambled near the hut, quietly browsing and seemingly content, though its hair was slick with sweat.

He shook his head. "Don't worry. No one else knows about this place."

Picking up the satchel, Sorcha took a seat on the edge of the granite slab. Once past her initial fear of being caught off guard by a rapist—and she was convinced that Conall was no threat in that regard—she was no longer concerned by her lack of clothing. Still, she dug into the satchel, pulled out a clean linen shift and slipped it over her head. Donella was much smaller in the bust, a petite elfish girl, but it fit perfectly. She dug back into the bag to see what other treasures were hidden inside and felt something hard.

"What's this?" she asked, pulling out a sturdy white comb. The length of her hand from fingertip to wrist, it had been carved in one narrow piece perhaps from the bone of a sheep or calf.

"Do you like it?"

"Aye. It's gorgeous." She'd read of a crannog near Sligo where they'd dug combs of bone and horn. She ran it through her damp hair.

"Here. Let me. I used to do my mother's hair."

"Is she gone now?"

"Yes, last winter. It was a wasting disease." His gaze shifted and he stared beyond her as if at a bevy of ghosts. "Many people grew sick with the cough but only the very old and the very young died. My mother, Criofan's wife, Ruairí's aunt ..." His voice drifted off with the memory.

Tuberculosis, Sorcha thought. With all of them living together under one roof and sharing the same stale air, the bacteria would spread like a plague. "I'm sorry."

"I did her hair until she died. My mother was a proud woman and hated to appear disheveled and sickly."

Sorcha handed him the comb. "As long as it doesn't bring bad memories." She closed her eyes as he ran the comb through her long red hair and gently teased out the tangles. Then, after placing it beside her on the rock, his fingers encircled her scalp and he began a firm head massage.

"God, that feels amazing." Closing her eyes, she allowed the drowsiness to descend, feeling pampered as he began to divide her hair into sections and twist and curl.

"Donella sent hair pins. Can you find them?"

She dug around and extracted a small leather case. "This?"

"Yes." Opening it, he took out several gold pins. "Can you hold them?"

She opened her hand and he dropped the gold pins onto her palm. *These are real,* she thought. *A real druid bard is putting real gold pins in my hair. A bard with a gentle touch and a gentle heart.* She remembered the music he'd played at Tarbfeis.

"Did you bring your pipes?" she asked, handing him the pins one by one as he held out a manicured hand.

"Always. A bard never goes anywhere without his pipes."

"And will you play a song for me?"

"I will *compose* a song for you. A melody has been teasing me as I rode here. I think it must be yours."

"Like I'm your muse?" The old stories spoke of bards who'd gone beneath the earth to the palaces of the Tuatha de Danann to learn their craft and be gifted with music. Sometimes, all it took was sleeping on a faerie mound. She wondered if he knew these stories and believed she was fey, as did Ruairí and Bres.

"Something like that." He stood back and assessed her hair, then nodded. "Bean Rua."

Bawn Roo-ah. Red-haired Woman. She liked the sound of that. "What's in this?" she asked, fingering the tip of a tiny sheep's horn stoppered with a rolled piece of leather.

"Ah, it's a *ruaim* for your lips."

Roo-im. "Do you just apply it with a finger?" A powder made from crushed dried berries, it appeared to be harmless enough.

"Yes, but let me," he said, and putting down the comb, he dabbed his fingertip into the crushed red powder and spread it on her lips. "And a dash for your cheeks. Charming."

Reaching back, Sorcha patted her hair, all twisted and plaited and pinned with gold. She could get used to this pampering. "All dressed up and nowhere to go." She sighed. "You are quite the artist and also a crafty messenger. You completely avoided my question about Ruairí. Why didn't he come? What haven't you told me?"

Perching on the rock beside her, he rubbed his eyes. Whatever news the bard carried was causing him anxiety. All this pampering was just a prelude to the bad news.

Sorcha felt a sudden tightening in her chest. "He's not hurt, is he?"

Conall shook his head. "No. Ruairí was fine when I left. Just concerned for you. But he needed to stay because—" He sighed. "Criofan died in his sleep and ..." His words tapered off.

Sorcha's stomach heaved and she swallowed back her fear. Criofan was her way back into the fort. Now what would become of her? "And ...? How did he die? Illness? Old age?"

"Mushrooms. Ruairí suspects Ana."

"Ana?" *A murderer? Bres might stoop to murder, but Ana?* For a moment Sorcha was breathless. *Could it be true that Ana, the Queen of Tuath Croghan, was a killer?* She wasn't fond of the woman, especially after hearing her that night with Ruairí, but still, it was a shock.

"She and Bres drank wine with Criofan last night. Criofan wanted to hold another Tarbfeis and was going to send a party south this morning to find another bull. But now he's dead and instead of Tarbfeis, we're holding another funeral."

"But why would Ana murder Criofan?"

"For Bres."

"Ana wants Bres to be king?" Sorcha couldn't imagine why *anyone* would want Bres to be king. "Will she marry *him* now?"

Conall's lips flattened in disgust. "When we all played together as children, Ana always had to be queen. As the physical embodiment of the Goddess of the Land, she has more power than any other woman in the tuath. She will do whatever is necessary to keep it."

Even kill an old man? Sorcha had appreciated Criofan's gentle ways, even though he'd banished her. And she was sure Ruairí would have convinced him to overturn her sentence. She frowned. "What will happen?"

"Bres has declared himself king. The day following Beltane he will be inaugurated."

"When is Beltane?" Sorcha was confused. In her world, Beltane had already happened on May 1, the weekend she'd spent with Cernunnos. Had the horned god taken her back to sometime before that or did they celebrate Beltane at a different time? Of course, asking about dates would mean nothing to Conall. The modern

Gregorian calendar was centuries in the future and even Julius Caesar's calendar wasn't implemented until 46BCE.

Conall eyed her curiously, as if she should know something so fundamental. "Twelve dawns. Bres has dispatched messengers to other tuath where he has kin, even to the High King at Tara. I met the rider on the road."

"But surely Bres is subject to the High King? He can't just proclaim himself king."

"No, but Bres and the High King are old friends and one of Bres's aunts married the High King's brother, so they are also kin."

Sorcha stood and began to pace. "But if he is to blame for Criofan's death …?"

"There's no proof that he or Ana had any knowledge of it, and Bres is a rich man. He would pay and no more would be said."

Honor-price. Could he simply compensate the family for their loss—a few cattle and some gold for the life of a man?

She left off her pacing in front of Conall and looked him straight in the eye. "So, Criofan is dead. Ana may have killed him, and Bres has declared himself King of Croghan. Where does that leave Ruairí?"

He scraped a hand through his long brown hair. "Ruairí is meeting today with Criofan's son. You know that Bres is skilled in the art of persuasion. You experienced it yourself."

Yes, she most certainly had. He could convince a man to jump off a cliff.

"When we met in council this morning, Bres argued that Criofan's dream must stand and provided another interpretation."

Sorcha huffed. "How can you interpret a man standing in a bloody field of cattle around the bones of his people in any other way?"

"He said it meant that if famine struck, he would do whatever was necessary to feed his people. Even slay the cattle."

"Well, that's just rubbish."

"The council agreed with him for the most part and Bres is now king. Also …" He paused and bit his lower lip.

"Also, what?"

"Bres convinced the council that *you* are to blame for Criofan's death."

"Me?" she cried, raising her hands. "But I was nowhere near there. I'm banished." Sorcha's mind reeled with worst-case scenarios. Bres could send an assassin or an army of assassins. Ana might slip her poison somehow like she'd apparently done to the old druid. Worst of all, she might have to get down on her knees and beg the horned god to come and take her back to her own time. Somehow in all this chaos, she'd grown to love it here with Ruairí's family and friends. She wanted to stay with him and be his wife, whatever that entailed.

"Bres claims you were invisible and sent the sickness through a curse."

"A curse? Why would I do that?" Sorcha's legs turned to ribbons and she sat down hard on the rock.

"Revenge. Criofan banished you from the tuath."

"That's ridiculous! Do they believe him?"

He nodded. "Many do, and others fear him."

"And you? Do you believe him?"

Reaching down, Conall touched her cheek. "No."

Sorcha hung her head in her hands. *Feck. Now, I'll never get back there. I must be delusional, thinking even for a second that I could have lived happily ever after with Ruairí at Croghan Hill.*

"I'm here for you, Sorcha, and I'll guard you with my life."

Sorcha stared up into Conall's eyes. They were the eyes of a concerned friend, nothing more.

"Aye, I know you will."

Later, they huddled inside by the fire. By dusk, the sky had clouded over and the rain begun again. They'd eaten thinly sliced lamb, bread, and cheese, and were on their third horn of ale. Sorcha's queazy stomach had settled and she was finally able to relax. She laid against the driftwood slab, wrapped in her cloak, and wished Ruairí lay behind her.

Conall produced a leather case, carefully took out his pipes, and played a haunting melody that made Sorcha both smile and sniffle. *I have to find a way through this. I won't live in this spider-infested hut forever. Not without Ruairí.*

"That's the song of Bean Rua," Conall said, brushing a tear from her cheek. "Don't despair, Sorcha."

"What's the song about?" she asked, sniffing.

"A red-haired faerie that falls in love with a mortal."

She glanced up. "How does it end?"

"The Bean Rua spirits him away to her underwater world where they live happily for three hundred years."

"Then what happens?"

"He passes into spirit and is reborn and they fall in love again."

"Ah, you're a romantic," she said, and kicked his leg with the edge of her foot.

Conall smiled. "It's both a gift and a torment but that's the life of a bard." Holding out the pipes, he presented them to her.

"You're going to let me hold your pipes? I didn't think a bard would let anyone touch his instruments?"

"Just this once."

"Lord," she said, taking the instrument from his outstretched hands. She'd seen the Wicklow pipes once. They were carved from yew and carbon-dated to 400BCE. These were worn, but solid and beautifully formed. Music was as old as humanity.

Conall moved closer and held her hands as she put them to her lips. "The breath comes from your belly and passes over the surface of the mouthpiece."

Like a flute or a panpipe, she thought, and taking a breath she blew a brief peep. "Ah, I'm shit at it."

He laughed. "It takes time and practice."

"Apparently not for you. Winnie said you played a stone flute when you were still a baby. *She* has a crush on you."

Conall took back the pipes and cradled them below his lower lip. The tones shivered with his embarrassment.

"Does Ruairí know how you feel?"

Conall's glance rose questioning.

"Does he know that you love him?" It was obvious to Sorcha from the moment she'd seen them together.

Dropping his hands, Conall fondled the pipes. The instrument gave him comfort. "It doesn't matter what I feel. I am sworn as the king's bard. It's a position of honor and obedience."

"But the king is dead." Narrowing her eyes, she cocked her head in sudden awareness. Aristotle had written that Celtic bards shared their patron's bed. Homosexual sex was esteemed and some kings expected sexual favors.

"Can we *not* talk of this?" Conall appeared to be reading her mind.

"We *must* talk of this. If your king expects or demands sex, it's wrong. And you, such a beautiful, gentle man. It's more than wrong. It's criminal. Did Adamair …?"

Conall squeezed his eyes tight and turned his face away. "When we traveled abroad he took me to the high courts, flaunted me, and yes, I shared his bed." When he opened his eyes again, they were glassed over. "It happens to other druids. Even a warrior can be singled out."

"That's horrible. Especially when your heart lies with someone else. Does Ruairí know what Adamair did to you?"

Conall shrugged.

"You must've been relieved when Adamair went after the white bull."

"Who do you think encouraged him to steal it?" A corner of his lip rose in victory. "I sang him a song of his exploits."

"Clever." She grinned, but then another thought, a horrifying thought, the most gruesome of them all. "What about Bres? If he becomes king …"

"I am sworn as the king's bard." Conall's bottom lip quivered and Sorcha's heart broke.

"We cannot let Bres succeed in his lies. Tomorrow, I'll go with you and we'll help Ruairí take down Bres. I'm not afraid of him."

It was a lie. The more she heard of Bres, the more she feared him.

"No," Conall said, firmly. "I must return alone. They'll be watching me and Ruairí said you must stay here where you're safe." He shook his head. "I will come back whenever I can and bring you food. But I cannot take you back. I cannot go against his wishes."

"Well, I can. You'll have to lock me in this hut to keep me here and then I'll crawl out the smoke hole or call on my spirits! I applaud your loyalty to Ruairí, but he needs us. We must find a way to draw out these murderers and prove that they conspired against Criofan. Surely, that's treason."

The Hill-Fort

Estrada could hear the excitement in Dylan's voice as they bounced along on the black draft horse and approached Croghan Hill. On its slightly flattened top was a timbered wall like a palisade. Around them the land was lush and fertile, thick forests surrounding pasture and dark plowed fields.

"Ah, it's brilliant! Look at the ditch and the embankment."

What's so brilliant about that? Estrada thought. They'd dug an extensive ditch partway up the hill and likely used the excavated dirt to build up the bank above it. It was obviously a strategy to keep enemies from attacking the nobles housed inside. But not everyone lived inside. A small village of round cone-shaped buildings straddled the base of the hill and spread out into the fields. If anyone attacked, they'd be first to go. Dylan said this was a stratified society and it appeared to be physically layered as well.

Estrada was more excited by the women washing clothes and bathing in the ponds in the red glow of the setting sun. It reminded him of photographs he'd seen of the Ganges River in India. Not surprising. Dylan said the Celts weren't really Celts at all, just several culturally-connected tribes that migrated northwest over thousands of years and spoke a common Indo-European language—a language Estrada could currently speak and understand, though he still thought in English. Apparently, Old Irish and Sanskrit shared several words. Estrada was sure that, given the chance and a knowledge of Sanskrit, Dylan would be able to rhyme them off. His friend was positively vibrating with excitement as everything he'd ever read appeared before his eyes.

The smoke from kilns and hearths drifted through the valley with other odors—braising meat, sweat, and manure. Both animal and human. It wasn't pristine, but the people were busy about their evening chores and looked content enough.

"It looks like the ponds at the base of the hill are flooding," Dylan said, peering over his shoulder. "Aye, they're building some kind of track road and bridge."

Indeed. The rutted trail they'd followed the past couple of hours had widened and wound its way up the hill, but water had covered it where it crossed the lowlands in the valley. Leftover lumber was still stacked at its edges in case they needed to add on. The horse plodded through the wet grass and puddles and crossed the bridge without flinching.

"Hey, looks like they're closing the gate," Dylan said, urging the horse on from behind. It began to trot and they bounced their way up the hill.

Estrada's shoulder was sore, but not as sore as his thighs and ass. Dylan must have been feeling a similar ache because as soon as they got close to the guards, he slipped off the back of the horse and hustled to the gate. Estrada hoped they weren't walking into something serious. First the posse, and then the horseman who'd warned them of chaos and the death of someone important.

"Aye, Ruairí Mac Nia," Dylan was saying. "Conall Ceol said we should see him."

The guard grunted and closed the gate.

"What happened?" Estrada asked.

"I don't know. He seemed pleasant enough. Maybe with the death of the chief druid this morning they've upped the security."

As they stood and waited to see if the gates would re-open, Estrada glanced down the hill. Perhaps they could find a place to sleep down below if—

The gate opened and a young, dark-haired woman stared at them. She was just a teenager and was accompanied by a rather large and handsome man who stood behind her flanked by the guards.

"You're looking for Ruairí Mac Nia?"

Estrada sniffed. "We're actually looking for—"

Dylan elbowed him in the leg. "We had a wee accident on the road. A man who introduced himself as Conall Ceol ran into my friend as we crested a hill." He pointed to Estrada who looked down from the horse and raised his eyebrows.

The woman laughed and brightened. "Conall is a gifted bard and generally a good horseman, but sometimes his mind is with his muse. I'm sorry if he hurt you."

"It's nothing," Estrada said, shaking his head.

"It was our fault really. We were wandering up the hill in the middle of the path. He didn't see us until it was too late." Dylan pursed his lips.

"Come in." She signaled to the guards to open the gate so the stout horse could pass. "You must rest and eat. Aengus will look at your shoulder. He's a gift for such things." Her face flushed as she glanced with wide eyes at the man beside her.

When Estrada slid down from the horse, one of the guards caught the reins and walked off with it. "It belongs to one of the farmers," Estrada shouted after him.

"Don't worry. He'll look after her," the woman said. "My name's Donella. Ruairí's my brother."

"Oh." Estrada didn't know what else to say. He didn't know Ruairí or Conall or anyone here. All he really wanted to do was find a pub, have a drink, and eat something. Still, he lagged behind, trying to get a feel for the place. His gut told him small talk with Donella was the least of his worries.

She led them into the largest of the round cone-shaped buildings. The reason for the cone soon became apparent. At its base was a huge central hearth. The smoke caught a draft and rose straight up until there was too much activity around the fire, and then it drifted. Large trenchers of meat were laid out at the edge of the hearth along with flat breads and wooden bowls containing butter and cheese. His nose led him to the huge casks of ale. This would do just fine. A good feed, a few ales, and some sleep was exactly what he needed. His shoulder would take care of itself.

The people seemed lighthearted, which seemed strange, given that the chief druid had died that morning. Perhaps, it was a wake. Several parts of the round room were partitioned off and, from one, he could hear a raucous party.

Donella pointed to the hearth and told them to help themselves and then join her and Aengus.

"He's her fiancé," Dylan said. "They're to be married at Midsummer."

Estrada nodded and nibbled on a pork rib. Then he slipped his arm out of the sling and spread a flatbread with cheese. He rolled it up and popped it in his mouth. "They're missing jalapeños," he said, dipping a metal cup into an open barrel of ale. His shoulder was feeling good despite the day of bouncing. A few more ales and he'd be healed.

Dylan shook his head. "Try not to get drunk. Remember, Sorcha's our priority. And don't mention her name. We don't want them to know we know her; at least, until we find out what she's done."

"Right." The ale was good. Damn good. Dark, bitter, and yeasty; as thick as the milk, which was also sitting out in metal pails and dotted with black bits. Estrada wolfed down his roll, ate three more ribs, and dipped back into the ale, three or maybe four more times. He was beginning to feel human.

By now the loud party behind the partition had spilled out into the hall. A group of men, with women hanging off their arms, was heading in his direction. All of them were inebriated, well beyond anything he'd seen in a while. They must have been drinking for hours.

The man in the middle of this mob was the ugliest motherfucker Estrada had ever seen. Not ugly so much in his facial features, but some inner ugliness that bloomed like red tide. He was short, maybe five foot five, which could account for some of his small dog syndrome. He shaved his head and wore an enormous mustache and beard that hung from his chin to his waist. It was tied in horse tales just below his Adam's apple, which was stupid really. In a fight, that would be the first thing Estrada would yank.

The ugly man approached, then stood sneering and weaving, a scantily clad woman on each arm. Behind him lurked the reason for his cockiness. His bodyguard was enormous, barrel-shaped and burly as a bear.

"How is it, you've come into our hall, eaten our food, drunk our ale, and not yet shown your submission to the new king?" the ugly one said.

"Who would that be?" Estrada asked, though he knew the answer. Arrogant assholes always talk about themselves in the third person.

"Me!" He laughed and, dropping the women from his arms, caught the two beard tales in his fist. Pulling them apart, he puffed out his naked hairy chest.

Squinting, Estrada cocked his head.

"You may submit," Ugly said.

"Ah, jeez." Dylan, who was standing beside Estrada, looked mortified. Covering his mouth, he muttered, "I think he wants you to kiss his nipples."

"What?" Estrada snorted.

"I read it somewhere. It's like kneeling before the king."

"No fucking way," Estrada growled.

The bodyguard had shoved his way forward and was now hovering so close to Estrada, he could feel the man's bushy red beard tickling his good arm. They all had knives hanging from their belts, but so did he. The fire was to his left. He could easily hurl this asshole into the coals. But he'd have to fight the big man and when he glanced around the hall could see the king now had his boys in position. There was no getting out of this save for a scrap he'd likely not win. Still.

"As much as I'd like to *submit*, I don't even know your name." Estrada winked, then looked Ugly right in the eye.

"His name is Bres Brecain," the bodyguard said, "and he's King of Tuath Croghan. Now show your submission or eat *this*." He held up a fist the size of a baseball mitt.

"Just do it," Dylan said.

The whole room hushed.

Now, Estrada hadn't been a magician for years without learning a few things. He was a decent hypnotist, but it was hard to hypnotize a drunk. You had to have a coherent mind to manipulate. He was as dexterous as some of *the52* with a deck of cards, but cards hadn't been invented yet. And he was a wizard knife-thrower. However, these guys were right in his face. With no other props, that left ...

As their eyes moved right, Estrada scooped left, so fast they didn't see it happen. Leaping atop one of the trenchers, he suddenly held in his fists two flaming torches from the fire. He tossed them in the air and did some fancy juggling just to catch everyone's attention. He could hear *oohs* and *ahs* and the sound of laughter through the hall. It might be enough to shift the mood.

But no. The big man lunged.

Leaping down into a crouch, Estrada tapped the torch to the frizzled bottom of that heavy red beard. It took a few seconds for the big man to register that his beard was burning, and then the jumping and screaming began. The girls were laughing. Dylan stood mortified. Estrada's shoulder ached and he knew if he did this next maneuver he could pop it again, but the performance bug had bit.

He took four seconds to focus, then did a double backflip across the room and disappeared into the madness. The crowd cheered when he appeared by the door.

In a very loud voice, a young man shouted, "Not on the night of my father's death. Show some respect."

The big man, beard still aflame, was leaping and hollering, which was only making things worse. Suddenly, one of the bystanders picked up the pail of milk and flung it over the big man's face and chest. The ox stood, mouth hung open in amazement, milk dribbling down his sizzling beard.

The king had disappeared. Nipples and all.

Donella and Aengus appeared beside Estrada with Dylan in tow. "You probably shouldn't have done that," she said. "Follow me."

"Let's hope they're too drunk to remember," Dylan said.

"They won't *all* be."

"I didn't have much choice." *Kiss his nipples? Seriously?* Estrada, at least, knew his way around a man's nipple. "Would *you* have kissed his nipples?" he asked Dylan. "Because *you* would have been next." His friend's face reddened. "That's what I thought."

"Let's talk outside," Donella said.

Darkness had fallen and the untainted sky above was studded with stars. Aengus led them to a shadowy corner of the fort where they'd be undisturbed.

"So, kiss his nipples?" Estrada squinted suspiciously. "Is that *really* a thing?"

"He's from Iberia," Dylan explained. "They have different customs."

"At a king's inauguration, and sometimes after, people kiss his nipples to show submission. Bres was just drunk and being an ass tonight."

"And his bodyguard?"

"Ah, that's Fearghas," Aengus said. "The two of them together maybe make one man. I shouldn't talk that way about the new king, but—"

"Aengus and I have been talking. I know we've just met, but we feel that we can trust you, and since Conall sent you ..." Pausing, Donella cleared her throat. "We can't find my brother. He wasn't at supper and no one's seen him since this morning."

"Would he have left the fort?" Estrada asked.

"His horse is still in the pasture." Donella caught one of the wavy tendrils that had fallen around her face and twisted it.

Stepping up beside her, Aengus gathered her in his arms. "When Bres declared himself king this morning at council, Ruairí laughed at him. Bres is not the kind of man to suffer public humiliation."

"Would Bres have him killed?" It wasn't the question Estrada wanted to ask the anxious sister, but he didn't know what kind of culture he was dealing with.

Donella swallowed hard.

"Or imprisoned? Do you have a jail?"

"They've more likely beaten him and left him somewhere in the woods," Aengus said. "Of the nine men in the inner circle, Ruairí and Bres were closest to Criofan. He needs Ruairí's submission."

Or his death, Estrada thought. "Have you searched everywhere?" There were buildings outside the perimeter of the fort—sheds, shelters, and all the villagers' houses at the base of the hill.

"We'll do that in the morning. Aengus is sleeping in the men's hut. I think you'll be safe enough there tonight. But you must leave before dawn. Bres will not forget you and neither will Fearghas. He'll have his stinking beard to remind him."

One side of Estrada's mouth pulled up in a grin. *The stench of burned hair was a bitch.*

"I can provide horses but you'll need to ride swiftly. A small army of Bres's kin have already gathered for his inauguration."

As they walked toward the cone-shaped hut, Dylan said suddenly, "We encountered a group of warriors today. They were searching for a red-haired woman. Do you know who that might be?"

"Sorcha!" Donella was visibly shaken by this news.

"What's *she* done to enrage the king?" Estrada asked. He remembered Dylan's dream of Sorcha being held prisoner. Was she in hiding or had someone taken her hostage?

Aengus answered quietly. "At council, Bres accused Sorcha of murdering Criofan in his sleep."

"She's our friend," Dylan confessed. "I know she'd never do such a thing. We're searching for her ourselves."

Estrada released a breath. It was good to know Sorcha had made friends among the people here and they could stop lying. Donella and Aengus were good people and would make strong allies.

"Oh." Donella's eyes widened with surprise.

"Aye, sorry. We didn't want to tell you until we knew what she'd done."

"Bres claims she cursed Criofan," Angus explained.

"Cursed?"

"I don't believe the Tuatha de Danann are *all* evil as Bres claims. I think the fey come to bless us. Ruairí liked Sorcha. I know he did," Donella said.

Estrada glanced questioningly at Dylan. *Did these people think that Sorcha was a faerie?* Of course, *he* knew faeries existed. Primrose had told him about the Tuatha de Danann, and he'd seen them himself that night on the mounds near Cong. *But Sorcha? Perhaps if someone saw her suddenly materialize in the middle of the woods.*

"When did you last see her?" Dylan asked.

"Ruairí took her away four days ago when Criofan banished her."

"Banished her?" Dylan's lip trembled.

"And returned without her?" Estrada asked.

"Yes. Early the next morning."

"She can't be far." Dylan looked like he was doing some kind of mental math. "In the morning, we can search for them both."

"Would Ruairí have gone back to her if he'd hidden her somewhere close?" Estrada asked. Sorcha had a way with men.

"Not without his horse. But I'm sure she's safe," Donella said brightening. "Conall came to me this morning in a rush and asked for some women's things. He didn't explain but I assumed they were for Sorcha. Your friend may be in danger but she's not alone. Ruairí sent his best friend to protect her."

Estrada nodded. "But we need to find Ruairí." If Bres or Fearghas got a hold of him there was no telling what would happen.

Horse Thief

When Dylan dipped his hands in the rain barrel and washed his face, the water dripped down his beard. "If Ruairí sent Conall to look after Sorcha, she must be somewhere down that road we came in on," he said, rubbing it awkwardly with his palm.

They'd arisen just before dawn to a threatening sky and stood in the shadows outside the circular hall where Aengus still slept. Estrada wanted to slip off all his clothes and climb right into the rain barrel. Instead, he dropped his cloak and took off his red jacket and white linen shirt. The fabric was remarkably strong and smooth, better than the linen they were mass producing in the twenty-first century.

"So, Conall was on his way to Sorcha when he took out my shoulder. That's bloody ironic." Leaning over, Estrada thrust his head and shoulders into the water, then popped up and washed as much of his bare skin as he could reach. That shouldn't contaminate the water supply too much. He sniffed the linen shirt. *No showers, no deodorant, no laundromat. It doesn't get more natural than this.* He slipped his shirt back on and pulled on the red jacket against the morning chill.

"It's logical. There must be more than one wormhole. Cernunnos must have brought us through the one closest to Sorcha. We'd likely be with her now if I hadn't chosen the wrong direction."

"Don't sweat it. We'll find her."

It would have been more helpful had the horned god just told them where she was. Then Estrada wouldn't have had to bounce on a draft horse all day, get a sore ass, piss off the ugly king, and make an enemy of his sidekick. But that was Cernunnos—he didn't *interfere* in the affairs of men unless it was entertaining.

Aengus appeared, nodded, and went to piss in a hole behind a stack of wood. It didn't take a scientist to imagine the rain would wash the sewage downhill into the ponds at the base—the ponds where people bathed and drew their drinking water from. Aengus helped himself to the rain barrel in much the same way Dylan had, and beckoned them to follow.

As they passed by the hall, he signaled them to halt and wait outside, then he disappeared for a few minutes and came back with Donella and a sack full of supplies. The four of them wound silently through the fort until they came to a gate just big enough for a single man on horseback to pass through. A guard slumped beside it sleeping off last night's ale. They walked through quietly and continued down the well-worn path to the pasture.

Cattle and horses mingled together. The moiled cattle laid in pale spotted clusters under the oak trees. Many of the horses stood; some with one hoof drawn up elegantly. Birds were beginning to twitter in the leafed-out trees, while the odd owl still hooted from the darkness. It was a beautiful pastoral scene—this in-between-time on the land—if you disregarded the fresh cow flaps and piles of horse dung, the biting flies, and the rain.

They watched as Aengus and Donella went into a timber shed and emerged with ropes and sheep skins. After looping rope halters around two of the horses' necks, they spread the hides on top.

Dylan looked teary-eyed. "We'll find them both. I promise."

Donella threw her arms around him and Aengus's eyes widened with surprise. "Sorcha's a fortunate woman to have two such loyal and gifted rescuers. If we have news of her or my brother, we'll send a message to you."

Turning, she hugged Estrada. "There's an old crooked faerie tree on a lone hill not far from here. I'm sure you'll know it when you see it. In the valley, there's a stream where you can camp."

The instructions seemed odd. There must be hundreds of old crooked faerie trees. And then it struck him—*Donella thinks we're faeries too.* Guilt by association. But there were smiles all around, so Estrada decided to let them think they were fey, at least for the moment. It might give her hope.

They'd just mounted the horses when a commotion erupted at the main gate.

An old man shouted, "I must see Criofan."

Had he not heard that the chief druid died the day before? Dressed in varying shades of brown, he seemed vaguely familiar.

Estrada and Dylan stayed near the shelter with Donella, while Aengus went to investigate. It wasn't really necessary. In the predawn hush, they could hear every word being spoken by the irate farmer.

"I've ridden all night and I must see him. I've known him since I was a boy. You must let me pass."

There was a pause and Estrada assumed the guard was explaining that it was impossible to see the dead druid.

"Then I will see the king! I caught this horse thief red-handed and I demand justice. It's the law."

A body slumped over the back of a draft horse similar to the one Conall had acquired for them yesterday. Estrada took a closer look and realized why the man looked familiar. This was the farmer who'd leant them Ebony. *What had Conall said about stealing horses? We take it seriously? What would they do to the horse thief? String him up? Hang him from a tree, without a trial or lawyer or any chance to offer a defense?*

It was not the ox who appeared then, but the little king himself, flanked by his retinue. Estrada recognized his bald head and that double-forked beard he ached to yank. The complainant fell to his knees—he obviously knew Bres—and the talk quieted.

Needing to know the outcome of this commotion, Estrada slid off his horse, despite Dylan's silent protests, and loped up between the lumps of cattle through the shadows until he stood alongside the timber posts. Then he crept along the rounding wall and stopped close enough to eavesdrop without being discovered. The sun had risen over the eastern horizon and light was slowly climbing up the hill.

"He stole my breeches right off the line," the farmer was saying, "and left these." He dropped a pile of garments on the ground at the king's feet. One of the king's men picked up what appeared to be a pair of bleached blue jeans.

How the hell? Estrada thought. *Did someone else slip through the wormhole?*

"And I caught him stealing my only riding horse."

"A horse thief, heh?" Bres seemed delighted with the prospect of this. "Did this man provide any explanation as to why he might steal from you before you knocked him unconscious?"

"When I questioned him something came from his mouth but I couldn't understand a word."

"A foreigner, heh? And a horse thief?" Bres signaled to his man to lower the thief from the work horse, which he did by cutting the rope and letting the body drop at the king's feet.

The man had obviously received a blow to the head that had rendered him unconscious. By now, the sun had risen far enough that its first rays lit the level of the mens' feet. Estrada gasped with sudden recognition.

The blond surfer boy hair, the ripped blue jeans. *Christ! That's Guy Fairchild! How the hell did the boss's son end up here? Had he followed them through the vineyard and got caught up in the spell when he invoked Cernunnos?*

"Stand him up," Bres commanded, and it was so. "You stand accused of horse thievery. What say you in your defense?"

Guy mumbled something incoherent.

"He says, 'I would have stolen the horse had I not been caught. Do with me as you see fit.'" Bres smirked and turned to the farmer. "Do you pay your food-rents on time to the king?"

"I do. I've served the King of Croghan all my life."

"What would you have me do to this man who's stolen your best clothing, would have stolen your best riding horse had you not caught him in the act, and made you lose an entire night's sleep to bring him here?"

"Hide him," the farmer said.

Hide him? In a shed? In prison?

"Very well. When you speak to the other farmers and villagers, you'll tell them that your new king is honest and just." Bres flipped a piece of silver into the farmer's hand and turned away.

The man beamed. "I'll tell everyone I meet. Thank you, lord."

Estrada waited. The guards dropped Guy to the ground and picked up the long rope that had bound him to the horse. As they looped it around the horse's halter, Estrada suddenly realized what was about to happen.

Aengus, who'd seen Estrada hiding in the shadows, signaled him to back off. Estrada shook his head. This was like a scene from the Wild West. Could a man live through a hiding?

The guard slapped the horse's flank and sent it cantering off through the pasture with Guy in tow.

Bres cleared his throat and spat. "If he lives take him to the slavery."

The farmer stood with his arms crossed, a big smile on his face, as he waited for his horse to return.

Estrada loped back down to where Dylan waited with Donella behind the shed. "I know that guy."

"Know him? How could you …?" Dylan stood, eyebrows furled, completely baffled.

Estrada ignored him. There was no way to explain the intricacies of gods and time-travel to Donella and Aengus. "If he lives through this, they're taking him to something called the slavery." Donella's face told him it was doubtful the horse thief would live.

The ordeal was difficult to watch. The horse raced through the pasture trying to free itself from the weight that bounced along behind it. Mercifully, after a few minutes the rope caught on a jutting rock and the heavy horse stopped abruptly, then stood pawing the ground.

Aengus joined the guard and the farmer in inspecting what was left of the would-be horse thief. Considering he hadn't even succeeded in stealing the horse, Estrada thought this unjust punishment. Finding him sufficiently hided, the guards tossed Guy's body over the back of the horse and walked it down the hill toward the village. The happy farmer danced alongside clutching his silver.

Aengus returned to where they were standing in the shadows of the cattle shed. "Well, he's alive. Though he'll need to grow a new layer of skin and he'll forever reek of cow shit."

"Estrada knows him," Donella said, signaling her partner to go easy.

"Will they lock him up?" Estrada was already orchestrating ways to rescue Fairchild. He might be annoying but he couldn't leave him to a life of slavery and beatings and God knows what else.

Aengus shook his head. "They'll leave him in the dust for now. He's unconscious and no trouble to anyone."

"Good," Estrada said.

"You're not going after him?" Dylan stood with his arms crossed over his chest and shook his head. "If we get caught trying to rescue a horse thief, how are we going to help Sorcha?"

Estrada didn't like the idea any more than Dylan but he couldn't walk away. He shrugged. "We'll just have to save them both."

"Aengus and I will walk down to the village," Donella said, "and see what's become of him." Hooking arms, the couple followed the trail of the farmer and his horse.

"Who is he?" Dylan demanded when they were out of range.

"Guy Fairchild. My boss's son."

"How the hell did he—?"

"He must have followed us through the vineyard and hid when I cast the circle. Whatever glamor Cernunnos gave us didn't apply to him. He was wearing jeans and he doesn't speak the language. He'll never survive here. Especially as a slave under this tyrant."

Dylan's jaw clenched. "Bloody hell."

"Let's just wait to see what Aengus and Donella say. If they don't think we can get Guy out right now, I'll come back tonight when it's dark."

"We should be gone *now*." Dylan stared up at the sun which had now risen over the horizon.

"I wouldn't leave *you* in a situation like that."

Dylan's cheeks flushed. "I know. Are you mates or …?"

Estrada shook his head and stared at his fist, remembering their altercation the previous morning. Guy had likely followed him through the vineyard because he wasn't prepared to take no for an answer. His schoolboy crush had nearly got him killed and Estrada couldn't help but feel bad for him. "He's just a guy I know. Still, I can't—" He elbowed Dylan in the arm and pointed up the hill to the side gate. "Hey, isn't that …?" He gestured with his chin.

"Aye, with most of his beard cut off."

Fearghas had stopped and was taking a piss against the timbered wall. The two guards fumbled about waiting and then followed behind him when he walked on.

"Where do you suppose he's going?"

"Somewhere you'll not want to be. He looks like he means business."

Estrada watched until the trio stepped out of sight behind the rounded wall. He tested his shoulder. It was fit enough for a fight.

When he turned back, he saw Aengus and Donella walking up the side of the hill accompanied by a rider on a white horse. "Is that Conall?"

"Aye, so it is," Dylan said, bouncing on his toes.

Donella became engaged in an emotional discussion with Conall, who dismounted and walked beside her. Stopping suddenly, he threw his arms around her and, for the first time, Estrada saw how terribly upset she was at her brother's disappearance.

Seeing the same scene, Dylan slumped and bit a nail. "I hope it's not bad news."

"Hello again," Conall said, when at last they were all hidden in the shadow of the cattle shelter. "How's the shoulder?"

"Perfect," Estrada said.

"Conall just left Sorcha," Donella blurted out. "She's safe. I told him you're here to help. He'll take you to her."

"But the guards will soon be patrolling. You must leave now." Aengus obviously didn't want to take a chance being seen with them.

"What about *him*?" Estrada nodded down the hill toward the slaves' quarters.

"The slaves are up and working and guards posted. We can't just walk in there without word getting back to the main hall."

"Bres has kin everywhere," Donella added.

Estrada nodded. They couldn't risk getting caught trying to rescue Guy when they now had a clear route to Sorcha.

"I'll speak to my woman and find out how your friend fares."

"Here's a fresh mount." Aengus passed Conall the reins to a sleek brown horse. "I'll see to Capall." He stroked the nose of the white horse and whispered in his ear.

"What's back there?" Estrada asked, gesturing toward the southern section of the fort where it backed onto pastureland.

"Just the bull pens," Conall said.

"Are there bulls in there now?"

"No, they're all out to pasture with the cows. We only lock them up to fatten them before a slaughter."

Estrada felt his belly flip and swallowed. "Fearghas went down there with two guards."

Conall, Donella, and Aengus all exchanged glances.

"We didn't check there," she said, leaping onto the back of Conall's white horse.

The Bull Pen

Ruairí was huddled in a dark corner of the bull pen, naked and shivering, his knees pulled up to his chest. They'd taken his clothes, anything that made him feel human, except his armband. That revealed his rank and would anger the gods if it were removed for any reason. Rain poured down against the thatch in a steady stream and seeped under the logs. Rivulets and puddles formed around his body and the water bit his bare ass.

Hours had passed, how many he didn't know. But he did know the fear the white bull had felt before it was taken from the pen and sacrificed. His face felt pulpy, his nose broken, the inside of his mouth shredded. His ears rang, and his head still pounded from Bres's punch. But most of all, he felt stupid. He should've known better. Bres had packed a bronze spear butt in his palm since they were kids. Ruairí had felt its kiss before. It was the only way Bres could turn a fight his way.

He coughed and spit to clear the blood that dripped down the back of his throat. His hands were tied behind his back with leather thongs; his eyes so badly swollen he could just make out shadows in the darkness.

The bull pen was a simple lean-to constructed of rough-hewn saplings, posted vertically and attached to the main wall of the fort. There was a door on each end, big enough to fit a bull. Fearghas had designed the pen so the bull could be pushed in one door and pulled out the other. There were no windows though as the sun rose shafts of light slipped through the spaces between the thin jagged trees.

What did a sacrificial bull need with a view? It was a divine creature whose view encompassed eternity, provided them with meat, and communed with other gods. The white bull had given both him and Criofan the dream of Bres, and the dream would soon come true unless Ruairí could stop it. How was another matter.

Fearghas had locked him in here after pulling him from the sacred pool. Then, he'd come back late last night with two guards, so drunk he could barely stand, his frizzled beard, burned and reeking. The big ox must have fallen into the fire. It happened on occasion. Ruairí hadn't done it himself, but he'd seen men permanently disfigured by their drunken clumsiness. Fearghas smelled worse than the tannery where they burned the hair off hides. Ruairí had smirked to see the ox's folly and that was enough to set the big man off. Fearghas put a knife to his throat while the guards tied his hands behind his back, then shoved him to his knees. Then the ox went to work on his face. Fearghas hadn't mentioned Sorcha at all. The beating was simply a means to release his rage.

Now he was back. Ruairí could hear his lumbering steps as he approached the door.

"You just watch." As Fearghas shoved open the door, Ruairí leaned back against the other door. "Put it there," he said to the guard, and pointed to the ground by Ruairí's bare feet. It was a thick slab of wood with two round cut-outs in the center.

Crouching, Fearghas leaned into Ruairí's face, his breath reeking of the night's ale. "I've made you something special." He was always proud of his creations. Then he turned to the guards. "Sit on his legs." They balked, and Fearghas snarled. "Do it, or I'll do you." They knew he would. He'd killed and maimed more men than any of them. His ropes of skulls ran down the wall beside where he slept in the hall.

Ruairí was six-and-a-half feet tall and his long legs were muscled from years of running and riding. In the blur of his mind, he pulled up his knees and tried to imagine what Fearghas was planning. But the ox drew his sword and cracked Ruairí's kneecaps with the flat side. Pain riveted through his body and his legs dropped. Then, his battered face fell forward over them.

"Hold his shoulders back," Fearghas shouted. The guards leaned over, wrenched him up, and held him firm.

When Fearghas lifted the top block off his new contraption, Ruairí could see that it was built of two blocks strapped together. Each block had two half-circles gouged into it, and when he stuck them together, they created two empty holes. He jammed Ruairí's ankles into the bottom half, slapped the other on top, and tied both blocks together with a leather thong.

"Now sit on his legs," the ox thundered.

The two guards squatted and settled themselves on top of his legs: one on his shins, the other across his thighs. His eyes met those of the man closest to his face and he saw a flash of sympathy. He'd known these men since they were boys. They'd been his uncle's men until his death and now served Críofan. And they'd been bullied by Bres and Fearghas just like every other boy in this tuath.

Pulling his knife from his sheath, Fearghas smiled and slashed upwards across the bottom of Ruairí's right foot.

Ruairí shrieked, bolted upright, and knocked the closest guard off with his shoulder. Still his feet were caught in the holes of the wood blocks and the weight of the other guard crushed his legs.

"Hold him down, I said!" And the guards shoved him back against the dirt floor with his bound hands jammed beneath his back and put their full weight against his shoulders. "You always thought Fearghas was an oaf and a fool," he said, tapping his head with his free hand. "Well, Fearghas is no fool."

Struggling, Ruairí raised his head and stared at the blood-drenched knife.

"Now, tell me. Where is the de Danann woman? Your king wants to know."

"*F-F-FECK.*" Ruairí spit. It was a fey word Sorcha used frequently and he prayed it had as much power as it seemed to have when she said it.

Fearghas drew his arm over his head and slashed down. Same foot. Opposing angle.

Ruairí clamped down on his tongue and swallowed his scream.

Then Fearghas grasped Ruairí's big toe, pulled it and wiggled it. "I just sharpened my blade on the whetstone. She can slip through bone she can, just like it's butter." He coughed and spat. "Where's the faerie?"

Ruairí held the big man's stare and refused to speak.

"Have it your way."

When Ruairí's toe fell away, he bit through his tongue as every muscle in his body contracted. The guard beside him gagged and swallowed back his disgust.

Fearghas wiggled the toe in the air, leering, and then dropped it on the ground. "You know," he said, dragging the knife along the edge of Ruairí's ankle. "I bet I could take your whole foot off with one stroke. I have all day. A toe. A foot. A cock."

"Tell him," the other guard urged.

Fearghas raised his arm again but before he could bring it down, Ruairí's rage erupted from somewhere deep within his core. Screaming his battle cry, he bolted upright and swinging his shoulders and chest he twisted and shoved the startled guards.

A blast of sunlight lit the bullpen as the door slid open and a backlit warrior stood holding his sword aloft.

Fearghas turned, raising his arms to block and gut the intruder. But in a breath, the sword came down and slashed both his hands clean off. They hit the floor by Ruairí's feet with a dull thump, thump. Fearghas gasped, then bellowed. The shock of it registering in his mind.

The astonished guards jumped up and drew their knives.

"Conall," Ruairí whispered in a rush of breath.

Then Donella leapt ferociously into the pen and brought her knee up into Fearghas's balls with such violent force, Ruairí was sure they'd been driven into his belly.

Blood spurted from Ruairí's missing toe and he felt suddenly woozy. Sliding back against the door, he watched it all in a daze. Fearghas on the floor, curled up and crying, and Donella grabbing the bloody knife and cutting through the leather thongs that bound his feet in the wooden blocks.

"Go," Conall said to the guards, "and don't raise the alarm." They shook their heads and ran.

Fearghas was blubbering like a baby. "Shut up," Donella said, and picking up one of the wooden blocks, she brought it crashing down against the side of the ox's head.

Then Aengus was in the room and two other men. Strangers.

"We'll need to seal those arteries with a hot knife," the shorter man said. He'd already ripped up his linen shirt and was binding Ruairí's feet to stop the bleeding.

"Manus," Conall said. "The blacksmith. He lives outside the village and his woman's a healer."

"We've got you now, brother," Donella said, helping him sit up. When she cut the leather thongs that bound his hands, Ruairí rubbed his wrists and struggled to stand. Then spying his toe lying in a pool of blood on the floor, he leaned over and picked it up. He'd leave nothing of himself here for these bastards to curse.

Conall took off his cloak, wrapped it around Ruairí's shoulders and pinned it tight.

"I'll help." The other stranger was tall and dark and muscled. Shoving his shoulder under Ruairí's armpit, he braced him. Conall pulled the hood up over his head and supported his other side, and together they carried him out of the bull pen and into the rain.

"I'll take him with me," Conall said, as they boosted Ruairí up onto the white horse.

"What about *him*?" Aengus gestured to Fearghas, who lay bleeding and unconscious on the floor.

Donella slid the door across, then brought the heavy plank down to bar it. "Forget him." Standing beside Aengus, she patted Ruairí's hand. "You'll be fine, brother. You've survived worse than this."

"You and Aengus should go back inside the fort," Conall said to them. "Those guards owe nothing to Bres or Fearghas and no one will suspect you of having a hand in this. Perhaps, you can maneuver things from inside. Bres will send someone here eventually and when he finds Fearghas, he'll come after us."

"Where will you go?" Donella asked.

"First to Manus," Conall answered, "and then we'll pray to the gods."

"I need my horse," Ruairí said, as Conall turned the white mare and they began a slow trot. His foot felt as if it was on fire and though he held his toe in his hand a pain ran up his leg eclipsing that of the banging in his temple.

"I'll send someone back for Púca once you're settled with Manus. Dylan's right. We must tend to your wounds before we do anything else."

Dylan? Why were these strangers telling us what to do in our own land? "Who are these men? Why do you trust them?"

"They're friends of Sorcha's."

"Sorcha? Are they de Danann?"

Conall shrugged. "If they are, perhaps it's a good thing."

"But why have the fey suddenly come here?" Ruairí was suspicious. One woman was understandable. An entourage was not.

"They'll help us fight Bres. Estrada set Fearghas's beard on fire. Donella says he's a magician."

"Is that right." *So, it was this magician who enraged the ox and got me a battered face. What good did it do to set a man's beard on fire?* "Will his magic kill Bres?"

As Conall's head turned, Ruairí saw him raise his lips in a grin. "Perhaps. But his head will still be yours."

Ruairí turned and stared at the tall, dark, man who rode behind them. Magician or not. If he went anywhere near Sorcha, he'd kill him. Ruairí had claimed her and given her a child and would tolerate no interference from anyone.

I'm No Mercenary

The blacksmith wasted no time in putting a red hot iron to Ruairí's maimed foot. Estrada surmised that in a warrior culture where sharpened iron was the norm, losing a limb was a common occurrence. Manus, the blacksmith, certainly didn't need Dylan to advise him on how to proceed. The stench of burnt flesh was nauseating. Ruairí's suppressed scream gut-wrenching. Estrada tensed and looked away while he helped Conall brace the poor man's back and shoulders to keep him steady. But Dylan hovered alongside watching the whole procedure with interest.

When they finally laid Ruairí out on a bed of straw and sheepskins, Estrada saw the full extent of his injuries. His face was pulp, his wrists burned from the bindings, and his foot ... Well, he wouldn't be walking anytime soon. He needed stitches and butterfly sutures, but the blacksmith's daughter was collecting spider webs off the walls in the hut. It was ingenious really, the webbing so sticky when she applied it to the wounds, it cinched the flesh tightly together.

Conall sat beside Ruairí, the devoted friend, whose feelings ran deep for the injured man. Again, Estrada was reminded of Michael's face when he stared at Conall. That look that said, *"Don't leave me. I can't go on without you."* Estrada wondered if the feeling was reciprocated or if Conall was caught in some unrequited love hell like Michael had been before he'd finally confessed his true feelings.

The blacksmith's wife scuttled from the kitchen carrying a wooden bowl that contained a foul-smelling herbal paste and slathered it on Ruairí's wounds. She'd given him something she called "flower sap" to calm him as soon as they arrived and Estrada suspected it was derived from poppies. Ruairí was certainly much more docile than he'd been when they first found him in the bull pen.

Dylan, who'd joined the blacksmith's daughter in assisting, bound clean strips of linen around his feet. Máire washed the blood from Ruairí's face and dabbed some of the concoction on the goose egg at his temple. She was pale and dark and grave, a healer who appeared to have considerable skill, though she couldn't be more than fourteen.

Ruairí's eyes were nearly swollen shut, so Estrada was surprised when he turned to Conall and said, "We must go to Sorcha. If Bres finds her …"

Sorcha? Was Ruairí the bog man Cernunnos had brought Sorcha here to see—the king who'd be ritually killed and dismembered and his torso sunk in the pool at the base of the hill?

And what of Conall? He appeared to love Ruairí, who, it seemed, loved Sorcha. Leastways, something had occurred between them.

Conall touched Ruairí's shoulder. "Sorcha is safe. As soon as you can ride, we'll go."

"I can ride now." Grunting, Ruairí pushed himself up on his elbows. "Feck," he cried, staring at his bandaged foot.

It was horrible but Estrada had to smile. Sorcha had taught Ruairí the one word that worked when no other would. She'd already changed history; at least, altered the vocabulary.

"Rest," Conall said, pushing him back down into the straw. "I'll send a boy to spy on Bres, and another to get Púca. They won't think to come here, even if they find Fearghas."

"Bres did this," Ruairí growled, "and I will take his head."

Estrada had no doubt the man was capable of such a thing. He'd do the same himself given the situation. Vengeance could be a noxious lover.

The blacksmith's farm was set far back from the fort in a clearing alongside a stream. There was plenty of fresh water and the smell and noise of clanging metal from his forge didn't bother the other people in the village. The place was bouncing with dirty happy children and it was the two eldest Conall enlisted, though they were only eight or nine.

Horses were sheltered close to the house beneath an overhang roofed with timber and straw. The rain streamed from it, creating puddles and rivulets in the grass and mud but the animals looked content.

Estrada was *not* content. Now that Ruairí was settled, he found Dylan and wrestled him away from the blacksmith's daughter.

"Máire's mother is the local hedge witch, although they don't use that word in this century. She's got herbs and powders for every kind of ailment. Even the queen comes to her."

"Then Sorcha's king is in good hands." Estrada sat on a bench and scratched his beard.

"Aye. If he rests, Ruairí should pull through this." Fatigued by the crisis they'd just experienced, Dylan hunkered down beside him on the bench and exhaled.

"You do remember how this story ends," Estrada said. "This is the bog man and Cernunnos said we can't change history. Even if he survives this—"

"Fuck Cernunnos."

Estrada sat back in surprise and stared at his friend. Dylan wasn't inclined to swear unless he was really riled.

"After seeing what that brute did to Ruairí, I'll do whatever I can to save him. I'm sure that's what Sorcha wants too."

Sorcha wants Ruairí and Ruairí wants her. That's why she refused to leave with Cernunnos. "I'm sure it is. But listen. I'm going back to the village to look for Guy Fairchild."

Dylan shook his head. "Stupid move, man. Bres has spies everywhere."

"Maybe so, but I can't leave Guy living as a slave in this nightmare."

"Well, if you're determined to go, I'm coming with you." Dylan stood and braced his hands on his hips.

"I think you should stay here and look after Ruairí. Conall's exhausted." Indeed, the man looked like he hadn't slept in days. "I can ride back with the boys and they can show me where this *slavery* is." The word gave him shivers. "On a day like this, no one will be out. I'll grab Guy and find my way back." He gestured to the blacksmith's daughter, who kept glancing Dylan's way. "Your girlfriend can nurse *him* too."

Dylan ignored him. "Aye, if your friend lived through the hiding, he'll need tending." He sniffed and rubbed his nose with his fist. "You know they sacrifice slaves in this society."

"Actually, I didn't know that." Estrada's hands went icy cold as the blood rushed to his heart.

"So, don't get caught."

The blacksmith, who'd heard the last part of their conversation, took a step closer. "If you're determined to head into the village, you best change your clothes. I've an old brown cloak that'll keep out the rain and prying eyes. With my boys near, you'll look like a farmer or craftsman in need of supplies."

"Good idea." It would also keep anyone from associating the blacksmith's boys with the magician who'd set Fearghas on fire.

They followed a double-rutted trail, that looked more like a cow path, up over the hill and into the flattened pasture. The cattle laid in clumps under the trees, chewing their cuds contently though the rain poured down. As in some parts of India, this was a splendid place to be born a cow. You might end up slaughtered but you were pampered throughout your life. The grass was rich and plentiful and you were free to roam with your herd. It was a better life than that of some of the men and women who lived and died here, Estrada soon saw.

The *slavery* was near the bottom of the road to the fort where the flooding was the worst. He sent the boys home when he saw how bad things were. With the continuous rain, the water in the pools had risen and formed a lake that crept ever closer to the overhang where slaves slept on whatever dirty straw they could claw together.

Guy lay in a mud puddle beneath the thatch. He seemed concussed. His shoulder was dislocated, his ankle busted, his skin scraped raw, his flesh reeking and smeared with cow shit. And possibly his own. Which was why he'd been banished like an untouchable. He whimpered when he recognized Estrada.

"I'm going to get you out of here." He pushed past the lump in his throat. "Will you let me fix your shoulder?" Guy said nothing but didn't object when Estrada laid him out and took his arm. "It'll hurt like hell and then it'll feel better. Trust me."

Guy's eyes were clouded with fever. He was broken and it made Estrada feel sick to see him so destroyed.

"I'm sorry it took me so long to get here," he said, as he lined up Guy's arm with the joint. "We had a little trouble ourselves." He shoved the joint. Guy bit his fist to stifle his scream, then exhaled at last.

"Can you walk?"

With a half shrug, Guy sniffed.

"We need to get out of here," Estrada said, helping him up. "Let's try."

Guy swayed and gasped. "Ankle."

"Lean on me."

Together, they managed the few feet down to the water, Guy hopping and Estrada alternately dragging and steadying him.

"Water," Guy said, and Estrada lowered him into the pond. He was dirty and dehydrated and rain barrels were not evident in this part of the village.

As Guy rolled in the shallow water, Estrada used what rags were left on his body to wash off the worst of the shit and blood. His tanned surfer-boy skin was a mess of bruises and abrasions. "Looks like you hit a big wave," Estrada said to lighten the mood.

Guy gasped when Estrada touched his ribs. There was no way to tell the extent of his internal injuries but with a concussion, dislocated shoulder, bruised ribs, and broken ankle, he likely would've died of dehydration had he been left lying in that shit puddle much longer.

"The blacksmith sent clothes for you." Estrada helped Guy into a long linen shirt and baggie brown breeches. The yellow wool cloak matched his wet, matted, blond hair. "Can you ride? We'll go slow." He knew the bouncing would only make things worse but if they could get back to the blacksmith's farm, he could get Guy a dose of opium to ease his pain. And if no one else got injured, they might be able to get Sorcha and actually make it back to the two oak trees and the wormhole that would take them all home.

He'd boosted Guy up on the wet horse and just mounted himself when three riders approached and cut them off. The first two were men. The third, a woman. There was no way Estrada could fight them off alone and Guy was practically falling off the horse. He'd be no help at all.

Estrada had never seen her before but she had an air that projected nobility. "Come with me," she said.

He sucked in a breath. What choice did he have? His horse followed hers and her two thugs trailed behind. Guy slumped forward over the horse's neck and Estrada had to hold him to keep him from slipping off. Another fall would do him in.

They arrived, at last, at a circular dwelling set apart from the others. She signaled to the guards to take Guy from Estrada's grasp. Which they did. Roughly. Then they dropped him under the thatch, where he was, at least, out of the rain and covered by the woolen cloak.

The woman slipped off her horse and glanced at Estrada. "Come," she said, raising her chin.

Inside the circular dwelling was a small central hearth from which hung a bronze cauldron. A fire flickered in the hearth, but the hut was dark, damp, and musty. Split logs had been set up as benches on either side of a small table in one corner. She motioned for him to sit but, not knowing the etiquette, he paused and waited for her to seat herself first. This seemed to please her and she smiled.

"My name is Ana." She didn't ask his name and he didn't offer it. "We're a small tuath and we all know each other. Most of us are related by kin and few strangers come our way. Yet, in the last few days, four strangers have appeared, one after the other. First, the de Danann woman, then you and your friend, and now this horse thief that I caught you with near the slavery." The dancing fire reflected in her eyes as she glanced toward the wooden door. "I cannot help but think you're all connected." She paused, waiting for him to talk but still he remained silent. "You'll speak or I'll have the slave killed."

"You didn't ask a question," Estrada said, nervously scratching his beard.

A corner of her lip pulled up. "Who are you?"

He looked into her eyes, as dark as a midnight sky, and then looked away. What could he say? What lies could explain or even twist the truth into something plausible? "I'm called Estrada."

"Why are you here?"

"I've traveled from a land far away across the sea."

"That much I gathered. You speak our language with a strange accent and you're not of our people." Reaching out, she touched his hand and he sat back, surprised. "Do you know I am the queen?"

"No, I …"

Somehow, he'd missed seeing her during the commotion last night. If he had, he'd have remembered. She was beautiful and bewitching—two qualities he found most attractive and difficult to ignore.

She touched her lips with a gold drenched hand. "I can have you imprisoned. Tortured. Killed."

He furrowed his brow at this casual threat. The woman was direct. So, he'd take the risk and be direct himself. "So, why haven't you? Why are we still here talking?"

Pursing her lips, Ana cocked her head. "Because I need a hero."

The shift in her demeanor was so sudden it left his head spinning. "A hero? But I'm a stranger, a foreigner." He shrugged. "Why me?"

"*Because* you're a stranger and a foreigner. You hold no allegiance to any man here, except perhaps the horse thief." She stood, then stepped forward and appraised him. "You're fearless and uniquely skilled. A bold warrior who'll take a risk." She sighed. "And there is no one else."

Estrada considered. The queen was tall and raven-haired, stunning, and charmingly haughty. Standing still, she radiated like a moon beam—or a lightsaber. She held her power in her rigid cheekbones and indigo eyes; the rest of the package was all glitter. And glitter she did. Her pale neck was ringed in a serpentine gold torc and stacks of gold bracelets jangled from both wrists whenever she moved.

"Why do you need me? There are armed guards outside the door awaiting your command."

She sat on the bench then and took a deep breath, as if this utterance took all her energy. "My husband is dead. My lover missing. And my enemy has declared himself king."

Bres was her enemy? The bearded weasel who'd suggested Estrada submit by kissing his nipples? And who was her lover? Ruairí?

"What exactly do you need this hero to do?"

"Kill Bres." Her matter-of-fact reaction twisted his gut. "Kill him, and I'll pay you well." Slipping off one of her gold bracelets, Ana pushed it across the wooden table. It was exquisite. Incised with lightning bolts. "There's more. Much more. I can make you a rich man."

"I'm no mercenary." Locking eyes with her, he slowly pushed it back.

"Guard," she said, loudly.

"Wait." Estrada placed his hand on top of hers. The guard opened the door and she waved him off. "I'll help you if you help me."

"Go on." Ana lifted a finger and touched his hand. The action was so strangely intimate and their conversation so dangerous, it sent shivers riveting up his arm.

"If you let us go free—*all of us*—I promise to rid you of your problem." Killing Bres would be no hardship and might gain him a powerful ally.

The soft pale skin beneath his palm pulsed. "I want you to understand something, Estrada. This is no personal revenge. Bres plans an inauguration ritual the morning after Beltane. It must not happen. A king must be honest and good. He must care for the land and his people more than himself." When she closed her eyes, he saw the strained muscles in her face clench as if she'd bitten something bitter. "I will not join him in a sacred marriage. I cannot. I'd rather die."

"You have to marry Bres if he becomes king?" He didn't understand their rules.

"I am the Goddess of Sovereignty. I must wed whoever becomes the Sun King."

Suicide, rather than be forced to marry her enemy? How could he not help her? Knife? Sword? Garrote? He was already imagining ways to kill this ugly king. "I understand."

"And you must tell no one that we spoke here tonight. If you do, word will get back to Bres. Word always does, and he will kill me as he killed Criofan. By rights, Ruairí should slay Bres, using Bres's sword. That way he could take the kingship."

Ah, so that was it. Ruairí was her lover. She wanted him to become king so she could marry him. What would Sorcha think of that?

"But Ruairí has vanished."

Indeed. What did she know of his predicament? Dare he tell Ana that they rescued Ruairí this morning and left the big man to die in the bull pen? That at this moment, he was in the blacksmith's home being tended by his wife? No. He just needed to be free of her and get Guy Fairchild somewhere safe. Then he could figure out what to do about Bres.

"Will you do it?" Her dark eyes flashed in expectation. She already knew what he'd say.

"How can I not?" If he refused, he'd never get Guy out of here and he'd likely end up in the slavery himself. Or dead—now that he knew of her desire to have Bres murdered. She'd given him a blast of power that must be handled carefully.

"Give me your word, Estrada."

"You have it, if I have yours. Will you set us all free afterwards? Sorcha, my friend Dylan, the horse thief, and me?"

"I will."

This was the Iron Age. Men died every day in battle. It wasn't much different from the gangs he'd known in L.A. Two thousand years later, men still killed for the same reasons—power, territory, wealth, vengeance, and to keep their women and children safe. He thought of Alessandra and what he'd done to avenge her death all those years ago. Did he regret it? Yes. Would he do it again? Yes.

When Ana stood and stepped back from the table, Estrada stood as well. "Take off your shirt," she said suddenly, "and loosen your breeches."

"What? Why?"

She unpinned her cloak and handed him the gold pin. "Take this, at least, and embrace me. It's better for them to think I seduced a handsome stranger than that we were conspiring all this time."

"But what about your reputation?" he asked, slipping the pin in his pouch and pulling off his shirt.

"I'm a free woman and a queen. I do as I wish." Her eyes widened when she saw the raven tattooed inside his bicep. Blood dripped from its beak and its body broke into a terror of tiny, winged ravens as terrifying as the creature who'd inspired it.

Her finger swept down the raven's head, then stepping up on her toes she embraced him, running her cheek along his beard to give her skin a flush. Her breath swept his ear and he felt a rush of familiar pleasure. When she noticed the tips of the black angel's wings tattooed on his back, she slipped behind him and ran her hands over the whole tattoo. "Ah! Magnificent! The mark of the fey!"

The massive wings were indeed magical—a gift from his first lover, Alessandra.

"The Goddess told me you were the one. You will save my people from this usurper who's claimed a kingship that's not his to claim. You will put the rightful king on the throne."

Stepping forward, Ana pressed against him and ran the tip of her tongue along his bottom lip. He opened his mouth to catch her and draw her in. Her long, exquisite kiss awakened a need that had lain dormant. She was dangerous, and that danger made her all the more alluring.

When her hand strayed down his leather breeches, she smiled at the effect she'd created. She thought she had him in the palm of her hand. "We'll speak again when you've fulfilled your part of the bargain. You need not be a mercenary to claim a just reward."

Estrada wondered just how many of the horned god's rules he was about to break. If he killed Bres was he changing history? Or had he been sent to do this task in order for history to unfold as it did? With Bres out of the way, Ruairí could become king and marry Ana. Then they could all go home.

Ana opened the door and walked out. "Let them go," she said to the guards.

"But he's a slave, lady."
"A slave who escaped his owner and has now been returned."

A Ruairí Sandwich

By midday, Sorcha was bored and lonely and aching to give Ruairí a piece of her mind. *Damn him!* After a night of amazing sex, she'd awoken alone, and now he'd been gone four days! Conall had abandoned her before dawn after making her promise not to follow him back to the fort. Well, she hadn't, had she? She was still in the bloody hut.

Rain poured down outside the open doorway and drizzled through the smoke hole. No matter how often she fed the meager fire, it just smoked and sputtered. The wood pile had dwindled to almost nothing. The spiders had feasted on her legs as she slept and around their v-shaped fang marks her red skin was swollen and itchy.

"Feck it," she said, aloud. "Sorry Conall, but I'll never save Ruairí stuck in this hovel."

She didn't care that she didn't have a plan. She just had to go. Somewhere. Anywhere that wasn't this feckin hut.

Grabbing Donella's leather bag, she crawled outside and pulled the hood of the emerald cloak up over her head. Low dense clouds covered the valley, so she could barely see the edges of the dark lake beyond the boulders.

Rowan stood under the trees, a small, soggy, depressed shadow. Ponies, Sorcha surmised, despised rain and loneliness as much as humans. Plus, the poor creature'd had nothing to eat for days but shabby grass. "Come on, then. Let's go back to the bloody fort and see if we can find you some oats. Anything is better than this." If she stayed just off the main road she could find her way and, hopefully, not be seen by Bres's posse.

The pony was much livelier on the homeward journey. No doubt, she'd been dreaming of oats for days. Sorcha bounced along with the cloak wrapped around her legs, her boots splattered by the pony's hooves as it dipped through the mud. She'd finally got the knack of holding both reins in her right hand and pulling them across the pony's neck to steer it; unfortunately, once the creature hit the main road, she stopped responding. Sorcha tried to move her into the trees but Rowan would have none of it. They traversed the forest without incident but when they reached open farmland, Sorcha worried she'd be too easy to spot.

"Come on, you stubborn thing," she cried, kicking its belly and pulling with all her might. Finally, Rowan turned onto the grass when she saw the farmhouse looming in the distance. "Ah, no you don't!" But it was no use. Rowan wanted food and shelter as much as she did. The pony broke into a canter and Sorcha had to squeeze its belly with her legs and hang onto its mane to stay upright.

Then the damn thing stopped short and Sorcha just kept going right over its head. She landed on her hands and knees, then slammed sideways into the water-filled ditch. "Feck! Not again!"

Free from her burden, Rowan dashed into the shelter.

Sorcha crawled out of the ditch and glanced around. She was more embarrassed than hurt and couldn't get any wetter than she already was. No one appeared to have seen the incident. No one, in their right mind, would be out on a day like this.

She found the pony in the shelter nuzzling an empty grain bin. Grasping the reins, Sorcha tugged. "Come on, you feckin mule. We can't get caught here." Rowan held her ground, her velvety muzzle flicking along the bottom of the empty bin. Glancing around, Sorcha spied a bin with a few bits of rotten apple stuck in the corners. She scooped up the best-looking bit of the bunch and held it in front of the pony's face. "Come on, then. You want this? Follow me." That, at least, got Rowan's attention.

She was just luring the pony out of the shelter when she spied a little lad watching her from behind a post.

"Sorry. My pony's hungry."

"You're the faerie," he whispered, his eyes wide and curious.

"Aye, and you know, faeries can either bless ye or hex ye, depending on their mood."

He screwed up his dirty face and backed up a few steps.

"All we want's a bite to eat. Me and Rowan here. And I can pay you." Reaching behind her head, she pulled out two gold pins. "A pin a piece."

"If my da finds me with those, I'll get a hiding."

"Bury them then. In a secret place only you can find. Be sure to mark it. It'll be your very own buried treasure."

His eyes gleamed at that.

Really, she just felt compelled to do something for the poor child.

"Then when you're older, you dig 'em up and give 'em to the girl you fancy. A gold pin will get you a long way with a girl."

"I hate girls." He screwed up his nose as if he'd just landed face-first in a cow flap.

"Of course you do. At any rate, you'll have a bargaining chip down the road worth more than this farm."

The lad stepped out from behind the beam. "One now, and one when you bring us the food." His breeches were ripped and sagged like maybe they'd belonged to his older brother or a host of brothers. His dirty feet bare. His cheeks were sunken and his limbs thin and Sorcha suddenly felt like a shit, like she was taking the food from his mouth. Reaching out a dirty hand, he took the gold pin and fondled it. "It's real," she said. "Have you any grain? My pony's half-starved."

He dashed off then, his fist wrapped around the gold pin. Sorcha waited and hoped she wasn't being set up. She had a gold pin. What had Bres offered for her return?

But a few minutes later, the lad was back, carrying two sacks and a mug of warm milk that had bits of straw floating in it. Sorcha felt the bile rise in her throat and swallowed before she gagged. He set them down on the ground and backed away.

She opened the first sack and discovered a fair amount of dried grain. "Ah, this one's for you, Rowan," she said, emptying it out by the pony's mouth. The other held a flat bread and a chunk of cheese.

"Good lad," she said, handing him the other pin. "If you ever want to catch yourself a fat red trout, there's a lake just up the path a piece. The gillaroo there would feed your whole family." The words were barely out of her mouth when she realized she probably shouldn't have given away Ruairí and Conall's secret hiding place. But the child was such a wretch, she couldn't help herself.

A corner of the lad's lip twitched and he dashed out of the barn into the rain. Faeries were fickle. A gold pin could easily turn into a wriggly worm.

Hunkering down in the straw, she bit into the cheese. Ireland was famous for its dairies. She remembered all the butter that had been discovered preserved in the peat bogs—votive offerings to the gods of the water. The white cheese was tart and creamy and salty all in the same delicious bite. She took turns eating the bread and cheese and wishing she had a good bottle of red wine to wash it down. After dipping her finger in the milk, she took a taste, then decided against it. It might be organic, but it was none too clean.

Sorcha discerned a presence even before the pony's head turned. Muscles suddenly tense, she spied a pitchfork and tried to determine how long it would take to snatch it and stab a man. When she turned, she saw the horses before the men, whose faces were in shadow—a white horse and a black.

She let out the breath she was holding and clamored from the straw pile. "Is it you?"

They nudged their horses further into the barn.

She felt her body sag with a sudden sense of relief.

"The last man who stole from this farmer nearly lost his hide this morning." Ruairí's face was swollen and bruised. His nose broken.

"I didn't steal. I bargained. But you. You've been scrappin'."

Her fingers flew to the fey butterfly tattooed on the back of her neck and she stroked it. Her friend, Yasaman, had designed it for her when she finished grad school. It was her symbol of freedom. Sorcha never wanted to be a professor bound to lecture halls—all she ever wanted were the wild places and the stories. Now she was deep inside Ruairí's story. Sometimes the butterfly brought her joy; other times, inspiration … but always a sense of hope. And she needed all three in this moment for her heart was breaking to see her man so broken.

She took a breath, and when she spoke again her voice cracked. "How did you find me?"

"It was easy enough to follow a pony track across a wet field. You're lucky it was us and not Bres's men."

"You promised to stay by the lake." Conall was angry and now he didn't trust her.

Her hand rose pleading for understanding. "I just couldn't spend another day alone in that hovel."

"You wouldn't have." Ruairí looked strange, like maybe the beating had done more than mar his handsome face.

"Who did this to you?"

"We should go," Conall interjected. "Before the boy brings back his brothers. Faerie gold is no small prize."

"How do you know?" Touching the tresses that had fallen around her face, she realized how. Conall *was* her hairdresser, after all. "Aye. Rowan's finished her grain." Sorcha gathered her belongings and mounted the pony who followed the other horses obediently. "You little shit," she whispered to the pony.

Halfway across the field, she kicked her pony with her heels like she'd seen them do and it trotted up beside Ruairí's horse. That's when she saw his foot—swathed in yards of linen and stained with fresh blood. "Tell me what happened to you."

Conall shook his head to warn her off and Ruairí cast her an evil glance. His eyes were shadowed, bruised, and feverish. He'd taken a hell of a beating. "It's nothing." He made a clucking sound to his horse that urged it on.

"It's something," she yelled after him. "Was it Bres? Did he do this or did he set his mongrel on you?"

Conall rode in close beside her. "This is your doing. If you can't be quiet, I'll bind your mouth." Pulling his dagger from the sheath at his waist, he flashed it in her face, glaring with angry eyes. The man he loved was injured and she was somehow responsible.

Sorcha was stunned into silence. When he'd left in the night Conall was her friend. Suddenly she felt like she was their prisoner.

"He needs peace. Let him be," Conall said, his tone softening.

"Don't be mad at me. I'm short on friends."

She'd come here to save Ruairí and now he'd been hurt because of her. The extent of it, she was afraid to ask. She wanted to race up to Ruairí, hold him, and tell him how sorry she was. But every time she urged her pony closer, he urged his horse farther ahead. There was a gap between them.

Conall rode along behind, his eyes watching the landscape. When they reached the main road, Ruairí turned the black horse east toward the lake and the spider-infested hut.

"Ah, Jesus, don't tell me we're going back there."

The rutted trail was deep in puddles and they were sopping wet when they finally rode into the glade by the lake. A faint blue ribbon puffed from the smoke hole.

Conall leapt down from his white horse and waited for Ruairí to dismount. When he did, it was an awkward fall onto his one good foot. Conall helped him limp into the hut while Sorcha slipped off Rowan and gathered the reins of all three horses. She tied them to the trees where they'd get some cover from the rain, and then went back to the hut.

Ruairí was licking something from an open leaf in Conall's hand. She looked at him curiously but didn't ask. Pushing back her long red hair, she wrung it out and tied it in a knot at the back of her head.

"Come and tend him," Conall said when he saw her, and passed her one of the bull horns full of ale. "I'll fetch some wood." He'd already prodded the fire back to life and added the few remaining branches.

"How will you find dry wood in this deluge?"

As he pushed past her, Conall caught her arm. "He's lame because of you. If you have any magic, now's the time to use it."

"Magic?" she echoed. "How bad is it?"

"He should have stayed with the healer but he had to come to you." Conall shut the door and the sound of his voice and the pounding rain were suddenly mute.

Sorcha got down on her knees and began to unwrap Ruairí's foot. He laid back on the earth and let her, seeming only half-conscious. Was he drunk or drugged? What had Conall given him? Blood leached through the linen bandage. When she finally saw the raw, naked, mutilated foot, she gasped. Ruairí's big toe was gone. The skin black and oozing blood. She put pressure on the wound to stop the bleeding. The sole of his foot was sliced deep with an x, as if the assailant had slashed him twice—an upstroke and a downstroke. This was no accident. The cross was covered in a white sticky substance and crusted with herbs.

Without antibiotics, Ruairí could lose his foot, his leg, his life. Sorcha tried to remember all the plants that were natural antibiotics. Lavender was one, and tea tree, but neither grew here. Someone—she assumed it was the healer—had slathered a herbal plaster over the amputation which had been cauterized with what? A hot iron? Shivers riveted through her body.

Dear Lord! Perhaps some kind of tree bark would help? A hot tincture to soak in? A tea to drink?

The Iroquois in eastern North America gave the European explorers stricken with scurvy a pine tea rich in Vitamin C. She'd seen tall pines in the forest surrounding the lake. It couldn't hurt.

She touched Ruairí's cheek and forehead. He was burning up. Red. Sweating. But that was good, wasn't it? That meant his body was fighting the infection. In his semi-conscious state, he didn't seem to be feeling any pain. Something black scuttled by her, drawn by the scent of blood, and she flinched. "Feck you!"

"Feck," Ruairí whispered, and one corner of his mouth drew up in a cock-eyed grin.

"Ah, good lad. You're still with me."

One of the women at her camp last year had taught her about healing with your hands and that's the only magic Sorcha could think of. Sitting by his feet, she held her palms a few inches above the wounds and closing her eyes, she prayed for him to be healed. Praying wasn't something she did much, other than to shout blasphemies now and again, but if ever there was a time, this was it.

When she felt Ruairí relax, she rummaged around in Donella's bag and pulled out a clean linen shift. Using his knife, she ripped it into pieces and re-bandaged the foot. Then, she lifted his foot and set it on top of the bag, so it was raised.

By the time she'd finished, he was asleep. She laid down beside him, put her hand on his heart, and prayed some more. After meeting Cernunnos, she could no longer assume that humans were at the top of the heap.

Whoever's out there, please hear me. Heal this man. He's a good man and he doesn't deserve such pain and hardship. He also doesn't deserve me messin' in his affairs but I'm here now and it is what it is. Just please keep him safe and help him get well. I'll stay out of it from now on, I promise.

Sorcha heard Conall enter, pile wood in the corner, and leave again. What must he be feeling? The man he loved beaten and maimed? She waited for him to return, but he didn't. Eventually she dozed, and when she awoke it was dark. The fire had burned down to coals and Conall still wasn't in the hut. Ruairí's breaths were loud and even—on the edge of a snore. He was deep in sleep.

She built up the fire, then crawled on her knees to the doorway and stared outside. The rain had lightened. She was thirsty, her throat parched from the smoke, and she had to piss. She grabbed one of the branches from the fire to use as a torch and tramped down to the edge of the lake. Kneeling on a granite slab, she washed her face, cupped water in her hands and drank. She found her way to the edge of the woods and, as she lifted her skirts, saw a flash of flame from the place where she'd tethered the horses.

Conall had rigged up a shelter in the trees from leather ropes and cattle hides. It was just a roof really, like a tarpaulin, but the horses looked dry and content. She found him sitting by a small fire.

When he saw her, he jumped. "Is he—?"

"He's all right. He's sleeping. Feverish, but I think that's a good thing." She sat down and looked into his eyes. They were blotched red from crying. "Tell me what happened."

Conall sighed. "Bres and Fearghas. They locked him in the bull pen and ..." He shivered. "Fearghas brought men and held him down."

"They *tortured* him." Her gut heaved and she swallowed to keep from puking. "Why?" Surely Ruairí wasn't that much of a threat to his throne.

"Bres wants you and Ruairí wouldn't tell him where you were."

Christ! Tortured because of me? What other harm might come to him because I was too feckin stubborn to leave with Cernunnos? That decision was impetuous and selfish and could end up costing the poor man more than a big toe.

Sorcha turned her face to the bushes and puked, then wiped her mouth with the back of her hand. "Sorry Conall, but I don't understand. Why am I such a feckin prize?"

"You're de Danann." Conall raised his eyebrows as if she should've known the answer and it hit her like a fist. She'd been playing along but they *really* thought she was a faerie—one of the old gods with magical power. What would happen when they discovered she wasn't?

"Someone's got to stop Bres," she said.

Conall glanced away and she knew what he was thinking. Ruairí had tried and this was the result. What if she told him the truth? If he believed in faeries, surely time-travel wouldn't be too far-fetched a concept?

"I hope you *are* de Danann for his sake."

"What is it you think I can do?"

"Save him."

Was she suddenly their only hope?

"He loves you, Sorcha."

"He doesn't even know me." An archaeologist from two thousand years in the future who drank and cussed and gave allegiance to no man? Who broke all the rules and did as she pleased? Who was now stranded in a past she didn't understand with a man who seemed willing to die for her? A man she loved.

"Ruairí dreamed of you and when he saw your face he knew you were the woman he'd been waiting for."

"Christ!" *Fated love?* She'd felt the same love for him when she envisioned his face in the museum lab years ago. She was fourteen years old and, in that moment, she knew she'd be an archaeologist. Ruairí was her muse. Her inspiration. Perhaps even, her destiny.

"You should go to him."

"Not without you." She touched Conall's hand. "You love him as much as I do. Maybe even more." Unrequited love felt like a spear through the heart. She'd known it once in uni and sworn never to love like that again. "And he loves you too. I know he does. You have to tell him, Conall."

"No, I ..." His words faded as his face dropped into his hands.

"You have to. Tonight. It'll help him heal. If there's any de Danann magic I can share, that's it. Love is what will heal your man."

"He came here for you."

"Well, he's got me. But he can also have you. And in the morning, we can do each other's hair!" Laughing, she patted his cheek. "Come on. We'll make a Ruairí sandwich. Keep him warm and fend off the feckin spiders."

Conall followed her into the hut. After building up the fire, they crawled alongside Ruairí, one on either side.

"A friend taught me that you can take the energy of love from your own heart and send it down your arms, through your hands, and into the heart of another. Lay your hands on his breast like this."

Conall touched Ruairí's breast, then leaned over and kissed his nipple. "You will always be my king," he whispered.

And Sorcha's heart broke.

The Flaming Circle of our Days

The blacksmith's wife made a bed for Guy in the straw and Estrada laid him in it. Máire brought a long linen shirt and slipped it over Guy's head, pulling it gently over his body to shelter him from the rough straw, and Estrada removed what was left of his reeking rags and tossed them aside. Then, she spread a rough wool blanket over him to fend off the damp. His bare twisted ankle hung out the end. Estrada assumed whatever footwear Guy had been wearing had been confiscated by the farmer. He recalled a pair of expensive suede sneakers that would be an inexplicable prize here and, yes, might just change history.

"Don't you need this?" Estrada asked, touching the blanket. The blacksmith's family weren't rich like the nobles in the fort. There were several children and he wondered how they survived. Manus had a decent position as a craftsman but there were many mouths to feed. He thought of Ana's gold pin in the bottom of his pouch. He'd give them that and more if he could.

"Oh, we've a stack," Mrs. Manus said. "There's a sheep farmer up in the hills who brings his tools for my husband to sharpen. He could do it himself on a whetstone but he likes the clean edge Mac can get. 'Sharpest blades in all of Croghan,' he says. Murph always brings us mutton and bolts of wool for Máire to spin and knit. This is her handiwork."

Estrada squeezed the blanket. The wool was thick and so greasy with lanolin, it could be used for lotion.

"I need to set that ankle," she said. It was swollen and twisted at an odd angle.

Guy was fortunate that was the only bone fractured. The rest of his injuries were sprains, abrasions, and bruises. That ankle, though, would set him back. And them. He wouldn't be walking on it anytime soon.

"I can set it for you," Estrada said, "if you have something to make splints."

Máire produced two stout sticks and a lengthy strip of linen.

"I'll give him a dose of the poppy sap first," the missus said, "to calm him. Works like magic, it does."

She opened a large flat leaf and Estrada examined the dark oily substance. It looked like hash oil. Magic, indeed. He'd always assumed opium came originally from China or the Middle East.

"You don't grow poppies here, do you?" He'd seen wildflowers but nothing resembling poppies.

"No, it's from a Gaulish trader who comes by here every couple of years. The last time he visited, Mac forged him a dagger and he gave me a good supply."

"Opium from France," Dylan said quietly, his eyes wide. "I can hardly believe it."

"If you put it on an open wound it has a quicker effect than taking it by mouth. But both will ease suffering."

Estrada thought he'd like to scoop some onto the head of a pin and smoke it. With everything that was coming up, he could use a few moments of peace.

"I put some in the cuts on Ruairí's foot," the missus continued. "Anything you rub onto the bottom of the foot goes directly into the body."

No wonder Ruairí calmed down so fast. The opium was having the same effect on Guy. His eyelids fluttered and his muscles relaxed. The missus finished stirring up her foul-smelling herbs and began spreading the paste over Guy's bruises and abrasions. Then she slathered it over his foot and ankle. "It's knit bone. Grows in the pasture."

When she'd finished, Estrada felt the bones in the injured foot and ankle.

"Dylan, can you hold him while I do this? It's gonna hurt."

"Aye, sure." Dylan knelt behind Guy's head and held his shoulders.

"Do you have those splints ready, Máire?"

She held up the wood.

"Alright." Estrada moved the bones gently but firmly into position and held on. Guy cried out and bucked forward but Dylan held him down. Máire set the blocks of wood between Guy's skin and Estrada's hand and he held them while she wrapped the linen in a figure-eight pattern under and over the foot, around the back of the ankle and over the top. Once it was done, Guy settled. Máire had a gift. She was knowledgeable and efficient and, Estrada supposed, had tended many breaks and sprains in her young life.

"Prop his foot up on this," the missus said, setting down a short three-legged milking stool. She smiled at Estrada. "Your friend will be up and walking in a few days and he'll be grateful you saved him from the slavery."

"He's not a horse thief." Estrada felt compelled to defend Guy, who'd landed unprepared in a strange world quite by chance. "He just got lost and was trying to survive."

"I'm not judging your friend," she said.

"I don't know how we'll ever repay you for all you've done," Dylan said.

But Estrada knew. Ana had offered him gold. He'd claim it and give it to the blacksmith.

They all jumped when they heard the pounding of horses' hooves outside the shelter. Donella and Aengus suddenly appeared just beyond the open door of the barn.

"We had to leave!" she exclaimed. "Bres's men found Fearghas. He's near dead, but he named me and Conall as his attackers. What are we going to do? My sister's still there."

Aengus held her horse's halter as she slipped down, then leapt down himself. "Your father will protect Winnie. You mustn't worry." He flung his arm around her shoulder but she was too excited to stay still.

Shrugging him off, Donella glanced around the barn. "Where's my brother?" Pausing, she waited for a response.

"Ruairí and Conall left this morning," Dylan said quietly. He'd wanted to go to Sorcha too, but they'd left before he awoke.

"Well, we'll have to find them," Donella said. "There's only one solution. Ruairí must challenge Bres. Take Bres's sword and slay him with it. Then he can claim the kingship."

That's what Ana wanted too, but how could Ruairí fight Bres? Estrada had seen the foot. He couldn't win a fight like that. Not on his own.

"Have they gone to Sorcha?"

"They didn't say," Dylan said, but his face revealed his feelings. He was still lovesick over Sorcha and annoyed that he'd been cut out after traveling through time to rescue her. "Do you know where they might be hiding?"

"Probably in their secret place." Donella shook her head. "They've never told anyone where it is. When they were boys, Bres and Fearghas tried to follow them many times and never found it."

"Then Sorcha will be safe there with them," Estrada said, more to reassure Dylan than himself.

"Yes, but Bres's men are looking for *me* now too," Donella said. "We must raise an army and fight him."

"*You* can raise an army?" Dylan's eyes widened.

Estrada didn't know why his friend was so surprised by this. It was a warrior culture and from what he'd seen of Donella, she was a warrior. Kids grew up fighting, if they were lucky. Some never grew up at all.

"Ruairí can. Everyone loves him."

"That's true," said the blacksmith's wife. "Ruairí's the true king. Mac and the boys will fight Bres for you and Ruairí."

"And me," Máire said. Dylan glanced at her strangely but her mother only smiled proudly.

"Donella and I will go to my tuath and bring back warriors," Aengus said.

"Then, it seems we must find Ruairí and hope he's healed enough to lead us," Dylan said.

Or I go to the fort myself, Estrada thought. *Kill Bres and save all these good people from the possibility of being killed in a battle not of their own making.* It seemed the most logical solution, plus he'd made that promise to the queen. If he could find a way to take out Bres, he could save them all.

"Bres's inauguration follows Beltane," Donella said. "While fires blaze on hilltops across Ériú, we will kindle a fire of our own!"

Estrada had spent days fretting over a decent plan that would allow him to get into the fort and assassinate Bres. And so far, he had *nada*. The blacksmith's boy said all the gates were well guarded. Foolishly, he'd made a spectacle of himself that night with Fearghas and everyone knew his face. Guests were arriving for Bres's inauguration which was to take place the day after Beltane in three days' time.

Donella and Aengus had fled to his tuath to rouse their warriors. Ruairí and Conall hadn't returned from their secret place, and Guy was being tended by Dylan and Máire. Estrada was alone and in his moments of loneliness, pined for the people he'd loved and lost. But nature was his solace and his strength. So, in the gathering dusk, he slipped outside.

The stream sang as it tumbled over the rocks. Overhanging ferns caressed the water, creating secret places for wildlife. A river otter played in the shallows and several deer browsed in the whispering willows. The night throbbed with bird song. He heard the guttural croak of a raven and glanced up nervously. Not long ago, he'd dispatched a flock of venomous ravens who'd threatened his family. And once, in what seemed another lifetime, his spirit had entered the body of a raven and flown over a town called Hope. As he watched the ravens cavorting in the birches, he wondered if he might use that shapeshifting gift again.

It would be impossible for him to walk into the hill-fort undetected but a raven could easily fly through the shadows and right inside. From there he could find his way to Bres. But then what? Drill a hole through the bastard's brain with his beak?

That thought conjured memories of Michael and a lump so thick in his throat he couldn't swallow his own spit. He picked up a stone and hurled it into the water. It sunk and the ripples fled in ever-widening circles. He was thinking too rationally. A raven wasn't the answer.

Sitting beside the stream, he leaned back against a thick yew tree, closed his eyes, and followed his breath. Sitting in nature dissolved the loneliness as he connected with other sentient souls. The tree's energy surged up his spine and a shower of stars erupted within the darkened theatre of his mind. From the sparkling canopy, he conjured a cloud of pink mist and sent it spiraling through a funnel-shaped opening in his crown chakra. From there it descended, opening and cleansing his third eye, his throat, his heart, down his arms and fingers, through his solar plexus, his belly, and his root, and down his legs to the soles of his feet where it streamed back into the earth.

As he settled into his third eye, images appeared. Primrose, her large elfin eyes shifting colors below her shaved and tattooed head. She was no porcelain doll and he'd loved her with his whole heart. Then he saw Lucy, safe and happy in her mother's strong arms. Reaching out, he took her from Sensara and swung her in the air. She screamed, giggled, and his heart ballooned. Lucy was the best of him. Handing her back to Sensara, an image of Michael flashed before him, his straight blond hair touching his pale cheeks, his eyelids closed in death. And then the tears came—a grief more intense than anything he'd ever felt before.

Holding his shoulders, he rocked and swayed and cried until he felt drained. There was no filling this hole in his heart. Michael was gone and wasn't coming back. "I chose you, amigo. I'm sorry I chose you too late."

"I know, compadre. It's always been us. Through moments and lifetimes. So, don't fret. We'll be together again."

Estrada opened his dewy eyes and turned. Hovering beside him in the woods was a shifting ephemeral figure. "Michael? Is that you? Are you really here?" His heart thudded in his chest.

"I'd like to say, *in the flesh*, as you know how I feel about the raw friction of skin on skin." Michael grinned sadly. "But alas, that's not the case."

As Michael moved closer, Estrada reached out his hand but could feel nothing but a cool mist like the touch of a cloud.

He pulled back, his grief exploding in a massive sob.

"Don't despair, compadre. Close your eyes and I'll blend with you."

"Blend?" Lying back against the tree, Estrada wiped his eyes and left them closed. The images that came then were raw and real, flesh and muscle, and he trembled.

"Be still and breathe. We're joining in here," he said, touching Estrada's heart. "Breathe and open to me ... body, mind, and spirit. Let me inside. Feel me. Everything we've ever experienced together, exists now, between us, within us."

"Michael, I love you. I've always loved you."

Michael touched his cheek. "I know. I should've told you long ago how I felt about you. It was only *after*, I realized. I was the one who left it too late. I should never have let you go. To Ireland. To Scotland. Anywhere without me."

"I want to hold you and make love to you," Estrada whispered. "I wake up dreaming of you and then I reach for you and you're not there." Michael leaned over and kissed him and he felt the sensations of that kiss as he'd never felt a kiss before. Surging from his toes, it filled him with desire.

"I'm here," Michael breathed. "As real as you. I'm inside you. Filling you. Can you feel me?"

"Yes." Estrada gasped. His body was on fire and Michael's spirit penetrated every cell, more real than he'd ever been. More potent. More visceral. Hearts throbbing. Breath quickening. The intensity building until they both screamed.

Afterwards, Michael laid in his arms, his lips against his neck. "I've never experienced anything like that," Estrada said.

"Well, now you know you can. I don't have to walk beside you in the flesh. We can skip the lattes and meet in the Otherworld. We'll have the most sordid affair you've ever imagined."

"But I want *this*. I miss *this*." He gestured between them.

"You're not listening, compadre. We can still have this."

Since the blending, Michael seemed more corporeal. Perhaps there was a chance.

"But you mustn't keep grieving for me. It breaks my heart to see you alone like this. Find a partner even for just a night. Better yet, a string of nights. A string of partners." He smirked. "You know I like to watch. I'm not the Empress and I detest monogamy. I want you to express yourself fully and deeply. To live. To love. Will you give me that?"

Estrada bit his lip. "But I haven't felt like …"

"You will. You must. For me and for you." Michael kissed him again and all the old feelings surged. "And for the record, even if I *could* come back, I wouldn't."

"Why not? We could play at Pegasus like we used to. Go for coffee. Get drunk on Chateau Margaux. Get high. Host fabulous parties. Be the men we once were. Don't you miss that?" Estrada realized that he missed that himself. Somewhere along the line he'd changed and life had become much too serious and complicated.

"I killed a man, compadre. An innocent man." Michael turned away so Estrada couldn't see his face. "There's no coming back for me."

Estrada caught Michael's chin with his fingers and turned him back to face him. "You never told me that. We shared everything and you never told me." He shook his head. "When did you …?"

"Before we left that morning on the yacht."

"What?" They'd made love the night before in Michael's flat. When Carvello arrived, Michael had left. Estrada remembered Michael's intensity, his rage at seeing Victor Carvello on his doorstep. Had he really gone out and killed a man?

"*That's* why I didn't tell you."

"You had the virus. Diego bit you. It wasn't your fault."

"It *was* my fault. I made a choice and once the line is crossed, there's no going back." Michael sighed. "Ironically, his name was Christian. I can still see his face. That's *my* personal hell."

Estrada bowed his head. He didn't want to believe that Michael had killed an innocent man and kept it secret.

"Look at me, compadre. You need to understand this *now*—before you walk into that fort and kill a man. It doesn't matter what a bastard he is or how much you hate him or what he's done. It will change you completely and irrevocably and it will never leave you."

Estrada thought of all the men he'd ached to kill and let go free. Of a woman he wanted to strangle. Of Primrose, who'd cleansed him of his demons. Of the vampire and his blood-thirsty ravens. Of the night Alessandra died in his arms and the rage that swallowed him whole. "I know. I killed a guy once. It was a long time ago. I'm a killer too."

Michael shook his head. "No. You're not. Some truths aren't evident until we pass through. It's a kind of quickening. A judgment by the god inside your soul." He shrugged. "Suddenly, you know the truth about everything and everyone." He touched Estrada's heart. "And the biggest truth I know is that *you* are not a killer. Trust me."

But Estrada remembered flashes of that night. The bullet holes in Alessandra's blood-ragged chest. His rage. The running. The garbage truck. The splayed body in the street. It was his doing. And everyone in the rival gang knew it and shouted it to the streets.

"No, compadre. You've got that wrong. Someone else was there in the shadows. Trust me. One day you'll discover the truth. You did not kill that boy and you cannot kill this man. It will destroy you."

Estrada's throat ached. He couldn't think. "Then tell me what to do. If I don't kill Bres there'll be a war. Donella is raising an army. Guy is wounded. And Dylan. If anything happens to Dylan ..."

"You must finish it."

"But how? Donella says Ruairí must slay Bres with his own sword to become king, but Ruairí's injured. How can he fight Bres like that? And Ana ... She wants me to kill Bres for *her*."

"The Crow Queen is using you."

"The Crow Queen?" Tears welled up in Estrada's eyes. "Michael, help me."

"Give the Crow Queen what she wants. Use her as she uses you. The solution lies with her." Leaning over, Michael kissed the tears from his cheeks. "And trust me. This weasel is not *your* kill."

The Proposal

Sorcha awoke feeling inspired. "I need a cauldron," she whispered to Conall. Their arms were crossed over Ruairí's chest. The poor man was still asleep, his eyelids riffling in dream.

"A cauldron?" Conall repeated.

"Aye. Something that'll hold water to boil over the fire. If you want to see my magic, get me a cauldron."

Conall sat up and rubbed his eyes. Reaching into his sack, he pulled out a leather-wrapped cheese and a loaf of bread.

"As good as your cheese is, himself needs something more substantial." She'd awakened with a vision and had it in mind to brew pine needle tea for Ruairi. Towering Scots pines grew in the grove beyond the lake. She'd flood him with it. Mega-doses of vitamin C. "Actually, I need two." There were plenty of waterfowl nesting around the grassy shores of the lake. She'd stew a goose or a duck, whatever she could get her hands on. It shouldn't be too hard. The fearless wildlife here were unaccustomed to human predators.

Ruairí slept through the entire conversation. It must have been the flower sap.

Conall devoured his food, then opened the bull horn and took a swig of ale, while Sorcha tossed another branch on the fire. When he offered what was left of the bread and cheese, she took it, though she'd been dreaming of vegetables. Giant salads.

They left him sleeping in the hut and stepped outside. Clouds hung over the horizon. It was close and gray and cool but, for once, no rain fell from the bleak sky. Conall picked a handful of dry grass and wiped down his horse. "Capall is happier today."

"How can you tell?" The white horse pawed the ground, tail quivering as he swatted the flies that hovered in swarms.

"He has a look in his eye." He winked. "Is there anything else you desire, my fey queen, besides two cauldrons?"

"A new updo and a manicure," Sorcha teased. She was relieved he wasn't angry anymore. When you have two friends in the world and one is injured and the other pissed at you, every moment is a struggle. "I'd love to eat something green. Vegetables? Lettuce? Cabbage?" The blank look on his face revealed he had no idea what she meant. "Onions, garlic, oregano?" Surely, they flavored their meat with herbs. "How about salt?"

"Salt. Yes."

Conall leapt onto Capall's bare back. "I won't be long. I'll try the neighboring farms."

"Won't they be looking for you? Surely Bres has sent his posse out by now."

"Perhaps, but the farmers know us well and would never betray us. Ruairí and I have been coming here all our lives."

"You mean, I was in no real danger back at that farm?"

"I wouldn't say that. That wee lad has a passel of brothers just coming into their prime and if his father caught you …"

"Go on, then." She didn't fancy that thought. "I'll look after himself."

"Ah, I almost forgot. Two strangers came to Croghan. I met them on the road. Men looking for you. They said they were your friends."

Sorcha squinted suspiciously. "I've no friends here."

"They helped us rescue Ruairí. They're good men. I was going to bring them to see you but Estrada's friend got hurt and—"

"Did you say Estrada?"

"Yes. Estrada. The other man is Dylan."

Sorcha clutched her heart and stared skyward. "Oh my God, Cernunnos. You did not forsake me!"

Conall smiled. "So, they *are* your friends."

"Oh aye. Good friends from very far away. And where are they now? You said his friend got hurt? Dylan?"

"No another man. They're staying with friends of ours. Ruairí wanted to see you so we left them there."

"Ah Conall, this might be the best news I've heard. With Estrada and Dylan on our side we've a grand chance of besting Bres and all his feckin kin."

After Conall rode off, Sorcha stripped and dove into the cold lake. She scrubbed her skin and hair and emerged feeling alert and refreshed. A new woman. A woman with hope in her heart. Wrapping up in the emerald cloak, she crawled back into the hut, stoked up the fire and nestled down beside her man.

"Ruairí Mac Nia, you handsome devil, it's time you woke up." She touched his cheek and kissed him gently on the mouth. His skin was still mottled from the beating but the swelling had decreased. He opened his mouth and kissed her back. "You may have an injured foot but the parts that matter are working perfectly."

He opened his amber eyes and grinned. "Sorcha, I've missed you."

"And I you."

When she freed him from his leather breeches and caressed him, low, soft moans escaped his throat. "Don't move," she teased. Then, mounting him, she held down his hands and rode him until he cried out and sank back into her kisses.

"There's something you should know," she said afterwards. "Yesterday, we thought we might lose you, so I'll not play games." Curling up beside him, she traced rings around the soft amber hair on his chest. "I love you, Ruairí Mac Nia. I've loved you since I first saw your face when I was fourteen years old." She looked into his eyes and waited.

He raised his eyebrows. "I would've wed you, had I known."

"No, you wouldn't. I was a chubby, loudmouthed, troublemaker."

"You've changed?" His lip curled up into a lopsided grin.

She ignored it with a kiss. "Listen to me. Conall loves you too. He's afraid to tell you, but he loves you very much."

"I know. Brothers don't need to say such things." Pausing, Ruairí stared at the woodpile. Finally, he made a gruff throat-clearing sound and spoke. "I've offered to share my women with him but he's more interested in his music."

His music? Christ! Do I need to spell it out?

Ruairí shrugged. "He's still a virgin."

No, he's not, Sorcha thought. *Adamair stole that moment.* But that was not her story to tell. Did Ruairí really not understand what she meant? She decided to take a different tack. "Aye. Well, I know some men who lie together and give each other pleasure."

He pursed his lips. Surely, he knew what went on. Men fought together and slept together on the battlefield. If Ruairí hadn't seen it, he'd have heard about it. All that testosterone in close, violent quarters begat sex. There must be those born gay and bisexual in this time just as they were in her time. The gold at the end of the rainbow was the freedom to love and be loved for who you truly were.

"Anyway, if you ever feel so inclined, you should know that Conall's your man."

He furled his brows.

Sorcha shook her head. "Really, I wish you'd just make love to him. I hate to see him suffering."

"Why are you telling me this? Don't you want me for yourself?"

"I want you. I do. But I can share you with Conall." Leaning up on her elbow, she gave him a long soft kiss on the mouth. "Life is short and perilous. If you love someone you must tell them. And you must show them. That's all I'm going to say."

"I somehow doubt that."

She ignored his jibe. "I love you, Ruairí Mac Nia."

He licked his lips and opened his mouth to speak, then closed it again.

"It's fine if you can't say it back. I'm just happy you're so much better this morning. You scared me yesterday with your foot and the beating you took." Relaxing, she laid her head on his breast. "Conall and I slept here with you last night and both of us sending you love had a miraculous effect. Magical even. Love can heal in all kinds of ways."

He caught her chin in his hand and lifted her face. "When I'm king, I'll marry you, Sorcha O'Hallorhan. Conall can sleep in our bed and you can take him as a lover."

"Christ, you're thick. But if that's a proposal, I'll take it, Ruairí Mac Nia. Then *we'll* take Conall as a lover."

Ruairí sat across from Conall in the hut, the fire burning between them. He'd always known of Conall's desire for him. It was something he couldn't reciprocate or talk about with Sorcha. It was easier to feign misunderstanding than explain his relationship with Conall to the woman he loved. Some things were best left unsaid.

When they were very young and discovered their cocks, Ruairí and Conall had explored each other's bodies for a few years with wide eyes and eager hands. Then Ana came along and took Ruairí down a different path. That didn't mean he loved Conall any less. His love had grown in a different way. He protected him and loved him as a brother and that was stronger than any lust he'd ever known.

"Do you remember when we built this hut?" Ruairí asked.

"Yes. We were seven and you were already a head taller than me."

"My cock was longer too … and thicker."

When Conall grinned, his brown eyes flashed. "But mine was always harder."

They both laughed at that.

"It was like holding the branch of a sapling." Ruairí snorted and mimicked by squeezing his wrist. "Do you remember why we built this hut?"

"How could I forget?"

"Has Fearghas ever touched you again like he did that day by the river?" Bres tormented them with clever tricks but Fearghas found other ways to humiliate and torture. That's why Ruairí wasn't surprised when he'd appeared in the bull pen with wooden blocks and leather straps. He was sadistic and had a particular fetish for Conall who was always the gentlest and prettiest of them all.

"Fearghas grew fat and couldn't catch me," Conall said, but his gaze dropped.

"Has anyone else—?"

"What does it matter? We are warriors who live for today."

They never talked of death. What mattered was how a man lived his life.

"Who was it? I'll kill him." Ruairí felt a rush of blood at the thought of Conall being forced by anyone.

"Too late. He's already dead." Conall tossed a branch in the fire and sparks flew up.

"Adamair?" Ruairí had sometimes wondered why Conall had changed when Adamair claimed him as the king's bard. Two winters ago, he'd taken him traveling to Gaul. "Is that why your songs grew so sad?" Conall hardly ever played his flute anymore but when he did his tunes had an air of melancholy.

Conall's eyes glassed over.

"Come here, brother." Ruairí held out his hand. Conall grasped it and moved around the fire to lie beside him. "You should've told me. Adamair was a bastard king who loved no one but himself. I'd have found a way to end him."

"No matter. I did."

"*You* ended Adamair?"

"Who do you think told him about the white bull? It was a legend. No one was safe with that bull."

"Oh, we should've let it live! That white bull was a hero." But Ruairí knew its death was fated. The white bull was a divine creature and had shown Criofan the truth about Bres.

"Yes, the white bull did the work of the gods and just to be sure I gave the king one last kiss with the tip of my sword."

Ruairí cheered and wanted to kiss him for that act but knew better than to start something he couldn't finish. Instead, leaning up on his elbow, he drew Conall in close against his chest and for a long while they laid staring at the fire.

"Tomorrow is Beltane and Bres's inauguration is planned for the following afternoon," Conall said, breaking the spell.

They'd both been thinking the same thing. Bres must be dealt with.

Growling, Ruairí sat up straighter. "I'll kill him before that happens. I dreamed his death and I have a plan."

"Tell me."

"Help me up. First I have to piss out a barrel of this pine tea that Sorcha keeps making me drink. Then I'll explain everything."

Ruairí's breeches lay crumpled on the floor where Sorcha had tossed them. Conall leaned over to get them. "Leave them. I need to wash. I can't stand my own stink." When he touched his right foot to the ground he was unsteady with the pain but could limp along, and the foot could take most of his weight. "Perhaps, Sorcha's magic is working."

Conall smiled. "Yes. You're much better."

Sorcha was sitting on a rock by the lake plucking feathers from a duck.

Ruairí stood at the edge of the glade and pissed, then tugged off his shirt and tossed it aside. It was filthy and stained with blood.

"What are you doing?" she asked staring at his naked body.

"Washing my stinking hide."

"Wait! Let me take off the bandage. I want to see if it's healing."

"Bah," he complained, but sat down on a flat rock and let her unwind the linen strips. Conall knelt beside her, watching intensely. "We've seen much worse in battle. Many limbs lopped off."

"But not yours," Conall said.

"Feckin miraculous," Sorcha said. "The cuts are sealed. Your burn is healing and there's no sign of infection. You'll be walking in a week or two."

"I'll be walking now," Ruairí said, putting his foot to the ground and standing up. "Right into that feckin lake."

Sorcha laughed, as Conall stripped off his clothes. "What are you doing?"

"Going with him. I used to love swimming in this lake."

"That makes one of us," Ruairí quipped.

Conall smiled proudly. "I could swim from this end to the other and back again."

"Well, feck. If you're both going skinny dipping, I'm coming too. This duck is ready for the stew pot." She stretched out her hands, sticky with blood and feathers.

The three of them waded into the cold lake, splashing each other like they were kids.

Ruairí ducked under and Conall scraped the mud and resin from his hair. For today, he'd let it dry long and free. In the water, he felt like a new man. Even without his big toe.

The Crow Queen

Estrada left his horse at the base of the hill with a friend of the blacksmith's and paid the man well to tend it for the night. If he didn't return by midday, it would be taken to Manus.

He'd borrowed one of the blacksmith's heavy iron swords in case he ran into a problem and drawing it from the leather scabbard, he cast a glamor.

The wizard, Merlin, was a man unknown in this historic moment but would one day become a Celtic legend. The night of King Arthur's conception, Merlin had cast a glamor over Uther Pendragon so Igraine saw her husband rather than his enemy. She'd taken Uther to her bed and conceived a legendary king. Who better to impersonate? Anyone who looked at Estrada, would see only what he wished them to see.

This was a new form of magic that had come to him in the night after his time with Michael. He could use his skill as a hypnotist to appear as another man. One who no one had seen before. One who had power and sway.

The sword became a tall straight walking stick and his black cloak faded to a dusky purple to denote nobility. When he touched the wrinkled skin on his face and ran his fingers through his long silver hair, he wished he could take a photograph. This was a glimpse into his future—if he lived that long.

"Don't die, for then you will have changed history."

Cernunnos need not worry. Estrada had no intention of dying.

The sun had just set and they were shutting the gates. Bloody heads hung from the posts. Uninvited guests? Was this new threat

Bres's idea of a welcome to his inauguration? Or were his kin settling old scores?

"Name and tuath?" the surly guard asked abruptly. No doubt, he was craving the ale he'd swill when finally free for the night.

"Merlin. I'm an old friend of Bres's uncle. I hail from Tara." He'd been to Tara once; at least, the grassy hill on which the legendary fort once stood.

The guard narrowed his eyes and snarled.

Tara had been peopled for a few thousand years. It was the residence of the High King, though when exactly Estrada didn't know. Producing the heel of a loaf from the leather bag that hung at his waist, Estrada held it up to the guard's insolent face. "Let me pass." He flipped the heel, which now resembled a fat piece of silver, into the greedy guard's open hand and the man stepped aside.

The population and activity had tripled since that first night he'd arrived with Dylan. Was Bres so popular? Or was it the idea of a celebration that drew crowds from the neighboring communities? Estrada was excited himself to experience the fire festival of Beltane as it was in the beginning, when the whole island was peopled with true believers.

The open acreage east of the dwelling flickered with bonfires and torches. Tents had been erected from poles and the smell of barbecued meat made him salivate. An enormous pile of wood was stacked on the high ground in preparation for the ritual fire.

Máire had said that fires burned atop all the hills. From here, they could see the fire of Uisneach, the very naval of Ireland. One day she vowed to go there for the Beltane celebration. Dylan had looked far too interested and Estrada reminded him that when this was done, and they had Sorcha, they were going home even if he had to knock her unconscious and drag her through that wormhole.

A space beside the ritual fire had been staked out. In its center was an enormous flat stone. The Stone of Destiny? Had the ritual started so far back in time? In the myths, the king stood on the stone at his inauguration and if he was a true king the stone screamed. Surely, when Bres stood on the stone, it would only shriek, "Tyrant!"

If Estrada's plan worked, Bres wouldn't live long enough to step on the stone.

He walked into the largest of the three circular dwellings. It was the main hall where he'd first seen Bres, the night he'd arrived with Dylan and set Fearghas aflame. It, too, was jammed with people. Eating, drinking, talking, flirting, and cavorting.

Fearghas was there. Alive. Sitting with his back wedged against a massive log for support. His stumps were bound in red cow hide that matched his greasy hair, and two women—slaves by the look of them—were feeding him meat and ale. Not that he needed more ale.

Estrada felt a pain in his gut. He knew that what Fearghas did to Ruairí was horribly wrong. If they hadn't arrived when they did, he would have sliced off the man's feet and God knows what else. But he didn't wish this fate on anyone. He was shocked that Conall had slashed through both Fearghas's arms without hesitation. The ox would never harm another man or woman. He couldn't even piss or wipe his own ass.

Still. This was war. The only way to ensure Ruairí would be made king was to assassinate Bres. Donella and Aengus would raise an army to wipe out any remaining supporters and life would go on at Croghan Hill. Estrada could take Sorcha, Dylan, and Guy back home.

Ana sat on Bres's right but her demeanor and the space between them revealed her discomfort. As she scanned the room, he took a chance and lifted his glamor just for her. Ana sat back, surprised, then shifted only her eyes to signal he should follow. Standing, she excused herself, then threaded her way through the room and out a back door. Estrada followed her progress and caught up with her in a lush garden.

Her shiny black hair was done up elaborately, plaited and pinned with indigo crow feathers. She'd painted her eyes and lips and wore a gold torque around her neck engraved with feathers and lightning bolts. Her black cloak was fringed in gold. The Crow Queen, in all her power, wore the perfume of death. The gold bangles on her wrists jangled as she raised her arms and placed her cool hands on his shoulders.

"Why are you here?"

"To do your business, lady." Narrowing his eyes, he placed a hand over hers.

"Come," she said, drawing him deeper into the trees. It was a private garden—the centerpiece, a stone pool with an altar lit by pine torches and vats of burning oil. "You are too bold. If anyone sees you, they will hang your pretty head from the gatepost."

"Not tonight. I wear a glamor. No one can see my true face, but you."

She sat back, impressed by this. "A true and beautiful face it is," she said, running a long sharp fingernail down his cheek. "And honest, I hope. What do you know of Ruairí Mac Nia?"

He paused, considering an appropriate response.

"Fearghas brags of cutting off Ruairí's feet," she continued. "But he cannot produce them. They seem to have walked away." Kneeling beside the pool, she leaned down and ran her fingers through the water.

"Ruairí still has his feet, but I don't know where he walks."

Looking up, she searched his face for lies and found none. "I've heard many old stories of men who slay the king with his own sword and then become kings themselves."

"I've heard that too," Estrada said. It was Donella's plan for Ruairí. And his.

Standing, she approached him and wiped her wet hand on his linen shirt. When she touched his cheek, her fingers were still damp.

"If *you* were to slay Bres with his own sword, I would wed you as the Goddess of Sovereignty and take you to my bed."

Estrada leaned back, shocked by this turn. "You would make *me* King of Croghan?"

"I would. This thought has pecked at my mind since we last met, and now that you're here, I can think of nothing more pleasurable." Reaching up, she grasped his jaw and pulled his face close to hers.

Estrada took a deep breath and swallowed. "But what of Ruairí? Surely he is the true king."

When she pressed against him, he hardened against her belly—a physical reaction he couldn't control. One hand fell and her long nails trailed down his leather breeches.

"Ruairí Mac Nia is blemished and consorts with the Tuatha de Danann. His time has passed."

Was she serious? Had she discarded Ruairí so soon? Estrada had once read the myth of Nuada, a Tuatha de Danann king who'd lost his hand in battle and, by his own rule, was forced to give up the throne. A king must be whole and unblemished. Ironically, Nuada's successor, Bres, was cruel and cowardly and had the de Danann people enslaved. Nuada's brothers crafted him a silver prosthetic hand and then used magic to create a flesh and blood hand so he could retake the throne from Bres.

Perhaps this need for wholeness was what Ana alluded to. Though it was more likely a ploy to spur on her assassin with promises of power.

"She has the solution," Michael had said. He need only play the game.

"If I'm to do as you ask, there are two things I need."

As her thumbnail ran up and down, a corner of her lip turned up, intrigued.

Estrada took a step back to keep his focus. "First, I'll take that gold bangle you offered."

"I thought you were 'no mercenary' and now you ask for gold?"

"It's for a friend."

"Ah, an altruistic mercenary." She slipped one gold circle from her wrist.

When he held out his hand, she drew a circle with her fingertip against his palm. The sensation sent another rush up his thighs. She dropped the bangle in his hand and he closed it. "One now, and two more when the deed is done."

Estrada slipped it into the sack on his belt. "Fair enough."

Laughing, she shook her head. "There is no fair. What is your second request?"

"Where can I find Bres alone and vulnerable?"

Grasping his hips, she pulled him tightly against her and whispered in his ear. "Must I do your job for you?"

Leaning in, his lips brushed the soft flesh of her neck.

"Bres is heavily guarded as he prepares for his inauguration, but he comes here alone to meditate each morning. He leaves his sword by the altar. This is where you can kill him." She ran a sharp fingernail across his chest and set her lips close to his nipple. "If I am to submit to you as king, you must first submit to me. Stay here with me tonight and kill him in the morning."

Estrada considered this command. Glancing around the garden, he marked off the trees, the clearings, the pool, the altar where Bres's sword would stand. It would be easy enough to hide in the trees and assassinate the weasel. He'd never be expecting it.

But Michael had said, the weasel is *not your kill*. There must be some other solution. Something she hadn't yet said.

"How will I escape?" Estrada asked. He could spin a glamor but if she betrayed him, he'd never get out of the fort alive.

"There is a way. Come."

Taking his hand, Ana led him through the trees to a globe-shaped boulder that rested on a large square slab. A raucous murder of crows flew in and then settled silently in the dark trees.

"Tomorrow night, when we celebrate Beltane, I would rather lie with you by the fire than Bres." Leaning forward, she caught his chin in her hand and kissed him. She tasted of French wine. Michael's favorite was Chateau Margaux and Estrada knew the taste well.

"We were talking escape," he said.

"After." Ana's fingers circled the back of his neck as she drew him in, then slid down his back and caught his hips. Her fingernails scratched like small barbs in his skin. Leaning back against the stone, she raised her skirt.

Estrada braced his thighs against the hard surface and gave her what she wanted. When he caught her in his arms, she arched, flinging back her head, crying out, the crow feathers dangling from her hair.

"You're pretty and shiny," she said, when she straightened up. "I think I will keep you."

Another bangle for your wrist? "When Bres is dead and I've left the fort unharmed, we can meet again." Taking her hand, he kissed it. "Now. Escape?"

"Ah yes. Fearghas showed me this once when we were young. He thought I'd be impressed. I suppose I was, though not enough to—"

"Do you want Bres dead or not?" Estrada had grown impatient with her game.

Ana huffed. "Beneath this stone is a tunnel that leads out into the valley."

"A tunnel?" *If a man could exit unseen from this place, he could also enter. Here was the solution he sought.*

"Yes. I haven't seen it, but I trust it's there. Fearghas knows better than to lie to me."

"Well, let's look," Estrada said, stooping to push off the stone that capped the thin slab.

"After," she said, sitting back on the rock. "Take off your shirt. I want to see those black wings again. They remind me of my companions."

Reunion

Sometime later, Ana left Estrada in the garden assured that her lover-assassin would take the bait. If Michael was there watching along with the crows, he'd certainly got an eyeful. What man wouldn't want to be king and wed the stunning Goddess of Sovereignty? Merlin had fallen for a witch-queen—a liaison that didn't bode well for him—but Estrada knew better. He wasn't egotistical enough to believe she'd keep him around after he performed his deadly task and had no intention of meeting his demise at the hands of the Crow Queen. He'd found the solution and that was all he needed to set things straight.

In the quiet of the garden, he rolled the rock from the slab. It weighed almost as much as he did. He was winded in the end and cursed as he caught his breath. Then, shoving the square slab aside, he stared into the black hole. Though it was too dark to see anything, he could hear the musty murmur of the Earth's heart beating below.

Grasping one of the pine torches from the altar, he laid on his belly and swung it down into the cavern. The hole itself was giant-sized, created by Fearghas to allow him passage. A solid ledge jutted from the wall about three feet below. The ledge led to the side of a magnificent cavern. Water dripped from the sacred pool into a dark hole hundreds of feet below. How deep it was, he couldn't imagine. This must be the core of a dormant volcano. To move from base to top, a man would have to climb up the side.

Ruairí would need both his foot and his courage to scale this wall. And they'd need rope. Plenty of long strong rope.

As Estrada shoved the slab back in place and rolled the rock on top, he smiled to himself. Ana would be surprised to find Bres alive after his morning meditation and even more surprised to discover him dead the next day. Slain by Ruairí Mac Nia. The man whose time had passed, according to her.

After donning his glamor, Estrada slipped out the side gate. The night was lit only by a muted moon and a fine rain fell as dawn broke over the far eastern mountains. He found his horse tethered to a long line in the shelter and rode slowly and carefully back along the rutted trail.

When he arrived at the blacksmith's home, Dylan was up and pacing. Livid. He must have heard the splashing of the horse's hooves in the wet ruts because he met Estrada in the glade just outside the dwelling. "You didn't even tell me! How could you just go off like that and not even tell me? I thought you'd been captured by Bres's men. We still haven't found Sorcha and—"

"I'm sorry, man, but I knew you'd try to stop me." Estrada slipped off the horse's back and set it free in a thorn-hedged paddock.

"Aye, you're right about that."

"I needed to understand Ana's game." Estrada stretched and yawned, exhausted from a night of sex and scheming.

"And do you?"

"She offered to make me king if I assassinate Bres."

"Assassinate?" Dylan's jaw dropped. "What? Wait. King?" He took a step back. "You slept with her."

It was an accusation Estrada felt uneasy with himself. "I needed information." Though Dylan never judged him, he always felt immoral in his friend's eyes. Clearing his throat, he looked away.

"So? Was it worth it?" Dylan asked.

What? The risk? The sex? Playing The Crow Queen's game? "Yes," Estrada said. "I found a solution to our Bres problem."

Dylan stood up straighter and cocked his head.

"There are guards posted at the gates checking everyone coming in because of the Beltane celebration and Bres's inauguration. Unless Donella arrives with an army and they storm the gates, Ruairí will never get through. They'll kill him and Conall on sight.

But there's a secret entrance and a garden where Bres goes alone every day at noon."

"Aye?"

"If I can get Ruairí in there unseen and he slays Bres with his own sword—"

"He can claim the kingship." Dylan sat down on the edge of a giant oak that had cracked and fallen in a windstorm.

The frayed trunk thrust up slivers that reminded Estrada of Ana's crow feathers. She was beautiful, but deadly. His flesh was raw and marked by her talons.

"I wish they hadn't left," Dylan said. "If Ruairí and Conall were still here we could—"

"Let's go find them." It was all Estrada could think about on his ride back to the blacksmith's farm. "We don't have much time. Bres becomes king tomorrow night unless we can stop him."

Dylan cocked his head and squinted. "But we have no idea where they are? How can we possibly—?"

"Listen. The day Conall ran into me on the road he was racing to see Sorcha. If we take *that* road and follow our intuition ..."

"Ach, I don't know. I don't fancy getting lost out there in the woods searching for a secret hideout."

"Then, we take someone with us who knows the land. Someone who can track. Come on, Dylan. This is our best shot. A way to avoid war and save lives."

The household had begun to stir with the dawn. Smoke streamed from the hole and the smell of porridge wafted through the air. The older boys stumbled out the door and down toward the stream to fetch water. Their younger sisters smiled shyly and giggled as they passed on their way to milk the cows and feed the livestock.

Estrada gestured to Dylan and they walked toward the dwelling.

Then Máire appeared, looking distraught. "Your man's taken a turn. He's a fever and pains in his belly."

Did Guy have internal injuries Estrada had missed when he'd bathed him in the river and checked him over? "I'll go to him."

"My ma's with him now. Best keep your distance. We've seen this before. It's not from the hiding." Máire's lips flattened. "It's his gut."

Estrada and Dylan exchanged looks. Appendix? Virus? Illness wasn't something they'd anticipated. "What can we do?"

"Nothing. My ma will tend him. Some survive. Some don't. After his hiding, he's weak." Her face matched the grimness of her prognosis.

Fuck. It was more than an illness. It was something that could kill him.

"Máire, we need to find Ruairí. Do you think one of your brothers could come with us? We need someone who knows the land and can track," Dylan said.

"I'll come," she said, standing straight with her hands on her hips. "Ma can look after your friend."

Estrada knew Celtic women were strong. He hadn't met one who wasn't. But he feared for her. "We need someone who—"

"Máire's the best rider of the lot," Manus said. A big man, but remarkably agile, the blacksmith had slipped into the glade unnoticed. "She can track a deer through the pasture where a herd of cows have strayed. She knows the land. How it lays. All the herbs and their uses. And she's known Ruairí and Conall all her life. You could do no better than to have my Máire as your guide."

Dylan grinned shyly and the tips of his ears turned scarlet. Estrada had seen this before and feared he'd be heartbroken when they had to leave the girl behind in another millennium.

"Her mother can do without her for a day or two."

"Thank you, Da." Máire hugged the strong man who turned to mush in his daughter's arms. "I'll get my stuff and pack some food." And off she went before they had a chance to object.

Estrada was torn. He felt obliged to stay near Guy, especially knowing his illness could be fatal. But he had to find Ruairí and tell him what he'd discovered about the secret garden. And then there was Sorcha, who was the reason they'd come in the first place. His gut told him she was safe, but he wanted to see her with his own eyes.

The trio set out an hour later, bellies full of porridge and tea, with Máire in the lead. A light rain continued to fall. At times, it was like riding through a cloud. As they crossed the stream, Máire commented on how high the water had risen from the continual rains. And it suddenly struck Estrada that Guy had been so dehydrated when he found him in the slavery, he'd drunk water from the bog pools—water where people washed their dirty clothing and their dirty bodies. *Christ!* He'd washed the shit from Guy in that water. And they all drank it.

Slaves carried it up the hill to the kitchens inside the fort and the people of the village dipped their buckets in it every day. He remembered the image of the Ganges that he'd had when he first saw the people in the pools. Plagues and disease ran rampant where people didn't have access to clean drinking water and antibiotics.

"Dylan, is there a disease people get from drinking contaminated water? Máire said, they'd seen it before."

"Aye. Typhoid. It's a bacterium that attacks the stomach and intestines." Dylan sat back on his horse. "Hang on. Do you think that Guy has typhoid?"

Estrada raised his eyebrows. "What's the recovery rate?"

"Without antibiotics?" Dylan shook his head.

"We need to find Sorcha and get Guy out of here. Now."

They'd been riding half the morning when Máire veered out of the pasture and headed toward a vibrant forest. Estrada rode at the rear of their single line but could hear Dylan's voice as they passed beneath the quiet trees.

"Where are we going?" Dylan asked, trotting up beside her on his horse. He hadn't taken his eyes off the back of her head for the last hour.

"Did you not see that flock of geese that passed east of us?"

"Aye, a flock of geese. So what?"

"Geese fly to water," she said, tossing her long dark hair back over her shoulder.

Dylan opened his mouth to speak and then thought better of it. Estrada chuckled to himself. Ever the practical man, Dylan analyzed every situation based on the facts.

"Aye?" he said at last.

"There's a string of lakes and ponds back here that mark the edge of our territory. No one from Croghan strays beyond our borders. If Ruairí and Conall have a secret place, it'll be out this way and they'll have built it by water."

"That's a good point," Estrada said, his mind spinning in a different direction. Water, to him, conjured Buntzen Lake and Hollystone Coven and their rituals. What if he never returned? If he died here in Iron Age Ireland, what would Sensara tell Lucy? He hadn't even told her he was going. He'll have simply disappeared just like his father.

"But how will we find it?" Dylan furrowed his brows. "There's no trail."

Glancing back over his shoulder, Estrada saw the horses' hoof marks in the bent grass. They were definitely leaving a trail.

"The horses are thirsty. They'll find water." Máire chittered to her horse. "Mind the branches," she said, as they passed through a hole in the brush and entered a woodland dense with oak, ash, and rowan. "As children, we were warned never to pass beyond this tree line. None of us ever did, but I always longed to come this way and explore."

Another portal into a magical land of Druid trees. The canopy overhead riffled in the misty breeze and Estrada felt a rush up his arms. "Are you frightened, Máire?"

She giggled. "Not among the fey."

A small bright blue bird flitted from the holly bushes that rambled between the tall trunks and Estrada suddenly thought of Magus Dubh. His blue-tattooed friend would love this place. Vibrant with bird song, scolding red squirrels, and buzzing insects, this was an ecosystem in the raw.

A part of him wanted to stay in this pristine land where he'd conjured Michael's ghost. California had given him no peace and no hope, but here ... Michael was somehow more *real* here. And surely, if he'd conjured him once, he could do it again. As they passed through the forest, his mind rolled in memories until the acrid scent of woodsmoke drew him back.

They'd come to an opening in the woods, a lake edge, where the wind blew ripples across the water. Máire's gray geese floated along its grassy edges, dipping their orange beaks in the clear water. On the far shore was a granite-strewn beach. And beyond it, a trickle of smoke spiraled skyward.

Their horses picked their way to the lake edge and drank, long necks drooping, soft mouths slurping. Iridescent dragonflies whizzed by and skimmed the surface of the ripples.

With her horse's thirst sated, Máire turned her mount, and they threaded single file through the thorny brambles. It took another hour to negotiate the thick brush in the lower reaches by the water and the bloody midges were biting. At times, they stumbled through only to be blocked by a boulder or thorns so dense there was nothing to do but turn tightly and backtrack or back the horse out. Estrada learned quickly that if he pulled back on the reins and asked nicely, his horse would back up. He pulled his hood up to deter the swarms of biting flies that ravaged his skin. Humans were nothing but giant blood bags to them.

Máire suddenly pulled back on her reins and the horse stopped.

"What's wrong?" The head of Dylan's horse was close enough to nuzzle the flank of her mount.

"We best not surprise them."

"Are you sure it's them?" Estrada asked.

"As I said, it's beyond our tribal borders and far from the other tuath. If I were them, this is where I'd build my secret place." Her eyes were wide with anticipation.

Estrada felt another rush himself. Of course, Ruairí and Conall would be armed. Both warriors wore scabbards slung over their backs so they could draw their iron swords and bring them crashing down across their enemy's shoulders. The knives that dangled from their belts were sharp enough to shave a head or a beard, though most preferred to grow their facial hair. Ruairí shaved the sides of his head to accentuate his mohawk and glued his long top hair straight up with mud and resin. On the battlefield, Ruairí Mac Nia would be terrifying and Estrada hoped never to have to face him in combat. He was the most intimidating man Estrada had seen since they'd arrived here. No wonder Sorcha was smitten.

Sticking two fingers in her mouth, Máire whistled like a hawk. Once. Twice. Three times.

The answering call was close by in the trees and followed by the appearance of a grinning Conall. "Máire Manus! As sweet as a new spring day. I recognized your call. How did you find us? Ah, you're a legend, girl. Of course, *you* could find your way through this."

Máire beamed and giggled, and Estrada felt a ripple of jealousy from Dylan whose ear tips reddened.

Conall nodded to Estrada and Dylan. "Lads. I expect you've brought news."

"Aye," Dylan said. "Some good. Some not so good."

Ruairí appeared as they entered the glade. Leaning on a walking stick, he ambled toward them. His long hair fell free and blew in the lake breeze and Estrada felt he radiated contentment despite the situation. Though his chiseled face could still spawn terror, his bruises had faded and his demeanor softened.

Then Sorcha walked out of the lake naked, her flesh as pink as the humungous fish she carried and Estrada understood what had befallen Ruairí. The bog man was in love.

Slipping off his horse, Estrada raced across the glade.

Sorcha dropped the fish on the rocks and threw herself at him. "Jesus, Mary, and Joseph! I can't believe it!"

She clung to him like a package from home. Goosebumps broke out on her skin and Estrada took off his cloak, wrapped it around her bare shoulders and covered her. Her dark red hair was dripping, her green eyes flashing tears of glee.

Then she saw Dylan and her grin riffled. "Dylan McBride. Of course, you two came together." She shook her head. "Ah jeez. Was it Cernunnos?"

Dylan slipped off his horse, then walked over and hugged Sorcha. "Aye," he whispered.

Ruairí stepped between them and jammed his walking stick in the earth. "Why have you come here?"

Dylan's face blanched and the hair on the back of Estrada's neck stood straight up.

A Grieving Man Breathes Water

Sorcha patted Ruairí's cheek. "Relax, big fella. Estrada and Dylan are two of my dearest friends. I trust them with my life. We slew a Viking together."

His eyebrows furled.

"You haven't met the Vikings yet, but once you do you'll never forget them." Sorcha huddled closer to Ruairí, who cocked his head curiously. She could see the tinge of fury in the flush at his cheekbones and took comfort in it. Ruairí loved her and she loved him. She hadn't meant for it to happen but now that it had, she was on fire. Seeing him get jealous just drove up the heat.

"Who's this now?" she asked, gesturing to the lass who sat proudly on her horse.

"*This* is Máire Manus." Conall beamed. "We've known Máire since she was born."

The girl was a pretty thing and couldn't have been more than fourteen—although that was marriageable age in a culture where the average woman died in her early thirties if she lived through childbirth, war, and plagues. Sorcha's Irish grandmothers were strong and feisty—warriors like herself—and she much admired that.

Máire tethered their horses in the trees and then hovered close to Dylan. Sorcha was relieved to see the lad blush. He was smitten with this girl and their tryst from last summer could remain in the past. For her, it was just a fling coddled by her feelings of guilt for landing the poor lad in jail, though she suspected it meant more to him. Still, Dylan was no threat to Ruairí.

Having a love of his own would do the lad good, especially if they were marooned here forever. But perhaps they weren't. The mention of Cernunnos had buoyed her spirits. If he'd brought the lads here to find her, he hadn't abandoned her completely and must be planning to bring them home.

It was Estrada who had Ruairí's hackles up. He could feel her attraction to the sexy magician she'd never managed to entice into her bed. It wasn't for lack of trying. Estrada was loyal to his friends and would lay down his life for them. He was a man she very much admired and could depend on, and she was relieved to see him in this dangerous, chaotic world.

The gillaroo flopped on the rocks, trying to find its way back to the lake, and startled them all.

"You're in luck. We've trout for supper. This lake's teeming with them. I've never seen anything like it. You can scoop them out with your hands."

There was an awkward silence and then Estrada stared directly at Ruairí. "We need to talk, man. There's a shit storm brewing at Croghan."

Ruairí nodded once and produced the bull horn from where it hung off his belt. He offered it to Estrada.

Sorcha breathed a sigh of relief. Men. There was nothing that couldn't be fixed with ale or a fist. Though sometimes it took both.

Estrada hoisted the horn, guzzled some ale, and passed it back.

As the hut was simply too small to house them all, they hunkered down among the rocks. A thin sun shone through the low stratus clouds.

Convinced that no blood would be spilled, Sorcha knocked the trout's head against a granite slab and went into the hut to dress. She could hear the low rumble of men's voices and hurried to get back to the conversation.

"And what of Fearghas?" Conall asked, as she emerged from the hut.

"He's alive," Estrada said.

"For now." Conall's frown spoke reams.

Sorcha squatted next to Ruairí and placed her hand on his shoulder. "So, what's the craic, lads?"

"I know when Bres will be alone and vulnerable."

"I know that much myself." Ruairí huffed.

Estrada turned to him. "*And* I know how to get you into the fort unseen."

Ruairí's eyes widened.

"Well, spit it out, man. We've been waiting a feck of a long time for this."

Estrada raked his fingers through his beard. "Both gates are guarded at all times but there's a third entrance. A tunnel."

Ruairí snorted. "How is it that a stranger knows this when we, who've lived our lives in the fort, do not?"

"Ana told me." Estrada made a clicking noise with his mouth as if the whole story could be garnered from that one sound.

"Ana?" Ruairí's laugh made Sorcha's skin crawl. "How the feck does *she* know about a secret tunnel? Does she bring her lovers in that way?"

Estrada smiled. "Fearghas told her years ago when he built it."

"Have you seen it with your own eyes? Is it real?" Sorcha couldn't believe no one knew about this.

Estrada tilted his head and smiled. "I lifted the capstone and looked beneath the hill into the volcano. Apparently, there's a passage below that leads out. I didn't see it," he confessed. "With all this rain it's likely underwater, but the plan still can work."

She nodded, then turned to the lads. "Where were you while Fearghas was building a secret tunnel? How could you miss that?"

Ruairí scoffed at Sorcha's question, but Conall explained. "Ruairí and I went to Priteni for training. We lived across the sea for years."

Like going to uni. Druid training was said to be intense. She wondered what Ruairí had learned in Britain and if it had changed his life. "Was it difficult?"

Ruairí's lips flattened. "We do not talk of it."

"It was a relief," Conall said. "Fearghas and Bres stayed here to apprentice with their uncles."

There's more to this story, Sorcha thought, judging by the somber look on Ruairí's face.

"When we returned, Fearghas had built the garden."

Ruairí sneered. "And told Ana about a secret tunnel." Leaning back against a rock, he folded his arms across his chest. "And Ana told *you*. A stranger."

"Yes."

"She took you to her bed." Ruairí grunted.

"Actually, she took me to a stone," Estrada said, flippantly.

"What the feck does it matter *who* Ana took to bed or told about the tunnel?" Sorcha flung her hands in the air. Ruairí was acting like a jealous boyfriend who'd caught his girlfriend with another man. A sudden rush of heat hit her cheeks and she felt like she'd been slapped.

Ignoring her, Ruairí stood suddenly, his muscles tensing.

Like an echo, Estrada stood and faced him. "It's a very important stone."

Christ! Were they going to fight? Jumping up, Sorcha stood clutching her churning stomach.

"It marks the tunnel. It's a flat slab with a round boulder on top of it."

"It's in the garden." Conall's eyes lit up. "We know it."

"Ana paid me to assassinate Bres," Estrada confessed.

"And offered to make you king." Conall had obviously heard this play before.

"Indeed." Estrada nodded. "I know it's a game and I'm not interested in being king." He hadn't taken his eyes off Ruairí. "That's *your* destiny and I support you fully."

Sorcha hovered on a spark of hope. If Ruairí became king, he was a step closer to his grisly fate, but Cernunnos had sent Estrada and Dylan and their presence surely changed history as much as her own. That meant the god was willing to help them and together they had a chance to save Ruairí from his fate. They could exterminate the enemies that might depose his rule. Possibilities glimmered now where before there was only fear. If they succeeded, she would stay here with him and rule as his queen. And if they failed, she would fight to take him back through time with her into the future where they could raise their child together.

"You're a smart man," Ruairí said, slapping Estrada on the back. "Now tell me about this tunnel."

As dusk fell, Ruairí and Sorcha wandered into the forest to build their own Beltane fire. Estrada had never seen her react with such emotion and wondered how he'd ever get her away from this place. "*Don't form bonds,*" Cernunnos had said. "*That's what happened to Sorcha.*" The horned god was right about that.

Dylan had also formed a bond. He could hear Máire's laughter and Dylan's answering "Aye, it's true!" from where he sat cross-legged on a granite slab by the lake.

Conall was swimming, his strong arms cutting through the waves like an Olympian. He'd touched the far shore and was on his way back.

The clouds parted and Estrada became entranced by a veiled moonlight trail on the rippling water. This was a between place: between night and day, between earth and water, between spring and summer, between this world and the Other. Between time itself. And they were caught in it.

Conall swam as far as the shallows, then stood and walked toward him, water streaming down his naked body.

The cool night breeze raised goosebumps on Estrada's arms and he rubbed them. "We're running out of wood," he said, dropping the last branch into the fire they'd built between the rocks.

"I've missed this place," Conall said, climbing into his breeches and linen shirt. "Come on."

He led Estrada to a small glade where he'd strung several hides to shelter the horses from the worst of the rain. He lifted another hide to reveal a humungous pile of dry wood. "I used to come here often before we went to Priteni. It was my refuge. While I collected dead wood, I prayed. Seed. Shoot. Sapling. The mature tree flowers and rains its seeds down upon the earth and life turns again. Sometimes a branch will catch in the wind, crack and fall, then wait years in the silence for some lowly druid to pick it up and say a prayer." He smiled.

Chop wood. Carry water. How Zen. "Why did you stop coming here?"

"The lowly druid became an exalted druid. Chosen by the king as his bard." He picked up one of the dried, crooked branches. "Now I'm like this."

"You're not old," Estrada said, ruffling Conall's hair. He was stunning. In his prime. It wasn't age that had bent the boy. He was talking something beyond the physical.

Conall sighed. "In time, I'll be reborn through fire and fly like a spark into the Otherworld."

Estrada said nothing. He knew what it felt like to be a dry, crooked branch waiting to be reborn.

They each gathered an armful of wood and ambled back to the rocks. While Estrada stoked the fire, Conall took out his pan pipes and played a melancholy tune. The notes growled and then skittered up an octave, landing in minor drops and hanging. The music conjured thoughts of Michael. *You can come to the Otherworld,* he'd said. But it wasn't enough. He wanted more.

"That song conjures sorrow," Estrada said, when it ended.

"Without sorrow, we wouldn't know joy," Conall put down his pipes and leaned back on his elbow. "I see, you're a man who's known both."

"My partner died not long ago." Estrada rubbed his eyes with the back of his hand. "I miss him."

Conall glanced up, perhaps surprised by this confession.

"I have regrets. I keep thinking if I'd made different choices, Michael would still be alive."

"Choices are as eternal as the soul. You can always make another."

"I can't bring Michael back." Estrada tossed another stick into the fire and it hit the rocks with a crack.

"If you'd made a different choice, you wouldn't be here now saving the people of Croghan from a monster."

"Sometimes, it seems like I've saved everyone but the people I loved most." He thought of Allesandra, who'd taught him to love. Of Primrose, who'd exorcized his demons. Of Michael, who'd sacrificed himself to save him from eternal torment. "Too many people are dead because of me."

"They love you still and haven't left," Conall said quietly. "Their souls dance around you like fireflies."

"You can see them?"

Conall nodded. "I'm surprised you can't. You have the ability. Do you not hear their voices?"

But Estrada wanted more than sparks and voices and spirits. Yes, the soul was eternal but so was grief and he was a flesh and blood man. He bunched up his cloak and laid down on the flat rock. The sky was a maze of stars, a thousand universes and he, a flicker.

Conall picked up his pipes and another tune emerged from his fingers and his breath.

"I don't fear death," Estrada said, when it ended. "I just hate this loneliness."

"You'll live a long life this time," Conall said prophetically, "and lose others you love. It's the way of it. But you can cross into the Otherworld, especially on nights like this when the veils are lowered. Then you won't feel such anguish."

"Michael told me much the same thing. But I can't spend all my time in the Otherworld. I'm a man."

"A grieving man breathes water and floats beneath the surface of the sea." He touched Estrada's shoulder. "It will pass."

"Will it?"

Conall stretched and glanced around the glade. "When this is over, I'll live here again. There's room for another hut."

Estrada eyed him curiously.

"There's no reason for loneliness when the wind showers us with deadfalls."

Into the Abyss

They weren't even married and already Ruairí was barking orders at Sorcha. "You will wait here with Manus until I come for you."

They'd arrived at the blacksmith's farm just as dawn broke over the horizon. Dylan wanted Máire to stay there where it was safe and Máire refused to stay without him, so both of them were staying behind. Now Ruairí wanted Sorcha to stay behind as well. There was no point arguing. Ruairí Mac Nia was as stubborn as she was. It was easier to kiss him goodbye and follow on her wee brown pony at a safe distance. If he was going to do this, she was going to do it with him.

Rowan trotted along, glad to be moving again after so many days of foraging under the trees. Conall's white horse was easy enough to spot in the gray light of dawn. In the distance, Sorcha could see a trail of smoke and ash rising from the Beltane fire at Croghan and farther west, high on a hill, the fire at Uisneach still glowed like a matchstick in a darkened room. Uisneach was the center of Ireland and the Beltane fire festival was the highlight of the year. It was still celebrated in her own time. All the major ritual centers would have celebrated this night including Emain Macha in Ulster and Cruachan in the west.

The realization startled her, riffled the ends of her red hair, and sent goose bumps careening down her arms.

I'm riding a pony through Iron Age Ireland on Beltane. I'm going to kill a king! I could die here. Or become a queen and reign beside the man I love. Or take him back to modern Ireland and show him my world!

As they closed in on the village, more and more hide tents appeared, strung across tree branches or propped up using five poles. Basic architecture—two crossing at each end and a fifth laid horizontally through the center. Dark lumps appeared on the ground—celebrants who'd drunk too much mead or ale, or lovers still entwined. Beltane was the ancient fertility festival and this celebration one of orgasmic delights.

After *they'd* made love, Ruairí had told her that many couples met and made babies this night. Some were strangers who found each other around the fire, then ran for the forest and the fields. Weddings often followed at Midsummer when the woman knew she carried a child.

Reaching down, Sorcha rubbed her belly below her navel. She was sure she carried his baby now. Her breasts were tender and tingled to his touch. She felt the presence of a new spirit and sometimes heard her name shouted. *Ma.* She was no longer alone in her body. The thought made her teary. Rubbing her eyes, she pushed down the emotion. She'd need her wits to fight these bastards. She was fighting for her family now.

She caught up to the lads in a wooded patch northeast of the hill. The ponds had risen several feet and the three men were arguing about the possible location of the entrance.

"Oh, for feck's sake. If the cavern opening is underwater there's only one way to find it."

Ruairí stared at her with fire in his eyes. "Sorcha, I told you to—"

"*I'll* find it." Dropping the reins, she leapt off Rowan and raced toward the water. The beat of horses' hooves thundered behind her, but before Ruairí could catch her, she was splashing through the shallows. When the cold water hit her breasts, she dove.

Opening her eyes, she swam toward the side of the hill. The rainwater was fresh and clear enough to make out shapes. She popped her head up once to see the three men, sitting on their horses by the edge of the pond. She waved to signal she was safe, then dove again. Following the slope of the hill, she searched for cracks and hollows. Openings.

She felt it before she saw it—a kind of current like a waning tide pulling her sideways. She let it carry her along, popped up for a few breaths, then held the last one and sunk again. Along the side of the rock, she felt dents and ridges and then a gap.

Formed of irregularly shaped rock, it wasn't much bigger than she was. She caught the edges with her hands, pushed in with her head and shoulders, and kicked out with her legs. As soon as she wriggled through, she kicked up. It was a long haul and her lungs were burning when she finally burst through. Gasping, she opened her eyes to darkness. Pitch. She waved a hand in front of her face but saw nothing. Not even a shadow. They'd need torches to scale these walls. But the space itself felt large and open and cold as a cathedral. Or a tomb. She listened and heard nothing but the steady drip of water on water.

Turning, she swam back in the direction from which she'd come, then couldn't find the wall and quelled a rush of panic.

Something touched her leg and she screamed, then a hand grabbed her foot and she fought to kick it off. A splash beside her and then, "Sorcha. It's me."

"Conall?"

"Come on." Grasping her hand, he pulled her back to the wall and down through the hole. When they finally emerged on the other side, she was never so happy to see the light of day.

"It's dead feckin dark in there," she said, when they'd crawled out of the pond. "Wouldn't it be easier to just come in through the gate? The guards must be drunk and passed out by now."

Ruairí's anxious face relaxed as he drew her close. "Sorcha, this place ... I saw it once in a vision. It's sacred. Ancient. The belly of the mother."

Estrada stepped up. "Listen, we can do this. I'll go through the side gate, open the passage from above, and come down with torches and ropes." He mounted his horse and rode a few steps, then turned back. "Oh yeah. Don't drink the water. We think that's how Guy got sick."

"What? You couldn't have told me that before?" Sorcha rubbed her mouth but knew it wouldn't matter if she drank it. She'd opened her eyes—a portal for infectious diseases.

"Actually. No. I didn't get the chance." His lips flattened. "Dylan thinks it might be typhoid fever."

"Typhoid! Are you kidding me, man?" Typhoid fever killed one-third of the population of Athens in 430BCE. The plague turned the war with Sparta.

With travelers arriving in Ireland from the continent and the continuous rain and flooding ponds ... *Feck!* Dylan was never wrong.

"Just be careful," Estrada said, and galloped off.

Sorcha didn't much like the idea of Ruairí wading into a typhoid-infested pond with wounds that had barely closed but they didn't have much choice. The plan to sneak into the hill-fort and surprise Bres in the sacred garden was unfolding whether she liked it or not. They tethered their horses in the forest and walked to the water's edge.

"I'll lead," Sorcha said. "Ruairí, you hold tight to me and Conall can follow behind." He opened his mouth to object, then closed it again and stepped into the pond. "It's black as pitch in there and easy to get separated once we're through the hole. So, hold onto the bottom of my skirt."

Ruairí was tall and broad and long in every way. Six-and-a-half feet of warrior with an arm that could slice a man in two when he swung his iron sword, an excellent horseman and brave as feck. But she'd seen how much he feared the water that day with the gillaroo. And the night they'd gone skinny dipping, he hadn't ventured in deeper than his waist. Even now, she could smell his fear.

"No gillaroo in here," she joked. "And Estrada will be waiting with torches. We'll be in the garden before you know it."

Just before they went under, he pulled her against him and kissed her hard on the mouth.

"I love you too." Sorcha kissed him back, then taking his hand, she placed it flat against her belly. "We can do this. We must. For our child."

Ruairí smiled and kissed her again. "I do love you," he said. Then, throwing an arm around Conall, he pulled him in close beside them. "And you, brother. Today, everything changes. For the people of Tuath Croghan, we fight and win."

Now that both Sorcha and Conall had been through the hole in the hill, it was easy enough to find. Sorcha pushed herself through, then turned and held out her hands to guide Ruairí. His shoulders were so broad he barely fit. Once she had his hand, she refused to let go. They popped up together and then she heard a splash as Conall surfaced.

"I've never been anywhere so dark," she hissed.

"And cold," Ruairí said.

She could feel his fingers trembling and knew it was not so much from the cold as from fear. He was trying to tread water and it wasn't easy with one hand. She moved her hand in tandem to help him keep afloat.

"Come this way," Conall said, pulling them along. "There must be footholds." They floated along together until Conall suddenly stopped. "Here. I've found the wall and there's a ledge near our feet. I can feel one above us too. I think we might be able to climb up out of the water."

"How's your foot? Can you touch the ledge?" Ruairí's wounds were still wrapped in bandages to protect them from further damage, but it made climbing difficult.

"I'm on it. And I can feel another one above."

The ledges were narrow, not more than eighteen or twenty inches wide and slick with algae. Conall helped Ruairí turn and balance with his back against the wall. Once they'd settled, the cavern went silent.

Sorcha had once tried a float tank. Though she loved the feeling of floating in salt, the complete darkness was unnerving. Then, as now, she could hear her own heart beating in her chest.

Ruairí and Conall were breathing quietly beside her. As druids they must be used to meditating in isolation. Sorcha hated it, but she curbed the impulse to speak by counting to sixty in her mind. That was one minute. She began again and then she heard splashes in the water beneath their feet.

"What the feck was that?"

Ruairí cleared his throat. "Whatever it is, it's found us."

Estrada had to shove with his shoulder to open the gate. A heavy body blocked the other side. Once he got it open far enough, he squeezed through. There were bodies everywhere, though no one stirred. Beltane had kept them celebrating until dawn. But why had the fort not been secured? Was Bres so confident in his rule and his gruesome decor? Like warnings, more bloody heads decorated the main gates.

Then, just as he was stepping over the body, a fresh young guard appeared brandishing a sword.

"Blessed Beltane," Estrada said, hoping to calm the surly man with small talk. "Quite the party last night." Wearing his Merlin glamor, he was no threat, just an ambling old man. A traveler come for the celebration.

The guard grunted and kicked at the drunken man but all he did was roll over on his side and further block the door.

"Let me give you a hand." Grasping the drunken man's arm, Estrada dragged him out of the way. "Your friend spent his night with a cask of ale, it seems. I hope you, at least, had a tumble with a pretty girl."

That got a smile.

"Ah." Estrada winked. "Good lad. I remember many Beltane Eve's from my youth. Enjoy life while you can. That's what I always say."

But the boy was getting bored and wasn't interested in stories from an old man.

"I'll leave you to it," Estrada said, and walked off, tiptoeing through the spaces between and holding his sword at the ready. Avoiding the hall completely, he threaded around the outside toward the druid's garden. Conall had told him that Fearghas designed the sacred garden with its labyrinth, trees, pool, and altar from a dream he'd had as a boy. The ox was a gifted engineer who'd built the stone pool with his own two hands—hands that were now gone. Estrada still felt bad about that whenever he thought about the big man.

He was just about to open the gate into the garden when he heard voices behind him.

"I want seven steers roasting in pits for this evening's feast."

"Seven? But that's twice as many as we need to feed everyone in the fort and the village."

"You'll do as your king instructs. My family are here and we will show our wealth."

Bres. Slaughtering cattle to flaunt his power.

Estrada hid in the shadows as several of Bres's men passed behind. There were patrols as he suspected. When the way was clear, he slid open the door to the garden and peered inside. It looked empty. He wondered how often people came here. If it was just a sanctuary for the druids, Conall said there were only nine of them living in the fort. The eldest, Criofan, had been murdered so that left eight including Ruairí, Conall, Fearghas, and Bres. Estrada suspected any rituals would have already been conducted when the moon was high for Beltane and the garden would be deserted until Bres's daily meditation at high noon.

Pine torches still burned on either side of the stone altar. A murder of crows fluttered and pecked in the fire pit where they'd roasted their ceremonial white bull. When one saw him, all five looked, then launched into the air and hung in the trees. There'd been crows here the night he had sex with Ana. Were they hers? Michael had called her "The Crow Queen" and he remembered she'd mentioned her companions.

A feeling of unease crept through his belly and evoked a memory. They were too like the ravens who'd perched in the trees the night his daughter was stolen from her bed. The ravens who were vampires.

He hoped these crows were only crows. They watched him curiously, cocking their heads and shifting their beady eyes, the odd one screeching in some language known only to carrion.

Estrada took a breath and whispered aloud, "Powers of Light, protect me from evil."

Then, grasping the torches from their stands in the garden, he hastened to the rock that marked the entrance to the cavern. Below him was a thin, solid ledge that ran underneath the garden; the means from which Fearghas had built the sacred pool with its interlocking stones and drain. A thin stream from the removable bottom stone dripped into the water at the base of the cavern so the pond wouldn't overflow in the heavy rains. It was an amazing feat of engineering, like the corbeled roof he'd seen at the Newgrange tomb near Tara, only upside-down.

Clutching a rocky handhold, he eased down onto the ledge below, then grabbed a torch and peered into the cavern. "Are you there?" he shouted.

"Estrada!"

First, he heard Sorcha's excited voice and then the lower tones of the men. Lying on his belly he swung the torch. "Keep talking so I can find you."

"Here," Sorcha said. "We're on a ledge just above the water line."

He found them, pressed up against the sides of the rock wall. The cavern appeared to be molded from molten lava that had cooled suddenly and created rock formations: stalactites hanging from above, odd ledges, and depressions.

He tied the leather rope around a solid finger of rock at the far side of the ledge and gathered the rest in his hands. They clung to the sheer sides two or three hundred feet below him. The rope would never reach.

"The rope's too short. I'm going to lower it, but you'll have to climb up." He let it go, then shone the torch and watched it fall down the length of the cavern wall. It was at least a hundred feet too short. What was he thinking? This was, perhaps, the stupidest plan he'd ever conceived. "I'm coming down. I'll bring a torch."

"No," Ruairí shouted. "If we don't make it ..."

His words drifted but Estrada knew what he intended. *If we don't make it, you must kill Bres and save my people.*

"You'll make it," Estrada yelled. "I have an idea." He pulled up the leather rope and tied it around the end of the pine torch, then lowered it like a ceiling light into the cavern. The flame spun in wide circles from the end of the rope and illuminated the fabric of the rock wall—striations, mottling, a myriad of colors: rose, sand, charcoal, ivory, wine.

"Jeez. This is amazing. We're inside the feckin volcano, lads."

"There are many ledges," Conall breathed.

Turning their bellies against the wall, they began to climb.

They were halfway to the torchlight when Estrada heard voices above his head. Standing up, he peered out into the garden. It was Fearghas with a woman. He was bragging about building the sacred pool. Nodding, she backed into the stand of trees. The ox moved against her. His stumps were covered in dark leather and just visible below the ends of his sleeves.

"Women aren't allowed in here. You can fuck me now or I'll tell them I caught you here and you'll be fucking me later. Understand? Now, bend over."

She was young and scared, a slave no doubt, and had stumbled into something vicious. Fearghas would need to be dealt with, now or later, and Estrada decided it might as well be now while his companions climbed.

He hoisted himself out of the hole. "Hey big man. Why don't you try bending *me* over?"

As Fearghas turned his face hardened into rage. He obviously recognized Estrada from the night he'd set his beard on fire. Possibly even from the morning he'd lost his hands.

"Run!" Estrada yelled to the girl. "And keep your mouth shut."

She ran. Confident in his ability to kill, hands or no, Fearghas lumbered across the garden to where Estrada stood above the hole. When the ox saw the capstone lifted from his secret tunnel, he forgot about anything else. "What are you doing? No one's allowed down there but me."

Estrada drew the knife from his belt. The ox had no hands but he moved like a bulldozer. "Just admiring your *handiwork*." He glanced at the stumps. "Oh sorry. Poor choice of words."

Fearghas lunged and Estrada leapt aside, intending to draw him away from the hole and buy them time. He didn't relish killing a man with no hands and no weapon to defend himself. It was too much like slaughtering a whale and the idea sickened him.

Grasping an oak branch, he swung up into the tree. When the ox came at him, he jumped onto the big man's back and the two of them jostled through the trees in some bizarre rodeo scene—Estrada still clutching the knife, hesitant to make the kill.

Then the crows came wheeling in. Black wings striking. Talons slashing. Beaks stabbing.

Estrada buried his face and clung to the ox's back, but he need not have worried. Not one bird touched him. They all went mad for the big man's eyes.

Fearghas was screaming and jumping and turning, trying to cover his face with the stumps of his arms.

And then they fell. Through the hole. Hit the ledge.

Estrada bounced sideways and sucked in a breath, clutched the rock and watched in horror.

Fearghas landed on his ass with the crows still at him, stabbing and slashing. Blood flying. The big man teetered for long seconds like a transport truck on a bridge, and then he tipped.

Estrada yelled as Fearghas caught his foot in the crook of his arm.

And over they went together.

After The Fall

Fearghas hit the water first, breaking with the force of a humpback's breach. Caught in the splash, Estrada held his breath and tried to curl mid-air, then both knees slammed hard against the water. Pain surged up his legs and spine.

He caught the rocky bottom with one palm, still clutching the knife with the other. Bending his arm, he used the force to rebound. Somersaulting. Fingers pointing skyward. Arms pushing, pulling. Legs kicking through the pain in his knees. Bursting through. Ears aching. Mind screaming.

"Holy feck! Are you all right?"

Sorcha? Breathing. Treading water one-handed in the pitch. Clutching the knife with the other.

"Estrada!"

Glancing up, he saw them balancing on the ledge, two, maybe three hundred feet above him. Ruairí. Conall. Sorcha. Shadows against the mottled wall. The torch light swaying above their heads.

"Yeah, I'm ... Yeah." Still treading water. Freezing. Trying to think.

Then the ox surfaced. Estrada lurched in the surge. Water up his nose. Sputtering and coughing. He blinked and stared at the wet hulk.

A shadow face up in the water. Stumps sticking out the sides like fins. Blood seeping from a crack in his head. The muscles in the ox's jaw throbbed like a fish's gills. And then he bobbed upright and snarled. One eye gone and streaks of bloody scratches and holes marring his face.

Estrada's arm moved and he stuck the knife into the fat, pale, neck. The artery burst and blood spurted in his face.

The ox's eye rolled back.

He pushed away the body with one foot. *God damn it. It was the merciful thing to do.*

"Estrada. Answer me!" Sorcha was calling. Demanding.

"Give me a fucking minute, will ya!" *I just killed a man—a man with no hands and no way to defend himself.* He wanted to run and hide. Take a Houdini breath, dive down, and sit in the bottom of the pond, the way he used to when he was learning his trade.

He took a deep breath. Then looked up. Half-way up the rock face, they still clung to the ledge. Waiting. For him. To do something to save them.

He swam to the watery edge and hoisted himself out and onto the first ledge. Craned his neck to see them again, up above. Strained his eyes to see through the dark below. Rock climbing was on his bucket list. But here, there were no ropes, no picks. Nothing but his fingers and slick dripping rock. Maybe three hundred feet of it.

A shiver ran through his belly. *Fuck.* He'd expected *them* to do it.

Gripping his first handhold, he began climbing the bubbled, mottled walls. It became a meditation. Like Conall's prayers. Nothing but the feel of the rock at his fingers. At his feet. Reaching. Searching. Gripping. Testing. Pulling up and finding the balance. Then again. And again.

The farther he climbed, the more the dim torchlight illuminated the rock at his face. A volcano had once erupted here, molten fire cooling quickly, leaving a flash of mottled rock. Sand, ivory, charcoal, a streak of red like spilled wine. Or blood. Cracks and fissures, bumps and ledges. Smooth flat patches.

Climbing diagonally and eventually hoisting his body onto the ledge. Then Sorcha's hands were on him, holding him. "Feck, man. I thought we'd lost you."

He exhaled.

Ruairí was balanced on his haunches sideways on the ledge. "Don't look down," he warned.

The thought scrambled in Estrada's brain like a suggestion. He looked and adrenalin rushed up his thighs. The ox floated, a dark hulk in the water and all around his body, the water roiled. "What's happening to Fearghas?"

Ruairí glanced down at his bandaged foot. "Eels. Bottom-feeders. Raised by the scent of blood."

Sorcha caught Estrada's cheek in her palm and looked into his eyes. "Listen. You survived that. You can survive this."

Estrada stared back at her then glanced at Ruairí. "Where's—?"

"Conall kept going," Sorcha said. "He's almost at the top."

Estrada looked up. Conall was climbing the steep wall like an acrobat.

Ruairí pulled his knife from its sheath, slipped it through a strip of linen and cut it away. Then he unwrapped the bandage on his foot and a yard of dirty, blood-stained linen fell away. "That's better. I couldn't grip."

Estrada nodded. "We got this."

They climbed one behind the other, leaving enough space for slips and re-grips. Estrada, Sorcha, then Ruairí. Another fifty feet and the torch dangled. Estrada skirted around the flame but kept his hand on the rope, feeling for handholds. He could hear them behind him. Still breathing. Focused. Concentrating. Their breath keeping him going.

Then a hand reaching down. Lying on his belly on the last ledge, Conall caught Estrada's hand. "I got you." An enormous tug. A clutch. And Estrada was on the top ledge, exhaling, fingers hot and trembling.

He found his balance, stood gingerly, looking out from the hole. Listening. It was silent, save for the wind in the trees, the sluice of water against the edges of the rock pond and the odd beating of wings.

Where are the crows? When Estrada thought of them, Ana came to mind, bent back against the rock, feathers jutting from her hair. *Had she set them on Fearghas?*

Climbing out, he waited above and helped each of the others. Conall came last and was barely out of the hole when they heard Bres's voice.

"If you're lying, I'll cut you." He was dragging the woman who'd been with Fearghas in the garden and flanked by several armed men. Estrada recognized her now as one of the slaves feeding the ox ale in the hall.

Ruairí and Conall drew the swords from their wet scabbards and advanced. Bres shoved the screaming girl into the fray and raised his sword.

Estrada caught the girl and shoved her aside. And then he saw Ana standing behind Bres.

She was dressed all in black as she had been that night, her hair long and loose, streaming in dark waves. She made an odd chirping noise and crows flew from the trees, careening around the warriors whose swords clanged as they fought.

They *were* Ana's crows. Ana's crows had attacked Fearghas. Would she turn them on Bres too?

Ruairí was fighting Bres, backing him toward the pool, their swords clanging, their breath heaving with each blow.

Conall brought up his foot and booted one of the guards in the gut. The man bounced off a tree and as he turned to recover, the bard struck low, catching the backs of his legs. He went down blood spurting from the gaping trenches behind his knees. Then two more were on him.

A leering warrior advanced on Estrada. Grabbing one of the torches from its bracket by the pool, Estrada swung it while the crows flew in mad circles around their heads. The man came in fast and sliced through the pine branch, barely missing Estrada's fist. He laughed. Then his face contorted.

Sorcha stood behind him with a bloody sword. Bracing on his body with her foot, she yanked it out and kicked. The guard fell forward. Sucking in her breath, she puffed out her chest, then squealed, her wild eyes connecting with Estrada's.

Then Ruairí almost hit them. Wavering on his wounded foot, he deked around them, followed by Bres. The clash of iron hurt Estrada's ears.

He looked back. Ana stood absolutely still. Watching. Only her dark eyes flashed. Was she communicating with the crows telepathically? Sending directions? Her birds were attacking Bres's guards. Beaks and talons thrashing and ripping. But none came near him.

Estrada picked up the sword his opponent had dropped. He was unskilled but when he swung the blade, he felt a force he'd never felt before. Magic or weaponry, he couldn't tell. A new man ran at him. The warrior, who'd grown up with an iron sword in his hand, quickly dashed the metal from Estrada's hand.

Estrada dodged and dipped and came up with his knife in his fist, then brought it up and caught the man under the ribs. The man dropped his jaw and hammered Estrada in the skull before he fell. For a moment, he wavered, dizzy, his vision blurred.

When it cleared, he saw Sorcha across the glade, holding a sword above her head, muscles were bulging with the weight of it. She drew in her breath, gaze fixed on Ruairí and Bres. Then she brought it down, catching Bres's wrist with the tip and slicing open the inside. Had she caught it with the blade, she would have taken his hand clean off. It was unexpected and Bres screamed as blood spurted from his wrist. Pulling back his hand, he dropped the sword. Ruairí went for it at the same time as Bres and they collided, wrestled, and then Ruairí stumbled over his sore foot and Bres retrieved it.

Conall had killed the last of Bres's guards and the two friends stood shoulder to shoulder panting, watching, hearts pounding, as Ruairí and Bres fought on. Then, Estrada heard a screeching sound and turned.

Sorcha had Ana bent backward over the pool. Her fingers were wound tightly around the queen's neck. Thumbs pressing. Eyes crazed. Above their heads, the crows circled, then dove.

Lunging, Estrada shoulder-checked both women, a move that sent them all careening into the pool.

The shock caught Sorcha by surprise but didn't slow her down. After wiping the wet hair from her eyes, she went after Ana again.

"Leave her," Estrada yelled, grabbing Sorcha by the shoulders and holding her against his chest. "She wasn't even fighting us."

"*Feck!* I hate her," Sorcha screamed, baring her teeth. Her fists shook with a vehemence she'd yet to release. And then she let fly, pummeling his chest.

Bracing himself, Estrada took the barrage as Houdini had done. Then, as the energy dissipated, he gathered Sorcha in.

"Feck. Feck. Feck."

Estrada knew what she was feeling. They'd both killed men today. The vicious edge of iron blades severed your sanity. "It's all right. It's gonna be all right."

And then it wasn't.

Warriors burst into the garden and surrounded them.

Ruairí and Bres were still fighting, though Ruairí looked exhausted. And then Ruairí lifted his sword and brought it down. The shoulder blow cut deep into Bres's neck and he crashed to his knees blood spilling out onto the rocks.

Estrada held his breath.

Ana raised her hand in a gesture that halted the fighting. Emerging from the pool, she shook back her black hair and walked toward the two men. Leaning over, she whispered something to Bres, then wrestled the sword from his fist and handed it to Ruairí. "Finish it."

Ruairí raised the sword with both hands and then brought it crashing down.

Bres's head fell.

Leaning over, Ana plucked it up by one of the straggling bits of beard and swung it. "The king is dead." A cry of amazement rose from the warriors. A few scowls, but also a few cheers. Turning to Ruairí, she handed him the bloody head. Then Ana held both his shoulders and kissed his blood-spattered nipples.

Estrada's stomach flipped and he swallowed to quell the nausea. Their blood lust sickened him.

Sorcha growled. "Why'd you stop me?"

"To *save* you, crazy woman." Estrada threw his arm around her. "To save us all."

An hour later, Estrada sat beside Conall in the hall, cleansed of all traces of blood and wearing a clean, dry linen shirt and soft leather breeches. Conall had combed out his long chestnut hair and was spinning the top into a man-bun. The hearth fire blazed as they drank French wine from bronze bowls and nibbled bread and cheese. It was only mid-morning, yet Estrada struggled to stay awake. His body was crashing after the sustained adrenaline rush.

Sorcha and Ruairí lounged together on a platform of sheepskins, no doubt, feeling much the same release. Criofan's son had announced that the inauguration would take place as planned but with the *true* Sun King. People were pouring into the fort. Ailill obviously believed, as did many others who refused to acknowledge it, that Bres's death was a sign from the goddess. Ruairí had slain him with his own sword and that was enough to legitimize him and his chosen queen.

Ana had disappeared and Estrada wondered what new tricks the Crow Queen had up her sleeve. Though she was not to be trusted, he was more concerned about Sorcha, who'd claimed Ruairí and was embracing her new role as Queen of Croghan. She'd tried to kill Ana once and he knew she'd try again. Another attempt on Ana's life could get them all killed.

Estrada had felt Ana's power that night in the garden. She was wild and savage. A woman who wouldn't be thwarted or maligned or easily killed. And she'd take revenge for the humiliation she'd suffered in that choking incident. How and when were the questions. By custom, Ruairí must marry Ana, but the two women would not make compatible wives. One of them would end up dead.

He decided it would be best to leave right after Ruairí's inauguration. Between them, he and Dylan must get Guy and Sorcha to the wormhole in the woods. Guy would be easy. Sorcha might be tougher to convince. Especially now that Bres and Fearghas were dead and she'd cozied up to her man.

There was nothing to do now but rest, so Estrada laid down on his side and pillowed a rolled-up sheepskin under his head. The hall, with its rustic beauty, gave him comfort. As did the silence between him and Conall. A new closeness forged by shared experience and respect.

Glancing at the bard, Estrada saw scars he'd not seen before. A thin wavy line too close to his brown eye. Another along the side of his long, tapered nose. His skin was freckled, his beard flecked with amber and gold.

Conall looked back at him and smiled, then laid his hand on Estrada's arm just below the shoulder. "Close your eyes, friend. You've earned a rest."

Estrada liked the feel of Conall's warm, strong hand and placed his palm over top. They'd climbed the crater of a volcano with these hands, wielded blades, and killed.

"What will happen now?" Estrada asked, glancing at Ruairí and Sorcha.

Conall sniffed. "Ruairí will wed Ana this afternoon during the ceremony."

Estrada's stomach clenched. "What about Sorcha?"

"He's already wed Sorcha."

Fuck. How would he get her out of Croghan now that they were wed? And what did wed actually mean? It was obviously a polyamorous culture. But how did it work? Was wed synonymous with bed? Or were there other obligations? Family alliances? Children? Power?

"Does Sorcha know what's about to happen? Is that why she tried to strangle Ana in the garden?"

Conall nodded, then pursed his lips. "It's Ana's right, but I think it will be hard for my friend, Sorcha, to watch."

"What about you?" Conall obviously loved Ruairí, and Sorcha had told him how the three of them bonded during their stay at the hut. "What will you do?"

"I'm the king's bard. I will sing his story." He squeezed Estrada's arm. "And you?"

"I must leave."

"I'd like you to stay." Conall stared into his eyes. "I'd like to sing your story too."

Inauguration

The next time Estrada saw Ana, she glowed in an indigo cloak, bejeweled in gold. Her hair, her neck, the brooch between her breasts, her wrists, her ankles, even her feet flashed in gold circles, swirls, and spirals.

"Behold the Goddess of Sovereignty," Conall said, an edge of sarcasm in his voice.

"She's stunning," Estrada said.

"Like a lightning bolt."

Estrada glanced at his friend curiously. What did he know about Ana? They suspected her in the murder of Criofan, but had there been others? Estrada had never seen a woman wear so much gold. Her family must be quite wealthy; or perhaps, it was her position that offered such riches. She still owed him two gold bangles and he wanted them to pay the blacksmith for his trouble.

She stepped into the chariot and set the sable horse prancing. Her crows circled high above her head, and when the sun burst through the clouds it seemed for her alone.

Then Ruairí appeared. His long top hair had been glued up with resin to stand stiff and straight. His amber eyes were lined in kohl and his entire visage had been dabbed in gold fleck. Mounted alone on his chariot, he appeared statuesque. Nine feet of rigid muscle and pride. He wore an azure cloak the color of the Mediterranean Sea, and his feet were encased in bronze boots. No injury apparent. Flawless. Impeccable. A glorious king.

People bowed their heads and Estrada heard murmurs. "The Sun King. He will save us."

Save us from what? War? Disease? Famine? All were possible. He watched for Dylan in the crowd but could see no sign of him or Máire or anyone from the Manus family. He'd heard that people were getting sick in the village and he prayed it wasn't typhoid. As soon as the ceremony was over, he'd go back to the blacksmith's home.

Ana and Ruairí set off in their individual chariots and drove down the long winding road. The bridge had been fortified especially for the occasion. With so many people crossing during the flood, it sagged and threatened to fall. Estrada followed Conall to the gate and watched the procession. People lined the roadways and cheered. This new king was a man they knew and loved.

The chariots completed a circuitous route, down the main road and around the village and neighboring farms, then back over the bridge. As they trotted back through the gates, Sorcha strutted from the hall dressed in a deep red cloak held tightly across her breasts by a gold brooch. With gold pins in her upswept hair she looked every bit the queen, though he knew she wasn't feeling it. How could she, knowing that her man was about to wed the Goddess of Sovereignty in a public ceremony?

Estrada caught her hand and they walked together to take their places close to the Inauguration Stone.

Conall moved closer to flank Sorcha's other side. He too was dressed impeccably in a fine pink woolen cloak, the shade of summer roses. His bright hair shone like chestnuts in the sun and Estrada found himself staring.

Taking both of Sorcha's hands in his, Conall looked her in the eye. "You must not stop the ceremony, my friend. No matter what you see or feel. Even if your heart breaks or rage threatens to blow you apart."

Sorcha bit her lip and stared down at her feet.

"I know you want him for yourself but it cannot be. And if the Goddess is displeased, we'll *all* suffer. Do you understand?"

"You can do this. You know that Ruairí loves you. He's *your* man, no matter what happens here today." Estrada hadn't known her long, but Sorcha certainly had seemed a free spirit when they met in Scotland. She'd never had a problem with polyamory but then she'd never fallen in love before as far as he knew. Something incredible had formed between her and Ruairí. Something perhaps destined. And yet, it seemed Ruairí was destined to marry Ana too.

Though he knew Sorcha planned to stay here in Croghan with her man, he couldn't let that happen. The two women could never live together and share Ruairí. Somehow, he'd have to wrestle her back through the wormhole.

When the chariots returned, Ana and Ruairí stepped down and approached. Ruairí stood at the head of the stone and Ana at the foot. Conall and the remaining druids stepped up behind them and gathered in a circle, their rainbow of cloaks riffling in the slight breeze.

Criofan's son, Ailill, approached and stood at the side of the stone between them. Then, he began to speak. "Today, in view of all here assembled, you, Ruairí Mac Nia, pledge the oath pledged by your fathers and grandfathers from the beginning of time."

Ruairí was somber. The sharp lines of his face appearing almost as if cut and shaped by a sword. Estrada could only see the back of Ana's head, a mass of crow feathers and black plaits woven in gold, but he was sure she wore the same grave expression. This making of a king was a solemn, serious affair.

Ailill then began to recite a list of fathers and sons much like the *begets* Estrada could vaguely remember from his childhood. He was surprised to hear the name Bres repeated several times. It was no wonder he'd claimed the kingship. Bres obviously felt it was his ancestral right. And then Estrada heard the name, Lugh, and shivered thinking of his daughter, Lucy, two thousand years away in time. His mind drifted and when it returned again to the ritual, Ailill was reciting laws and customs. After each, he asked Ruairí, "Do you swear to uphold this ..." To which Ruairí replied, "I swear by the gods of my people."

Estrada didn't see or hear anything that might upset Sorcha and wondered why Conall had given her so stern a warning.

The druids all recited their names and their father's and grandfather's names. Estrada was starting to feel antsy and thought of his own response. *Sandolino Estrada, son of Antonio Estrada, son of ...* He didn't know who. He'd never asked.

Black clouds were gathering overhead when Ana suddenly threw back her head and raised both her arms. The druids all bowed and the bowing spread throughout the crowd. When they were the only two still standing, Estrada grabbed Sorcha's hand and pulled her down to her knees.

"The Goddess of Sovereignty blesses us this day in her earthly form. We ask that her union with the Sun God be one of fertility."

When she unclasped her brooch and threw off her cloak, Estrada blinked. Then Ruairí followed suit. They both stood naked on the stone facing each other, their bodies sprinkled in gold. As the clouds parted, Ailill threw down a white and orange cow hide upon the rock and Ana laid down on her back.

"*Fuck,*" Estrada breathed, as Ruairí knelt over top of Ana. He was no stranger to the idea of sexual joining in ritual. *As the chalice is to the goddess, so the blade is to the god.* He'd uttered those words many times before, though he'd never convinced Sensara to act it out as boldly as Ana and Ruairí were about to do. He glanced at Sorcha who held one hand on her belly and was squeezing his fingers with the other. "Be cool," he whispered, clutching her hand.

Then, Ana spread both her arms and her legs. The druids in the circle picked up branches of oak, ash, and rowan leaves and spread them around her so her body was bathed in greenery.

Ruairí, whose blade had assumed its full strength, leaned into her and the union began.

Estrada assumed, Ruairí's flat expression is what stopped Sorcha from a full scale rebellion. His biceps bulged as he performed his pushups, but there was no kissing, no lovemaking, no enjoyment; except, perhaps, in the final moment. After which he stood and exclaimed, "I swear by the Goddess of Sovereignty to uphold the laws of my people and perform all duties that are required of the king." Leaning down, he held out his hands to Ana, who clasped them, and he pulled her to her feet. The two of them stood naked on the stone with their arms raised, hand in hand.

There was a great banging of wood blocks through the crowd and everyone stood and cheered. Everyone except Sorcha, who was so red-faced and rigid, Estrada had to haul her up. "He loves *you*. That was just a show. Nothing more. He'll be in *your* bed tonight."

"I'll feckin kill her," was all she said.

Indeed, she might.

Then Conall picked up his trumpa and blasted it three times. The sound was so intense, it hurt Estrada's eardrums and he let go of Sorcha to cover his ears. When he glanced back, she was gone. Vanished into the crowd.

Suddenly there was a commotion at the gates and a host of warriors burst through on horseback. Donella and Aengus. They'd come. Estrada glanced at Ruairí and Ana still standing naked and glittering on the rocks and shook his head. Surely, Donella had seen the inauguration ceremony before, but Ruairí was her brother. It wasn't the kind of thing a sister would want to witness. But a naked brother didn't seem to bother her. Donella rode through the crowd, jumped off her horse and embraced him. The solemn ceremony was over and a party had begun.

"Sorcha seems happy now," Estrada said. He and Conall both looked over to the platform where she was kissing Ruairí. His gold flecks were pasted over her cheeks and glittered in the firelight. The Goddess of Sovereignty had disappeared. Crows and all. The hall was packed. The liquor flowing as hard as the rain that beat on the thatch above their heads. The scene heartening.

"Bean Rua." Conall scoffed. "He didn't stand a chance with that one."

Bean Rua? *Red-haired Woman.* Sorcha was that and Conall was right. Ruairí couldn't escape her. Estrada barely had himself.

"I've got something for her," Conall said. "My good friend, Sorcha, held her ground and her tongue today." And standing suddenly, he picked up the pitcher of ale, threw back his head, and guzzled it down. He was already drunk and Estrada wondered what effect this would have on him. Heads turned. People held out their bowls, guzzled their ale, and banged the empty bronze cups together. Into the midst of this cacophony, Conall strolled, arms raised, and body wavering. He arched backward so far Estrada worried he might tip, then closed his eyes and cleared his throat.

Estrada sat up, curious to hear his voice. He'd been impressed by Conall's flute and astounded by his ability to blow the giant trumpa but had yet to hear him sing.

What emerged was a wordless stream of melodic intensity: syllables and sounds, building from moist velvet whispers to hectic modulations. A sonic rhythm of breath that silenced the crowd and brought them to tears.

Fuck, you'd be a rock star in my time, Conall Ceol. A fucking rock star.

One August, Estrada had come upon a six-hundred-year-old yellow cedar tree that had been split by lightning only minutes before. Its flesh was shredded in long furls and its raw smoky perfume caught in his throat and brought tears to his eyes. Electricity shook the leaves like a shaman's rattle. Somewhere between smoke and brandied sap, its sticky blood drizzled down the rasps. He folded forward into its golden smoke. He thought of it now as he listened to Conall's voice. It caught his gut like an iron fist and drew him in. Leaning over, he closed his eyes. He wanted more. He wanted to curl into Conall's yellow cedar soul and steam.

When it ended, someone cried out, "A satire! A satire about our king!"

It broke the spell and then Donella suddenly appeared carrying Conall's lute. Smiling at her, Conall shrugged and plucked a few strings, then swaggered up in front of Ruairí and Sorcha and made a production out of tuning. "Just sing," the same man shouted, and Estrada thought of a sawdust and tooth country bar he'd stopped at on his way to California where the bikers were rowdy and the band not so much.

The last of the ale had gone directly to Conall's brain and his words came out with enough of a slur to reveal his total inebriation. His voice was thick and low and rich, a rasping shiver. This time, there were words.

"There was a king of Tuath Croghan much loved by a fey"

He held the note with a vicious vibrato, arms trembling along with his voice.

"A red-haired prize, she came disguised, and stole his heart away—

Though she had witnessed Tarbfeis, been banished, and castrated Bres"

A few eyes narrowed at the mention of Bres being castrated. While some of his relatives had died in the garden, many others still lived in the fort. Conall took a deep breath and continued singing undaunted.

"He took her to a secret place where things transpired that were unchaste"

Eye rolling and cat calls from the audience.

"But, oh, they were to Sorcha's taste—"

Applause and bowl banging on the wooden trenchers for that line, and Sorcha actually flushed and yelled, "Too much information."

Conall laughed and went on.

"He bore the pain of Fearghas's knife and climbed rock walls to take a life—

And now he has himself a wife ... or two."

He whispered the last two words and Sorcha picked up a bronze pitcher and hurled it at him. He dodged and someone in the crowd yelled as it hit. But even that didn't faze Conall. He took it up an octave.

"Oh, on his foot the scars are found, and Fearghas's knife with Fearghas drowned

Still, Bres is dead, and Ruairí's wed. The foot that bled is still stained red.

And there is much that can't be said about what happens in his bed"

More cat calls from the audience.

"But at the foot and at the head there's faerie hair that sparkles red

Our Sorcha is a thoroughbred—"

Another brass pitcher flew across the room. Conall leapt aside and continued to sing nonsense syllables with his beautiful voice, then finally took a deep breath and whispered, "Ruairí Chos Fola."

Ruairí Blood Foot? Estrada couldn't stop laughing. He banged his bronze bowl with the rest of the crowd as Conall leapt onto the platform and fell on top of Ruairí and Sorcha. Ruairí hugged him. Sorcha slapped him. And they tossed him back into the crowd. Conall was passed around for several seconds and when he got close enough, Estrada grabbed his hands and hauled him back down on the sheepskin where they were sitting.

"That was the worst *fucking* song I've ever heard. How did you even get this job?" Estrada laughed.

"Come on. I made it up on the spot. Let's see *you* perform. Go on. I dare you."

Never one to back down from a dare, Estrada said, "If you insist." He glanced around the hall looking for props and considered what kind of display he could put on to dazzle the crowd. Then he looked at Conall, who was watching him intently with those bright copper eyes and decided to make it personal. If he really wanted to see what Estrada could do, he'd skip the tricks and show the bard his power.

They'd been guzzling ale from two very large bronze bowls for the last few hours and Conall's was now empty again. Estrada tilted back his head and drained his own bowl—it was a two-handed operation. Then he picked up Conall's bowl, flipped it into the air and caught it with his fingers. He set it spinning, like a basketball, on the tip of his pointer finger. Then he flipped his own bowl up and set it spinning too.

Conall laughed. "A juggler. Very good."

Estrada raised his arms as the bowls continued to spin, then caught them in his palms and held them aloft. Conall didn't see the move, just the bowls change places.

Closing his eyes, Estrada directed his energy into the palms of his hands. He could feel the heat surging up his spine and down his arms where it culminated in his palms. Steam rose from the bowls. Estrada drew his arms together as a great cloud grew above their heads. Then he lowered his arms to eye level. The bronze bowls bubbled and boiled with a gold, oily liquid.

Conall gasped. "How did you—?"

"Flamicio," Estrada breathed. It was one of his favorite Latin words and never failed. The liquid burst into flame—orange, gold, blue.

"Unbelievable!"

"You wanted to see my magic? Feel my magic too. Touch it."

Gingerly, Conall reached out his finger and touched the flame. "But it's cold. How can it be cold?"

Estrada focused again. The flames turned blue and sunk into the bowl becoming water and then crystalizing into snow. Bright blue snow.

Estrada flipped the bowls over onto the ground and lifted them. Both were empty. "We need more ale," he said, slyly.

Conall's mouth hung open. When he was finally able to form words, he stammered, "De-de Danann."

Estrada smiled. "Magician." He'd never performed a trick like that before, but he'd certainly directed energy. "And something else. Wiccan."

"Wiccan." Conall mouthed the word he'd never heard before.

"From what I hear it's similar to Druidry. I can teach you."

Conall was the best surprise in this whole ordeal. Estrada could stay here and play with him all night, if it weren't for Dylan and Guy. He'd already stayed longer at the party than he'd intended. "One more round," he said, holding up the empty pitcher.

When Conall returned with a full pitcher of ale, they each downed another bowlful. Rain pounded on the thatch and sprinkled through the smoke hole causing the fire to sputter. Conall had turned melancholy. A certain amount of liquor can have that effect. Sitting with his knees drawn up to his chin, he stared across the fire at Ruairí with glassy eyes.

Estrada didn't much care to go out riding in the storm, but he was concerned. "I'm going to find Dylan. He didn't show up today. No one did from Manus's farm."

Conall leaned sideways and belched. "I'll come with you." His eyelids were heavy, his cheeks flushed. He looked like he was about to pass out.

"What Ruairí did today ... What we saw out there ... It was just a ritual."

"I know. I was there. *Right* there." He pursed his lips and Estrada had to laugh.

"Listen, man. Sex is just sex. It means nothing. It only matters when you feel something for the person you're fucking."

"What if you hate them?" Conall's lip curled, and Estrada realized they weren't talking about Ruairí and Ana anymore. Conall was someplace else, someplace Estrada had never been.

"Then you shouldn't be fucking them," he said, seriously. Picking up the bronze pitcher of ale, he refilled Conall's bowl. "And they shouldn't be fucking *you*."

Conall tilted his wolfish head and guzzled the whole bowl of ale. Then, he slammed the empty bowl down on the ground and his brown eyes flashed. "Want to have sex?"

Estrada laughed. "Indeed, I do. But not when you're this drunk. And not when you feel like this about *him*."

Peace Comes Dropping Slowly

When Estrada arrived at the blacksmith's farm, a sense of doom pervaded the dwellings and surrounding forest. The downpour had stopped and a faint moon silvered the sky. He was still half-drunk and feeling jittery. Frightened deep in his core. *Trepidation.* That was the word.

Conall had passed out, so he'd left him to sleep it off in the hall and ridden the dark trails alone. The horse plodded along slowly and gingerly, careful not to turn a hoof or trip on an upturned root. Night birds chittered in the bush and the distant howl of a wolf sent a chill up his spine. When the woods broke into cleared pasture and soggy fields, the feeling intensified. Closing in on the farm, he smelled woodsmoke and something else—something that turned his stomach.

The children had always awoken before dawn, exuberant, and full of mischief. But now there was only silence. The door was ajar to the summer kitchen, so he wandered in. The missus was burning honeyed candles and bitter herbs, but it didn't cover the stench. Dylan was on his knees in a corner, holding a wooden bucket while Máire vomited. Her mother huddled behind, bracing her daughter and uttering soft incantations.

"Jesus, Dylan. What's happening here?"

Dylan turned, his face smeared with dirt and tears, and Estrada's gut clenched. When Máire collapsed in her mother's arms, he set down the bucket and staggered across the room. "You should go."

"Is it typhoid?" Estrada's hand went to cover his mouth.

"I'm no doctor but …" Dylan shook his head. "They've got the symptoms and with all the rain and the flooding …" When he rubbed his eyes, Estrada could see that his nails were bitten down to the quick.

"How many are sick?"

"All the kids. It started with the two boys who went to the fort. Now it's all of them. The two youngest bairns, it's hit them the worst." He shook his head. "And Máire …"

"Christ! What can we do?"

Dylan shrugged. "I don't know. If it *is* typhoid, the only cure is antibiotics and they won't be invented until the 1900s."

"I'll conjure Cernunnos and go back through the wormhole. I'll take Guy with me, and I'll bring back enough antibiotics for everyone."

Dylan shook his head. "Guy won't make it." He gestured to the far corner of the barn where they'd made him a bed of straw away from everyone else. Not that it mattered now. He'd been here for the past two weeks and had already infected them all. Guy laid with his eyes half-closed. Dying. "He's exhausted. Hasn't kept anything down in days."

Fuck. Another death because of *him*.

Hunching his shoulders, Dylan stared down at his feet. Watching everyone sicken around him, he'd lost hope.

But there had to be something they could do.

Estrada grasped Dylan's arm and squeezed. "I'll go back on my own. I'll break into a hospital if I have to. Just tell me what to get."

"Cernunnos will never let you do that. You can't change history. Remember his rule?"

"We're not going to *teach* them how to make antibiotics. We're just going to help them through this. Heal them and set things straight." Estrada had brought Guy here. It was his fault the kids were sick.

"Heal people who are destined to die?"

"We don't know that." Estrada threw up his hands. "Jesus, Dylan. Maybe we were sent here to save them."

When Dylan's eyes filled with tears, Estrada stared off into the distance. Did they cause this?

"They're just kids," Dylan muttered and turning, he walked back to Máire, hunkered down beside her and held her hand.

Estrada looked at Guy, suffering alone in a filthy corner, walked over and knelt beside him. A faint glow encircled his body, like his spirit was expanding and preparing to leave his diseased body. "I'm sorry things didn't turn out the way you hoped, man."

All Guy had ever done was proposition him. It was nothing. Estrada thought of some of the guys he'd had sex with over the years. Young men who'd finally acknowledged who they were and wanted their first time to be with someone experienced. Someone they could trust to be patient and gentle. Usually it was Michael; sometimes it was him. Guy had just caught him at a bad time when his world had imploded and he had no sympathy for anyone.

"Fuck, man. Why'd you have to follow me into the vineyard? You should be riding the surf back in L.A. Not puking up your guts in Iron Age Ireland."

Picking up Guy's hand, he squeezed it. No response. Guy's skin was cold and clammy. His belly distended. He didn't appear to be in any pain and Estrada wondered if the missus was dosing him with opium. "I'm sorry, man. I shouldn't have hit you." Sitting, he laid his other hand over Guy's heart. The beat was so faint, he could barely feel it. "I'm with you, and I'll stay with you. I hope you can hear me, Guy. You're not alone."

Estrada closed his eyes and calmed his own breathing. There was nothing more he could do. Guy's heartbeat was fading.

Time passed. How much he didn't know. An image of Lucas Fairchild—rich and suave and unapproachable—flashed through his mind and with it came understanding. Guy was just working through his father issues with all the homophobic comments. That was all. What he'd really needed was a friend and Estrada had pushed him away. Punched him even. He should have done better. He should have, at least, listened.

When Estrada heard a sound, he opened his eyes and stared at Guy. His raw, blistered mouth had opened. A small round O in the fragile face. Suddenly, Guy's eyes opened wide. He exhaled and like warm breath on a frigid day, a mist rose from his lips. As it dissipated into the air, his eyeballs sunk red-rimmed back into his head.

Reaching over, Estrada closed his eyelids. That image would haunt him. *"For peace comes dropping slowly."* Why those words? Perhaps Yeats had found peace at his Lake Isle of Innisfree and Guy would find peace too.

Estrada took a ragged breath. For him, there was no peace.

Staring and shaking, he placed Guy's empty hand across his chest, then stood and walked outside. He made it as far as the edge of the stream before the rage ravaged his core and erupted through his fists. A tree took it. A tall, strong, tree. And as his fists pummeled its tough bark, he raved.

Fuck! I brought a sick man into this family and infected them all. This one's on me.

That day he'd rescued Guy from the slavery, he'd taken him to the pond and let him drink the water. That had to be where it started. How many others in the village were sick? With all the chaos over Beltane and the king's inauguration, no one had noticed what was happening at the slavery. It wasn't fair! It was always the poorest people who suffered. Everyone at the fort drank ale or wine or milk. But the slaves drank water from the ponds. And washed in it. And washed their dirty rags in it.

Emptied, he sank to the ground. His hands were raw and bloody and throbbing but it didn't matter. There was one thing he *could* do.

Climbing the hill through the forest he searched for the right place, and at the top of a rise he found it. A glade encircled by tall trees. Working on his knees, he pushed back the low-lying plants with his bloody hands. Then he began collecting dead wood from the forest floor repeating Conall's Zen prayers. Most of the wood was damp and he had to search under branches and shrubs to find anything dry enough to burn, but at last he had a considerable heap.

Back at the house, Estrada found Dylan sleeping beside Máire in the corner. Her mother had gone. Probably tending the other children. He gathered Guy up in his arms, along with as much of the straw as he could manage, and carried him down to the stream, talking as he walked. "I know you liked water, man. You would have liked this stream." Guy's body felt light, like his spirit had weighed more than his flesh.

Estrada walked along the bank, then climbed up through the forest to the glade. He placed Guy's body on the wood, then realized he had no matches, no lighter, nothing to spark a flame.

Fuck. Nothing in this world can be taken for granted. If I only had Michael's lighter. Unfortunately, it hadn't come with him through the wormhole.

Never mind. He'd kindle his own fire. Not a trick fire like he'd conjured for Conall. It would need to be hot—hot enough to burn flesh and bone. He'd seen Sensara shoot light from her hands, and that night the vampire attacked them on the yacht, their combined force had set Diego ablaze. What was fire if not transfigured light? Energy. All he had to do was raise it and focus it like they did in ritual.

Rubbing his hands together, he closed his eyes and chanted. *Fire. Rise up. Rise up in me.* He blew gently on his hands and felt the warmth of his breath against his palms as he repeated the incantation. *Fire. Rise up. Rise up in me.* He focused on the image of a flame at the base of his spine. Sucked it up through his core and across his shoulders. Spun it down his arms.

Small yellow flames popped like match heads from the lines in his palms—spreading, whirling, orange and blue, crackling and quivering. He flattened his hands and held the fire to the straw. Watched as it kindled. The flames danced, catching the dry straw, the twigs and the wood, then the ragged linen clothes around Guy's vacant corpse.

Estrada backed up. Dragged cedar branches from the woods and spread them over top. Smoke billowed and he felt a shiver of dread. *Burn you bastard!* The fire burst through, sparks splintering through the smoke, raging and pounding like his heart.

He stood watching, hypnotized by the spectacle of incremation, until the sun rose and the smoke and ashes of Guy's pyre smoldered and crumbled into the earth. Then turning, he stumbled back down through the forest.

When he came to the stream's edge he stripped off and stepped into the rushing current. As he laid on his back, the cold water tugged and spit and washed over him, catching his limbs in a wild rhythm.

An image came of Guy sitting in his yellow convertible with his surfboard sticking out the top. And then the Pacific, cool and blue and beckoning. The sun shining and Guy cresting a white wall of waves. Bright eyes flashing as he braced atop the board. Perfectly balanced. Perfectly focused. While all around him the blue water surged—

"Estrada! For feck's sake. We've been looking for you everywhere!"

He sat up too quick. Gasped, and breathed through the head rush. Then smoothed the wet hair back from his face. "What? What are you doing here?"

"I came with Conall," Sorcha said, gesturing to the bank of the stream where the bard stood looking sheepish and grim. "When he said you'd gone to find Dylan, I figured we'd better come and find *you*." She went to grab his hand, then pulled back. "What happened to your hands."

Estrada shrugged a ragged breath. The worst of the dirt was washed away but his knuckles were frayed and bruised to the bone, fresh blood seeping through the flayed flesh.

"Come on, man. This water's freezing."

He let Sorcha take his arm and hoist him up from the stream bed. Once upright, he felt dizzy again, wrapped his arms around her back and held on. She smelled fresh and real and alive and the feel of her plush breasts against his bare chest brought comfort.

"Guy's dead," he said.

"I know. Dylan told us. I'm sorry you lost your friend."

"Sorcha, I brought him here. He drank the water and now everyone's sick. If it's typhoid ... If they die ..." His jaw trembled.

"Come on, handsome. You need to get warm. Get some tea into you." She touched his forehead, then ran her hand down his cheek and along his bare shoulder. "Your skin's like ice. How long have you been lying here?"

He shook his head and stumbled along behind her to where Conall stood on the bank.

After wrapping his gray cloak around Estrada shoulders, Conall gave him a sharp slap across the cheek. It was unexpected and Estrada startled.

"You left me," Conall said.

"You passed out."

"So? I told you I'd come with you." He stared into Estrada's eyes. "And you left me."

Fuck. Not this again. Michael had said those same words. "I should come with you. You always leave me."

"Fuck off," Estrada said, and tried to pull away. His dark hair was plastered to his head. His knuckles throbbing. His chest aching. But that was nothing to what Guy had suffered the last few weeks.

Conall held him firm. "You didn't have to go through that alone." His face was close, their foreheads touching. "And you don't have to go through *this* alone. We build a shield wall and fight as one no matter who or what the enemy."

Estrada shook inside. Those red-rimmed eyes washed up from the darkness. Dead eyes like Michael's eyes. Ripping up the past and twisting his gut. Shuddering, he squeezed his eyes tight and buried his face in Conall's beard.

They stood holding each other tightly for what seemed forever. Just the two of them and the scent of earth and rain and fire and horse and sweat.

Then Sorcha pounced like a gentle lion, throwing her arms around them both, purring. "Alright lads. We'll get through this shite. I have a plan."

It is Women Who Fortune Or Misfortune Give

Ana sat cross-legged on the stone altar between the glowing torches. "Have you been here all night?" Too late Ruairí heard the jittery rasp in his own voice. He'd come to pray alone and hadn't expected her to be here. Hadn't seen or even thought of her since the ceremony yesterday afternoon.

Nothing was out of place. Slaves had been sent to bind Bres's body in linen, mop the blood from the stones, and set things right. The rain had done the rest. Bres's body, minus his head, was laid out in the hall. Since he was a self-proclaimed king and not inaugurated, the druid council had decided to delay the cremation until after Ruairí's inauguration. His bald, rain-soaked head hung from a post outside the hall. The Usurper.

Estrada's plan had worked and Bres was overthrown without a war. Estrada said it was Ana who'd given him the idea to surprise Bres in the garden. It was also Ana who'd given Ruairí Bres's sword and told him to "finish it." Ruairí furrowed his brows. Ana had handed him the kingship as she'd handed him the head of Bres. And this thought terrified him. What did she want in exchange for her patronage?

He was still unsure of her guilt in the deaths of Adamair's family, though, in his mind, he'd cleared her now of Criofan's murder. That was Bres. If she'd had a hand in it, it was only to provide the mushrooms. She was a conspirator perhaps, but not necessarily a cold-blooded killer.

The queen stared up at the crows that perched atop the fence in the rain but did not speak. Her hair was still plaited and bejeweled, though drooping slightly from the damp. When she turned, the torch light caught speckles of gold dust on her skin. She was wrapped in the black cloak she'd worn yesterday at the ritual. A gold circlet bound it together. It had been given to her, along with several other gold and bronze treasures, by her great-grandmother who'd come from the north.

When Ana rubbed her eye with a pale fist, her gold bangles clanged against the silence. The kohl above her cheeks was smudged. Her lids heavy. She hadn't slept. Raising her eyes slightly she glanced up at him. "There's much to contemplate. I hear there's sickness in the village."

The hair lifted slightly on the back of Ruairí's neck. Ana was now his wife, but he didn't know what she planned or thought or felt. She was fed by spies. Men who worked for her. Women in the slavery. And all feared her. Even her crows.

He still remembered the day she found the nest of fledglings in the woods. She'd been displeased with his sexual performance and distracted by the squalling above their heads, she'd shoved him away. The mother had likely just gone to find food, but that hadn't stopped Ana from climbing the tree and taking the baby birds, nest and all. She had no real friends in the fort and the crows quickly became her pets. She fed them from the meat trenchers in the hall. Stole bones from the roasting pits. Trained them to peck from heads taken in battle. No one could ever stop Ana from doing anything.

His gut quivered as he hovered by the side of the dark pool, not knowing quite what to do. He was still alarmed by what he'd heard her whisper to Bres in the garden. *"My secret dies with you."* What secret had Bres held over Ana that demanded his death? And what had Bres taken from Ana to keep his silence? Whatever it was, she'd grown weary. And then another thought. Was she aware that he'd overheard her final words to the usurper?

"Where have you gone, husband? I hope you're not getting sick too."

Ruairí took a deep breath, rolled his shoulders and exhaled loudly. "Sick? No. Sorcha's gone to Manus's farm. Her friends are there and she's worried the sickness may be too. No one came for the celebration."

She croaked something incoherent.

He'd made it clear last night that he'd taken Sorcha as his wife—Sorcha, who'd tried to choke Ana to death right where he now stood. Might as well get it out in the open. It was his right and he didn't intend to hide it. He was the king and partnerships were based on mutual consent. Ana had no say in who he wed or took to his bed. Just as he had no control over her. Still, the thought of warring wives turned his stomach and he belched.

"That fey cow will be the death of you," she said disparagingly, then smiled. "Come talk to me." She beckoned with a spiked fingernail and the bracelets clinked against her bare arm. When Ruairí didn't move, her face tensed and she ran her fingers through the water indicating he should enter the pool and come stand before her.

But the water looked cold and after his swim in the cavern below, he didn't much feel like stripping off his clothes and getting wet again. "I'll come around," he said, turning.

"No." Her voice cut him midstride. "You will not ignore me, husband." Unclasping her brooch, she let the cloak fall.

Oh. It wasn't talk she wanted. The sight of her aroused him as always, but his nostrils itched with the scent of danger.

"Will you have me right here on the sacred altar?"

"I will have you whenever and wherever I desire. I am the goddess and you are the god."

That much was true. The god and goddess were wildly sexual beings whose couplings strengthened the community.

Reaching up, Ana pulled the pins from her hair and let it fall in a dark rush. One of the crow feathers fluttered down into the water.

Ruairí tugged off his shirt and tossed it aside. When he started to step out of his breeches, he looked down at his foot. It still hurt to walk on the deep cuts that scored his sole and his missing toe ached constantly. Without the poppy sap, he'd taken to drinking wine to dull the pain, but his belly was empty now. He'd need to take off the soft boot to wade into the pool and he didn't want Ana to see his wounds. Sorcha didn't mind. She'd tended him. But Ana would find him blemished.

He shook his head. "No, it's not right. This is a place of prayer."

"Prayer comes in many forms." She raised her arm and one of the crows flew down and perched on her wrist. Together they made chucking sounds that made Ruairí's flesh crawl. "Do you wish to displease the goddess, husband? She already punishes us."

That too was true. The goddess had sent unrelenting rain. The crops were stunted. The lowlands flooded. And now this sickness. To please Ana was to please the goddess.

Ruairí sat and pulled off one boot and then the other. For a moment he stared at the foot bound in linen, then he stood and began to pull down his breeches.

"Wait. Take it off."

"What?"

"The bandage. Take it off. I want to see what Fearghas did to you."

He sat at the edge of the pool and began unwinding the linen. "Conall called me Ruairí Blood Foot. I am a blemished king. Perhaps I shouldn't have been inaugurated." As much as he wanted to be king, a part of him knew it was true. His inauguration was risky. If the goddess took offence, sorrow was not far off.

"We'll see," she said, then smiled. "The goddess doesn't mind a missing toe if the king is just and can uphold his duties."

"I will do as I swore to do," he said defensively. Did she think he would not?

"Come to me," she repeated, and spun the crow off with a flick of her wrist.

Ruairí dropped his breeches and stepped into the pool. The cold water was a shock but numbed the pain in his foot. Perhaps it would help. This sacred water was blessed by the druids unlike the water below in the bog. Slowly, he waded across the stony bottom. In the center, at the deepest point, the water kissed his nipples like many people had done in the hall last night after his inauguration. Even some of Bres's most loyal men had come to him to show their submission.

By the time he reached Ana, the water just brushed his thighs. He held her cheeks in his palms and pulled her face forward. His deep hungry kisses made her growl and claw at his shoulders. When they made love she was a different woman. A woman he could love.

Uncrossing her ankles, she dropped her legs over the side of the rocks into the pool. Her scent invoked intoxicating memories. She'd spent hours teaching him how to please a woman and he knew every inch and quiver of her skin.

Leaning forward, he kissed the soft dips where her neck met her shoulders. "You're perfect," he said, running his fingers along the straight hard horizontal bones. He kissed the hollow of her throat and his lips trailed down the cleft. Her breasts were small and hard, so unlike Sorcha's that threatened to delightfully suffocate him. Every man should have at least two wives that were so different.

Leaning back on her hands, Ana arched her back, and he answered her silent request with a flick of his tongue. She moaned softly, and then whispered, "Ruairí, my king. I have something to tell you. Shall I tell you now or after?"

"After." Sinking to his knees in the cool water, he pulled her hips close to the edge and held her in his palms. Lying back against the stone, Ana surrendered to his long deep kisses. He loved the sounds she made, never caring who heard.

When she screamed with delight, he stood, water rushing from his limbs. Tugging her hips in tightly to meet his, he pushed inside, locking them together and scooping her up in his arms.

Everything she'd ever done washed away in this moment when all he wanted to do was kiss her and hold her. "You're my Ana. You've always been my Ana," he whispered.

In the rush that followed, he bent his knees and they sank into the pool, laughing and gasping. The water was cool and calmed him after the exertion.

Pulling himself out of the pool at last, he sat on the high ridge by the altar, cradling her in his arms. "What is this thing you have to tell me?" With all the problems happening around them, he prayed it was something good.

Taking his hand, she laid it on her belly. "I'm carrying your child."

"Ah, Ana! This is the best news." His heart swelled and, smiling, he touched her cheek. "The night of Adamair's death, I'd hoped we—"

"Do not speak of him. That was *our* night and this is *our* child."

"Of course." It was unwise to speak of the dead and rouse their spirit. "But you must be careful and not get sick with this disease."

As the words left his mouth, he thought suddenly of Sorcha. She too had delighted him with the news that she was carrying his child, and this morning she'd gone to a place where people might be sick. He'd tried to stop her but there was no stopping his fey queen.

"What is it?" Ana had felt the change in his mood. She knew him too well.

"It's cold in here." Placing her back on the altar, he rose and picked up her cloak. As he wrapped it around her shoulders, he kissed her on the forehead. Then, he stumbled along the edge of the pool to retrieve his linen shift and pulled it awkwardly over his wet skin.

Sorcha was at the blacksmith's barn, perhaps surrounded by illness. He should go to her. But his relationship with Ana was marked by certain rules of her design—one being, he couldn't leave until she dismissed him. At times, in their youth, it had been immediate. Other times, she'd made him stay beside her for hours. Once his father had given him a hiding for disappearing so long. He hoped this wasn't going to be one of those times. After sharing the news of her pregnancy, he dare not rush. If she suspected he was concerned for Sorcha, who also carried his child, she might never let him go.

"What do you know of this sickness?" he asked. "It worries me."

"It should. It was sent by the goddess. She is much displeased."

As the physical embodiment of the Goddess of the Land, Ana knew her thoughts. Her powers of divination were more developed than any of the men and Ruairí trusted her to know the goddess's wishes.

During the last plague, Ana had advised a sacrifice. Criofan and the druids agreed, but Adamair held back. People died. Ruairí's aunt. Conall's mother. The eldest and the youngest. The most vulnerable. Finally, when Adamair began to plan a trip to Gaul, the druids sacrificed three young male slaves without his consent. As was their right. It was the blood of the third that finally satiated the goddess and stopped the plague. Some people had never forgiven Adamair for his hesitation.

"You must choose a slave," Ruairí said. "We won't wait this time."

"It's true, a sacrifice must be made but a slave will not do." Ana's face seemed split in two—one half lit by the light of the torch, the other shrouded in darkness.

Ruairí shivered and rubbed his hands together anxiously, then walked carefully back along the edge of the pool. He sat beside her on the altar and covered his maimed foot with his cloak. "Cattle, then."

Ana shook her head. "No." Reaching over, she grasped his hand and squeezed so tightly he felt her nails dig into his skin.

He wanted to pull away but knew that would only delay his leaving. She had something on her mind—something his churning gut told him was vicious and impossible and would end in tragedy.

"The de Danann woman has beguiled you, husband. She shrouds your sight so you cannot see."

His throat felt dry and tight and he longed for a pitcher of ale. Coughing, he leaned back and pulled his hand from hers. *What can't I see?* He dare not ask the question but she heard his thought and answered.

"The day she came Adamair died. Perhaps that was good; perhaps not. For Bres replaced Adamair." Pausing, she rubbed her eyes. "I know you've wed her, but I believe Bres was right. Adamair, then Criofan, then Fearghas, then Bres. Since Sorcha appeared four druids are dead, almost half our council, and the goddess drowns the land."

"What are you saying, Ana?"

"The goddess wants her blood. Fey blood. If we are to save our people you must sacrifice the de Danann woman."

"No!" This was the raving of a jealous wife. He would not do it.

"You are king now, Ruairí Mac Nia, and you must think and act like a king. Your duty is to the people of Croghan and *she* has brought this down upon us."

"But I love her."

She scoffed. "Do you not love the goddess more?"

But Sorcha carries my child, a powerful, half-fey son who will one day rule Ireland. I've seen it and know it to be true. I must keep her alive so Rónán can fulfill his destiny.

"I love the goddess and I love this land, but we must find another way. I don't believe Sorcha is responsible for the deaths of those men. Adamair tried to steal a bull to gain fame. Bres murdered Criofan because he would not make him king. And I slew Bres with his own sword. You were there. You helped me do it. And Fearghas… He was trying to kill me when he fell with your crows scratching at his eyes. Sorcha had nothing to do with any of it. She's done nothing but help me."

"Yes, the de Danann woman helped you become king. But would you have *become* king had those four men not died?"

A King's Choice

Sorcha pointed to Estrada's discarded clothes. "Leave those here and don't touch them. We'll burn them with everything else."

Estrada glanced down at the black wool cloak, the scarlet jacket and breeches, the linen shirt smeared with dirt and reeking of smoke. "I need my knife," he said, pulling it free from the belt. This was no place to walk without a weapon and he couldn't defend himself with an iron sword. They were heavy and awkward and he'd had no training. Ruairí and Conall's strength and skills both astounded and terrified him. Then he took the gold pin and bangle from the pouch and held them in his hand, as the crumpled shamrock fluttered to the ground.

Back at the dwelling, people were awake. The missus was stirring a pot of porridge on the hearth fire. Beside it was a slab of honey and bowl of cream. The older children were hovering, anxious for food. But not Máire. She lay curled up on her side, covered in one of her knitted blankets, her long brown hair shading her pale face.

Dylan was hunkered down beside her but bounced up as soon as he saw Estrada walk in the door. "Jesus, man. I'm sorry about Guy. You should have told me. I would have come with you."

Estrada's gaze shifted from Dylan to Conall, who hadn't left him since their moment at the stream. He touched his cheek, warm and imprinted with the bard's fingers. Conall smiled easily and Estrada looked back to Dylan. "I burned his body."

"Aye, good. That's smart."

Estrada glanced at the empty corner where Guy had lain. The straw had been removed and the dirt floor scraped clean. Smoke drifted from a dried branch of herbs stuck into the earth. Mrs. Manus had a remedy for everything. The smell of corruption was dissipating along with the energy of decay.

"I don't know as these clothes will fit you, but they're clean," Manus said, handing Estrada a pair of leather breeches and a pale linen shirt. "You can choose a cloak from the pegs." He gestured to an area by the door where several woolen cloaks hung in varying shades from gray to green.

"We've just brought them in off the line," the missus added. "I boiled everything and hung it out. Whatever this is, you needn't worry, son. We've been through plagues before and survived them. We'll survive this too. Your man was weak and injured from the hiding so his body couldn't fight it."

Estrada took the blacksmith's hand, dropped the gold pin and bangle on his palm, and closed it. No words were needed. Their eyes spoke gratitude on both sides. Then, he pulled Conall's long gray cloak tighter around his naked body. It felt awkward to dress in front of the family, so he turned his back to them and slid into the breeches. Manus was broad-shouldered from years of heavy labor at the forge, but his hips were narrow and the breeches were a decent fit. He took off Conall's cloak and handed it back. Then, he pulled the linen shirt over his head, attached his knife to his leather belt and cinched it tightly around his waist.

As soon as he was settled, Conall draped his cloak back around Estrada's shoulders. "Sit by the fire and warm yourself, friend. You've had a shock."

Sorcha, who'd remained unusually quiet throughout this interaction, spoke up. "You make a good point, Missus. The only way to fight this disease is to strengthen our immune systems." Kneeling close to the fire beside Estrada, she swirled a wooden spoon through a steaming cauldron. "I made Ruairí a pine needle tea when he was injured and it worked a charm. I'm brewing some now."

"Sorcha's de Danann magic is strong," Conall said. "Between Máire's herbs and Sorcha's tea, and the healing we gave Ruairí with our hands, his wounds closed in no time."

Estrada raised his eyebrows. "A healing with your hands? Sounds witchy to me."

"Love can work miracles. As can megadoses of Vitamin C," Sorcha said.

He narrowed his eyes. Where the hell did she get Vitamin C and why was she talking about it so casually in front of Conall?

"Scots pines," she said, catching his confusion.

He nodded, impressed by her ingenuity. "Can I talk to you outside?"

"Aye, sure, but I've just spent my wedding night with my beloved so don't be expecting any favors. You missed your chance in Scotland." Grinning, she put down the spoon and tweaked his cheek.

Estrada took a deep breath of clean fresh air. "Wind's changed direction and the sun's broken through. That's something."

"I'd like to say, the weather's the least of our worries, but it's not." Huffing, she flattened her lips. "Things have been coming back to me."

"Things?"

"During my undergrad, I took a course on dendrochronology. That's the study of tree rings."

He nodded. "I've heard of it."

"Aye. When you slice a tree horizontally, its rings reveal what years it grew well and what years it didn't. In Ireland, the bog oak died out around 200BCE. Probably as a result of severe weather. Climate change."

"Climate change? Like what's happening to our world?"

"Something quite pivotal. Perhaps a cataclysmic event." She paused, waiting for his complete attention. "Around 208BCE, Greenland experienced something so powerful it created a dust veil. I remember the date because it was 2008 when I read the papers. It was my first year at uni, and it kind of stuck with me."

"A cataclysmic event in Greenland? Bog oaks dying? What's that got to do with—?"

"I'm getting to it." She crossed her arms over her chest as if bracing herself. "Then, there's the bog bodies."

Estrada didn't like the idea that there were flattened preserved bodies beneath the ground in modern day Ireland or that people in this time were responsible for putting them there. He grimaced.

"Ruairí Mac Nia's not the only ritually-killed king unearthed in the bog. Six months after a bog-cutter dug *him* up in 2003, another fella surfaced. They called him Clonycavan Man. He's a short fella with hair like mine."

"How do you know?"

"Because he's on display in the National Museum in Dublin along with Ruairí. Hair and all."

"That's creepy." Estrada ran his fingers through his own damp hair. How could hair be preserved for two thousand years?

"What's creepy is that they both could have been alive at the same time in 208BCE when the event occurred. Radio-carbon dating placed both men as living between 300-200BCE. We can't place them exactly in time but we can ballpark it."

"What are you saying?"

"I think that's where we've landed."

"In the middle of a cataclysmic event?" A flush of adrenaline ripped through Estrada's body. Climate change was on everybody's mind back home. He stared up at the gray veil of clouds to the north of them. Was it possible for a dust veil over Greenland to be affecting the rainfall in Ireland?

"I agree with Sorcha."

Estrada jumped at the sound of Dylan's voice.

"They don't mark their years like we do, but it's logical. The cold relentless rain. The flooding. The disease. Paying homage to the Goddess of the Land."

"Jesus," Estrada said. "You think that's why they sacrificed these kings? Because of climate change?"

"Because they believe the Goddess of the Land is angry," Sorcha said.

"Crops need sun and heat as well as rain." Dylan scratched his beard. "They've just celebrated Beltane, which happens in late spring. But it doesn't feel like May. It's more like February or March."

Estrada remembered looking at the budding trees when they arrived. "But we can't stop the rain," he said. It was once believed witches had the power to affect the weather. If only that were true.

Sorcha exhaled loudly. "No, but we can help fight the sickness. I'm almost certain it's a bacteria and Salmonella Typhi spreads in the monsoon season."

"It's in the water by the slavery." Estrada's thoughts drifted off. If only he'd listened to his intuition. He never should have put Guy in the pond and let him drink. Then another thought. "But Máire didn't go near that pond."

"She nursed Guy," Dylan said. "The bacteria spreads through vomit and feces as well. It can easily spread under these conditions."

"Oh." Estrada didn't want to think about that.

"Ah, we're not fecked yet lads." Sorcha's voice trembled with excitement. "Scientists have studied the mud in the peat bogs and found it has antibiotic properties. It's even being marketed to rejuvenate skin."

"But the bog is infected with bacteria."

"No, the pond at the base of the hill is infected."

"Aye. Someone likely carried it from the mainland unaware," Dylan said. "Bres sent messengers everywhere inviting people to his inauguration and the Beltane ceremony."

"Here's the thing, boys. A peat bog is made up of decayed plants and sphagnum moss. The layers create an acidic, oxygen-free environment that's dense in nutrients."

"Aye. Things don't rot in there," Dylan said. "That's why they find such amazing artifacts."

Estrada thought of Ruairí's leathered body. Twenty-two hundred years? He looked at Sorcha's wrinkled face and knew she was thinking the same thing.

She shrugged. "At the very least, if we bury people in the peat bog, it'll bring down their fever."

"Bury people?"

"Not completely, you daftie." Dylan smiled. "I agree with Sorcha. The bog's worth a try. At best, they'll absorb nutrients, maybe even antibiotics that'll help fight the bacteria. Along with the pine needle tea and the herbal remedies …"

"You really think?" Estrada wanted to believe the bog was the answer.

"Oh, aye." Dylan nodded.

"I'll stake my reputation on it." Sorcha said, then took a deep breath. "And there's one more thing I need to do."

"What's that?"

"Tell Ruairí the truth."

She bit her lip and Estrada realized her fear. Whatever she said to the man she loved would change their relationship forever.

"I'm tired of him thinking I'm fey. I want him to know who I really am and why I stayed here. Ruairí may be king and Bres may be dead but his fate's still in jeopardy.

"Where *is* Ruairí?" Dylan asked.

Ruairí raced from the garden to the stables and mounted Púca. There was no way he was going to let Ana anywhere near Sorcha. *Sacrifice the De Danann woman? A woman who carried his child in her womb? A son who would one day rule all of Ériú?* He would never let that happen.

He knew Sorcha had gone to Manus's farm with Conall. He'd wanted to go with them, but he was a king now and that came with obligations. He wouldn't be like Adamair, who indulged his whims to travel and flaunt his wealth. Or Bres, who only wanted to impress people with his power. Ruairí Mac Nia would be a righteous king. A just king. A king who led his people by example and made choices with the entire tuath in mind. He would be a king who cared for the land above all else. But sacrificing Sorcha was not the answer.

As he raced through the village on Púca, he saw that the land was drowning. The people dying. Bodies were piled outside the slavery at the edge of the water—water that rose steadily. Puddles had become ponds. Ponds had become lakes. Water crept up the hill and the fort was now only connected to the village by a makeshift bridge they kept having to reinforce. He remembered a dream he'd once had of the fort surrounded by water and when he turned back, shuddered to see the exact same image.

"Burn them," he ordered, as he passed by the people. "Burn them now."

The sickness was spreading as had the plague last winter. Something must be done.

But even as he trusted Ana to know the goddess more intimately than any of them, he also knew that Ana wanted to control him. She resented Sorcha as she'd resented Adamair's wife and child. He yanked on his reins so hard, poor Púca stopped short.

Was this the secret Bres had discovered? Could he prove that Ana had poisoned Adamair's wife and child? If it could be proven, she'd be banished. Even the Goddess of the Land was not exempt from judgment when it came to the murder of women and children. There was no honor price high enough. He fumed as he rode. Is that why she'd called for a fey sacrifice? He would not allow it. Sorcha had saved his life. The flesh of many men wounded in battle, turned green and rotted before they died in agony. But Sorcha had saved him from that fate with her magic, her tea, and her healing hands. He would not allow Ana to take her life.

He spurred on his horse and galloped down the rutted road, veering off to take the old trails that wound through Manus's woodlot and farm. The blacksmith's moiled cattle stood in a wide-eyed row blinking at the streak of horseflesh that was Púca.

When the first of the screeching crows appeared above his head, he veered the black horse into the stream, splashing through the water and clomping over rocks. The crows kept with him. Circling. Talons down. Ready to stab and tear and destroy. He pulled up his horse and turned, leaned back and drew his sword to slash at the attacking birds. That's when he saw Ana's warriors. Holding swords and spears, their horses' hooves thundered behind him. And then he saw her. Driving the twin horse chariot alone, Ana careened down the rutted trail.

"No!" he bellowed. He would not let Ana take Sorcha.

He followed the stream where she could not go and near the blacksmith's house, he leapt off the horse and burst inside.

"Ruairí. What's happened?" The missus sat by the hearth fire stirring a cauldron.

"Where's Sorcha?"

"Gone. You've missed them." She dipped a bronze cup into the brew and offered it to him. "She made us a healing tea."

He waved her hand away. "Where? Where did they go?"

"The peat bog. They've taken the children. Sorcha thinks it will heal them."

Two of Ana's warriors burst through the door on horseback; one of them as wide as his horse.

Ruairí raised his sword above his head. "Get out," he commanded. "You will not come into this house. Manus was my uncle's closest friend. You'll be respectful or you'll feel the edge of my sword."

The men backed off their horses in the face of this new formidable king. Storming from the house, teeth bared, Ruairí waved his sword.

The warriors flanked Ana's chariot as she careened into the glade and skittered to a halt. Like him, she'd raced from the garden after their tryst, not bothering to dress. Her face was moist and flushed, the gold sagging in her windblown hair, the cloak over her linen dress askew.

He'd never seen her so disheveled and, for a moment, it unnerved him. Gathering his courage, he puffed out his chest. "Sorcha's not here. You will not have her."

Refusing to acknowledge his decree, Ana looked beyond him and addressed the missus. "Your queen is thirsty. Will you leave her standing unbidden at your doorstep?"

"Of course not, my lady. We've a cauldron of tea. You must have some. It'll settle your stomach."

"My stomach is not—" She stopped mid-sentence and touched her belly.

Many women came to the missus for ailments and solutions. Ruairí remembered that when he'd accused Ana of poisoning Adamair's wife and child, she hadn't denied seeing a healer. Was it the missus? Surely, Mrs. Manus wouldn't provide poisons. Still, she knew which herbs could harm and which could heal. If she didn't know Ana's intention, she'd do her best to help. That was the missus.

"I'll try your tea," Ana said, stalking by Ruairí. Turning to her warriors, she raised her hand. "Sorcha is close. Find her."

Ruairí swung up onto his horse's back and kicked it hard. The brute and another of Ana's warriors followed, fearing her more than him.

Wheeling Púca around, shield and sword raised, Ruairí attacked. The smaller man held back, but the brute charged with all the bluster of a cornered bull. Ruairí had the advantage in height. Raising up, he held his sword high and slashed in a downward curve, catching the brute's shoulder, drawing first blood, and knocking him sideways.

Grasping the moment, he raced off into the woods. Near the top of the rise, he glanced back. Strange. They weren't in pursuit. Still, he wondered what threat Ana had invoked to incite them to attack their king. As he sat astride his horse, watching the trail and listening for signs of riders, he realized, he didn't know which peat bog the missus meant. There were several lowlands around the stream that Manus cut for fuel. His gut told him to try the bog beyond the ridge, but he must be careful not to leave a trail that could be followed.

As he ascended the hill, the scent of smoke and burnt flesh tickled his nostrils. Bits of bone and ash were scattered in a gray circle in the center of the glade. The remains of a body. One of Manus's children? Surely not. The missus would have said, not offered him a cup of tea. This was someone else.

Something must be done soon. The sickness was spreading. Sprouts rotted in the fields. They'd had off-years before, but nothing like this. The business with Adamair and Bres had riled the Goddess beyond anything he'd ever seen or imagined. If nothing was done, they'd be forced to slaughter their cows this winter. There'd be no grain to harvest, nothing to feed people or cattle. His dream of Bres standing in a field of slaughter, surrounded by the bleached bones of his people, would come true.

But it won't be Bres standing in the center of this carnage. It will be me.

When Ana's crows appeared in the glade, cawing and careening around his head, Ruairí knew she was coming. Then, from the trail on the opposite side of the glade, he glimpsed a white flash in the woods, heard the snort of a horse and the sound of muted voices. Conall came first, riding Capall and holding Manus's youngest son in his arms.

Ruairí galloped toward him. "Take the children and ride from here. Now."

Conall asked no questions, simply checked his horse and turned. Then Sorcha was riding toward him, smiling, her skin dappled with bog mud. Conall stopped. Waiting.

"Sorcha. Go with Conall. Hide in the woods. Ana's coming!"

"I'm not hiding from her."

The others drew around Ruairí on their horses. Her friends, Estrada and Dylan. Manus. Máire riding with the other children. They were all covered in mud.

And then Ana appeared with her warriors, whooping and brandishing their swords.

Conall dropped the boy to the ground and drew his sword. Manus pulled an axe from the sheath behind his back and together with Ruairí, they fought.

Sorcha was behind him when he heard her cry out. Wheeling, he saw the two women grappling. Ana held a knife to Sorcha's throat. "You'll come, faerie, or I'll spill your blood now. The Goddess will have you. Here, or on the hill."

"No," Ruairí yelled. "Do not harm her. You'll have your sacrifice. But let Sorcha go."

"What are you saying?" Ana continued to hold the knife to Sorcha's throat though both women looked confused.

"The Goddess will have her blood—the blood of The Sun King."

"No, you can't!" Sorcha stomped hard on Ana's foot, then elbowed her in the belly. Gasping, Ana curled forward.

Sorcha ran to Ruairí and grasped his leg. "Please. Listen to me."

"I've made my decision. Will you argue with the king?"

We Are Between

Ruairí and Sorcha were back in the garden. Ana had accepted his suicidal offer and they'd been awarded this time alone before he went to purge for his sacrifice.

He leaned back against a tall ash tree; the leg of his injured foot stretched out on the grass. Sorcha leaned forward and laid her palm on his thigh. How could she convince him to change his mind? He was the most stubborn man she'd ever met and also the most noble. She'd come to save him from his fate and now he was sacrificing himself to save her. It was the most horrible thing imaginable and she couldn't get through to him no matter how hard she tried.

They'd been talking for over an hour and she still hadn't got to the crux of what she needed to say. Time-travel wasn't something you just blurted out. She'd told him about the rain and flooding—how these phenomena were the result of a climatic event that would take years to resolve. She said, the bacteria that caused the disease was likely brought by travelers from the continent and multiplied in the flood water. He hadn't asked her how she knew this. He just listened wide-eyed.

"Everything that's occurring has a scientific explanation and can be fixed *scientifically*. The climate will eventually ameliorate." Ruairí raised his eyebrows. "It will get better," she said. "Meanwhile, we can eat the red trout. Find herbs in the forest and make teas like I did for you. Use the bog mud to heal people and treat the disease. Move to higher ground. We can survive this. Your people can survive this. There's no need to sacrifice yourself."

Ruairí shook his head.

"*Please.* You *must* listen to me."

"I *have* listened, Sorcha. I know all these things are connected." Interlacing his fingers to signify the interlocking of the problems, he tucked them under her chin. "And I know your fey magic is strong. Your solutions have merit. But *you* don't understand the Goddess. This *climatic event*, you speak of, is a sign of her anger. If she's not appeased, she'll send more events. More rain. More plagues. More death. We're farmers. We can't survive her anger."

Sorcha ran her fingers through her long red hair. She felt like ripping it out. She was tired and frustrated and annoyed and beginning to feel like this was all her fault. If she hadn't come here and meddled in his life. Fallen in love with him. Conceived his child. Let him think she was a faerie.

She bit the inside of her cheek. If Cernunnos hadn't sent Estrada and Dylan to rescue her, Bres and Fearghas might still be alive. Was she responsible for their deaths too? And what about Ana? *If I hadn't pissed her off, would Ruairí be offering himself as a sacrifice to save my life? Feck! Am I the reason Ruairí was ritually killed and thrown into the bog?*

This last thought was too much. *Cernunnos warned me not to change history, but what if I'm the reason history unfolded as it did? I have to tell Ruairí. Even if he hates me forever for lying to him, I have to tell him the truth.*

"Remember the day you found me out in the hills?" she asked quietly.

"Of course. I'd never seen a woman so beautiful. I felt your power and wanted you then, right in the middle of the rampaging cattle."

"Well, then why'd you spend the night with Ana?"

He watched as three crows flew into the garden, their black wings barely visible in the growing darkness. The crows played among the tree branches, pecking at morsels only they could see, then settled along the fenceposts.

"Because she asked me to," Ruairí said at last. Leaning in, he ran his fingers through Sorcha's windblown hair, pulled it to his face and breathed it in. Tilting her face up to meet his, he kissed her. "And I wanted you to know I was a good lover."

"You didn't have to advertise. You could have just shown me."

"I've shown you many times since. Shall I show you now?" Ruairí's pupils widened in the flash of his golden eyes, and he leaned into her like a great fox, his copper mane, spiked and tangled from the wind.

She rubbed a lock of his hair between her fingers. In this moment, when the world seemed about to end, she found comfort in his raw and ragged breath, the salt and sweet of his skin. He was a vision made real by some impossible miracle.

Catching her in his arms, Ruairí pulled her down and they sank into the Earth while the crows flapped and fluttered along the fence.

"The first time you made love to me, that night in the hut, I knew you were the man I'd been searching for my whole life. Do you know how much I love you?"

He answered her with a force that shook her to her core.

"We may not understand each other completely, Sorcha O'Hallorhan, but there are some things we do well," he said after.

We won't be doing them if you're dead, she thought. Picking up his hand, she examined the manicured nails she'd first seen on his preserved fingers in the museum.

"Tell me what you're hiding," he said, reading her mind. "There can be no secrets between us."

"No," she said, glancing up. "No more secrets." New lines had appeared around Ruairí's young eyes, etched by the weight of this kingship. He was aging overnight. Time was running out.

"That day you found me ... I wasn't alone."

"No, you were with your sister's husband, the invisible man from Connachta." He smiled sarcastically.

"I was with Cernunnos," she said flatly.

"Cernunnos? The god?" His eyebrows furled as he considered this.

"Aye. 'Twas him who brought me here."

"So, Bres wasn't lying. He really saw the god in the forest that night?"

"He did."

"Your fey power is greater than I suspected. Where is this god now?" Leaning back, he stared at her with awe—awe she was about to shatter.

"I don't know. He left me here." Sorcha moistened her lips. "And I didn't conjure Cernunnos. I can't do things like that. I'm not fey."

Ruairí stared with eyes so deep, she thought he must be looking inside her soul. "I see truth in your eyes. But, if you're not fey, what are you?" She was clearly not an ignorant woman from Connachta.

Grasping his hand, Sorcha clutched it tightly, afraid when she told him, everything would change. "Promise me, that when I tell you the truth about who I am, you won't stop loving me. I don't care if you give me to Ana. I can suffer through whatever she has planned for me. But I couldn't bear it, if you stopped loving me."

"I'll never give you to Ana. We are wed." He laid his palm against her belly. "And you carry my son. I feel his spirit and know that one day Rónán will rule this land."

"Rónán." Sorcha sighed, and pulling Ruairí in close beside her, she squeezed his hands. "I let you believe I was fey because it seemed easier than telling you the truth." She took a deep breath and exhaled. "I was born here in Ériú just like you. On the west coast in Connacht, just as I said. Only, I was born some twenty-two hundred years from now. I come from the future."

Ruairí laughed.

Was it the intensity of the moment or was the future too much for him to fathom? "Well, say something."

"I don't understand *future*. There is only the birth and death and rebirth of each season, of each being. Our spirits slip through veils, traveling within, between, beyond. Here," he said, placing his palm on her forehead so that his fingers curled over the top of her head. "Here, we are always."

"I don't understand," Sorcha said. Time had always been linear to her, marked by years, centuries, millennia. You could carbon-date an artifact. Count the rings in a tree. Record it all on a timeline. Analyze. Hypothesize. Interpret.

Ruairí drew a spiral in the earth with his finger. "Here's where I saw you in my vision." He pointed to a point on the spiral. "I see you there now, standing in a field of yellow flowers with the wind blowing through your hair. And I see you *here*, beside me. There's no difference. We are between." He smoothed the spaces between the rings with his fingertips.

But I can't be here and there, she thought. *I'm just me. Is he saying that time doesn't exist? That he has no concept of past, present, and future? Is this some druid belief?*

"I'm an archaeologist," Sorcha said, hoping to restore reality with fact. "I dig up the past and try to make sense of it. I saw *your* body"—she touched his chest with her palms, ran them down his arms, and picked up his hand—"I saw *this* beautiful body in a museum laboratory when I was fourteen years old. You were killed and your body was preserved in the bog. When I touched *this*," she said, fondling the tin and copper mounts on the braided leather armband he wore around his upper arm, "I saw your face and felt such love."

Leaning over, Ruairí kissed her and pulled her down against the earth. "It's as I said. We are wed here and here and here." He touched her head and heart and belly.

"Aye, but if you die..." Sorcha squeezed her eyes tight to hold back the tears, but they leaked out and dripped down her cheeks.

He rubbed them from her skin with his thumb. "What do they say about me in this place you call the future?"

"They say you were a king who was ritually sacrificed." Dare she tell him the details? That scientists had studied his body? That they knew he'd eaten cereal and buttermilk for breakfast that day? That he'd been struck in the heart with a sword? Decapitated? Cut in half? That his torso was tied down in the pond with rowan withies? That they'd slit his nipples to show he was no longer a king?

"And Ériú? In your future are there still people and cattle? Do crops still grow? Are there *giolla rua*?" His eyes had glazed over now too.

"Aye, I've fished gillaroo with my uncle. And there are many people and cows and horses and fish and animals of all kinds. It's grand. Ériú is one of the most beautiful places on Earth. It's my home." When the new thought struck she bit her lip and then it came racing out. "If we run from here *now*, Estrada can conjure Cernunnos and we can all go back together. Ireland can be *your* home too. Ruairí, we can escape into the future and avoid this whole catastrophe."

"Sorcha, don't you see? There are people in Tuath Croghan. Then and now." Taking her hand, he placed it on the spiral. "We continue."

"Continue? Aye, the people of Ériú continue. They've survived much. Plagues. Famine. Subjugation. A civil war that divided north and south. A battle for independence. An economic boom and bust. You could be part of that world. Watch your son grow up and change things there."

Ruairí's eyes sparkled as he considered this new possibility. "Perhaps Rónán is to rule *that* Ériú."

"Aye, well, with you as a father, Rónán may very well grow up to rule Ireland."

"If Estrada is not de Danann, how will he conjure the god?"

"Ah, well, Estrada has his own brand of magic. I was there when he conjured the Oak King and Cernunnos."

"Now *that* is something I'd like to see."

On the other side of the garden gate, Estrada and Conall sat listening to this ragged conversation. Though their talk curled in upon itself like the spiral, Sorcha seemed to be making headway. Estrada knew she wouldn't leave without Ruairí, but if she could convince him to give up this idea of sacrifice and agree to fight, they might all get out of here alive.

"Do you know what he's talking about?" Estrada asked. "I understand reincarnation. In meditation, I see and feel myself in other times and places, and I know I've lived many lives. But what does he mean about the space between?" He thought about the wormhole and how they'd slipped through time without feeling a thing. If ever there was a space between, the wormhole was it.

Conall looked at him oddly. "It is as he says. But, if you and Sorcha aren't de Danann, how—?"

"None of us are de Danann," Estrada said, cutting him off. He didn't want to explain time-travel right now. He was concerned for Sorcha. "I understand what Ruairí is saying about sacrificing himself for his people, but we can't let him do it. Sorcha will never get over it." Two people Estrada loved had given their lives for him and he knew the pain never left.

"I don't want him to—" Conall's confession was caught short by the weight of an iron sword against his throat.

Estrada leapt up and was struck between the shoulder blades by hard metal that propelled him forward. He fell to his knees, all the air forced from his lungs. His arms were yanked behind his back and as he was dragged, gasping and coughing, he caught a glimpse of Conall facedown, his hands bound behind his back.

Ana appeared from the darkness, crow feathers poking up around her head like a Vegas showgirl. Estrada heard the gate creak and then warriors swarmed into the garden. He heard Sorcha scream and swear and then her curse was cut short.

A Burden Not To Be Borne

Sorcha sagged from the hazel withies encircling her upper arms. They'd bound her to a cross pounded into the soggy ground. Estrada called out to her but she didn't lift her head, and he feared Ana had poisoned her. Perhaps rubbed some lethal powder into her skin while she'd lain bound and unconscious in the garden. The Crow Queen wasn't taking any chances. Sorcha had been held prisoner throughout the night—tied and gagged and guarded by her warriors, while Ana worked on Ruairí. She wanted him submissive, a willing sacrifice, and Estrada feared she'd coerced or beaten him into something pliant enough to kill.

Estrada, Ruairí, and Conall were bound to makeshift crosses just like Sorcha. If only Estrada's wrists had been tied, he might have found a way out. But the hazel withies were wrapped from wrist to shoulder. He was the only one bound so intricately, as if Ana knew he was an escape artist. The four of them formed a circle around the inauguration stone like macabre compass points with Ruairí at the head and Sorcha at the foot. Ruairí was barely bound at all and Estrada knew that the force compelling him was stronger than hazel cords. Ana had either convinced him to be a willing sacrifice or made him a deal. His life for theirs, perhaps.

Dawn was barely visible through the slate sky and driving rain. What was left of the inner circle of druids stood among them as they had for Ruairí's inauguration. Five men. The only one Estrada recognized was Criofan's son, Ailill. He stood in the center of the stone beside Ana and was obviously another of her instruments. Ana used men like tools. The other four druids stood between each of the crosses to which the prisoners were tied. Five druids, four victims, plus Ana. He wondered if the number nine meant something special—three times three—as it did in Wicca, or if she was just cleaning house. He assumed she'd orchestrated the deaths of Fearghas, Bres, and Criofan, just as she had this.

Estrada searched among the people assembled to witness the king's execution; for that's what it had become. Was there no one here who would stand up to Ana and her warriors? Where were Donella and Aengus?

One of the older druids stepped up to Ruairí. His long, gray-streaked hair drizzled from his head like a wet mop. The stoop in his shoulders and rounded back took inches from his height, so he had to crane his neck to look up into Ruairí's eyes. "I will meet you in the Underworld, son. The Goddess blesses you and is grateful for what you do here today."

"Father," Ruairí replied, his tone as flat as the muscles in his face.

Father? How could Ruairí's father sanction his own son's execution? Were they pagan zealots with religious beliefs so strong murder was acceptable? Or was it no longer considered murder when the victim was willing? Estrada didn't know what Ana had planned for the rest of them, but he knew they weren't just here to witness. Ruairí would be first and then ...

Estrada tasted something bitter in his mouth, tried to swallow and couldn't. Pulling at his bindings, he spun a spell to break the bonds, then called out to Cernunnos. The horned god had brought him here and didn't want him to die. He might be their only salvation.

Ana bent and picked up Ruairí's sword from the stone beneath her feet—the stone she'd laid on only days before when he was proclaimed the Sun God and she wore the mask of the Goddess.

"No!" Sorcha's sudden shout alerted them to the horror about to happen. She'd awoken at last. Fighting and cursing, she raged until Ana nodded to the warrior who flanked her. Without hesitation, he raised his sword and brought the flat end down on top of Sorcha's head.

The sound turned Estrada's stomach and the bile rose again in his throat. He coughed and spit.

Sorcha's head fell to the side and then forward as her body slumped. A blow like that could fracture her skull. Even kill her. At the very least, she'd end up with a concussion.

Turning slightly toward Estrada, Ana fondled Ruairí's heavy iron sword.

"Stop Ana, please," he pleaded, knowing it was useless. Turning toward the crowd, Estrada shouted loudly. "Ruairí's death won't change anything. You'll still get sick and die from the fever. The germs are in the flood water. Don't drink it and don't let her do this!" Estrada felt the guards behind him move closer and, in his periphery, swords were raised.

Ruairí straightened tall and proud, power wafting from his pores. "Leave him. I am still the king and you will do as I command."

The swords wavered slightly but remained upraised.

"Do not look to Ana for your orders. While I live you must heed your king."

The guards glanced at Ruairí and then at Ana, bewildered.

Ruairí went on. "You will not harm Sorcha or Conall or Estrada or any of my family. If you do, the Goddess will strike you down. All of you! With her power, I will reach out from the Underworld and destroy this entire tuath."

"Please ..." Conall's voice cut through the rain, soft, trembling, begging. "You cannot do this, Ruairí." The rain had washed the tears from his face, still his eyes were streaked red with grief.

"It's my choice, friend. I do this for you. For all of you." Ruairí's eyes ranged through the crowd, then settled on Ana. He'd made a deal with the Crow Queen. "Free them now. Give them horses and let them go as you promised—"

"Enough!" Raising Ruairí's sword, Ana brought it down against his chest, once and then again, quickly, deftly, slitting both his nipples.

Ruairí gasped, his eyes wide with shock.

"No!" Conall shouted.

"You are no longer king. Your voice is mute." Stabbing the bloody end of the sword into the earth, she smiled. "Your blood freshens the veins of the Goddess. Already her heart grows stronger."

Ruairí held his breath and stared at the blood streaming down his chest and staining the puddles by his maimed foot. When he growled, the hairs on the backs of Estrada's arms stood straight up. "If you harm them, I will come. You cannot escape me."

Estrada turned and glanced at Sorcha. Her eyelids flickered, and he prayed she wasn't conscious enough to witness this travesty.

As Ana wrenched the sword from the earth with both hands, he turned back. Ana stepped back and drew the blade to her right side. Then, staring straight into Ruairí's eyes, she thrust it forward and up, piercing the flesh between his ribs.

Ruairí's eyes and mouth opened wide and Estrada saw his spirit shift in the glow surrounding his body.

Ana held the sword for what seemed an eternity, rocking back and forth. A sadistic executioner. Then, dancing back, she pulled out the bloody sword and hefted it high.

When she swung, time slowed. Ruairí's head balanced on his neck for one terrifying second, and then hit the ground.

Conall gagged.

"We're fucked," Estrada muttered.

Ana swiveled, her hands and face spattered with Ruairí's blood. Still holding the sword, she stepped up to Sorcha, who wavered with narrowed eyes, then spit in Ana's face.

"The Goddess demands de Danann blood," Ana proclaimed. Muscles bulging, she held the tip of the blade to Sorcha's neck, then ran it down the front of Sorcha's body, and blood stained the pale linen shift. When she paused at Sorcha's belly, Estrada realized what she was about to do. It was the child she feared. The unborn prince who was, in her eyes, half fey.

"No, you crazy bitch!" Rage erupted from Estrada's belly, flew up his spine and into his skull. He opened his mouth to release the pent-up charge and fire blasted out.

Ana leapt back, hit Ruairí's father, and dropped the molten sword. Staring wide-eyed at her blistered hands, her lips curled into a dark line. "This is de Danann magic! Kill them. Kill them all."

But the warriors froze in terror as Estrada continued to huff and puff like a dragon, flames flying from his mouth and cutting through the rain-soaked air.

A hum arose as the druids began to chant.

Then, Conall's voice pierced the low wail of the druids, a high ululating pitch like the howl of a wolf.

Estrada focussed the flame at the cords that bound Conall to the cross and the woven branches began to smoke and pop.

Conall's cry grew higher as he pushed against his bonds. Breaking free, he picked up Ruairí's sword and turned on Ana.

"Forget her," Estrada yelled. "Get Sorcha out of here."

The pounding of horse's hooves added another layer to the cacophony. Everyone turned as Donella's horse raced into the fort and reared up on its hind legs. Holding up her sword, Donella brought it down against the bonds that held Sorcha and she tumbled into Conall's arms.

Estrada's arms dropped as his bonds were cut. He fell forward still breathing fire, then stared up into the grinning face of Aengus. The clash and clang of metal on metal rang through the rain.

"Take her." Estrada pointed to Sorcha, and watched as Aengus swept in and scooped her up from Conall's arms.

Picking up a sword, Conall raced into the fray.

"Take my horse." Donella leapt off and held the animal still as Estrada mounted. "Go, look after Sorcha."

Aengus was waiting just outside the gates with Sorcha in his arms. Thankfully, she'd passed out again. Estrada pulled her in front of him facedown so her head hung over one side and her legs, the other. Touching the artery in her neck, he felt a pulse. "She's strong. She'll live. I'm going to take her home."

Aengus nodded and then he was gone, riding back inside the gates eager for battle.

Estrada raced down the switchback and over the bridge, the horse's hooves clattering beneath him. He was heading for the wormhole, summoning Cernunnos, calling his name once, twice, when he suddenly realized he couldn't leave. Dylan was still at the blacksmith's farm.

Forever a Farewell

Estrada pulled Sorcha from his horse and laid her on the ground. As she regained consciousness, she was woozy and cursing and spitting fire. "I'll feckin kill her!"

He knew she wouldn't back down from Ana or the warriors or anyone. If he didn't get her out of this place, she'd get herself killed. Maybe get them all killed.

Dylan hung in the doorway of the blacksmith's house, his face furrowed and eyes red, wanting to help but reluctant to leave Máire.

Taking Sorcha in his arms, Estrada held her. "Easy now, woman. Let me take a look at your head."

"Ah, my head's grand. It's my fists that are itchin'."

"Just let me look." Kneeling behind her, Estrada held Sorcha steady, then pushed aside her hair to examine the raised welt across the top of her head. "That bastard knocked you good. No blood, but—"

"Don't touch it!" she yelled, elbowing him in the gut.

"I didn't. I just ..." He rubbed her arm. "Look, I've had my share of concussions. You have to calm down."

"Calm down? Are you mad?" Rising to her feet, she paced and ranted, her ripped, blood-stained shift askew. "That bitch murdered Ruairí. He was no willing sacrifice. He was going to come home with us until she threatened him." Turning her head suddenly, she retched and puked.

Estrada closed in behind her, holding her shoulders, careful not to pull her hair.

"She had no right!" Sorcha yelled, slamming her fists together. "She knew all along it would come to this. She set him up. Put him in power, just so she could break him publicly. Show them all what a formidable bitch she is so no one will ever dare come against her!"

Estrada sighed. Sorcha was right. Ana had used them all. She'd shown him the secret passage to the hill-fort so he could assassinate Bres. And when that failed, she'd set up Ruairí to kill Bres. Once that was done, she needed to dispose of them all. Estrada didn't think for a minute she cherished her religion the way Ruairí did. It was a tool, a means to obtain power. She played her part as The Goddess of Sovereignty, but the Crow Queen was as dark as Kali or The Morrigan. "Yeah, and you know she's coming. We have to leave before she gets here."

Sorcha scowled and spit.

"You have his child to consider," Estrada said, glancing at the blood-stained linen shift. "Ruairí did this for us and he wants us to live. Don't give in to your rage, Sorcha. We have to keep our heads."

"Literally," she said, and the image of Ruairí's head tumbling from his shoulders flashed through Estrada's mind. "Ah, but I want her to come. I want to scratch her feckin eyes out with her feckin crow's feet."

Grasping the reins of his horse, Estrada mounted. He wasn't a man to back down from a fight but Ana had an army and there were women and children here. He glanced at Dylan. They needed to leave *now*.

His friend stood silently in the doorway listening, his lips as flat and hard as stone. Dylan had changed. Grown from boy to man. He wore this place like an old pair of jeans. Like a story he'd told a thousand times.

Estrada raised his chin. "Dylan? Are you ready?" He knew the answer before Dylan shook his head.

"Máire's sick and ... No. I can't. I'm staying here."

Estrada felt a lump in his throat. Staying meant a short, hard life. An early death.

Dylan took a few steps forward and his voice softened. "You go. Take Sorcha home. Manus and I will hold Ana off."

"But you can't stay here. Cernunnos said we can't change—"

"Ach! Bollocks to that rule. We've done nothing *but* change history. Either Máire comes back with us, where I can get her real medicine, or I stay here with her."

Estrada could hear the clatter of horsemen on the horizon. "Dylan. Please."

But Dylan stood with his hands on his hips, his long copper beard dripping rain and Estrada knew no logic would break through. His friend wouldn't leave behind the girl he loved.

"Bring her then," Estrada said.

Manus and his missus walked through the doorway and approached; their eyes streaked with worry. "We can't let Máire go with you, son." The missus stopped beside Dylan; her arm drawn through her husband's.

"We can get her proper medicine," Dylan said.

"Máire's barely a woman." The missus shook her head. "She can't go off with you. It's not right."

"Then I'll marry her," Dylan said, falling to his knees. "Just tell me how."

"Let him stay," Sorcha said. Dylan's desperation had eclipsed her own. "Let him stay and marry the girl. He deserves to be with someone he loves in a place he loves." When she stumbled up to Dylan and threw her arms around him, Dylan's face colored. "Your girl will thank me one day. Everything you learned about sex, you learned from me. Remember, your woman always comes first."

Dylan bit his lip in a lopsided grin and his face flushed. "Aye. How could I forget?"

Sorcha kissed him on the lips and tweaked his red ear. "Do me one favor if you can. Find what's left of Ruairí. Bury him by the hut near the lake of gillaroo. He was happy there."

Dylan nodded. "I'll do my best."

Estrada could feel the earth vibrating beneath the weight of thundering hooves. "They're almost here."

Dylan walked up to where Estrada sat on his horse and held out his hand. "You probably don't know it, but you're the best mate I ever had."

When Dylan clasped his hand, Estrada's throat tightened. "Teach your kids to play bagpipes and talk to stones."

"Aye. Manus and I've been working on a set of bagpipes. Sweet sounding too with a drone like thunder and a blast like the cry of a banshee."

Unspoken memories passed between them as their eyes met. "You'll go see my granddad? Tell him the truth. I want him to know where I am, and that I'm happy."

Estrada nodded. "I'll go see Dermot first thing."

"And you'll say goodbye to *them* for me? Sylvia and Sensara, Daphne and Raine. Tell them I love them. Tell them that Hollystone Coven was the best thing that ever happened to me."

Estrada slid off his horse and caught Dylan in a tight clutch. "I'll miss yer arse, laddie."

"You'll ne'er get near my arse," Dylan quipped, punching Estrada in the shoulder. "Now get out of here. Donella and Aengus will help us rebuild. She'll make a grand Goddess of Sovereignty when Ana's turned to ash. Don't you doubt me. There's a new magic afoot. I can feel it here." He pounded his chest. "We're gonna be fine."

"Aye, laddie. I know you will. And Conall … I know he's enough of a warrior to escape that fray. You'll say goodbye to him for me?" Estrada's eyes stung. He wished there'd been another ending to that story. Wished with all his heart, he could bring the bard back with him through time. Their story felt so unfinished.

Dylan nodded. "We'll keep your tale alive. Don't you worry. We'll write a song about you and Sorcha and your escapades here at Croghan. One day you might even hear it sung in a pub."

Estrada leapt onto the horse, turned its head and urged it on. "Sorcha, it's time to go home."

Sorcha's eyes were wet. Once past her anger, she was numb. She'd tried to save the bog man and failed. Perhaps Cernunnos was right and you couldn't change a man's destiny. Estrada watched her mount the small brown pony and urged his horse forward.

Then turning, he glanced back for one last look at Dylan. "Name yer first born after me, laddie," he said in his terrible Scottish accent.

"Sandolino? I don't think so." Dylan laughed.

"Estrada. Just Estrada."

"Estrada McBride. Are you daft?"

Through his tears, Estrada smiled. They were going to be all right.

"Remember the two oak trees with the antler blaze," Dylan shouted.

Estrada kicked the horse and she charged forward through the wet pasture leaving a trail a baby could follow. He wanted Ana and her warriors to chase him and Sorcha. He needed to buy time for Dylan and the blacksmith to join up with Donella and Aengus and fortify against the small war that was coming.

All he could hope to do was find the wormhole before the warriors found them.

"We'll go the way Máire took us. Through the woods and along the lakes. I think I can find the wormhole once we get back on the main road near that farmer's field where Conall first knocked me off my horse."

"Conall! What happened to Conall?" Sorcha's eyes widened with dread.

Estrada's jaw hardened. "He was fighting when we left the fort, but he's alive." He sniffed and touched his heart. "I'd know if he wasn't."

"*Feck.* Did he see what she did to Ruairí? Was he watching when—?"

"Ride!" Estrada shouted and slapped her pony's flank.

He could hear the warriors on their tail. Horses' hooves clattered on the rocky lands and splashed through the swamplands. As they cut through onto the main road, he recognized the farmhouse they'd passed where Conall had borrowed the big black work horse.

Conall, who'd knocked him on his ass and made him feel something for the first time in weeks.

"Hail Cernunnos, Lord of the Hunt! Hail Cernunnos, God of Fertility! Hail Cernunnos, God of Love! Wherever you are, hear me. I have Sorcha and we're coming home. We don't have time for riddles or drama. Just open the fucking portal!"

He was thinking of a kiss. An inexplicable kiss and some whispered hint of intimacy and destiny. He hoped the god loved him enough to grant him this one last boon.

Then they were galloping into the woods along the rutted trails. If, for some reason, Cernunnos didn't oblige them and the portal didn't open, they'd ride straight to the hut by the lake. They were heading east toward the edge of Croghan territory.

With spirit eyes open wide, Estrada knew his way through this strange land. As the forest closed in, wet branches slapped them. Drenched trees acted as great umbrellas keeping off the worst of the rain but every once in a while they hit a clearing thick with mist. In the densest thicket, he heard the eerie howls of wolves from the liminal forest. The horses reared and then forged ahead.

Glancing back, Estrada saw Ana standing straight and tall in her horse-drawn chariot. Holding the reins, she careened over the rutted road, crows circling above her head. Faster and more deadly than men, the crows, with their resemblance to the vampire ravens, triggered him most of all. The spell came spinning out of his mouth, giving voice to his thoughts:

"Hail Cernunnos!
As in Macbeth, this world is 'out of joint.'
One man has given his life for love.
Another has given his home.
We ask that the power of love open all portals.
We fly as passengers of time and space.
From the old world to the new. From past to future.
We waylay our enemies with magical energies,
With the driving force of wind and rain,
The gods and all sentient beings.
Hail Cernunnos!
In the name of all that is sacred and holy and good,
Great and Ancient Horned God,
Open this fucking portal and let us pass.
Hail Cernunnos!
Do this one thing and you'll have my heart forever!
So, mote it be."

Estrada heard Ana scream as her chariot collided with a rock. The wheel broke free and the vehicle careened off the rutted road, horses going one way, chariot the other. Some of the warriors stopped to help. No doubt afraid of her wrath. Her arms waved but her body lay trapped beneath the wheels.

Estrada reined up his horse. For a split second, he thought of freeing her. He'd had sex with this sorcerer who wanted them dead and the energetic bonds of intimacy connected them still. Then he took a deep breath, raised his knife, and brought it screaming down. He saw the blade slash through the bond and it snapped back like a red rubber band.

Free of Ana at last, he kicked his heels into the sides of the horse.

Ahead, a glorious golden light radiated from the forest and drew him forward like a magnet. As they reached the oak trees, the air wavered and the blazing antlers danced like fire against the dark gray bark of the two oak trees.

"There!" he shouted.

My Heart Has Given Love

Estrada squinted to block the glaring sunlight. Before him, stretched a close-cropped green pasture, cut sharply and distinctly by a swath of oily black soil. An enormous yellow machine was cutting strips of sod and blowing the dark earth out into rigid stacks like some mechanized monster.

"*Jesus, Mary, and Joseph.*" The words had barely left Sorcha's mouth when a whoosh of wind nearly knocked Estrada off his horse and a white horse streaked by carrying a screaming rider. "Conall!"

The bard pulled his horse up so fast it reared. When he turned, Estrada saw that he was spattered in blood, still had his fist clenched around his bloody sword. He glanced around, his face a maze of confusion. "What happened? Where are we?"

"Croghan Hill," Sorcha said, pointing to a grass-covered hill in the distance.

"No." Leaping from his horse, Conall stabbed his sword into the earth. "Where's the fort? The trees?" He pointed to the yellow machine that ripped through the earth. "What is that?"

"*That* is a peat cutter," Sorcha said, "and *this* is where your ponds once stood."

Estrada leapt down from his horse vibrating. "I know this is fucked up but trust me. It's going to be alright. There are amazing musical instruments and bands and concerts and videos and—" He stopped mid-sentence when he realized he was babbling.

Conall stared at him blankly and Estrada sent him all the love he could muster. The man was in shock. He'd just watched The Crow

Queen execute his best friend, fought a battle, and crossed through the wormhole into a completely different world.

"The between," Conall whispered. "We've crossed between."

Estrada stared up at the sky. The sun was shining but his hair was still wet with the rain of Ériú. "Yes. Over two thousand years have passed between where we were and where we are." He sniffed. "But this is still your home."

"My home does not look like this." Conall took a ragged breath and his eyes filled with tears. His love of the land was as strong as his love for Ruairí. Druids. They held the land in their hearts. "How can it be so barren?"

Estrada threw an arm around his friend and drew him in. Millenia had passed, and yet, it had only been hours since Conall watched the man he loved be tortured and executed. And now this devastation. "It will pass ... this feeling."

Conall dropped his forehead against Estrada's shoulder. "I'm glad he's not here to see this. It would kill him."

"Remember what you told me back at the lake? A grieving man breathes water and floats beneath the surface of the sea." Somewhere in Croghan, Estrada had surfaced.

"You remember my words."

"You're a bard. The whole world will remember your words."

Sorcha chittered and the small brown pony walked up beside them. "Ah, boys. Our Ruairí was a good man. Will you write something for him, Conall? Something the world will remember?"

He nodded. "He walks with the goddess."

"Aye." Sorcha petted the pony's neck. "They never found his head. I hope that Dylan did as I—"

Estrada shot her an incredulous stare. "Jesus, woman." Either the bard's grief had eclipsed her own, or Sorcha was still in shock. He remembered her head injury, and knew how mind and body were tied.

"I loved him too, but that's the truth of it. Our Ruairí is gone. He's been gone for over two thousand years." She sniffed and pointed to a dark swath at the southwest base of the hill. "A peat-cutter found his torso down there in Clonearl Bog. You can see it in the museum in Dublin."

"I don't *want* to see it." Conall sat down hard on the grass, and rubbed his blood-spattered face with his bloody hands. "At least, he is avenged. This is *her* blood."

Estrada cocked his head. "Ana?"

"I took her head." Conall's skin was taut, his eyes cold.

Estrada knelt behind him and laid his hands on Conall's shoulders. He felt a sense of relief knowing Ana had been killed before she could do anymore harm, then felt guilty at the thought. "It's done, then."

"I'm a bard and a druid. I've killed thirty-three men in my life. Men I didn't want to kill but did in the heat of battle because there was no other way. Today, I killed three. And her." He shook his head. "But hers was not an honorable death."

Sorcha touched the top of Conall's head with her fingertips. Her white linen shift was slit and stained with the blood from Ana's sword—Ruairí's blood. "Ah, well, herself was not an honorable woman."

"That was her dishonor but *this* is mine."

Conall drew his knees up to his chin but Estrada could see that his bottom lip trembled. Was he so ashamed? What had happened to cause this self-loathing?

"The last time I saw Ana she was surrounded by warriors," Estrada said. "How did you—?"

"I fought my way through. She was trapped beneath the chariot, her pelvis crushed. But when she looked up at me, she smiled with such triumph and arrogance my sword spun out as if wielded by the arm of the goddess."

Or the god, Estrada thought, an image of Cernunnos flashing through his mind. He threw his arms around Conall's shoulders, pulled him tight, and whispered in his ear. "Listen, man, you saved more people than you killed today. If Ana had lived, she'd have killed anyone who supported Ruairí. You know that."

Conall stared at the bloody metal. "When I pulled back my sword, her warriors pulled back too. No one tried to stop me as I rode to you, except her crows." Breaking free of Estrada's embrace, Conall stood and lifted his sword. "Perhaps, you're right and there was justice beyond the act."

Estrada stood beside him. "I know I'm right." He thought of Dylan, back at the blacksmith's farm with Máire, Manus, the missus, and the kids. Of Donella and Aengus. With Ana gone, they would survive. Closing his eyes, he had a sudden vision of Dylan standing among a herd of children, and he smiled. Perhaps, Dylan's ancestors still walked here today and talked with stones. Perhaps, somewhere far back in Dylan's family tree was an ancestor named Estrada McBride. He smiled at his own mad thought.

"You should bury that sword right here and now," Sorcha said. She'd been unusually quiet. "The Gardai will have you if you get caught walking around with a weapon like that."

"That's true," Estrada said.

"Aye, and they'd have a fit trying to match the DNA on those blood samples."

Estrada touched Conall's hand. "Can you give it up?"

Conall stared at his sword. "I never wanted it."

"She's a beauty but as someone who's spent her life digging up such things, I'd suggest we find a secluded spot to put your sword to rest."

Estrada used the sleeve of his damp linen shirt to wipe the blood and tears from Conall's face. "What *you* need is a long hot shower and a few shots of Sorcha's Irish whiskey."

"Ah, Connemara Peated Single Malt. She's one smoky devil."

Conall dug a long thin grave beside a pile of stones and buried his sword with little ceremony. Estrada stood beside him feeling a sense of grief for this forged iron block that was like an appendage Conall never wanted. Perhaps the act of burial was ingrained in the Collective Unconscious. What came from the earth must be returned to the earth. Ashes to ashes. Dust to dust. And metal to the earth from which it was forged.

"Someday someone will dig it up. Come on, lads. Let's ride to the top of the hill."

They mounted their horses and followed her across the pasture toward the green hill. In the distance, Estrada could see farms and fields dotted with cows. It was much like it had been in the Iron Age, except the forests were gone, the ponds dried up, and the earth scarred and bleeding black blood.

Sorcha waited at the base of the hill on a two-track road similar to the one they'd ridden to the hill-fort. They followed it as far as they could, then tied the horses to a gate. Sorcha took off the red cloak she'd worn as Queen of Croghan and they all did likewise. Noticing the ruined linen shift, she hiked up her red skirt over her breasts and tied it like a strapless sundress. Bundling up their wet clothes, they left them by the gate and climbed over into the pasture.

A cow path wound up the hill and they walked single file: Sorcha, Conall, and finally Estrada. The sun was directly overhead and, as the sweat trickled down his back, Estrada realized how much he liked the feel of the hot sun on his skin.

"You see, Conall, Ireland's still a land of cows." Sorcha pointed to the curious cattle that followed them at a distance.

"They've changed." The red and white moiled cattle were as black as the earth.

"Aye. You'll find much has changed." She pulled the gold pins from her hair and let it fly free in the warm wind. "But much has stayed the same too."

At the top of the hill, they stood and stared at a cement marker. Nothing was left of the hillfort or the sacred garden, but they all knew what existed beneath their feet—a magnificent cavern that held the bones of a man the size of an ox.

"They say this is a Bronze Age burial mound and so it may be, but we know what else went on here, don't we lads?"

Sorcha seemed to have come back into her own. She'd lost the man she loved but, for the moment, her pining was at bay. Estrada knew this lucidity wouldn't last. He'd worn the shifting cloak of grief himself. Perhaps her concern for Conall kept her connected to Ruairí in a new and different way.

Conall looked out over the land in all directions. "It's the same and yet it's not."

Sorcha pointed directly west. "That hill is Uisneach. Beltane ceremonies are still held there every May."

"I wonder what day it is?" Estrada said, wiping the sweat from his brow. When he'd left it was the twenty-first of September, Fall Equinox, but when he'd arrived in Ériú it was sometime in May, near Beltane.

Below them was an old cemetery and he could see a dark-haired man sitting among the graves. As if sensing him, the man turned, and even from this distance, Estrada recognized his face.

"*Fuck*. I'll be right back."

As he walked down the hill, a sudden, brash idea set his body tingling.

"You're a contradiction," Estrada said, facing Cernunnos. The god's hair fell in black jags below his shoulders. He'd stripped off his shirt and was sunbathing in loose blue jeans and bare feet. How many guises had he worn over millennia? Estrada shook his head. "You say there's no time. But if there's no time, there's no history to change."

The god chuckled. "Shaman. I'm delighted to see you again."

"Yeah, I didn't die and mess things up for you."

Cernunnos shrugged. "Your fingers tremble. What is it you desire now?"

"Michael. I desire Michael. I never stopped desiring Michael and it just occurred to me that since there's no time, as you say, it won't matter when I surface. Take me back two years. To Mabon. To the night before we charmed the killer and everything changed."

"I could do that. I might even come with you." He smiled seductively. "But you would still charm the killer and end up in the same soup."

"How do you know that?"

"Because I know you, shaman. You're a man who saves wounded deer."

"Just take me back. No one will die. I'll do everything differently. I'll be a better man." Estrada chewed his bottom lip, remembering a time when things were simpler.

"Very well."

Staring across the pasture, Estrada saw Sorcha gazing out over the Ireland she loved and Conall sitting on the earth with his head in his hands. "What about them?"

"You'll never know them. What difference does it make?"

"I won't know anyone from the past two years?" Of course he wouldn't. If everything changed, he'd never meet them. He thought of Primrose, his fey lover, who, like Michael, had sacrificed herself for him. And Leopold, who'd carried him from immortal danger. And Magus Dubh, who'd saved his life more than once. He was a great friend and Lucy's godfather. "Wait!" he said aloud. "Lucy. What about Lucy?"

Cernunnos shrugged. "She will never be born. Now, come." Reaching out, he offered his hand. "We must go. The bard is coming."

Estrada glanced across the hill. Conall was walking toward them, his face a maze of shadows. He was yet to understand the depths grief could reach.

Estrada turned toward Cernunnos. "Are you saying I have to choose between Michael and Lucy?"

Michael's words floated through his mind. *In a world gone mad I'd choose you.*

"You cannot change history or alter certain events to suit your desires, shaman. You humans are all intertwined. One cannot be cut from the rest like a cow from a herd."

"I will not *cut* Lucy from my life." He spit the word. "She's my daughter."

"The memory will fade. Sometimes you may see a child and think *once I had a child*. And then the thought will be gone."

"But Lucy has a whole life to live and Sensara loves her too. And Daphne. And Raine. She makes us all happy."

"Michael makes you happy, does he not?"

"Yes, he ... Estrada sucked in a long breath and shook his head. "No. I will not sacrifice Lucy for Michael."

The god touched his cheek and pulled his purplish lips into a sexy grin. He could be so infuriating. Nothing was ever simple where he was concerned. "Very well. You've made your choice."

"Wait!" Estrada cried. "What day is this? And don't tell me you don't know because time doesn't exist. You're a god and you know everything."

"It's Midsummer," he said, and winked.

"Midsummer? June 21?" As the date registered in his brain, Estrada heard the sound of voices and muffled laughter. Turning, he saw several women walking up the cow path carrying backpacks and bundles. Sorcha was walking toward them.

"Is it true? Is it really only Summer Solstice?" Estrada asked, glancing back to Cernunnos. But his voice just shimmered on the wind. The horned god had vanished, grin and all.

Estrada turned and raced across the pasture. As he ran by Conall, he grasped his hand. "Come on," he cried and kept running, pulling the bard along beside him.

"Hill walkers," Sorcha said, as they caught up with her.

"I don't think so," Estrada said. There was something in the way they moved. Reverently. There were nine of them and though they were dressed in thin knee-length dresses and some wore brightly colored scarves that caught in the breeze, their feet were bare. They looked like pilgrims or ... "Witches." The word rippled through the air around him as he said it. His body was riveting with adrenalin and a sense of pure joy but he had to be certain.

When he caught up, the nine women stopped and formed a circle around him.

"Everything alright?" She had choppy turquoise hair with one pale streak down the side and like the others, wore sunglasses.

Estrada squinted, then raised a hand to shadow his eyes. "Are you here for Summer Solstice?" He held his breath.

"Aye. We came early to picnic and make a weekend of it. You too?"

Sorcha was suddenly beside him, flanked by Conall. "Who could miss Summer Solstice with the sun shining full on like this."

"Holy fuck!" Estrada swayed. The world was spinning, shapes and colors whirling around him. He closed his eyes, but still they remained.

"My mate's been out in the sun too long. We best find him some shade." Linking her arm in Estrada's, Sorcha yanked him down the path away from the women.

"What the feck's happening? Your face is as white as my winter arse."

"Sorcha, is Conall still here?"

"Right here," the bard said, grasping Estrada's shoulder.

"I gotta sit down," Estrada said, lowering himself onto the soft grass. He was dizzy with numbers and events and possibilities. Cernunnos had spun the great roulette wheel of life and suddenly everything seemed possible.

"Sit down, Conall, and hold tight," Sorcha said, grasping Estrada's other arm. "I've never seen him quite like this."

The two of them perched across from him on the green grass and waited.

Estrada cleared his throat and wiped his mouth with a sweaty palm. "I'm almost afraid to say this out loud in case it's not true. Because the truth, I've learned, is not always true."

"Oh, for feck's sake. Just say it, man."

"Alright. Here goes. When you left Scotland with Cernunnos it was Beltane, right? The first of May?"

"Aye."

"Well, when Dylan and I left California it was Autumn Equinox, the twenty-first of September."

"Go on."

"Well, in between those two sabbats are twelve weeks and one more sabbat—Lughnasadh, which falls on the first of August. That's my daughter's birthday."

"You have a daughter?" This from Conall, whose eyes were suddenly as wide as the full moon.

"Yes, Lucy. I didn't—"

"Just go on with the story," Sorcha said. "I'm sensing a climactic event here somewhere."

"Right. Well, a lot of things happened that I didn't get a chance to tell you about when we were ..." He motioned with his head toward the hill. "Like Lucy was kidnapped at Lughnasadh on her first birthday."

"Jesus, man. You should've said something."

"We got her back. But, in the process, my partner was killed."

"Michael Stryker's dead? Bloody hell, Estrada. You're too tight-lipped. No wonder you've been so broody." Sorcha fell on him and crushed him against her breasts.

"Yeah. Well. We had more pressing concerns."

Conall threw an arm around Estrada and converged on his other side. The three of them sat, heads touching, souls huddled in the heat for several moments. They'd all lost men they loved.

"I'm so sorry, man. I remember the day Michael turned up in Scotland. He flew across the ocean after taking one hell of a beating. Your man loved you."

Conall's eyes grew wide again. "He flew?"

Sorcha chuckled. "Easy friend. We'll have you flying in no time."

"Here's the thing," Estrada said, drawing them back. "If it really is June, those things haven't happened yet. They don't happen for another five weeks."

"You mean, your partner's still alive?"

Estrada caught an edge in Conall's tone. "Indeed, and you'll like him. Trust me. Michael is … liberating."

Sorcha cocked her head. "You think Cernunnos …?" Her voice drifted off. "What about his 'don't change history' rule?"

"I think that rule is pretty much fucked." Estrada raked his hair with his fingernails. "This is a gift; at least, I think it's a gift. Knowing Cernunnos, it could come with a price. Either way, I'm taking it."

Accept what is offered. That's what Cernunnos had once told him. And this was one miraculous offer.

Estrada knew how to cure Michael's disease. He knew his way to the vampire's lair. He could wipe the fucking vampires off the face of the Earth and stop innocent people from being slaughtered. It was a re-do on an epic scale—a piece of history needing revision.

In the distance, Estrada heard the god's sultry laughter. Had this been his plan all along?

"So, what are we going to do now?" Sorcha's eyes were brighter than he'd seen them since they rode through the wormhole.

"We?"

"Oh aye. Conall and I won't be missing out on this, will we? I want to see what cards you've got tucked up your sleeve."

Conall nodded his head. "I want to see your world."

"Well then, we're going home." Estrada's eyes brightened with tears.

"Home?" Conall's eyes brightened too.

"Yes, home. I need to see my family, and I want you both to meet them. But we have to make two stops along the way. I promised Dylan I'd visit his grandfather in Tarbert and explain."

"Oh, aye," Sorcha said. "That we must do first."

"And then, we're off to The Blue Door in Glasgow. There's a man there I need to see."

"Oh! The Wee Pict!" Sorcha grinned. "Ah Conall, you'll love Magus Dubh. He's one of my favorite people in the whole wide world."

Estrada stood and held out his hand to Conall. "It's gonna be good, man. Trust me. We'll do this together."

Conall took his hand and the two men embraced.

As the three friends walked down Croghan Hill, the witches turned and waved.

"Blessed be," they sang.

And Estrada felt his heartbeat quicken. He was indeed blessed.

Series Characters

The Witches of Hollystone Coven

- Sensara Narado: High Priestess. Therapist and psychic, Sensara created the coven, makes and enforces the rules.

- Sandolino Estrada: High Priest. Estrada is a free-spirited magician who performs weekly at Club Pegasus in Vancouver when he's not performing at other venues or out solving crimes.

- Dylan McBride: a Canadian archaeology student, raised by his grandfather in Tarbert, Scotland, Dylan travels the world playing bagpipes with the university pipe band.

- Daphne Sky: a landscaper gardener and Earth mother

- Raine Carrera: a journalist for an alternative press who recently joined the coven. Raine and Daphne are partners.

Supporting Cast:

- Nigel Stryker: entrepreneur and owner of Club Pegasus in Vancouver, Canada

- Michael Stryker aka Mandragora: Hedonistic manager of Club Pegasus, Michael is Estrada's best friend and lover. He believes himself to be the reincarnation of Lord Byron and likes to play vampire.

- Magus Dubh: the tattooed half-fey dwarf who is the proprietor of The Blue Door, an antiquities shop in Glasgow

- Sorcha O'Hallorhan: a fiery and rather unconventional Irish archaeologist

- Primrose: the sweet Irish witch who becomes a faerie. She is one of the loves of Estrada's life and one of my favorites.

- Leopold Blosch: chef and owner of Ecos, a vegetarian bistro in Vancouver

- Don Diego: Father of the Vampires, Diego can transform into a thunderbird

- Cernunnos: the Horned God, an ancient Celtic fertility god

- The Oak King: an ancient Druidic god discussed by Robert Graves in *The White Goddess*

- Guy Fairchild: a young California surfer

- Lucas Fairchild: owner of the Abracadabra Winery in southern California

Irish Cast:

- Ruairí Mac Nia: the "bog man" destined to become King of Tuath Croghan

- Conall Ceol: a gentle talented bard and Ruairí's best friend

- Donella: Ruairí's younger sister and a powerful druid warrior

- Aengus: Donella's fiancé and "One Love"

- Winnie: Ruairí's youngest sister

- Bres: Competitor. One of the more powerful druids at Tuath Croghan.

- Fearghas: a giant of a druid who is both strong and gifted

- Criofan: Eldest druid at Tuath Croghan

- Ailill: Criofan's son

- Ana: The Crow Queen. Goddess of the Land/Goddess of Sovereignty

- Adamair: former King of Croghan

- Manus and the Missus: a local blacksmith and his wife who is a healer

- Máire Manus: a young healer who catches Dylan's eye and then captures his heart

Acknowledgements

Every story comes from a seed. This one began when I was leafing through a National Geographic one night in bed and came across one of those famous photographs of Old Croghan Man's curled manicured fingers. As morbid as it sounds, that mummified fist spoke to me, and I had to tell his story. I wondered why he was still wearing an armband, how and why he'd been so brutally murdered, where the rest of him might be, and if he truly was a deposed king sacrificed to the goddess. The fact that he was 6'6" tall and only in his early twenties made him all the more intriguing. What was his name? What did he look like? Who did he love? Above all, I wanted to give his life and death meaning.

I did the main research for this book in 2017, before and during my third trip to Ireland. I sat with the body of Old Croghan Man in the National Museum, Kingship & Sacrifice Exhibit for several days asking for his name and story. The name Ruairí came on my last visit as a kind of burble of sound. Much of my Dublin time was spent at a library near Trinity College where I was staying and exploring research materials on Iron Age Ireland.

Most everything Sorcha says she did in the story, I did in Ireland that summer, including tying a clootie on a prayer tree at the Hill of Tara when I was alone and desperate for healing, and climbing Croghan Hill to the place of Ruairí's inauguration and ritual sacrifice.

As always, I did masses of reading and viewing. Then I left it all for two years to stew. When I came back to write the draft in 2019, my muse tapped easily into the plight of the characters and they became real. I hope they became as real to you as they did to me.

Remember always that this is a work of fiction. Nothing is written from 200BCE Ireland, so everything must be gleaned from the archaeological record and extracted from myths and stories that have been told and retold over millennia. At one point, I drew a T-chart and headed it "Known from the Archaeological Record" and "Imagined." Much is imagined, but the following are a few sources I'd like to acknowledge that helped situate me factually in Iron Age Ireland.

Simon O'Dwyer is an archaeologist with a passion for ancient music. I first discovered his work when I researched Irish Traditional Music in 2006. See original instruments on his site, Ancient Music Ireland, and check YouTube for videos of O'Dwyer rockin' ancient horns including a reproduction of the Loughnashade trumpa that Conall blows. He's a master at it.

Library Ireland provided online access to *A Smaller Social History of Ancient Ireland* by P.W. Joyce. Also, Dr. Joseph Rafferty's little treasure, *The Celts,* by Mercier Press, 1964, proved invaluable.

I'm particularly indebted to Dr. Eamonn Kelly, researcher, archaeologist, and curator of the Exhibit at the National Museum of Ireland in Dublin. His theories on the ritual killing of deposed kings form the basis of this story. For Kelly, the Croghan torso and other Irish finds are proof of the existence of a form of sacred kingship in which rulers entered into ritual marriages with the Earth Goddess in order to guarantee future supplies of milk and cereal (which is why he ate them for his ritual meal). These kings were killed if they failed to protect their people. Dr. Kelly's papers on Kingship & Sacrifice are available at Academica.edu.

In creating chapter headings for this book, I looked to Ireland, and paid homage to W.B. Yeats and Douglas Hyde, two great influencers of the Celtic Revival. Lines drawn from Yeats's early poetry include: Weary-hearted, From Kiss to Kiss, A Fatal Image Grows, Cruel Claw and Hungry Throat, Not a Crumb of Comfort,

The Flaming Circle of our Days, Peace Comes Dropping Slowly, and A Burden Not to be Born.

Forever a Farewell comes from Douglas Hyde's *The Love Songs of Connacht*, as does My Heart has Given Love.

Two other chapter titles come from Conall the Bard, a character inspired by one of my favorite bards and muses, Peter Gabriel, whose music is a constant inspiration. Conall gives us Bean Rua, his song for Sorcha, and A Grieving Man Breathes Water.

Thank you to Aingeal Stíobhart for help with Ruairí's Irish epithet.

Much gratitude goes to Yasaman Mohandesi who designed and drew the wonderful tattoos for this series. Each tattoo is one worn by a character. Sorcha's fey butterfly symbolizes magic, freedom, and new beginnings, and connects to both the elements of earth and air. If you get this tattoo, please send me a photograph. I'd love to see it. See Yasaman's work on Instagram @ ym_blackrose_art.

Thank you to my beta readers: Sionnach Wintergreen, Jackie Murdock, Linda Mah, and Sarah Kelly. I always listen to what you say and appreciate your positive feedback and suggestions for changes.

I asked author, mentor, and editor Eileen Cook to provide a developmental edit for *To Kill a King* because I enjoy working with her so much. Her keen eye, knowledge of writing, psychology, character development, and humorous comments in the margins of my Word doc kept me laughing, even as I struggled with revisions. In the first two scenes, Eileen was quite concerned that Estrada had left his pants back at the flat and was wandering around the vineyard naked. What can I say? Estrada is his own man and does as he likes. Without him, there would be no stories.

As always, much gratitude goes to you, my readers.

blessings and all good wishes,

Wendy

About the Author

W. L. Hawkin writes the kind of books she loves to read from her home in the Pacific Northwest. Because she's a genre-blender, you might find crime, mystery, romance, suspense, fantasy, adventure, and even time travel, interwoven into her stories.

If you like "myth, magic, and mayhem" her Hollystone Mysteries feature a coven of West Coast witches who solve murders using ritual magic and a little help from the gods. The books—*To Charm a Killer, To Sleep with Stones, To Render a Raven,* and *To Kill a King*—follow Estrada, a free-spirited, bisexual magician and coven high priest as he endeavors to save his family and friends while sorting through his own personal issues. Book Five, *To Dance with Destiny*, is expected in late 2023.

Her latest release, *Lure: Jesse & Hawk*, was a recipient of a Crowned Heart Award from InD'Tale Magazine and a finalist in The 2022 Wishing Shelf UK Book Awards. Lure is small-town romantic suspense story set in the American Midwest in the fictional town of Lure River.

As an intuitive writer, Wendy captures what she sees and hears on the page, and allows her muses to guide her through the creative process. She needs to feel the energy of the land so, although she's an introvert, in each book her characters go on a journey where she's traveled herself.

If you don't find her at Blue Haven Press, she's out wandering the woods or beaches of Vancouver Island with her beautiful yellow dog.

If you enjoyed this book, please take a moment to leave a few words with your favorite retailer. Thank you.

Are you curious to know more about W. L. Hawkin, Lure River, and Hollystone Coven? Come by Blue Haven Press, subscribe to Wendy's seasonal newsletter and follow her on social media.

instagram.com/w.l.hawkin/?hl=en

facebook.com/wlhawkin

pinterest.ca/wlhawkin/

goodreads.com/author/show/16142078.W_L_Hawkin

https://twitter.com/ladyhawke1003

Manufactured by Amazon.ca
Bolton, ON

32751613R00176